THE
HANG OUT GROUP
AND THE CREATURES OF THE GARDEN

TAYLOR J. GASE

Book Vine Press
2516 Highland Dr.
Palatine, IL 60067

CHAPTER 1

The Seven Travelers

Saturday, October 4, 1924

It was a late evening for the seven travelers who set up camp for the night. The full moon was wide, glowing over the mountains visible in the short distance, giving the gentlemen a stunning sight. The ground was a rocky terrain, with scattered shrubs surrounding their camping area. The barren landscape seemed to be on a tilt because they were so high up on the side of the mountain.

Four of the men sat around a small campfire for warmth. Parker, one of the men sitting around the fire, turned over a log burning in the fire with a thick stick, causing embers to fly toward Derrick. Derrick spazzed out in fear as the embers flew at him. Zach, sitting next to Parker, let out a small laugh at Derrick's discomfort.

"Sorry, Derrick," Parker apologized.

"No need, Parker…I love hot embers landing all over me!" Derrick uttered in frustration as he moved away from the flying cinders.

"It was pretty funny." Zach chuckled with a big grin. It was a long day of walking for the men, so Derrick was already grumpy. The latest hunt didn't provide much food, so they didn't have much to eat. A lack of sustenance and being exhausted took its toll on the men's morale. Once the fire was burning a bit brighter, Parker reached into his bag and pulled out his journal. Parker then turned to Kyle, the man sitting to his right, and asked if he could borrow his pencil.

"Writing another chapter for your logbook?" Kyle asked after he passed over his pencil to Parker. Before Parker could respond, Zack pointed out that Parker was only writing in his journal because Logan was doing the same thing. Kyle and Derrick turned their heads and saw Logan sitting by himself. Logan was writing in his journal by candlelight.

"Following in the steps of our leader isn't going to make him like you more," Zach added. Among the seven travelers, Logan was the most mysterious. After he lost his parents from yellow fever at the age of fourteen, he had been hiking from state to state for the past ten years, most of it being on his own. Parker was the first to join Logan on his travels; he thought following him would lead to adventure and excitement. Logan was the tallest of the group. He was strong as a horse and kept to himself mostly. He was a man of few words, but whenever an argument arose within the group, Logan knew when to step in to end it before things got out of hand. He was very much respected by the others; they looked to him as their leader. Logan didn't like the idea of being the leader, so he never fully embraced it. Logan liked it better being on his own. He wasn't good at making friends, nor did he ever want to improve on that. In his mind, he was stuck with these six men and wasn't rude enough to ditch them.

A voice rose from the sleeping area where the remaining two travelers were setting up the sleeping bags. In the group, the jobs rotated each night. Some would gather water for the canteens, some would go on a hunt for food, some would gather firewood, while the others would get the sleeping bags ready for the night. Logan, on the other hand, handled most of that stuff on his own. Even with the others chipping in, he still felt like he needed to be self-sufficient.

"Don't put my sleeping bag on the bumpy part of the ground! You want me to wake up with back pains?" Jake yelled at Ezekiel. "Move it away from there now!"

"Hey, take it easy on the new guy, Jake!" Parker hollered over to Jake.

"He put my bag on the bumpiest part of the ground!" Jake shouted back.

"It was probably an accident," Parker responded.

"No, he did it on purpose. I know he did!" Jake said, raising his finger at Ezekiel.

"It's dark over there, and he might not have seen it," Parker replied, defending Ezekiel. Jake then turned his head to Ezekiel to make sure he moved his bag. Over by the fire, Zach leaned into the others saying that he told Ezekiel to put Jake's bag there. Zach said he thought it would have been funny to give Jake the worst place to sleep or see Ezekiel get in trouble by Jake. No one really liked Jake; they were all pretty sure that he was wanted for a crime in his hometown and was walking with the travelers to get as far away from that town as he could.

Ezekiel wasn't the best person to travel with either. He was barely a month in, and the group was making bets on how much longer he was going to stick around. Ezekiel wasn't mean like Jake, but he simply had no survival experiences. He couldn't hunt and grew the most winded from the shortest of walks. Ezekiel came from a rich family and never went too far away from his home his whole life. He always fantasized about traveling into the great unknown, thinking it would be an adventure like the books of fiction he had read about when he was a child. But now, he found it to be the hardest work he had ever done in his life.

Parker started his writing, logging the hours of hiking the group had accomplished. Parker wrote about how mesmerizing the sights of the mountains were. He couldn't wait to continue the long hike up them in the morning. Kyle yawned and said that he was going to go to bed. Derrick said that they all should get some sleep; they knew Logan was going to want to reach the peak first thing in the morning. Parker reached for the bucket of water and splashed it onto the fire, putting out the flickering flames before retiring for the night.

Logan continued to write for a few more minutes after the others had dozed off. Once his writing was completed, he carefully placed his pencil and journal into his trusty bag that he always kept within arm's reach. He blew out the candle and rested his head on his folded-up jacket. As Logan was looking up at the moon, he spotted an unusual flickering light soaring in the distance. Logan immediately sat up, keeping his eyes focused on the object on the horizon. The object in the sky was on fire and crashing uncontrollably toward the ground. Logan quickly got to his feet. The sound of Logan's movement caused Parker to open his eyes and look back at him.

"What is it, Logan?" Parker asked with concern, which caused the others to open their eyes. There had been nights when the group had to flee from a wild animal. Some of the men thought that this was the case. Logan didn't say anything but just pointed to the sky. Parker and the others on the ground turned their heads toward the sky and saw a falling object hurling down in a frenzy toward the side of the mountain.

The object crashed not too far from them, causing the ground to shake on impact. All the men had their eyes glued to the object the entire time, gaining insight on where it landed. The men could feel the impact of the object striking the ground. They even saw small rocks jump off the ground among flames from the crash site. Parker turned back to Logan, but Logan was already running toward the crash site in a dead sprint with his bag strapped tightly around his shoulder. Parker hurried to his feet, telling the others to get moving. Leaving their bags behind, the men quickly grabbed their boots and ran after Logan.

Logan sprinted up the mountain as fast as he could; he wanted to see the crash site up close. When he got closer to the spot, the ground started to feel hot on his feet. When he reached the crash site, he saw flaming rocks lying around the surrounding large gash that impaled the side of the mountain. Logan came to a halt at the front of the gap. He stared at what looked to be a tunnel. In this moment of pause, the other travelers managed to catch up with him. The seven men all gazed at the tunnel in the mountain without saying a word.

Zach leaned in closer inside the tunnel, resting his hand on the side of the hole for balance support. As soon as Zach placed his hand on the rock, he yanked it away because of the heat that he did not expect to feel. It was like touching a hot stove. He slightly burned his hand. The men were all right standing on the hot crash site because their boots shielded them from the heat radiating from beneath. Due to the cold night, the warmth on their feet felt pretty good.

"Don't touch anything. The fire from the thing that struck this area is still cooling off," Derrick stated.

"Yeah, I'll try to remember that next time," Zach responded, looking at the burn on his hand.

"What was that thing anyway?" wondered Jake.

"A meteor, or an asteroid, I guess," Kyle replied.

"What's the difference?" Jake asked.

"I'm not really sure," Kyle answered. Most of the group turned their heads back to the sky to see if they could spot any more meteors. Logan, on the other hand, never turned his head away from the large tunnel formed by the falling object that crashed into the mountain. See, Logan was the first to the crash site, so he heard a sound coming from the tunnel. When the others got to the site, they were too distracted by the newly found tunnel and didn't bother paying attention to such a hushed sound. When they started talking, the sound was drowned out.

Parker looked at Logan's face as he stared down the tunnel. Logan would sometimes get lost in his own thoughts, so lost that he would forget about everyone around him. Parker knew when Logan entered this state, it meant he was going to do something dangerous, not caring about his or the others' safety. Parker slightly said Logan's name. But Logan didn't respond. Instead, he started to walk into the tunnel. When Logan started marching into the dark tunnel, the others stood still. From the looks of it, the tunnel shouldn't be too long, so they figured that Logan would just turn around after reaching the end. But they knew Logan wouldn't enter the tunnel for the fun of it. If any other person would have entered, they wouldn't have thought anything of it. But this was Logan; it felt that he would lead them to something unbelievable. Parker pointed out that they all have followed him this far, why stop following him now? Parker entered the tunnel, and the others followed. Inside, the ground and walls were emitting warm steam from the heat.

"How could one meteor cause all this?" wondered Kyle.

"The meteor struck the place pretty hard," Ezekiel said, walking behind Kyle.

"Yeah, but you'd think the meteor would have shattered, not dug its way deep inside the side of the mountain," Kyle responded. The men kept walking, way longer than they thought they anticipated. Parker caught up with Logan and asked him what he was doing in there.

"Don't you hear it?" Logan said as he continued to walk. Parker told Logan that he didn't hear anything. But a few steps closer, Parker saw a light at the end of the tunnel. Logan saw it too but didn't say anything. When the others saw it, they grew even more confused. Some started to worry about continuing on, but the desire to see the source of the light was their motivation to keep going. The light grew brighter as they walked closer, and by this time, the others were able to hear what Logan was able to hear from the beginning.

"What is that?" asked Zach. As they neared the end of the tunnel, the fear and excitement grew higher.

"Sounds like...*a waterfall?*" Derrick questioned in a confused tone. The people could not understand why they would be hearing a waterfall in a place like this. Logan reached the end of the tunnel, and what he saw was the most beautiful sight he had ever seen. The sight left him speechless and even drew a tear to his eye. The men all huddled round the hole at the end of the tunnel and were all shocked by the amazing sight.

The men saw a bright blue sky, with white billowing clouds, and a beautiful glowing sun. On the ground was the greenest grass they had ever seen with the healthiest fruit trees scattered about the land. Then they looked to the left and saw the waterfall pouring crystal-clear water into the bluest body of water beneath. "What is this place?" Parker asked.

"The Garden of Eden!" Logan said with wondering eyes.

CHAPTER 2

The Garden of Eden

Standing at the end of the tunnel, the men saw about a thirty-foot drop to the ground of the garden. The garden was bordered by a thick, smooth rock wall that reached up to the sky. The top of the rock wall was shrouded by clouds, creating the illusion that the wall's height was endless. Looking up toward the middle of the land, they saw the blue sky and the bright yellow sun. The men were still speechless from the sight; it took a moment to fully let the beauty of the land sink in. Jake was the first to speak; he asked how the sun could be out at this time of night.

Parker checked his pocket watch, saying that the time was 10:42 p.m., hours before sunrise. The men looked back at the tunnel they traveled through and saw that no light was shining in. It implied that it was still dark outside or, at least, dark on the other side of the tunnel. "How could it be dark out there but sunny in here?" Kyle asked with confusion.

"I think the bigger question is how can an entire garden be inside a mountain?" Zach pointed out.

"You're thinking way too out of the box about this. That meteor probably drove right through the mountain, creating a path to the other side of it," Derrick said, trying to make sense of it. They pointed out if that was true, then how was the sun out on one side of the mountain and not the other? Plus, the mountain was so wide that it would have taken them much longer to walk all the way through it. The men had to discuss every logical possibility before truly believing that this was indeed the Garden of Eden. As the men argued, Logan pulled out a rope from his bag and tied one end of it to an overhanging rock that was lodged near the exit of the tunnel. Logan tugged the rope to test if it would support his weight.

Logan tied his bag to the other end of the rope. Then he stood up, walked past the others, and reached the edge of the tunnel facing the garden. With all his might and without saying a word, Logan leaped off the edge toward the river where the waterfall poured into.

"LOGAN!" shouted Parker.

The men all stopped talking, and with a shocked movement, they turned their heads toward Logan. Logan tossed his bag away from him just before landing into the water. Parker took a knee to get his eyes closer to the bottom to see if Logan survived the fall. The men hovered around Parker's shoulders, also getting in close for a better look.

"How deep do you think that water is?" asked Parker with panic in his tone.

"Hopefully deep enough!" Zach shouted hopefully.

Waiting for Logan to pop up was very stressful for the travelers. All they saw was the splashing of the water from the waterfall and the swinging of the rope with Logan's bag tied to the bottom of it. The men took a reassuring breath when Logan swam up to the surface. The men cheered in celebration seeing that their leader was alive. Logan swam to the grass and hopped out of the water. He caught his swinging bag, and as he untied it, he shouted out to the others, "You coming?" Logan asked it with a smile. This might have been the first invite that the men received from Logan. Parker was the first to jump out of the tunnel into the river. Jake, Ezekiel, Derrick, and Kyle all took huge leaps toward the water, cheering in unison from the fall. Zach, admitting that he's not the best swimmer, opted to climb down the rope.

"That was awesome!" Jake stated as he tossed his head around to get the water out of his ears.

"And the water...perfect temperature!" Derrick added with a fancy hand gesture.

The men no longer talked about how strange this land inside a mountain was or how the sun was out in the middle of the night. It was like all their confusing thoughts and desires to make sense of this land washed away once they entered the grounds. Once Zach finished climbing down the rope, he checked the burn on his hand. The burn was all healed over, as if it was never even there. When he showed this to the others, the belief that this was indeed the Garden of Eden seemed to be the only logical explanation. The men felt that they had stumbled upon the greatest find any traveler could ever dream of. Overwhelmed with joy, the men shouted with glee.

Logan didn't participate in the group cheer, but his happiness for being in this place was visible; he had a joyful grin on his face that wouldn't go away. He really wanted to search the land as fast as he could. Normally, he would just take off on his own and the others would catch up. But this time, he waited until everyone was ready to move. When they started to walk, they had this feeling that the garden was endless. Every new direction they turned felt like it went on forever. A never-ending exploring location was Logan's vision of heaven.

The group stopped by a fruit tree. The fruit was at arm's reach for the men. The fruit was of the pear variety and looked fully ripe for the picking. Once they all had a pear in hand, they passed looks to each other, wondering if they should take a bite. They were not sure if they should eat it or not, but their hunger overwhelmed them, so they all took a big bite. They all felt fine and even felt a little silly for having any worry. They ate the pears they picked and took comfort in the shade of the tree. The men didn't feel like they traveled far into the garden, but looking back at the ground they covered, they could no longer see the rock wall from where they came. They weren't concerned about getting back as they figured the river would be their guide back, a trick they learned over the years of traveling.

The men grew weary, and the grass was so soft that they all lay down under the tree. They were about to fall asleep for the night before they saw the meteor crash on the mountain that led them to this wonderful place. So they decided to go to sleep, right there under the tree. Their thought was to take a quick nap and start exploring more when they woke up. It was easy to fall asleep once their heads touched the soft grass.

Sitting under the tree, a very peaceful place to get some sleep while the gentle breeze kept them at a comfortable temperature.

Sunday, October 5, 1924

A few hours passed when Logan woke up. He turned and saw only five others still asleep; Parker was the one missing. Logan got to his feet, grabbed hold of his bag, and headed to the stream for some water. When he walked toward the water, he saw Parker sitting on a rock alongside the stream. Parker was writing in his journal, unaware that Logan was awake. When Parker heard someone coming, he turned his head toward the sound. Parker saw Logan, and the two nodded at each other in greeting. Logan squatted down next to the water to scoop up some in his hands. He took a drink and then splashed water on his face.

Parker put his pencil down and asked Logan how he slept. Logan didn't face Parker but did respond, saying it was the best sleep he'd had in years. Logan then faced Parker and saw that Parker had his bag with him. Parker informed Logan that when he woke up, he climbed up the rope to exit the garden to fetch his bag. Parker said that he had to write this down in his logbook as soon as he could. Logan asked what it was like leaving the garden and then coming back.

"Pretty strange. When I walked out of the tunnel and was back on the mountain, the sun was rising. After grabbing my stuff and coming back to the rope, I realized the sun here never moved," Parker explained. It was clear that the garden had its own sun, which was such an unbelievable thing to acknowledge for them. Logan sat on the rock beside Parker.

"Why do you do that, write in a journal I mean?" Logan asked.

"I guess it started because I saw you doing it. But when I started, I liked the idea of writing down the places I've been, the places I've seen. Maybe when I settle down, I'll forget all this. If that happens, I'll be glad I jotted all this down so I can read about everything I did. Isn't that why you do it?"

"Yeah, I guess. I like to learn from my travels, the way I learn from my mistakes. Plus, it passes the time," Logan said, laughing at that last part. Parker laughed along with Logan. Parker pointed out that he didn't think he'd ever heard Logan laugh before. Logan said that being around the others, he felt like he had to put on this tough attitude. He said the group would tear each other apart if there wasn't someone who could take command, so he stayed emotionally distanced from the others and became a man of few words. He knew his distance made him come off as mysterious, but Logan admitted that he was never good at making friends. Being alone for so long, he believed that he never wanted to make friends. "Then one day this stranger asked to join me along my journey," Logan said, talking about Parker.

"You could have said no. I expected you to say no. Why didn't you say no?" Parker wondered.

"I guess after being alone for so long, it was time to attempt to make a friend," Logan replied with an awkward grin.

"You consider us friends?" Parker asked.

"I tolerate you, but if I knew you were going to be so welcoming to others who wanted to join, I would have never let you come with me," Logan said, once again laughing at the end of his sentence.

Parker found it nice to see Logan act joyfully for once. Maybe being inside the garden had allowed Logan to relax. Parker now knew why Logan acted the way he did; his being alone for so long made it hard for him to let people in. He, being the group leader, didn't make it easier to make friends. Being a leader is a hard position to be in, even harder if you never wanted the position in the first place.

Jake walked up to the two men, rubbing his eyes to wake up. He asked if the water was drinkable. After coming across contaminated water for so long, he developed a force of habit to ask before drinking. Logan and Parker both told Jake that the water was good to drink, so Jake shoved his face into the water. He took a huge gulp, popped his head out, and said, "I never want to drink dirty water again!" This made Logan and Parker laugh as they saw Jake drive his face back into the water.

Logan asked Parker for the time. Parker pulled out his watch and said that it was 9:42 a.m. Logan said that the others had slept long enough and that it was time to explore. After everyone was awake, the explorers walked around the area; they found some more fruit and even some planted vegetables for breakfast.

There was a thrilling feeling walking around this place. It felt like no man had even been there before, and if it wasn't for that meteor, they would never have found this place. The men thought they would have found some kind of life after a while, animals, or at least some sort of insects. They felt like they were walking for a long time, but according to Parker and his pocket watch, they had only been walking for an hour.

Then they came across a cave. The cave's entrance was a large oval archway. The opening was wide enough for all seven men to stand side by side in front of the entrance. They all turned to Logan, waiting for him to go in first. It was not because they were afraid, but because it wouldn't be right if anyone besides the leader went in first. Logan walked in first, with the others following. Inside, they saw stone steps carved into the ground leading down to a few stone pillars that held up the cave. Ezekiel emitted a shrieking whistle, and the sound echoed throughout the cave.

"This place is big," Ezekiel stated. As the men went deeper into the cave, they spotted a glowing white light in the distance. Following the light led the travelers to an archway leading them to a very wide, tall section of the cave. The light was coming from a giant-sized diamond buried deep into the wall. The men gazed at its beauty, for some of them believed that they just found something that could make them a fortune.

The diamond was glowing, emitting a bright white light, as if it was the North Star. The light lit up the whole room. It looked to be fifteen feet high and eight feet wide. Four feet of the diamond was sticking out of the wall, so they didn't know the depth of the entire gem. The diamond was not smooth; in fact, it was surprisingly rough all over. Derrick was the first with his hands on it; others were scared to touch it due to its odd glowing presence, but Derrick could tell from the touch of it that this was a real diamond.

"How do we get it out of here?" Jake asked, walking up closer to it.

"*How do we get it out of here?* Look at it! That thing probably weighs over a ton!" Ezekiel pointed out.

"It's stuck inside the wall. Who knows how long it'll take to dig it out?" Zach added.

"Guys, even if we could dig it out and could move it...it won't fit out of the cave!" Ezekiel shouted.

"If you're not going to be helpful, then shut up!" Jake yelled at Ezekiel. Jake, Zach, Derrick, and Kyle all tried to push and shove the diamond; but it didn't even budge. Ezekiel took a closer look at the diamond.

"I think I have an idea," Ezekiel said to the others.

"It better be helpful!" Jake threatened Ezekiel, no longer tolerating his negative input.

"This part right here." Ezekiel pointed to the largest facet sticking out of the diamond. "If we can chop this part off, we would be able to collect a very big payday!" Ezekiel was from a wealthy family, so he was very familiar with prices of jewelry and the value of diamonds in particular. The guys wished to bring the entire diamond with them, but realistically, this was the only option.

"Only problem…how are we supposed to chip this piece off!" Jake asked. They turned to Parker and Logan who kept quiet during this time. Getting money wasn't a priority for Logan. But Parker thought a nice and easy cash grab like this would be something smart to participate in. He could settle down and buy a house with that kind of money. Logan was silent, but Parker said that the only way to cut a diamond was with another diamond. Parker's idea was to have everyone to go on a search to hopefully find another diamond that they could use as a tool to slice off the section of the diamond.

The men liked this idea, so they all left the cave and headed out in different directions. Parker told them to be back in twenty minutes; he checked his pocket watch for the time and waited by the entrance of the cave. Logan stayed back with Parker. "You really think we could take a chunk of that rock out with us?" Logan asked Parker.

"It's worth a try, isn't it?" Parker responded.

"I guess," Logan uttered.

While the others were scattering all over the garden, Derrick was walking alongside the rock wall that surrounded the entire garden. The border had small hills around the land, giving him a chance to marvel at the endless scenery. He kept his eyes to the left, hoping to find another cave. Then by pure luck, he turned his head to the right, facing the rock wall. There he saw a crack in it, right at eye level. He looked in the crack of the wall and spotted something shiny in it. Derrick placed his right hand inside the crack and felt something. He grabbed it and pulled. The object took some force to remove, but when his hand came out of the wall, he was holding a long sword with a handle made of pure gold.

Derrick couldn't believe what he found just by luck. He felt mighty holding the weapon, like there was no challenge he couldn't win. He touched the blade and was immediately cut. Derrick looked at the cut on his finger. The cut healed up right away. The travelers discovered that the garden had the power to heal all wounds to any who stood on its ground. Derrick knew that this sword was special, and if there was anything that could chip off a piece of the diamond, it had to be this.

Back at the cave, the men were arguing with each other. The disappointment in failing to find another diamond had them all yelling at each other. No one even noticed that Derrick was still absent from the group. Some of the travelers were afraid of getting lost, so they didn't wander off too far. One of the men claimed that he saw a unicorn and ran away from it. The others thought that he was just making up lies to get out of searching.

Logan didn't step in to stop the argument this time; he just sat on the side alone waiting for them to stop on their own. Logan didn't care much for money, so he hoped that this idea of bringing a piece of the diamond home with them would pass due to their endless complaining. But from a distance came Derrick's voice saying he found a sword. The presence of the sword got all the men's attention, and the bickering came to an immediate end. The sword was so shiny that it was hard not to stare right at it. Derrick claimed a *finders keepers* rule on the sword. The group said they would only agree if the sword could do the job. Otherwise, they were going to sell it and split the cash.

The men hustled back into the cave to return to the diamond. "Okay, Derrick, slice it right here," Ezekiel instructed while pointing to the exposed chunk of diamond.

"Wait, why does he get to cut it?" Jake instantly asked.

"I found the sword, so I should be the one to use it!" Derrick stated.

"Maybe we should have someone with some muscle do this," Zach suggested.

"Like you, *scrawny*?" Jake said, mocking Zach's weak arms.

"We should give it to Logan!" Kyle yelled. This caused the men to grow silent and look at Logan. Logan was the strongest of the group, so they knew he was physically capable of doing it. Logan didn't say anything, just nobly stood by and watched.

"Yeah, I'm okay with that," Derrick said, agreeing with Kyle.

"Fine with me," Zach added.

After Jake agreed, Parker gave Logan a pat on the back saying that it was only fitting that Logan did this task. Derrick offered the sword over to Chuck. Logan paused before receiving it. Logan was skeptical. He took a quick look at everyone. If this was what they wanted him to do, then he'd do it. Logan took the sword from Derrick; once it was in his grip, he had this overwhelming feeling of confidence and pride. The feelings hit him like a splash of cold water. It was odd but delightful at the same time.

Logan stood right next to the diamond, eyeing his target. He raised the sword above his head with both hands. He took in a deep breath, and with all his might, he brought the sword down right on target, grunting during the motion. To his amazement, the blade sliced through the diamond with almost no trouble. But the moment the object was split off from the main piece, the glowing white light from the diamond was released from the cut. The white light blasted out as fast as lightning. The blast looked like a shock wave striking all seven men and knocking them down. The men hit the ground hard, and the diamond suddenly lost its glowing feature. Outside the cave, the garden's bright sky turned pitch black, the waterfall suddenly ran dry, the streams became motionless, and the gentle breeze became nonexistent.

CHAPTER 3

The Price of Fortune

Logan was the only one who passed out from the light wave blast, while the others were only knocked off their feet. As Logan was under, he had a mysterious dream. In the dream, he saw the garden; he was looking at the location where he and the others had entered. He saw an unknown person approaching the rope that dangled out of the exit tunnel. Logan couldn't get a good look at the person; the sight of him was blurry. The person seemed to be a tall male who looked very strong and wore dirty, raggedy gray clothes. Logan couldn't get a clear look at the face of the man. The stranger climbed up the rope and marched through the tunnel. Logan believed that he just witnessed something evil leave the garden and headed out to the outside world. Logan then was awakened by Parker who gave him a heavy shake.

Relieved that the dream was over, Logan opened his eyes. Parker asked Logan if he was all right; Logan nodded yes. "What happened?" Logan asked. Parker helped Logan to his feet.

"I don't know. Once you sliced off the piece of the diamond, we were all hit by some white light, and then…darkness," Parker explained.

The darkness didn't last long, a few moments at most. The diamond's glow came back, along with the garden's bright sky as if everything went back to normal. Logan looked around and perceived the frightened looks of his fellow travelers. Being hit by that blast that was followed by the total darkness made them apprehensive. Some of them thought Logan was dead when they saw him on the ground unconscious. Normally they would feel some relief seeing Logan was all right, but the shock of fear still covered them, resulting in a strange indifference toward Logan.

No words were said after Parker told Logan what happened. Logan carefully handed the sword over to Derrick. Derrick slowly took it, and once he had it, he embraced it close to himself for some feel of safety or protection. Logan turned and saw the chipped-off piece of the diamond he caused. Logan knelt beside it and eyed the object with concern. The chipped-off piece didn't have the glow it once did; being separated from the main piece must be the reason, he thought. Logan gently cradled the piece with both hands. He turned to the others as fear still shrouded their faces. Not even the success of the severing of the diamond caused them to smile. Logan reached for his bag and packed the diamond inside. With the diamond secured, he motioned toward the exit. The men got to their feet and quietly walked out of the cave in a single-file line with Logan exiting last.

Reaching the garden's sunlight made the group a little more relaxed. The men wanted to start heading to the exit. All the excitement of exploring the garden had passed, and they were eager to get out. They turned to Logan for permission to leave. When all eyes were on Logan, he pointed to the direction of the tunnel and started to lead the way. The men all walked with no distractions. The beauty of the environment didn't seem to impress them anymore. When they reached the rope, they all climbed one by one back up to the hole in the wall. Logan was the last to climb the rope. He took a moment on the ground to take one last look around.

He remembered his dream of someone else using the rope. Logan told himself that it was only a dream and that there was no stranger who exited the garden earlier. But Logan wasn't sure if he believed that. Parker yelled out from the tunnel, asking if Logan was all right.

"I'm fine, just taking one last look. Climbing up now," Logan replied. The travelers marched out of the tunnel and returned to their campsite before the sun went down. They lit a fire and started eating the food they had left over from their last meal, along with the food they took from the garden.

"How long were we gone?" asked Jake with a mouthful of food, anxious to break the awkward silence that had been haunting them since leaving the cave.

Parker checked the time and stated that they were in the garden for half a day. The group found it hard to believe that they hadn't even spent a full day inside the garden. Due to the sun never leaving its position, time felt like it moved differently inside the garden. Even though their time inside the garden was brief, some felt that days had passed. It felt like they spent a lifetime within the garden.

"When we were in there…did anyone see anybody else?" Logan asked the group. The dream that Logan had was still haunting him. He felt that the person he saw in the dream was real, so he was hoping someone else had seen him.

"I didn't see anyone…Now that I think about it, it felt kind of creepy, like a ghost town or something," Jake stated.

"I'm telling you, I *saw* a unicorn!" Kyle shouted. The group didn't believe Kyle, saying it was probably just a regular horse.

"Why do you ask, Logan? Did you see someone in there?" Parker asked Logan with a hint of concern.

Logan took a moment to think if he should share his dream with the others. He didn't want to worry the group about something that was just a dream, so he said that he was just wondering.

The men changed the topic by asking what they were going to do with their share of the money they were going to make selling the diamond. This topic got the group in a happier mood.

"People are going to wonder where we got it from," Kyle said.

Zach said they couldn't say they found it in the Garden of Eden; people would think they were crazy and the diamond was a fake. The group made an agreement that they wouldn't tell anyone about the garden nor the events that happened inside it.

The men said they had time to come up with a story on how they found the diamond later, so they continued talking about what they would do with the money they got from cashing it in. From the plans the men were making with their future money, it sounded like this was the end of the seven travelers. They all talked about buying a house and settling down. After everyone shared their plans, they asked Logan what he would do.

"I bet he'll continue his travels and find Atlantis," Zach said, making a funny statement. This made the others laugh also. Joking aside, the others did really wonder what Logan would do now. Logan said he wasn't sure as money was never a goal for him. Traveling was the only thing that interested him. He said they never headed up the mountain, and seeing the sun rise from top of the mountain was one of his goals. He said that after they sold the diamond, he'd work on crossing that goal off his list.

The men spent the rest of the day hanging out around the fire. The group was all getting along with no more pointless arguments or nasty attitudes toward one another. For once, Logan wasn't annoyed by being around them. The day grew late, so they settled down for sleep. It was a slow day for the men, which was nice because the next days would just fly by.

Monday, October 6, 1924

When the new day started, the goal was to get a boat ticket to New York. The group wanted to sell the diamond in a big city and chose to use a boat to get them there. The travelers always walked to their destination, but they made an exception taking a boat because they were impatient. The travel expenses were covered by Ezekiel who said he was happy that he finally got a chance to use the money he packed for the trip. After getting to New York, it wasn't until **Tuesday, October 7, 1924,** when they sold the diamond.

The diamond was huge news as it was the largest ever discovered. The men each received a small taste of fame after making the sale. Many reporters wished to interview them, but none of them were saying a word. Zach was the reporter of the group, so he handled the story himself. Finding a huge story like this was his reason for joining the travelers in the first place. With Zach's share of the money, he planned to buy his own newspaper business. Zach wrote a fictional story about how the diamond was discovered. Giving a location that was nowhere near the real location to help keep the garden from being discovered, he and the others agreed with the story Zach created. A photo was taken of the seven travelers for the paper. The photo was all seven men smiling with their hands on the diamond.

After the men had their money, they started making plans to go home. The men all headed off by train, boat, or horseback. By the morning of **Saturday, October 11, 1924,** the only two travelers were Logan and Parker. Logan and Parker's last trip together was back to Parker's hometown, not too far from New York; it was on the way to Logan's destination. They come to Parker's parents' home, a nice small house in the country. Parker was excited to see his family again. Before Parker walked to the porch, he was ready to say his goodbye to his friend Logan.

"It's been a great few years, Logan. Thank you for the unforgettable adventure!" Parker said as he shook Logan's hand. "Are you sure you don't want to come in, maybe spend a few nights before you get back on the road?"

"It's best for me to just take off now. I don't want to extend the goodbye for any longer," replied Logan.

"Well, you know my address, so drop me a letter sometime. We should stay in touch, you know. I'm going to be worried about you on your own."

"I was on my own long before I met you, Parker. I'll be fine," he said with a smile.

Logan was about to walk away, but Parker pulled him in for a hug. Logan couldn't remember the last time he was hugged. It must have been before his parents died back when he was fourteen. Logan realized that he did, indeed, have a friend; this was hard to believe due to his spending his life shutting people out for so long. The two said goodbye, and Logan took off.

Logan walked for a long time, and things were going well. No one slowed him down, there were no complaints from others, and he got to stop when he wanted. But thinking about the others did make him miss them a little. He even started to fear being alone again. He felt that his time of being alone should be over. He thought about how Parker was planning on settling down and starting a family. This made Logan wish to find a new friend, one whom he could love and call wife. He thought about ending his nonstop travels for once; he flirted with the idea of trying something new.

Logan was in such deep thought as he walked blindly forward, deep into the woods. Then his train of thought was interrupted by the sound of a nearby bear. Logan's head rose toward the sound of the animal. There was a large grizzly bear staring right in his direction. Logan, frozen with fear, had many thoughts rushing through his mind. Logan had heard many instructions on what to do when you came across a wild bear. Many instructions were different; he was once told to play dead, while another was to make yourself as large as possible as you screamed with hopes of frightening the beast away. The one instruction that had kept Logan safe for so long was do your best to avoid bears at all times. But that one was long past, and there was no way he could play dead now that the bear had already seen him alive.

Logan knew he would not be able to outrun the animal, so he felt his only option was to try to frighten the bear. The bear started to move closer to Logan; in return, Logan threw his hands high into the air and screamed out loud. The bear then rose to two feet growling at Logan. Logan pushed his hands toward the bear over and over, trying to make himself look more intimidating. Then out of Logan's right hand blasted out a violet stream of light. It flowed out of his hand and then struck the chest of the bear. The blast gave the bear a tiny shock, as if it was hit with a stun gun set on low. This was enough to get the bear to return to his four legs and walk away. Logan patiently watched the bear walk away. Once it was out of sight, Logan started to walk in the opposite direction of the bear. He was cradling his right hand, examining it, trying to figure out what just came out of it.

CHAPTER 4

More Than What They Were

Logan found a creek and squatted down for a drink. He gulped up a handful of water, followed by splashing himself with the refreshing liquid afterward. The shock, mystery, and fear of what just happened felt like a nightmare he couldn't shake. He checked his reflection within the water, wondering if he still looked the same. As he looked at his face, he didn't see any changes. He looked deeper into the water and asked himself, *Think you can do it again?* Logan talking to himself wasn't anything new to him. It was something he used to do all the time when he was on his own. Logan felt like he could think better talking out loud, a style of thinking that he had not done since Parker started to follow him. He missed it, and in a way, talking to himself again after all this time was like talking to an old friend.

Logan stood up tall facing a nearby tree. Logan faced the tree chest out, shoulders back, chin down, as if he was an action hero. He then waved his hand fast at the tree, hoping to let the light out once again. No light blast came out from his hand. Logan tried again with the other hand but still no light. He tried until he started to lose breath. In anger, Logan kicked the creek, splashing water and disturbing the serenity. "Come on, Logan!" Logan shouted at himself. Logan caught his breath and started to think.

How did you do it last time? Logan checked his memory of the bear attack. He even recreated his action from how it happened. "I was walking, and then I saw the bear…" Logan started to think how he was feeling when he saw the bear. "Fear…but that wasn't when the light came out." Logan then looked at his hand. "No, I was only afraid at first. After that, I called upon courage and confidence. I needed it if I was going to defend myself from the bear. I didn't want to die. I was just thinking about what I wanted out of life before I saw the bear. Friends, a wife, family…love." Logan wasn't sure if all this was connected, but he faced the tree once again. This time instead of shooting at the tree with a blank mind, he gave himself confidence that he could do this once again. This time when Logan waved his hand at the tree, the same violet color light blasted right out of the edge of his fingertips, flowing right at the tree. Bark went flying off the tree from the impact of the light. Logan was amazed, impressed, and jubilant that he was able to call upon the light once again.

Logan then walked toward the tree, firing off more light and blasting off more bark from the tree. He now knew the trigger as he walked through the woods, amused and amazed with his newfound power. Each blast of light he forced to come out caused him to grow exhausted, as if he was doing twenty-five push-ups for each blast. Despite his strong physical conditioning, the toll of this new discovery had driven him to a state of exhaustion. By blast number 12, he had to stop. He even knelt to catch his breath. He figured out that there was some muscle required to cause this act. This just fascinated him even more, as he couldn't wait to catch his breath so he could further study this new ability.

Thursday, October 16, 1924

Within the next five days, Logan got a new journal and was filling it with all his new abilities. He called the sorcery that was able to defend him from the bear a *defense spell*. After training a few days on his defense spell, he saw that the light started to turn into a light blue. When he fired off a blue, it felt as if he reached a new level of strength along with a new feeling of exhaustion. Whenever his defense spell reached a new level of power, his

25

body would react as any person who lifted daily. One morning after a light rainfall, Logan looked up and saw a rainbow. Logan grinned and believed he found a power-level chart in a way. He believed that the color revealed the strength levels of his attack; the stronger the attack, the darker the color reached until it gained the next color. He went from a light violet to a dark violet, and now he was strong enough to reach light blue.

Logan wondered what would happen if he focused all his new inner light power to do something amazing. Logan had a feeling that this power could take him places. With a gut feeling, he felt like he could muster enough energy inside himself to travel great distances in an instant. He couldn't explain this feeling, but it was something he knew he had to try. Logan went out to the woods to find a private spot. He thought if he could channel this power inside him, he could use it to take him anywhere he wanted. Logan began to focus in a meditative state. He could somehow feel the energy in him start to flow around his body like warm water. He stayed focused on his goal for a given destination. Then, in a blink, he was gone. The space where he once was quickly filled with air, creating a *poof* sound.

Logan appeared in Maine, on top of one of the mountains. The air around his body was blown away with high speed when he appeared, causing a gust sound. He looked around in a sense of wonder, not fully believing his experiment was a success. When Logan realized he was now standing on top of the mountain that he had pictured in his mind, he threw his hands up high, letting out a cheerful victory cry. He was fascinated; he could be in any place he could picture in his mind, with just a concentrated thought. This would make traveling a breeze and save so much time. Logan made camp on top of the mountain for the night. In his journal, he wrote down his newly learned ability, the power of teleportation.

Friday, October 17, 1924

Logan woke up early because he didn't want to miss the sunrise. Back when Logan's parents were ill, he was used to seeing depressing sights. After they passed, he no longer saw beauty in the world. He made it his goal to witness something beautiful, a chance to take in the wonders of the world; so he went out east, saying he wanted to be the first in America to witness the sunrise. What he ended up seeing was something far beyond what he ever thought possible: the Garden of Eden. Thanks to that place, he gained a new ability with his powers he still hasn't fully mastered.

The sun rose just like it did every morning, and Logan felt the beginning of a new day. Now that Logan completed his goal of watching the sunrise, it was time for something new in his life. He now understood the feeling that his fellow travelers had of settling down and finding a place to grow roots. That's what Logan desired now, and he was willing to make it happen.

Logan got to his feet and started walking down the mountainside. He wasn't ready to teleport again; he wanted to stretch his legs. As he walked down, he heard something in the area. It was the sound of people. He followed the sound to the source, and he couldn't believe who he found.

Right then and there were all of Logan's old traveling mates. They were all there, Parker, Jake, Zach, Ezekiel, Derrick, and Kyle. He could not believe his eyes and even wondered if this was a dream.

"Hey, he's here!" shouted Jake who was the first to see Logan. All eyes were on Logan with looks of disbelief and jubilation. The men were all waiting for Logan to arrive and began to fear that he would never show. The men rushed up to Logan to say hello. Logan was still so stunned by seeing everyone that he was speechless.

"What are you all doing here?" Logan finally brought himself to ask.

"Well, we're guessing by now you've learned that there is something different about you," Parker stated with a joyful speech. He was just happy that everyone was once again together.

"Yeah, I've been trying to study it for some time now," Logan stated.

"Study it? I figured it out pretty quick when one of my horses fell on top of me a few days ago," Ezekiel stated.

"Yeah, I knew I was stronger when these guys tried to pick a fight against me at a bar. I wiped the floor with them!" Jake added. Logan was puzzled, not sure what to think of all this information.

"Wait, what are you guys talking about?" Logan wondered.

"We're talking about how we learned about our superstrength," Jake replied.

"What did you mean by *superstrength*?" Logan asked.

"Were all stronger, Logan…like *Hercules* strong," Kyle replied.

"Aren't you stronger?" Zach questioned. Logan looked around. It was clear to him that none of them had the same powers he did. It was strange that they had something else altogether.

"You all have this *enhanced* strength, nothing else?" Logan asked the group.

The excitement of everyone being back had now passed, and now things started to feel intense. They only nodded; the group was now wondering what was on Logan's mind. Logan felt somehow forsaken, feeling out of place and alone. He told the men, as if it was a confession, that he hadn't received any enhanced strength; but he had the power of something different. Logan fired off a defense spell to show off his powers. This caused the men to jump back in shock. Some were even scared of Logan.

"What the heck was that?" Jake shouted.

The men looked at Logan differently, as if he now carried something unnatural inside him. Logan said that he learned of this ability not too long after the group spilt up. The group didn't understand why Logan had this power while the others didn't. It was a mystery; why didn't he have the enhanced strength was another question. Why couldn't the others do what he could do?

This mystery is why they all returned to the mountain. They believed that the answers were within the deep dark bowels of the garden. But none of them felt right going back inside without the others present. Within just a few days, every member of this group returned to this campsite, waiting for everyone to arrive. In the end, they waited for Logan to return. Now that they were all present and accounted for, they were ready to find the answers to what happened to them inside the garden.

The men wasted no time; they headed right to the tunnel of the garden's entry. It felt like years when these men first went down this tunnel, but it was only less than two weeks. Everything looked exactly as it did the first time they saw it. They once again heard the waterfall and then saw the light. The rope was still right where they left it; Logan climbed down while the others simply jumped down to the ground. With their new strength, a thirty-foot fall felt more like a simple hop to the ground. Their landing caused a small indentation on the surface. Once Logan had his feet on the ground, they all marched to the cave.

The beauty of the land no longer impressed the men as they walked past glorious sights totally unaffected. For some reason, the look of the place didn't have the same effect looking at it a second time. The shock that the men faced when they got hit by that blast from the diamond still gave them goose bumps. When they approached the entrance of the cave, the men froze in fear. Logan was the only one who didn't hesitate walking up to it. Logan passed out from the blast, so he wasn't awake when the light went off. He didn't experience the same fear as the others.

The men refused to enter the cave, saying they'd gone far enough. "Guys, we came here to find answers...They may lie in there," Parker stated.

The men refused to budge any closer to the cave. They told Parker that he could go in, and they'd wait outside. Logan said he wasn't afraid, so he went in to get a look at the diamond. Parker followed his friend inside while the five leery comrades waited outside.

"What makes them so scared?" Logan asked Parker as they were getting close to the diamond.

"The light that blasted all of us when you cut that sliver off of the diamond was just something that none of us expected. It terrified us," Parker replied.

"I was just as shocked as the rest of you."

"You passed out from the blast while the rest of us experienced total, complete darkness. The sunlight shining from the entrance was also gone. It felt like we would never see the light again. But it was more than that...we didn't hear anything. We couldn't hear wind, or even the water running through the river. It felt like all life vanished, and we entered a world of complete darkness."

Parker's walk came to a halt as he spoke this, like he didn't fully realize how terrified he was until he said it out loud. Parker needed a minute to take this in; he had to gather his courage once more to continue his walk. Logan could see that Parker needed a moment; bringing all that up brought fear to his tone. Parker then took a step forward, followed by another.

"And when the light came back on, we thought you were dead, which wasn't the best sight," Parker said as he walked next to Logan.

"I guess I'm a little happy that I passed out from the blast and didn't have to experience the fear of total darkness." Logan felt that he should have told Parker about his dream he had when he was passed out, the dream of a mysterious person exiting the garden. But he didn't want to add any more fear to Parker's mild panic attack. Since Logan didn't fully understand the dream, he felt that he should keep it to himself. The two made it to the diamond and were standing right in front of it. The diamond was glowing as bright as when they first saw it.

Logan squatted down to check the location where he chopped off the piece. The location should have been sharp, with pointy edges from the sloppy slash job Logan did on it. But it was fully smooth, as if there was never a scar on it. "It healed itself," Logan said, feeling his hand on the smooth location.

"How did it do that?" wondered Parker.

Logan looked up at the diamond and came up with an educated guess.

"Well, this land has the power to heal wounds. Remember Zach's burned hand healed right up as soon as his feet touched the ground of the garden. I think this the diamond was able to heal the cut I made on it," Logan explained.

"Okay, but that doesn't explain how we got our powers," Parker added. As Logan stayed in his squatted position looking at the glowing diamond, he ventured forth an explanation.

"Well, when I fire off my defense spells, the blast comes from the energy I hold inside my body. I believe this diamond is a container of that same energy. I think this diamond holds the fuel that keeps the garden the way it is. It keeps the sun glowing, the water flowing, the wind blowing. When I cut off a piece of it, that *fuel* was released striking us down, which would explain why everything went dark. I blew out the candle in a way," Logan said, trying to think of the best, easiest way to explain his hypothesis.

Parker understood what Logan was saying, that the garden was like a candle, and the diamond was the flame that kept it bright. Parker agreed that Logan's theory would explain why everything went lifeless after the blast. Logan said that the diamond was powerful enough to seal off the cut and refill the fuel inside, and after the diamond was repaired, it was able to do its job of keeping the garden beautiful. Logan added that the same energy that was contained inside the diamond had sunk its way inside his body, giving him his powers.

"But this only covers why you have your powers. This doesn't explain the advanced strength the rest of us possess," Parker stated.

As Parker went on talking, Logan checked the ground where he was squatting. "Maybe it was the food that we ate here. Was there anything we ate that you didn't?" asked Parker.

"I ate everything you guys did. And I think you're forgetting that the blast hit all of us, not just me," Logan uttered, having more focus on what he was digging up from the ground with his hand.

"The blast did hit you first. Maybe you absorbed more of the fuel than the rest of us, but you don't have any strength, which still confuses me."

Logan retrieved something from the ground; he stood up tall and turned toward Parker, holding what he found in his hand. "Maybe I just had a different side effect from the event."

It was clear that Logan no longer cared about thinking any further about this; instead, he was more interested in what he found. Parker looked at Logan's palm and saw little flakes of the diamond heaped on top of each other. He held them in his hand like small pebbles. Parker couldn't believe that none of the others noticed them the last time they were there; they must have been in too big of a hurry to get out. Logan searched the pile and found the largest piece. He handed it over to Parker, saying he could have it.

"No, we should tell the others about it. It isn't fair that I get to keep it without the others knowing," Parker stumbled to say.

"Oh, come on, Parker. For once be selfish. You were the only one brave enough to come back here, so in return, you deserve this," Logan replied.

Logan saw that Parker was caught between his unselfish attitude and the temptation of getting a free diamond ring–size rock. Parker thought that this could be a good gift to someone special, and if he wished to marry someone someday, he would love to give her a rock like that. So in thinking like that, Parker took Logan's advice and accepted the offer. Parker hurried and put it in his pocket, fearing that the others may come in and see it.

"What are you going to do with the rest?" wondered Parker.

The remaining pieces in Logan's hand were so small it felt like Logan was holding sand. Logan said he could study it to see if they had any power left in them. The two felt like they got all the answers they were going to get from the cave, so they headed out to tell the others what they'd learned. Once outside the cave, the two told the men their theory of the diamond being a container of power that kept the garden as it was. That same power was now inside all of them. The only explanation that the men could come up with was that the energy had a different effect on them, which was why six of them had advanced strength and Logan had sorcery powers. Now that they learned all that they could from this place, they wanted to leave.

After climbing up the rope, one of them mentioned that they shouldn't leave the garden open and exposed like the way it was. Logan proposed a method of locking the entrance up. He said that he could try to make a spell that would keep people out. The men agreed that the place should be sealed off and asked what Logan needed in order to perform the spell. Logan asked the strong men to find a boulder, one that would cover the view of the garden. Three of the strong men found a rock, a large heavy stone. The three rolled it down the path to where the garden met the tunnel.

When the three men rolling the boulder neared the edge of the tunnel, they were able to place it right where it needed to be to block the view of the garden. Logan said the rock would block the entrance, but to ensure that no one could move it, he was going to cast a spell on it. He told the others to wait outside the tunnel as he experimented with this idea. The strong men left Logan alone in the tunnel and waited at the campsite.

Logan took some of the pebbles he got from the cave and buried them around the bolder. He then placed both hands on the stone and started to channel the power inside him onto the rock. As the others waited outside, much time had passed, and they started to worry for Logan. The length of his absence started to concern them, so they all returned to the tunnel to check on him. When they found Logan, they found him lying on the ground asleep.

Parker gently woke his friend up, asking if he was all right. Logan said that placing the spell on the rock took a lot out of him. They asked if the spell worked as they were more concerned for that than Logan's health. Logan asked them to attempt to move it; Logan himself wasn't sure if the spell worked. Jake tried to move the rock; his blood veins popped up due to his heavy attempt to simply budge the rock to the right. The men were amazed by the steadfastness of the stone.

"How did you do it, Logan?" wondered Zach.

"I gave the rock some of the power from the garden. I charged it up with some of my own power as well. This rock holds the same kind of powers that we have in our bodies," Logan explained.

"But what if someone tries to smash it with a hammer or something?" wondered Kyle.

"Since I used small pebbles from the diamond, the healing spell is blessed into the rock, so it'll never crumble," Logan stated.

"But what if we want to get back in?" Derrick asked.

"Well…you'll have to depower the rock," Logan replied.

"How are we supposed to do that?" Parker questioned.

Logan said that the stone was made to absorb the same kind of power that lies within the seven men. Logan said that you could drain the door's energy when two people with powers were touching the rock at the same time. When the rock absorbed the two people's powers, it would overload it and then in a way be turned off and rolled out of the way on its own.

"This will take away our powers?" wondered Jake.

"It'll drain you, but only for a short while. It can't take away your powers, only make you feel so weak that you won't feel like you have them at all," Logan answered.

"So it takes two to open the door?" Parker asked, touching the rock. Logan nodded.

"That's good. It makes it so that this place is ours, and no one can share it without another's permission," Ezekiel reported. Zach wanted to know if it would really work, but no one volunteered to be a key. The seven kept the rock away from arm's reach from the fear of their power being drained. They believed Logan, and after seeing Jake fail to move the rock, they knew the garden was secured. So they never tested the door, taking Logan's word for it that two people were the key to unlock it.

So now that it was all over, the travelers once again all took off to return to their lives, now knowing why they were more than what they were. Parker was in a hurry to return to his hometown. He was hoping Logan could walk to the train with him to be able to catch up. But Logan said he was going to stay at the mountain for a while. Parker told Logan to come out to visit him someday. Logan, now developing a new sense of friendship, said if he was in the area, he would. Parker was the last to leave, making Logan alone at the campsite.

On the train home, Parker wrote in his journal about the garden's magic door and that it would take two people with power to open it. He wished to return to it someday, so he made a goal to stay in touch with the other travelers. He got their mailing addresses and promised to send letters updating them on what was going on in his life, and maybe they would do the same.

Logan was happy to see his fellow travelers once again. He was glad that he believed that he found the answer to the source of his powers. For the first time in a long time, Logan felt a sense of completion. He succeeded at his goal of being the first in the country to witness the sunrise, a goal he desired when his parents passed away. His love for traveling felt over, and now he wished to follow in his past travelers' footsteps by settling down. He also wished to continue improving his power skills. Logan was now ready to find a place to build a home.

CHAPTER 5

The Renshaw Mansion

By November 1, Logan had fully mastered his power of teleportation. After visiting a post office, he picked up postcards that had photos of locations all around the country. After getting a look at the locations, all he had to do was visualize the place in his head; and with his new power, he could appear there in a blink of an eye. Logan saw some amazing sights within just one week, which would have otherwise taken him years to see all these places if he had traveled on foot.

Logan moved to Ohio, the state where he was born. He wanted to live in a place where he could experience all four seasons. He said if the weather stayed one way for too long, he would get bored with it. Logan finally started to use his share of the cash reward from the diamond by buying a patch of land. He bought acres of woods. The location was a short distance away from a small town, so it was very secluded. Logan was planning to hire a crew to build him a house there.

Logan spoiled himself. At first, he thought a nice one-bedroom house was all he wanted, but he wanted to go big for once. Instead of the modest home he once thought would be adequate, he ordered a big mansion to be built. He named it *the Renshaw Mansion*, after his last name. As construction began, Logan had to find a place to give his powers a workout. Logan was able to buy some very cheap land in the Ohio area.

He bought a swamp. Miles and miles of dead land provided the perfect shelter to shut out unwelcomed guests. There was little chance of anyone running into him while using his powers there. The place smelled, bugs were everywhere, and the ground was all damp and muddy. It was an ideal atmosphere to ensure that he would be left alone.

After walking deep into the swamp, Logan knelt, removed his backpack, and placed it in front of him. He reached into his bag and removed the remaining pebbles he took from the diamond of the garden. He had a theory that he wanted to try. With the pebbles in his left hand, Logan used his right hand to dig out a hole in the land. He placed a leather cloth into the hole and placed the pebbles on top of it. He used some string to tie up the corners of the cloth containing the pebbles inside. He then covered the hole with the dirt with the bag still inside. Logan stood up and saw the land around him start to transform into something amazing. The mucked-up ground became solid and started to grow the greenest grass. The leaves on the trees grew bright green, the watering hole nearby suddenly became crystal clear, and the bugs scurried away. The displeasing odor faded and was replaced with the smell of fresh flowers that started to grow around the area. The reach of this beautiful land only stretched out for an acre. Outside this acre, the land was still a wasteful, dead swamp.

Logan loved this; the beautiful land was covered by miles of the swamp so no one would ever know about the nice spot nor venture out there. Logan could do his spells without anyone noticing. Logan built a small cabin right on top of the spot where he buried the pebbles so he'd always remember where they were hidden. Logan painted a name on the cabin, calling it *the Diamond in the Rough*. In the cabin, he had a desk where he could log into his journals. Logan hung a newspaper up on the wall. This newspaper contained the story of him and the others finding the diamond, including the photo of all seven men who found it. Logan started a new journal dedicated to how he worked his powers. He talked about his defense spells and the level of power strength it had. He talked about his power of teleportation.

Out in his cabin where he lived while construction was being done on the mansion, he tried out a new spell. While in the garden, he saw a burn from Zach's hand heal once touching the land. Logan thought if he could create a spell like that, wounds and injuries would be a thing of the past. Logan placed his hand on a hot log from his cooking fire. The burn caused him to hop up and down in pain. "Oh, this was a dumb idea!" Logan shouted. Logan was in too much pain to settle down to focus on his spell. After a quick moment of letting the pain sink in, he forced himself to calm down. "All right, now concentrate!" Logan yelled at himself, looking at the burn on his hand.

Logan was still stressed from his burn, and the pain was all he could think about. He took some deep breaths and then was able to focus. Then, like magic, the burn was healed up as if it was never there. Logan let out a huge smile, followed by a loud cheer of joy. "YES!"

Logan was able to recreate the healing ability the garden had. Logan wrote it down in his journal, calling it a heal spell.

"All right! Now to see if I can do it again," Logan said as he reached out for the hot log once again. Logan repeated the flinching reaction he had the first time, yelling at himself about why he would test it again. The second time around, Logan was able to execute the heal spell much faster and felt that he could get the knack of turning it on right away just moments after getting hurt by anything. There was a tree that still had some life in it just outside the acre being blessed by the diamond pebbles. Logan tried to fire out the heal spell form his hand onto the tree. But the heal spell didn't get released like a defense spell works, so Logan learned that he couldn't forward the heal spell to someone through the air. But Logan didn't give up; he placed his hand onto the tree, and then with his powers, he was able to transfer a heal spell to the tree. He added this in his journal, saying the heal spell couldn't be transferred through the air. He must be touching whomever he was healing.

Later that night, Logan grew the idea of reversing the heal spell. A *death spell* he thought but didn't see the reason to ever use a spell like that. He reasoned that he could never take a life; his defense spell would protect him if he would ever find himself in battle. Still, he had to know if he was capable of killing someone with his powers. He needed to know what he was capable of doing. He walked up to a flower that was growing. He grabbed the flower and started to focus on reversing the powers of the heal spell.

Logan quickly let go of the flower. He didn't want to be touching the flower when releasing his attack onto it, fearing that it would affect him as well. When Logan focused on his outcome, a dark-violet blast flickered out of his finger landing onto the flower. The flower instantly lost its petals and bent over, completely lifeless. Logan was surprised. The death spell was real but worked differently from heal spell. The death spell could only be transferred through the air, but the physical look of the blast looked wilder than the one of his defense spells. The defense spell blast looked like water flowing peacefully through a stream while the death spell moved like an unpredictable lightning strike. This was frightening; something that could cause instant death with no safe way of aiming it was very dangerous. He wrote this in his journal, saying that it should never be used.

Tuesday, September 22, 1925

Logan was at the market buying some more seeds to grow for his own garden behind his now-completed mansion. Logan's visits to the nearby town were very rare. He grew his own food at his mansion and got his own water from his well. His only human interaction was with the construction workers when they were working on his house. As he was leaving the town, he went into the woods. His house was a few miles away, but once he was far enough into the woods away from wandering eyes, he would just teleport to his house. As he walked deeper into the woods, he heard a woman in pain close by. The woman was in tears, crying in agony. Logan sprinted into action following the sound of her voice. Logan approached the crying woman. She appeared to be a hiker, and the direction she was heading showed that she must have been on her way back to the town. She wore a backpack and kept a walking stick in hand. She had a big snake bite on her ankle.

Logan squatted down next to her to check on her. "Are you okay?" Logan asked with a sense of panic and heavy concern.

"I was bit by a snake...a Buckeye herps to be exact," the woman responded.

"Aren't they poisonous?" Logan asked with great concern, feeling like he already knew the answer.

"Oh yeah, most definitely. But it was my own fault. I spooked it. It was such a gentle-looking creature…that is until it jumped out and sank its teeth into me," the woman stated, trying to be nice to the stranger.

"Let's get you to a doctor!" Logan said, trying to help her to her feet. The woman leaned on Logan, trying to stand up, but she struggled and fell back to the ground.

"It's no use. The poison will kill me by the time I get anywhere near a doctor," she said. "But thank you for trying…I know it's a lot to ask, but could you go tell someone that my body is out here? I see that you were heading away from the town, so if you're too busy, that's fine. Wolves need to eat too, I guess." This woman was overwhelmingly considerate and weirdly calm considering what was happening to her. Her acting like this made Logan a little uncomfortable; he was stunned by her reaction to all this, thinking that she should be more worried and panicked about this than he was.

The woman could tell that Logan was scared and nervous, so she thought one of the two should be calm during this, which made Logan even more uncomfortable. "Look, I can get you to a doctor. I'm strong, and I can carry you," Logan stated. Logan was ready to teleport her to the town right there and then.

"I don't want to be too much of a bother, and the trip would give me false hope. The odds of surviving this are very low," the girl said, still trying to sound like this wasn't a big deal. She was at peace with herself, willing to accept whatever happened to her. Logan looked at her. Her bravery was outstanding, her calmness was inspiring, and her acceptance was unnatural. While looking at this girl, he was able to absorb the strong fearless mode she was presenting during this moment. With a steady calmness, he performed the heal spell on her.

Instantly, the girl's body was fully cured, the bite mark healed over, the swelling was eased, and the poison was gone. With the pain gone, the girl stood up in amazement. Logan, still kneeling, looked up to her waiting for her to say something. "What just happened?" she asked with confusion. She then touched her ankle where her wound once was. "It's gone." She then looked down at him with her brown eyes full of wonder. "How did you do that?"

Logan didn't know how to answer that, and part of him didn't want to. He thought about keeping her in the dark about how he did it and just be happy that she was fine. Something told him that she would have accepted that and never asked about it again. But Logan felt that she should know; he felt that he could share the answer with her.

"Look, I see that you don't have any water with you," she said as she took out an extra canteen from her backpack. She offered it to him as a gift.

"No, thank you, I don't want to take your water," Logan responded as he got up.

"Oh, please do. I haven't taken a sip out of it yet, and it's *sadly* the only thing I can offer to say thank you!" She pushed the canteen closer to him, hoping that he would take it.

"No, thank you, miss. I think I should get going now. Glad you're okay." Logan turned and started to walk away. In a way, he felt embarrassed and thought he should just leave.

"It is a long walk until the next water supply, and I packed enough for two," she insisted as Logan just continued to walk farther away. "Do you mind if I walk with you?" she struggled to ask. She didn't want this mysterious man to exit her life for what could be forever. She felt that she owed him her life.

The question to have someone walk with him hadn't been asked in such a long time. The first person to ask that was Parker, and for the first time in a long time, Logan missed having someone with him. Logan was alone for so long that being alone felt like his only positive relationship. But she wanted to walk with him, and Logan was flattered by that for the first time ever. This girl's kindness was unlike anything he had seen before. He found it attractive. Logan turned his head to look at her. He could tell that she wanted to go with him, but if he said no, she would respect his choice and no longer bother him. After battling with this dilemma for a long minute, he made up his mind. "You may join me if you would like."

She emitted an uncontrollable joyful smile, a smile that Logan loved to see. She hustled over to his side, and the two walked deeper into the woods.

"I'm Logan."

"Katherine."

The two were walking to Logan's mansion. While they walked, Logan informed her of his many adventures, crossing the country on foot and seeing amazing sights. Katherine was amazed and a little jealous of all this. Katherine said that she loved being in the woods and found hiking to be more fun than anything, but she never left her hometown. She said she would love to get away like Logan had, but didn't feel like she could be away from her hometown for too long as she would get homesick.

As the two walked deeper into the woods, the conversation also grew deeper. Logan said that he started his travels after his parents died at such an early age. He said that he shut people out of his life for most of his life after that. He brought up Parker and the others who walked with him, saying that Parker was the only one he tolerated. Katherine felt sad for Logan and gave her condolences on losing his parents; she could understand why something like that would make him turn to isolation. She felt that Logan never experienced friendship; she could tell by the way Logan talked about Parker that they were friends, but Logan couldn't admit it. She saw that Logan was afraid of letting people in. He spent so much time being on the move because he didn't know how to carry a relationship for a long time, nor did he want to.

Katherine gave Logan a hug. "You're someone who needs a hug," she said with her arms wrapped around him. After she stopped hugging him, they resumed their walk.

Logan was now ready to tell this girl about his powers. He told her about the Garden of Eden, and the blast from the diamond that changed him and the others' lives forever. The study of his powers was what he'd been doing for quite some time now. After telling her all this, he was afraid that she would think that he was crazy or making all this up.

"I was saved by a magic man," she said so gently and gratefully. She was kind to him and believed every word he said.

"It was hard to let people into my life before…but now that I'm…something more than the others…I feel even more like an outsider," Logan confessed.

"I can't imagine what it's like having the powers you carry, but that doesn't have to make you an outsider. You can let people into your life, and the right people will see you as normal as anyone else."

Logan was touched by what she said. She smiled and stated that they had been walking for so long, it would be dark soon. "Safer to set up camp than risk the walk back to the town," she said, as she pulled out matches that she kept in her bag so they could start a fire. Logan grinned.

"You could set up camp if you want, but you're welcome to stay at my house."

"What, you live in a tree or something?" she joyfully joked, due to not seeing a house anywhere.

Logan pointed; she turned and saw the Renshaw Mansion hidden between two branches of close-by trees. "Yeah, I think that'll be cozier there than sleeping on the ground," Katherine said, smiling.

Once they got past the branches, there was a clear path to the front steps. She hurried up the steps and was overwhelmingly impressed by the look of the place. "Oh my gosh, it's a palace!" She wrapped her arms around a supporting porch beam, giving the place a hug in a way.

"I was saved by a magic man," she said in a romantic way; this time the magic man saved her by granting her shelter for the night. She then rushed up to the door and boldly told him that she had to get a tour. She ran into the house, leaving Logan standing out front next to the first step of the porch. He was in disbelief and took a moment to let this sink in. He was about to enter his house with someone he loved inside waiting for him. This was the happiest Logan had ever been.

CHAPTER 6

The Renshaw Family

Saturday, November 6, 1926

Logan nervously approached a house. With sweaty hands, he brought himself to knock on the door. The wait for the door to be answered was highly stressful. The thought that no one was home crossed his mind, but this could have been more wishful thinking than anything. The door opened, and Logan and Parker were seeing each other once again.

"Logan!" Parker joyfully shouted. Logan smiled, and the two gave each other a hug. Parker could tell that there was something different with Logan, as he sensed an aura of happiness surrounding him. It was almost like Parker was hugging a stranger.

"What brings you here?" Parker asked his friend.

Logan was excited to announce that he was getting married, and he needed a best man. Parker couldn't believe that Logan was planning on getting married; he'd never visualized him to be one to settle down. Nonetheless, he was very happy to hear that Logan found someone to spend the rest of his life with. Parker asked what date he planned for the big day.

"In like…a half hour," Logan uttered. Parker was dumbfounded by this statement. He hadn't seen the guy in a very long time, and without announcement, he showed up asking him to be his best man and that the wedding was in a half hour. Parker said yes and then asked where the wedding was going to be. Logan said the wedding would be at his house in Ohio.

"Okay, now I know you're kidding. Logan, there is no way we can get to your house today let alone in a half hour!" Parker yelled.

Logan emitted an uncontrollable grin before putting his hand on Parker's shoulder and teleported them to the front porch of the Renshaw Mansion. The trip happened within a flash for the two. Parker's eyes looked at Logan with open fields in the background, with the sun in the sky. Suddenly, the background changed; the sun was blocked by the shade of the trees from the woods that were now taking the place of the background. Parker's eyes widened, and his heart started to race.

"Calm down, Parker...I just teleported you to my home," Logan stated.

Parker felt a momentary loss of balance and put his hand on the porch railing while hunching over to catch his breath. Logan told Parker that he learned how to use the power inside him to transport to anyplace he had seen. He said it was very unnatural, but he got used to it fast.

"Well, the other guys and I can't do anything like that. We can work up a pretty strong running pace that can get us running fast miles, but we still need to take each step between point A to point B," Parker said, trying to catch his breath. Logan patted him on the back, telling him to take a moment and come on when he was ready. Logan then walked into his house. Parker quietly turned and followed. "This is where you live? I guess you're making the best with your share of reward from the diamond."

"Yeah, I figured if I was going to get a house, go big or go home, *right*?" Logan replied, hoping to set his friend at ease.

"Here I am living at my parents' old farmhouse, while all my money is invested in the bank," Parker said, looking around the rooms. "Wow! Look at that fireplace. It's huge!"

As Parker gazed at the design of the mansion, Katherine walked in the room wearing her wedding dress. "Logan, I see that you've brought him," she said, pleased to meet the best man.

"I have to shake the hand of the woman who was able to make this guy learn commitment!" Parker said as he rushed over to Katherine. "You must be a wonderful woman...Sorry if I'm acting a little nervous...I was just teleported for the first time!" Parker said, laughing joyfully. "You look beautiful by the way!"

"Thank you, Parker, and you're acting fine. It's an exciting day!" Katherine replied.

Logan told Parker that he had a suit for him and that they should change now.

The two headed to a room to get dressed. As the men got dressed, Parker wanted to know everything about Katherine: how they met, how long they had been together, and when did he ask her the big question. Logan hated small talk, so he informed Parker that he was regretting bringing him to his wedding for asking all these questions. Parker said he'd shut up if it would make Logan happy; he was just so excited to be there. He was bursting with more joy than the guy getting married. Logan was starting to sense he was slipping into his old ways. He felt that if he was going to change, he should open up to Parker. Spending time with Katherine had taught him to be nicer to people who were just trying to be his friend.

Logan told Parker how he met her, saying that she was hurt in the woods and he was there to help her. Logan said he never met anyone like her. She was kind, sweet…Heck, she was willing to let the wolves eat her! That made Parker laugh, saying that she sounded perfect for Logan. Parker said that this girl sounded like she had a big heart…and Logan was a man who needed a heart. Logan then asked how Parker had been coping with his advanced strength. Parker said that nothing had changed with it. Still much stronger than a normal man should be, he had decided to keep it hidden from everyone in town. He continued saying he had become accustomed to living with it and now no longer saw it as a big deal.

The men were both fully dressed and headed to the front entrance for the ceremony. Not many people were at the wedding, just Katherine's friends and what little family she had. On Logan's side was Logan's barber. Logan was told to invite people; however, being as distant to people as he was, he didn't have any friends to invite. So he just invited people whom he ran into the morning of the wedding. The barber was the only one who showed up. Katherine did make him get a best man, saying she wouldn't marry him without one, so Parker had Logan's wife to thank for being at the wedding.

The wedding was very nice; Logan had a big smile on his face the whole time, as did Katherine. Katherine said that she fell in love with a magic man, a slight change of words from the first night she met him. After the ceremony, the guests were welcome to stay at the mansion for food and drinks. Parker gave a speech, talking about the many days and nights of the seven travelers. He told Katherine what a great guy she just married, saying that Logan was a leader, a provider, and a protector. The only thing he was missing in his life was love. Now that he was with Katherine, he had everything he needed.

After everyone left, Katherine couldn't thank Parker enough for being the best man and giving his speech. It was truly a lovely wedding, and everyone had a good time. Logan then told Parker that it was time to go, so he laid his hands on his shoulder and teleported them back to Parker's house. Back at Parker's place, he took the teleportation trip much calmer this time. The two said their goodbyes, and after they exchanged mailing addresses, Logan teleported away back to his wife.

Thursday, May 30, 1929

Logan stood in his bedroom, staring at the full moon up in the dark night. He was once again lost in his thoughts. Logan then saw his reflection in the glass window. He had been looking at his reflection a lot lately. Logan's body hadn't appeared to show any physical sign of aging since his trip to the garden. His visit to the garden was now five years ago, and he still felt different from everyone else. The chilling dream he had while in the garden was still trapped within his memories.

Logan didn't let the effects of the garden keep him from living. Logan had been married to a woman who accepted him for who he was for almost three years now. They had gone on dozens of vacations during their time together. With Logan's teleporting powers, they were able to visit lots of places. When they made the choice to have a child, they spent all their time at the Renshaw Mansion. Logan was fearful of the child having the same powers as he did. He wished to monitor his wife's pregnancy for any signs of that being the case. The pregnancy was normal; the child did have strong kicks that caused discomfort, but that was it.

The child was born on May 27. A boy, they named him Cain.

Katherine walked in the bedroom holding the newborn, Cain. Logan smiled seeing his family as she walked over to the window to stand next to him. The two had a home birth; Logan was able to provide a heal spell for both his wife after giving birth and the newborn. They also wanted to keep the child a secret, just until they knew if he had the same kind of power as Logan.

"I went to check on him, and he was already awake," Katherine stated, holding the baby. The baby didn't cry much, not as much as a newborn should. This worried Logan as he always had a ton of thoughts going through his mind. Logan didn't think his son had any power to create spells as he did, but he wondered if he had the advanced strength as the other travelers had.

Logan picked up Cain from his wife's arms. Just after three days, the boy was already able to lift his head up on his own. Logan knew his son was strong and was slowly getting stronger every day. This was why the child didn't cry much. "I think he's like the others, the ones who got the strength."

"But you didn't possess the advanced strength, so how could it be passed down to him?" wondered Katherine.

Logan didn't know. Logan and Katherine were planning on going back to the entrance of the garden tomorrow. Logan said he had to be 100 percent sure that his son did have something extra inside him. Logan informed Katherine about the boulder that covered the entrance of the garden. He said that it took two people with powers to open it. If Logan's son did have the same type of powers, then the door could be unlocked from both of their touches. So they put their son back to bed and went to bed themselves.

Friday, May 31, 1929

The next morning after they ate, Logan teleported his wife and son to the mountain. Once there, Logan saw no one, and he guided his wife to the tunnel. Once they made it to the tunnel, Logan told Katherine to watch her step, to not trip on the loose rocks.

"Is it going to hurt him, Logan?" Katherine asked with concern.

"The lock was made to be drained by an overload. One can't overload it alone, so it takes two to do the job," Logan explained.

"Logan…would it hurt him?" she asked once more. She was told how the rock worked many times, so she knew Logan was avoiding the question. Logan stopped, turned to her, and hesitated.

"If the power that runs through me has been passed down to him… then the rock will start to suck the energy out of him," Logan struggled to say.

"So you're saying it could hurt him?" the worried mother raised her voice in fear.

"We don't need to keep his hand on the rock for very long, just long enough to see if it works. The second I know, I'll tell you to pull him back," Logan said, trembling.

He wasn't happy about this, but he didn't know any other way to find out. Katherine trusted her husband. She was nervous for her child, but she too knew how important it was to find out the answer. A few steps later, they were standing in front of the rock. This large boulder covering the entrance of the great Garden of Eden was exactly how they left it all those years ago.

Logan placed his hand on the rock; nothing happened. Katherine was concerned that nothing was happening. Logan said that until another with powers touched it, nothing would happen. Katherine looked down at the baby who was asleep in her arms. "Okay…here we go," Katherine said as she brought her child to the rock. She got him as close to the rock as she could and paused. "As soon as you know, tell me," Katherine stated. Logan nodded. Katherine, as slightly as she could, leaned Cain toward the rock.

Cain started to cry out loud, while Logan fell to his knees feeling as if he might faint, as if he no longer had the muscles to stand up. "PULL HIM AWAY!" Logan shouted. Logan couldn't remove his hand, as if the rock wouldn't let him go until the process was completed. Kate yanked her baby away from the rock. She did her best to comfort Cain while checking on Logan.

"Are you okay?" she asked Logan.

Logan let out a grunt and then said he needed a minute. "Well… the lock works just as I designed it," Logan grunted.

Katherine asked if he needed help up, but Logan said he was going to stay down for a bit.

"Wow, that really takes everything out of you," Logan stated while lying on the ground.

"Look!" Katherine shouted as she pointed to the bottom left part of the rock. The rock moved very slightly, just enough for some of the light from inside to shine out.

"He can open the door...That means he has powers," Logan stated, trying to catch his breath.

"But he seems to have that advanced strength as the others do," Katherine added.

This made Logan wonder why the baby would have the strength instead of the power to make spells. But this was a question for another time. They came to the rock to see if their son was granted powers from his father. After a while, Logan was feeling better; he cleared his head and gave himself a heal spell. He gave one to his son as well, which instantly caused him to stop crying. His wife looked at her husband with loving eyes. "I married a magic man," she said.

The three took a walk back out of the tunnel and walked around the mountaintop. They spent most of the day out there enjoying the sights. The three had their first outing with the baby, and they loved it. They felt like a family on a vacation. Last time Logan was here, he was surrounded by people when he would have rather been alone. Now with his wife and son, he never wanted to be away from them, ever. His wife was looking at the beauty of the mountain sights, while Logan only looked at his wife and child. A tear appeared in his eye, for he was truly happy. When they felt it was time to go, they huddled together so that Logan could teleport them home to the Renshaw Mansion, now housing a family of three. Once they returned home, Katherine walked up the porch steps saying she needed to feed Cain. Logan stayed on the ground in front of the first step of the porch. He looked at his house, knowing that his loving wife was in his home with his son, his heart full of pure happiness. Logan was about to take his first step onto the stairs of the porch but came to a sudden halt when he heard a familiar voice call out his name behind him.

"Logan," the voice said with a slight tone of fear.

Logan turned around and saw his old friend Parker. Parker didn't have that happy-to-see-you face he always showed in the past. Logan could tell something was wrong from looking at Parker.

"We need to talk," Parker said softly.

CHAPTER 7

The Past Comes Back to Hunt You

Questions arose in Logan's mind as he looked at his friend Parker. What was he doing here? Why did it look like he ran for miles as fast as he could to be here? What was so important? Parker had his guard up, indicating that he was preparing for an attack. He let down his guard and embraced Logan in a hug. "Glad to see you're okay, man," Parker gratefully said.

Logan could hear the worry in Parker's voice, as if he expected something awful had happened to him.

"Of course, I'm all right, Parker. Why wouldn't I be?" Logan wondered.

Parker took out a photo from his jacket pocket. He showed Logan the photo and asked, "Can you take us here?"

Logan looked at the photo. He saw a nice-looking house, the front yard, and the street the house was on. Logan saw enough to be able to teleport him and Parker there. Logan took his eyes off the photograph to look back at Parker. Parker was not playing around here; something in Parker's eyes put the fear of God into him. This had to be why Parker had come to see Logan. Without any questions, Logan placed his hand on Parker's shoulder, and they teleported to the house shown in the photo.

The two appeared on the street as seen in the photo. Parker was just at this house yesterday. Logan looked at the house and noticed the doors and windows were all boarded up as if it was quarantined. Logan asked Parker why they were at this house.

"You need to see something," Parker said as he marched up to the house. Parker had his defensive pose back up and suddenly lost that friendly tone normally found in his voice. He reached the door first with Logan behind him. Parker easily removed the large board nailed to the front door and tossed it aside. He then tried the doorknob to find it was locked. With a little force, Parker was able to push the door open with the frame of the door chipping off. Parker walked in with Logan right behind him. They entered slowly, as neither one knew if it was safe to enter or not.

They entered, and Parker hit the light switch. When the lights came up, Logan's eyes widened, for he saw blood everywhere. Parker wasn't shocked by the sight, for he had seen this before. Logan looked around. He could tell that there was a struggle in the room and not just there; he could see that the stairway was smashed up as well, as if a fight had started upstairs. As he continued to turn his head, he found a body lying on the ground. Logan could not believe whom he saw lying on the ground.

Parker squatted down close to the body and was grateful that the body hadn't been moved by the police. Parker looked back up to Logan and said, "It's Derrick."

Logan knew this. He may not have been close to his former travelers, but he never forgot a face and name. But looking at Derrick's face, it was still hard to tell if it was him. Logan squatted down closer to the body. "Who could have done this to him?" wondered Logan.

"Not too many people could have beaten him up this badly, not with his advanced strength," Parker stated.

"You think it might have been one of the other travelers?" Logan questioned as Parker rubbed his head with one hand.

"No, I know it wasn't any of the others," Parker painfully uttered.

"How could you be so sure?" asked Logan.

"We are the last two left alive," Parker answered. This shocked Logan even more than seeing Derrick dead on the floor. "I kept in touch with some of the other travelers after we split up. I went to go visit Kyle and found out he was killed. I wrote to Zach and Ezekiel. They too thought it had to have been one of us. Ezekiel was able to confirm that it wasn't Jake, for he had died just a month just before Kyle. After that, I lost touch with Zach, so I went to go visit him, and he too was killed. A few weeks later, I got a letter from one of Ezekiel's coworkers saying he was just killed. I looked up the dates of the murders. All were killed within the last days of a different month. Kyle died January 29, Ezekiel died February 28, Zach March 30, and Jake April 29. All died this same year.

"I didn't understand the pattern of the days of the murders, but they were all killed the same way: battered to death. Not easy to kill one of us with our strength, let alone being battered to death. I thought it was Derrick committing the murders. I knew it had to be someone very strong, and I knew it wasn't me. I went to go see Derrick to confront him. I only worried that if it wasn't him, then this visit would have turned into a warning."

"When I came here last night, I was too late. Derrick was already being attacked. I could hear the rampage from the street. I was so worried as I ran toward the house. If the murderer wasn't Derrick, then who was strong enough to kill four men with this kind of advanced strength? I ran to the house, thinking I could help Derrick. But I was too late. When I entered the house, Derrick was already killed. And that's when I saw the murderer. Well, I only saw his back. He was standing over the dead body, fist all bloody, but with a steady breathing rate, as if killing Derrick didn't even break a sweat. He must have heard me because after I saw him, he just disappeared in thin air…Only person who I know that can do that is you, Logan," Parker explained just before looking at him.

Logan replied right away, "He teleported…" Logan stood up straight in disbelief. "I didn't know anyone else could do that."

Parker rose from his squatting position too. Logan looked at Parker. "You don't think I did this, do you?" Logan was offended by having to ask that but remained calm, understanding Parker's reasoning.

"I did at first…you being the only person I know who can teleport."

"Parker, I didn't do this!" Logan stated honestly.

"The more I thought about it, the person had blood all over their hands. That means that the attacker was able to use their hands to beat them all to death. Plus…" Parker raised Derrick's hand up. "Derrick's knuckles are covered in blood and are broken. Whatever he was punching must have been very strong."

"So the attacker had superstrength…which is something I don't have! A punch from one of you guys would knock me out with ease!" Logan shouted, defending himself.

"Look…I'm sorry I wrote you down as a suspect, but while on my way to see you, I put the incorrect pieces together!" Parker replied with a yell. After that, the two grew silent. "I'm sorry I yelled. I should have known that you couldn't have done this," Parker said with an apologetic tone.

"No, you had every right to think what you did. I'm sorry I got upset…I'm just scared, that's all. Someone is out there killing us one by one. Knowing that we are the last ones still standing is a little unnerving," Logan said with a kinder voice. Parker understood Logan's fear, as he too was terrified of being the next one killed.

"What else do you remember about that attacker? Does anything stand out?" Logan asked curiously.

"Well, he was tall, a bit taller thin you, and…" Parker didn't like looking back at his memory of seeing the person. He only saw the man's back, but just a glimpse of that made him shake in uncontrollable fear. "He had these dirty, gray raggedy clothes on."

Logan's head popped up fast, as if what Parker just said triggered something he had spent so many years trying to forget. Logan knew who this murderer was, as he saw him only in his nightmare that day he was hit with that blast that came from the diamond. Suddenly, the air grew very thin, and the room's temperature grew, covering the area with a dry heat. A nasty stench of brimstone took over the area. "We need to leave now!" Logan shouted as he hustled over to Parker. Before the two could touch hands, giving Logan the ability to teleport them both away to safety, the man dressed in dirty, raggedy gray clothes suddenly appeared between the two. The man was facing the wall with Logan on his right, while Parker was on his left. The attacker pushed out his hands, slamming them into the friends' chests, pushing them across the room.

Logan was knocked right out through the window, landing on the front lawn as he gasped for air. That shove felt like it collapsed his lung.

Logan had to focus on his heal spell; he had to heal himself so he could get back to his feet. He had to find Parker and get them both to safety. He was able to calm himself down in order to perform the heal spell on himself. Being fully healed, he rose to his feet. He looked inside the shattered window. The attacker was walking toward him with a sinister look. Logan trembled at the sight of the man's face. He'd never seen anything more frightening; that man was not human. Logan wanted to perform a defense spell onto the attacker, but because he was frozen with fear, he couldn't move a muscle.

Inside the house, Parker ran up behind the attacker and swung an entire couch across the attacker like a baseball bat. The attacker was hurled across the room from the blow. Parker looked at Logan.

"Parker, get over here!" Logan ordered to Parker. Parker jumped out the broken window and ran to Logan's side.

"We got to get out of here!" Logan said with much panic in his voice.

"No, no, we can't. He'll find us just like he found all the others." Parker scrambled for words; a part of it was fear, and a part of it was adrenaline. "If we run, it'll find us, no matter where we hide!" Parker insisted.

"You want to fight back?" Logan asked, confused. "He's already killed the others. He's too strong!"

"Not unless we attack him together. He killed the others with ease because they were alone. We outnumber him. Together we can beat him!" Parker said with confidence. Logan was unsure, was afraid, and didn't fully trust Parker. Logan wanted to flee, but he wasn't going to leave without his friend. Logan wished he had the same high spirit as Parker did, but all he could think about was returning to his wife and son.

The attacker walked out the front door and slowly walked to the two. The fear was real for Logan, while Parker was ready for battle. Parker charged at the attacker, ready to fight. Parker threw a punch at the attacker across the face. The head moved, but the blow had little impact. Parker then shoved the bottom of his foot at the attacker's stomach, but the attacker managed to grab Parker's leg and swung him around, throwing him onto the street.

"PARKER!" Logan shouted.

Logan became determined to land a hit on this beast. He riddled off a stream of defense spells, releasing them from the tip of his fingers. The color of the blast was light green, striking the attacker head-on. Still, this blast barely emitted a shake out of the monster.

The monster looked at Logan with an almost-impressed stare and started to walk toward Logan. Logan was puzzled. He had just attacked him with his best shot, and the attacker seemed to absorb it like it was a dull breeze.

Parker hustled back over to Logan. "Is there anything else that you can hit him with?" Parker asked.

"There is another spell I've learned…but it may be too risky," Logan stated.

"Do you think it can kill him?" wondered Parker.

"I'm not sure," Logan said with a sense of concern. Logan told Parker of the death spell. Logan was worried about using it because the spell was hard to aim, and he was afraid of missing the target. Parker said he'd hold down the attacker, giving Logan a clear shot. Before Logan could rule out that idea, Parker was already on the move. Parker got close to the attacker, feeling more confident that their devised plan now could defeat and possibly destroy the attacker. Parker swung a right hook across the face of the monster. This time it seemed to cause some pain to the man. Parker threw a left punch, again landing some pain on the attacker; then Parker landed a strong punch onto the attacker's chest. This punch knocked the monster off his feet, causing him to fall back into the house. The monster grabbed hold of Parker and pulled him back into the house with him as he fell out of sight behind the wall. Logan could not see what was going on in the house, but he could hear Parker's voice screaming, "LOGAN, HE'S HEADING OUT THE DOOR! HIT HIM NOW!"

Trusting his friend's words, Logan was ready to fire off the death spell at the silhouette walking out the house. Certain that his life was threatened, he instinctively fired off the death spell. A blast of what looked like a jagged bolt of dark-violet light fired out of Logan's hand. The light twisted, flickered in a random style, and landed onto the man coming out of the door. The target fell to the ground lifeless, and Logan stood with his defensive pose still up, wondering if the spell worked. It was quite an uncomfortable silence. Logan was wondering why Parker hadn't said anything yet. The man on the ground was motionless, so Logan started to believe he managed to kill the beast. Still he proceeded with caution as he walked up to the house. As he drew closer to the house, he got a good look at the target he hit. He saw his friend Parker dead on the ground in front of the door. Logan's heart shattered, as he could not believe that it was Parker whom he hit. Then he shockingly heard Parker's voice from inside the house.

"Logan, he's heading out the door! Hit him now!" the voice echoed.

Logan was confused. If Parker was dead, then how could he hear his voice from inside the house? The voice spoke again, still sounding like Parker. "Logan, he's heading out the door! Hit him now." Logan caught a glimpse inside the house and saw the monster standing there, repeating the same phrase over and over. "Logan, he's heading out the door! Hit him now!" Logan was spooked by this. Logan backed away in fear as he tripped over Parker's fallen corpse. Arched on his elbows and his heels, Logan backed away from the house, keeping his eyes on the monster. The attacker exited the house and stood over Parker's body.

Logan rose to his feet and fired a death spell at the attacker. The spell struck the monster, but the impact did not faze him. "You're going to need something more powerful than that to kill me," the monster said, still speaking in Parker's voice.

Logan was panting heavily because he was fully exhausted from his unsuccessful attacks on the monster. The monster lifted his left hand and told him to save his energy. Logan demanded the monster explain how he could copy Parker's voice. The monster said that he could do a lot of things as he took a good look at Logan, as if he was studying him. "You're the last one. You're the last one with the Loomation inside you."

"Loomation?" Logan said, not understanding.

"Loomation is what lies inside you. It's how you're able to blast all those lights out of your hands. It's what gives you the power to teleport, and it is what's powering the garden."

"Do you have this power?" wondered Logan.

"I do, but mine is a mighty ocean, while yours is just a puddle."

"Why did you go after the others? They don't have this power," Logan questioned.

"Humans were not made to contain Loomation, so if any of it manages to sneak into them from a power source, it normally dries up inside the body, sticking to the bones, muscles, and skin. They can't use it for any spells, but it does make them very strong. It is possible for the element to become active inside a human body, which happens to be your case," the monster explained.

"You're killing us because we carry this power?" asked Logan.

"When humanity was made, I was disgusted by them. *They're too weak*, I claimed. But God loved them the most, saying that they were perfect. So I vowed to kill any human who was more than what God intended! You were not meant for this power, so I'm here to fix all of mankind!" the monster yelled.

"If you are so powerful, why didn't you just kill us right away? Why did you give us a fighting chance?"

"I like the fight. It gives me a bit of exercise. Plus, I like to give the illusion of hope. Let them get a few punches in, let them think that they have a fighting chance. Then I love to take that hope away and kill them with my bare hands," the monster said sinisterly.

Logan couldn't believe all this; he was clearly facing something very ancient. Logan wanted to go home and hope that all this was just a bad dream. "Why did you trick me into killing my friend?" Logan asked.

"See, I just killed that guy in the house a few days ago. I have a set of guidelines I must follow, got to spread out my kills over time. So I tricked you into killing this one here," the monster said as he kicked Parker's body below him. "Now, if you give me permission, I will kill you right here and now," the monster stated with an odd sense of compassion.

"Why on earth would I ever do that?" Logan asked, insulted by such a request.

"Because there is nowhere on earth where you can hide. I know you can teleport, so running is your only option. But trust me, I will always find you. It'll take about four weeks to track you down, but when I'm hunting my prey, that's all I focus on. I don't get tired, I don't need to eat, and I don't get distracted. So if you want to avoid the chase with the inevitable conclusion of me killing you, say the word, and I'll kill you right here and now. I'll show mercy and make it painless," the monster offered.

Logan thought about what the monster said. He was looking for humans who were more than what God intended. Logan knew that his son possessed this power the monster was hunting. If Logan gave himself up, it would only be a matter of time until the monster becomes aware of his son, Cain, and kills him too. The monster said that when he was chasing his prey, he stayed focused on it. If Logan could get the monster to only focus on him, then he'd never learn about his son. His son could be free from this nightmare and live a full life. Logan knew what he had to do to save his son.

"I'll surrender," Logan said as he walked up to the monster. The monster had these hellish-looking eyes; Logan felt a cold chill every time he looked at them. But to surrender, he felt that he should look him in the eyes. Logan put his hands in the air as he slowly walked up to the beast. Logan knelt in front of the monster and looked up at the monster's eyes.

"Start searching!" Logan then placed his hand onto Parker's body and teleported away. The monster had been tricked; Logan pretended to surrender just so he could get close enough to teleport away with Parker's body. The monster showed no rage once Logan disappeared. Instead, he emitted a rare smile. He knew that the human made a human mistake, but he welcomed the hunt.

Logan teleported to Parker's front porch. When he arrived, he felt grateful to be away from that place and the monster he fled from. But it was now time to mourn over the death of his friend. On the porch, Logan broke out in tears. All he could think about was how it happened. He knew using the death spell was a risky move.

"We should have run…You would still be here if we ran!" Logan said in tears. "It's all my fault. I shouldn't have used the death spell. I should have known it wouldn't have worked on him. Should have just used a defense spell…I should have waited until I got a better look at the target. I should have done it differently!"

As Logan was grieving, he started to think about his family. He knew he could never go back to them. He couldn't risk the monster finding him with them; he couldn't let the monster know about his son. Logan rose and placed Parker's body on the porch swing. He handled the body with care and took one last look to say goodbye. Then in a moment of silence, he heard someone coming from the yard. Fearful that the monster was hot on his trail, Logan teleported away as fast as he could, not bothering to look back at who the person was.

The person in the yard was not the monster but a woman, Parker's wife. She saw Logan disappear in thin air. She didn't even bother to look around, for she saw him take no footsteps in any direction; he just vanished. She had never seen Logan before and knew nothing of his powers. The woman walked up to the porch and found her husband dead on the porch swing. At first, she was in disbelief; and then she entered a stage of denial, trying desperately to wake him up. When she found that to be in vain, she stood back for a minute; and then realizing the truth, she poured out tears of devastation. The child she held in her hand sensed something was wrong and started to cry inconsolable sobs. The agony the two felt was unbearable. They were alone, so there was no one around to console them. After her time of grieving, the wife slowly walked away and retreated to the living room and fell asleep with her son from sheer exhaustion.

Logan was standing on a beach staring at the Atlantic with no one in sight; Logan gazed at the waves hitting the shore while the full moon was glowing in the night sky. For a moment, Logan had everything: a loving wife; a strong, healthy baby boy; and a family home to grow old in. But now he was robbed of all that. He was tricked into killing his best friend, and he could never return to his home to see his wife and son again. A long, lonely life of endless travels waited for him. He started his journey traveling alone. On his journey, he found friendship, love, and a family. But now it was all taken away by the devil himself.

CHAPTER 8

The Next Generation

The day Logan never came home to his wife and son, the Renshaw Mansion was never the same. The once-proud mansion started to fall apart. The weeds started to grow up along the side of the house, the paint started to chip away from the walls, the roof started to leak, and the harsh winters were taking a toll on the house. Cain quickly became the man of the house and gained a sixth sense of how to do house repairs. He started fixing up the house as soon as he could hold a hammer. Still, it felt like every time he would fix one thing, five more problems would arise. His mother was a single parent who made sure her son had everything: food, homeschool lessons, and as much love as she could give him. She felt sorry for Cain never knowing his father. She spoke highly of him, saying that he was a magic man. Cain loved his mother with all his heart but hated when she spoke of his father. His mother never knew the reason why he left them, but she waited on the porch most nights hoping against all odds for him to return.

On late nights, even when it was twenty degrees outside, Cain would find his mom sitting on a rocking chair on the porch, huddled in a blanket fast asleep. Cain hated seeing her wait for a man who would never return. The mother and son never knew why the man of the house left. Katherine said that there was no reason. Everything was fine, and then one day, he never came home; he just disappeared. Cain quickly became aware of his advanced strength, and both he and his mother discovered something new about his powers. The seven travelers didn't live long enough to discover this side effect, except for Logan. People who carry Loomation inside them age slowly. By the time Cain reached the age of six, he looked as if he was only three. When he reached twelve, he looked as if he was only six. For anyone born with Loomation inside them, whether it be active or not, possessed the body of someone half their age. Logan wasn't born with Loomation, but ever since he came in possession of it, the slow aging process began.

Due to Cain's peculiar growth pattern, his mother never took him to a regular school nor to a hospital, so there was no record of Cain's existence on file. No birth certificate and no social security card were ever printed. She was afraid of someone learning about his powers and taking him away from her. She didn't want to lose another family member.

Cain was told that he got this gift from his father's side. The last day his family was whole was the day they learned that he had inherited unusual strength but not the power to make spells like his father could. Part of that made Cain feel like his father leaving was his fault. Thinking that his father wanted a son more like him and not who he turned out to be haunted the unsuspecting son his whole childhood.

Cain thought his mother would stop waiting for her husband by the door if he declared him dead. His father was missing for years, and it was time to pronounce the man deceased. Despite his mother's best efforts, Cain could not see the justice in this world. How his father ran out with no explanation was incomprehensible. Every day his confusion turned to hatred. He felt he was wronged and was willing to do anything to find a way to get even. Eventually the hatred he felt would be directed toward society and would turn this once-loving child into a criminal who decided to use his strength for his own selfish purposes. Cain would go out at night promising his mother that he would return to her before sunrise. Cain was able to ride his bike all the way to Columbus. From an early age, he was getting into trouble, ranging from stealing candy from candy shops to robbing gas stations at gunpoint; he felt he had to pay the bills somehow. One of the boys who he stole with had a knack for graffiti, giving themselves the idea for the name of their group: the

Havocs. The Havocs were visited by some shady drug dealers looking for some new workers.

For a while, Cain and the other Havocs were drug dealers, transporting drugs and money to the buyers and sellers. Cain looking as young as a child made him look less of a suspect. With Cain never owning any kind of ID, this was the only job that didn't require that kind of paperwork. Over the years, Cain found himself doing more illegal jobs. He worked the docks when shipments came in; he managed to protect the product when police showed up. He took on four police officers on his own and managed to carry most of the drugs by himself out of the area before backup arrived. This landed Cain a seat at the head table for the drug lords of the town. They called him their little animal. Cain the Animal was the name of fear to anyone who stood in his business's way.

Over the years, Cain grew tired of easy money from selling drugs. He wanted a job where he was able to get his hands dirty, so he started taking hit man jobs. This job gave him a chance to hurt people who owed money to his group, but still he wanted more, so he started his own gang. As a kid, he liked the name Havocs, so he kept it. He became a provider for hit men assignments and private security, all led by the animal himself.

One night when Cain returned home, he found his mother had passed away. Cain found her sitting on the rocking chair on the front porch, right where he left her. She spent much of her life sitting and waiting for a husband who would never return. Cain was amazed by her loyalty, but on the other hand, he learned that people would always let you down. He never really made any close friends nor kept girlfriends around long enough to make anything last. Cain's mother was all he had. He put his business on hold to take care of his mother's funeral. Cain didn't want to return to an empty home. He, therefore, made his home the headquarters for his new business, opening it to the Havocs who worked for him. Years went by, and the Havocs became a wanted criminal gang. They were hired by mobs to supply guards or to act as gunmen in planned shoot-outs. It was a life of crime that Cain grew into, and he was good at it.

≈◦◦◦≈

"When you come across a problem where neither sciences nor logic can give an answer, start to seek out the supernatural for answers" (Jerrod Jochovo).

This quote was written on the first page of a logbook belonging to a man named Ray Mantus. Jerrod Jochovo was a celebrity hero to Ray. Ray admired the fact that even though Jerrod was a hugely famous scientist, he still believed that there was something stronger, higher, and even spiritual out in the world that science could not explain.

Ray lived his life studying the world of sciences. He was always at the top of his class, even graduating high school and college early. His IQ was rated at the genius level, making him the youngest to achieve that title. He loved to experiment with chemicals and even started his own chemical plant. He called it *Saltwater Chemicals*. They were known for making cleaning supplies. Ray created special items for secret deals that were kept off the books.

At a young age, Ray became quite wealthy and was running his own company. He took his success in stride, but he was still on the hunt to find the answer to a question that had been presented to him when he was born. Ray wasn't like everyone else; he was born with something that had always made him believe in a greater power that had yet to be discovered. Ray was born with advanced strength. Ray was able to lift a fully grown cow over his head with his bare hands. He was able to jump to a roof of a two-story house and was able to outrun a healthy young steed for a short distance. Whatever blessed him with this strength also slowed down his aging process. For every year he was born, his body would age only half that. It was said that he was the youngest to score that high of a score of an IQ test, but the truth was he lied about his age. This was something he had done his entire life.

The mystery of the source of his strength was loosely solved. His mother told him that his father also had this advanced strength, so it must have been passed down to him. The story of what happened to his father was a disturbing one—one that would haunt him with big lifelong questions. Ray was told his father was found dead on the front porch. He was told that his mother was out taking him for a walk, and when she came home, she saw a man standing on the porch, a man who vanished into thin air. The mother didn't even get a look at the vanishing man, but she assumed that he was the killer. Ray spent his life trying to figure out who this mysterious killer was though the search was put on hold for decades as he built his business. After that, his search was back on. He believed that a look into his father's past could provide answers.

Ray read all his father's old journals. There was one passage that Ray read over and over. This one talked about his father entering the land of the great beyond, a land that couldn't be located on any map, a land to only be talked about within the Bible. A land referred to as the Garden of Eden.

March 29, 1970

About four miles away from the bottom of the mountains, signs were staggered throughout the area saying, "WARNING NO TRESSPASSING: DEADLY CHEMICAL LEAK AHEAD. TURN BACK NOW!" The signs were real, but the warning was a ruse. No dangerous chemical leak in the area existed; it was just a way to grant Ray some solitude while he was out around the mountain. Ray returned to the location written of in his father's journal, the place where he saw the meteor struck the mountain. The journal was well-detailed on the location of the tunnel that would lead him to a stone door. Behind that door was what Ray wished to see.

It was written within the journal that the garden lay behind that rock. Ray was skeptical on this, not sure if it was true, but still curious. But when he approached the rock, he saw a small beam of light glowing from the bottom left. Ray dropped down to his knees. He stuck his face in close to the light. The light was warm and very yellow, as if it was sunlight. Ray knew that it was impossible for sunlight to be shining out from this area. It was nighttime outside the tunnel, so there was no chance that it was just a reflection from the sun outside the entrance. There was no logic or science to provide an answer for how a ray of sunlight was glowing outside of the rock. So Ray believed his father's writing, that what lay behind this bolder was indeed the Garden of Eden.

Ray spent a few weeks in that area. He tried everything he could think of to move the rock, but all attempts failed. The simple *push it out of the way* was the first to be checked off the list. Even with Ray's strength, he could not get the rock to budge. He used objects to assist him to move the rock out of the way but to no avail. Ray tried smashing the rock into pieces by clobbering it with a pickax, but the rock failed to gain even a scratch. Undaunted, Ray then started to dig around the door thinking he could get to the other side by making a new path. Ray dug more tunnels in hopes of reaching the other side. This was a waste of time, for he just dug into more rock. Ray did have the idea of using explosions to blast through the door, but the structure of the tunnel wouldn't withstand the explosion. The tunnel to the entrance would collapse, and the door could get lost within the destruction.

Ray knew that there was only one way to release the opening, and that was with the key. In his father's notes, he wrote that the rock could only be moved by two who were granted the powers. All that the two people would have to do would be to simply touch the door, and the rock would begin to move. Ray spent hours with his hand on the rock, lost in his thoughts. He knew that he qualified, but he was alone. For the key to work, he would have to find another. Now convinced that the journal was accurate, Ray packed up his belongings and left the mountain in hopes of finding someone who could be the second half of the key.

Ray studied the newspapers, trying to find anyone who stood out in any nonhuman ways. Ray learned that all his father's old traveling companions had passed away, and there were no official records of any of them having children. This made the odds of finding another like him woefully low. In time, he learned about a criminal gang called the Havocs, a dangerous gang wanted for abetting in many crimes. The Havocs were led by an unknown leader, a man with the muscle to take on six men at once, with no problem. Some believed that he was more animal than man.

A man like that was exactly who Ray was looking for. Someone with advanced strength like that could very well be a candidate for the second key. Ray had his connections with some higher criminals. Some of the chemicals he used for his experiments had to be bought off the black market, a place where Ray had set up shop a few times in the past. Ray was not a saint, but he never tried to be. It took just a few phone calls until Ray learned how to find the Havocs. It was just outside Columbus, Ohio, in an aging mansion with the name Renshaw written on top of it.

The name Renshaw rang a bell for Ray. He knew the name from his father's journals. Renshaw was Logan's last name. Logan was the most mysterious one of the group. He was referred to in the journal as the one who cast the spell on the boulder that sealed the garden. Ray read that Logan was reported dead a few years after Ray's father was killed. Ray was able to put two and two together, that this mighty leader of the Havocs was Logan's son, a man with advanced strength. Ray felt like things were coming together and it was his destiny to find Logan's son. Together they would open the door that his father placed and locked. Maybe Logan's son could help lead Ray to his father's murderer. There was much to think about. It was a day's trip to arrive at the mansion, so he started to move.

CHAPTER 9

The Two Keys

Thursday, April 2, 1970

A knock at the Renshaw Mansion alerted the man inside who opened the door a crack to get a glimpse at the visitor. The man took a quick look at the visitor before asking, "What do you want?"

Many people come knocking at the door at night, so this wasn't too out of the ordinary. Some were looking for work and knew that if they worked for Cain, they also got to live in the mansion. But this visitor said that he wanted to meet with Cain. The doorman said that Cain wasn't seeing anyone right now and he should come back in the morning.

The visitor was pushy, saying that he traveled a long way with no rest and insisted on meeting Cain now. The doorman showed his gun hanging in his shoulder holster to intimidate the stranger. Amused, the visitor let out a small laugh.

"Look, I know you're just doing your job, but trust me, I'm not just another homeless man looking for a place to stay. If you don't let me in, I'll beat your face in," the stranger threatened.

The doorman was not shaken by what the man said; instead, he pulled out his gun and aimed it at the visitor. Before the doorman knew it, the visitor had snatched the gun right out of his hand. The visitor then snapped the gun in two with his bare hands. "Your leader and I have a lot in common, so take me to him now!" the visitor demanded while maintaining a steady tone.

The doorman was shocked by this action, even frozen with fear. He believed that his leader, Cain, was the only one strong enough to do something like that. The man knew he was no match for this stranger, so he opened the door wide to lead him to the master of the house. The visitor at the door was Ray, and he was happy to finally arrive at his destination. As he walked, he heard the creaks within the steps and saw the cracks in the walls. He could tell that the place was once a magnificent structure but was now in high need of a new coat of paint and much more. It looked like one small stray flame could burn the whole place down.

Ray was led to the office door of the leader of the Havocs. The doorman then walked out of sight, fearful of what Cain would do for letting a visitor in to see him so late at night. Ray wasted no time with knocking; he just turned the knob and let himself in.

"I told you, I'm not to be disturbed!" Cain shouted as soon as he heard the creaking of the door opening. Cain was staring out the large window and looking up at the night sky. Cain found himself staring out this window all the time; it gave him a peaceful time to get lost in his thoughts. Cain turned his head to the door to see who opened it, shocking him out of his meditative state. Cain's eyes rose when he saw a stranger. The newcomers would never come to his door; only the longtime members who had a better relationship with him would dare to come to his door. "Get out!" Cain ordered with a holler. He was too tired to raise his fist, but a strong firm demand would surely scare the man away in a hurry.

Ray showed no signs of fear, not even a flinch; he walked with confidence into the room. "The great Cain…*Cain the Animal* I believe they call you. It suits you," Ray said with a sly tongue.

Cain was tall, a wide man with a heavy set of shoulders and large muscles on his arms. The man looked as strong as a horse, stronger even. Just looking at Cain made you feel weak; he always stood tall, with his chest out and shoulders back. Even Cain's jacket looked intimidating, a faded and beaten-up brown leather jacket. The jacket had stitches all over it, patches possibly placed to hide knife stabs or bullet wounds.

Ray, on the other hand, was wearing an expensive suit and tie, as always. Ray dressed for business, but his body language was giving off the impression that he was laid back. Ray marched right up to Cain for a handshake. "Ray Mantus," Ray said with his hand out there for Cain to shake. Cain looked at Ray with evil eyes, before refusing the handshake.

"Are you here for a job, Mr. Mantus?" Cain asked, thinking Ray was here to hire the Havocs.

"Kind of. See, we have a lot in common, and I believe that together we can open a door to an enchanted land," Ray said, coming off more as crazy than someone who was speaking the truth.

"I'll give you to the count of three to leave this room, or you will be dragged out," Cain threatened.

"That doesn't really give me a lot of time to make my pitch," Ray replied, undaunted by the threat. Cain started to count, beginning with the number 1. "There's just a lot to go over, and there might be something in it for you," Ray added. Cain continued the count, not letting Ray talk himself out of his threat. "If you want to hurt me, don't make me wait for it," Ray stated. At this time, Cain said the number 3 and delivered a powerful left hook across Ray's face. Ray was knocked off his feet, slammed into the side of the wall, and fell to the ground. Pieces of the wall fell off and crashed onto Ray's body. The entire room gave a slight shake. Cain took a few steps to the door to call on one of his men to drag what he believed to be a dead body out of his home.

Cain was about to reach the door when he heard Ray say something. "You really are an animal!" Ray said, grabbing his chin to make sure it wasn't dislocated. Cain was frozen with disbelief. He fully expected Ray to die from his punch, not just shake it off like it was just a small slap. Cain turned fast toward Ray and saw him getting back up on his feet, brushing off dust from his suit. "I saw the punch coming, but the delivery…wow! That was impressive!" Ray stated.

Cain was puzzled. He punched people all the time, but something felt different when he punched Ray. He didn't have that soft cardboard feel he got when he normally punched people. Cain's knuckles were slightly hurt, which made him conclude that this man he had punched also had advanced strength.

"How is this possible?" Cain asked the man.

Ray smiled and motioned to Cain's chair behind his desk, implying that they should sit and talk. The two sat with the desk between them. "Talk!" Cain ordered.

"Well, I guess I don't need to show off that I'm more than the average person," Ray said with a shrug.

"How did you get this way?" wondered Cain.

"Long story short, I inherited it from my father," Ray stated.

"What's the long story of that answer?" Cain knew that he got his strength from his father as well. But he could tell Ray had a story to articulate, one that could reveal the whole story of where his strength truly came from.

Ray pulled out a newspaper clipping from his pocket. It was a photo showing the seven travelers with the diamond they sold. He handed it over to Cain saying that both their fathers were in this photo. Cain looked at the photo and was informed that his father was on the far right, with Ray's father on his left. Cain saw the photo and for the first time got a glimpse of what his father looked like.

"Our fathers used to hike the countryside together. I read it all within in my father's journals," Ray said, beginning to tell his story. "They found a mystic place that they believed to be the Garden of Eden."

"Like from the Bible?" Cain questioned with some disbelief.

"The very one," Ray said with a grin. "While in there, they were exposed to some type of power source that granted them their powers."

Cain wasn't sure if he should believe this story, but it did provide some answers. Cain asked where Ray's father was now. Ray said that his father was killed when he was just baby, so all he knew about this was from his father's writings. Cain said that his father died when he was a child as well. Cain always claimed his father to be dead when speaking of him, even though he didn't really know it to be true.

Ray said that Cain's father put up a door to the entrance of the garden, putting an unbreakable lock on it. Ray said that it took two people with powers from the garden to open the door, which was why Ray had come to see Cain. Ray believed together they could open the door. Cain wasn't sure whether to believe Ray; what he was talking about sounded crazy, but Ray delivered the pitch in such a believable way. Cain may always deny it, but there was a small part of him that believed that his father was still out there somewhere. If there was a chance that his father was in this place Ray spoke of, he must find out. Cain didn't take longer than a minute to think about it. He said that they would head to the door first thing in the morning. Ray grinned, said great, and started to go into detail on the location of the garden.

Friday, April 3, 1970

Cain gathered a group of his followers and told them they were taking a train to Maine. They boarded the train and started the long trip. Ray and Cain sat next to each other on the train. Ray, busy writing everything down, expressed his excitement in his notes. Cain found this annoying, so he snatched the pen out of his hand and chucked it away. The two sat in silence for a while. They came from two different worlds but had so much in common. Both built their successes on their own and oversaw their own employees. Both had to grow up with an absent father and were raised by only their mothers. But what they had most in common, the one thing that no other person could relate to, was their powers: their advanced strength and slow aging process.

Over time, Ray started up a conversation. "Your father didn't have any advanced strength but had the powers to perform supernatural spells. I wonder why that didn't get passed down to you."

"You know, my parents were hesitant to have a child due to their fear that I could not control the power that could have been passed down from my father," Cain responded.

"But you got the advanced strength instead," Ray uttered.

Cain said that he believed his father left because he could not do what his father could. As they traveled, Ray and Cain were able to bond over the shared experience of having absent fathers. They also shared stories of how much they cared for their mothers. Both had great love for their mothers who did their best raising them alone. Not easy to raise kids like them.

Ray asked how his powers worked; Cain was unsure what he meant by that. Ray said that he'd been studying his advanced strength for years. He found out that when he was filled with joy and other positive emotions, he was at his strongest. When he was feeling negative emotions, he felt like he lost all strength.

Cain knew what he was talking about; he said that he still remembered his weakest moment. When Cain came home, he found his mother dead on the porch. Cain cried tears in that heartbroken moment. He said that there were a hundred people who wanted him dead, and the weakest one of them all could have beaten him to death with no problem in a matter of seconds in that moment.

Ray shared his weakest moment with Cain. It happened when he was reading his father's journals. The last one talked about his wife being pregnant. The last page talked about how happy he was that he was a father and how he planned to devote the rest of his life to be the greatest father he could be; he promised his son he would never be alone. Ray said that made him cry because his father died just days after he was born. Ray was devastated that he would never meet his father and that his father couldn't keep his promise.

Both had their weakest moments when it involved family. The two lived the rest of their lives being afraid of getting too attached, afraid of losing someone whom they would love, and afraid that weak feeling would return. They never wanted to feel weak again, so they only wanted to look out for number one. It turned out to be a lonely life with no family and no friends. The two really bonded during this train ride. Neither had shared their weakest moments with anyone before. Sharing this advanced strength really made the bonding process easy, easier than with any other person in their lives. It felt like no one could understand them but each other.

Ray even learned from the old kept letters his father received from his past travelers that they really didn't start becoming friends until after receiving their powers. It was easier for them to bond with someone who was like them than with anyone else. Ray and Cain never really had friends. Their feeling different from everyone else kept them from ever finding anyone who really understood them.

When they arrived in Maine, they headed to the mountain. As they hiked, it seemed like Cain and Ray already had inside jokes, as if they had become good friends. Cain's followers were shocked to see their leader putting down his tough-guy persona and sharing a laugh with someone.

They came across a sign warning about the deadly chemicals ahead; Ray laughed and explained that he put that there and informed them that there was no chemical threat.

The two walked up the mountain to the tunnel. Ray walked down the tunnel first with Cain and his men following. Ray pointed to the boulder, saying they had arrived. Ray pointed out the sunlight streaming from the bottom left side of the rock. Cain took a closer look and started to believe Ray more now.

"How do we open it?" Cain asked with a seemingly direct order. The idea that his long-lost father could be on the other side crossed his mind, so he wanted to get inside now. Ray said that all he knew about the way it worked was that it took two with powers to open the door, and all you needed to do was simply put your hand on it.

Ray put his left hand onto the rock and looked back at Cain, waiting for him to do the same. As Cain brought his right hand to the rock, Ray felt this huge nervous feeling cover him. If he was wrong, then he brought Cain and his men here for no reason. The moment Cain's hand touched the rock, both started to feel like they were being drained, as if they were giving blood. It was as if they were giving up their strength to the rock. They were unable to take their palms off the stone as they lost the strength to stand. Their legs were lifeless on the ground as the rocked moved out of the way. The sound of the boulder moving sounded like grinding stone on gravel; the tunnel started to light up from the sunlight beaming from the other side of the entrance. Once the rock was moved out of the way, both Cain and Ray were able to remove their hands from the stone. They both lay on the ground feeling so weak they couldn't stand. While on the ground, the two looked over and saw the wonderful sight of the Garden of Eden.

CHAPTER 10

The Creatures of the Land

Cain's men pulled themselves away from the fantastic view of the garden to help their leader to his feet. Cain grunted and struggled to stand. "Trying to kill me, Ray?" Cain used all his might to yell.

"You want me to kill him, sir?" asked one of Cain's men.

Before Cain could say anything, Ray started to say that once they entered the garden, they'd be fine. The men carried Cain past the rock and closer to the edge of the tunnel. Once he was past the rock, he started to feel better. He was able to stand on his own just fine. He ordered his men to help Ray to his feet and bring him closer. Once they were both past the rock, they started to regain their strength. On the edge of the tunnel, they saw the thirty-foot drop along with the waterfall close by. Ray looked down and saw a rope tied up leading downward.

"They must have been standing right here," Ray said, holding the rope in his hand.

"Who?" wondered Cain.

"Our fathers," Ray replied sentimentally. Ray felt an emotional attachment with his father at this moment, while Cain was hit with a feeling of disgust by the mention of his father. The two took a long deep look at the garden. "All right, we didn't come all the way here to just look at it," Ray stated. Ray, now feeling much better, jumped off the edge and landed on the ground unharmed. Cain then followed suit and landed next to him. Cain's men used the rope to climb down. After getting to the ground, Ray swung his bag off his shoulders to take out a sheet of paper and pen.

"What are you doing, Ray?" wondered Cain.

"I'm working on a map. Who knows how big this place is. If we forget how to get back, we could be lost for days," Ray said, thinking ahead.

Cain believed the map was a good idea because when he looked at the grounds, it seemed that the paths reached forever. The place was beautiful, but if you ever found yourself lost with no escape in sight, you'd be terrified. Cain was hoping to find his father in this land. Cain knew that it took two with powers to open the door, but his father made the lock, so if anyone could find a way around it, it would be him.

Ray and Cain jogged through the land. They covered miles and miles in a matter of minutes. They ran far past the cave that contained the diamond that powered the garden, the same place where their fathers received their powers. They stopped after a while, checking behind them and seeing that Cain's men were far out of sight. Ray took out two water bottles and gave one of them to Cain who took a big gulp from the bottle.

"It's nice having someone who is able to keep my running pace for once," Cain said after his sip. Cain's strong legs were able to carry him for miles at an unhuman-like speed. Cain had a history of running from cops and cop cars. Ray laughed, saying that he liked to keep himself in running shape as well. He said he'd thought of running the Olympic marathon but didn't want all that attention because he knew he could win and set a record. Cain laughed and said they could win gold medals in so many events if they would go out.

Ray took a sip out of his bottle, and as he took the bottle away, he saw something behind Cain. Ray was in motionless shock, his eyes wide and his jaw dropping. Cain could see that something spooked Ray, so he turned to see what it was. Cain could not believe what he saw.

"Is that a unicorn?" Cain asked in disbelief.

Ray simply nodded yes, still not saying a word. The unicorn was a full-grown, horse-sized pure-white animal complete with a spiral horn on top of its head. The unicorn was graceful, just posing in the slight distance.

Worried that a sudden move would frighten it, the men slowly approached the animal. Ray got close enough to put his hand on the creature's back. The horn on the horse's head changed color from yellow to violet. The creature seemed scared for a moment. Then it calmed down as if it realized there was no danger. The horn changed to light red after that.

"I think it likes me!" Ray said with much joy.

"I think you're nuts," Cain replied.

"Notice how the horn changed colors when it expressed a different emotion? Fascinating," Ray said. Ray then pulled himself up onto the unicorn's back. The horse remained calm and stood still. "I wish I had a camera," Ray said as he sat on the animal's back. Ray then asked Cain if he wanted a turn on the horse's back. Cain laughed and said that he was fine with his feet on the ground.

"You didn't say there would be creatures here," Cain stated.

"There was no mention of them in my father's journal. We ran far away from the door. Maybe our fathers never made it out this far out," Ray guessed.

Cain asked where the horse came from, puzzled on how it appeared to them just like that. Ray pointed to a nearby hill, saying they should go check out what lay beyond that hill. Cain started to walk up the hill, while Ray managed to ride the steed.

When they reached the top of the hill, the sight showed a stretch of land where many types of wild animals ran free. The garden had surprises around every corner. The animals were nothing like any Cain or Ray has seen before. But strangely, they knew them by names.

Cain pointed to a pack of creatures and asked, "Are they ogres?"

"I bel—"

"I'm sorry, but get off the horse. I can't take you seriously while you're sitting on that thing," Cain barked. This made Ray laugh as he climbed off the animal. Ray said that he believed Cain was right. Ray then started to point out other animals. He pointed out Sasquatches, trolls, griffins, and phoenixes.

"These must be the creatures God kept from the outside world," Ray uttered.

"Makes you think that this place is more of a prison than a paradise," Cain replied.

"Interesting thought," Ray admitted.

The two gazed at the animals on top of the hill for quite some time. Ray was amazed by the fact that they all were living in peace and harmony. The animals looked tall and mighty. The two wondered if they ate meat; if so, what race hunted down the other? There was no sign of any type of defections anywhere.

Ray spoke about how much he would love to bring some of them back to his lab for further study. Cain had the idea of taking one of the creatures home to use as an attack dog of some kind.

"Well, why not? Think of what we could learn from getting one of these things under a microscope. We could learn how they survive and how long they lived. Heck, they may taste good."

"You want to eat them?" Cain said with humor.

"Have you seen how ugly pigs are? Sometimes the best dishes come in the ugliest packaging," Ray said with a grin.

The two shared a laugh together. Then Ray started to sell his idea of taking some creatures out of the garden. "Some of these creatures look like they can do some real damage once they get to a rampage state. If we can somehow *aim* that, you'd be the best mercenary in the country. The Havocs would be the most feared group out there. And the rumors of the leader to be an animal would be almost true."

These ideas enlightened Cain; the thought of having a fully grown bigfoot at his command would be very empowering. He said they had to get a lot of prep work done first. The capturing, the transporting, and the cages would take a while to set up. Ray said if they worked together, they could have their own mystical zoo in a matter of months.

The two went back to find Cain's men and then headed to the door. They pushed the boulder back into place, causing the lock to activate once more. While on the return to the Renshaw Mansion, Ray made a design plan for a ramp that would stretch down the thirty-foot drop from the entrance of the garden. That would have to be the first project when they returned to the garden because they wouldn't be able to carry up all the animals up the rope.

Within the following days, Ray had bought an abandoned prison in Ohio. Ray said that the place would be perfect to hold the animals and would have plenty of room for him to build a lab to pursue his studies. Cain handled the cells; he knew that they would have to be heavily reinforced for these creatures. After the prison was remodeled, they started getting shipping trucks, the type that transfers zoo animals. They took several trucks out to the mountain that housed the garden.

Once inside the garden, the two started building the ramp that was formed from the logs and vines from the garden. It was a very strong structure, able to withstand heavy weights. Ray said that since it lay within the garden, it would never rot nor collapse. Now that most of the prep work was completed, it was time to get the beasts. They had strong chains and enough sedatives to take out a fully grown whale.

The unsuspecting creatures were very easy to transport out of the garden; it wasn't until after they passed the door that they became hostile. It took seven men holding chains to hold down one of the animals. Even Cain was pushed back from the beasts during the struggle of getting them into the trucks. Ray had to deliver large amounts of sedatives to the animals to knock them out. It was a pretty thrilling time for Cain and Ray as facing something that could hurt them was rare due to their strength. The trucks were full, and they drove back to the prison.

It was a long day. The animals kept waking up on the way to the prison, almost tipping over one of the trucks. Luckily Ray came prepared and was able to keep the animals tranquilized long enough for them to enter their cages.

"This is animal cruelty at its highest," Cain said as he listened to the animals howling while they were locked inside their rooms.

"Don't tell me you're growing a conscience, Cain," Ray said, fully knowing it wasn't true. "Besides, as far as the rest of the world knows, these are animals of fiction; so there are no animal rights to protect them," Ray added as he pulled a couple of beers from his bag.

Ray thought they should celebrate. Together, they had accomplished their own personal zoo. As they drank their beers, they were both thinking the same thing. They both went to the garden to find something. Ray was hoping to find answers on how his father died. Cain was hoping to find his father. They didn't find what they wanted, but the trip wasn't a waste at all. Cain had a chance to make his group stronger, and Ray found something new to study. And the two became good friends after that.

CHAPTER 11

What Matters Most

December 15, 1970

Three men were running for their lives down the hallway of the very large banquet hall. A very large ogre was chasing them. Suddenly, two of the men could hear the ogre smash the third man to death in an instant with its mighty fist. Not too long after that, one of the remaining two was whacked against the wall. These men were just trying to get to the door at the end of the hall, but none of them were able to outrun the ogre. The massive swing from the ogre's forearm would kill a normal man with ease. Things were not safer in the kitchen. The Sasquatch already mauled all the ones hiding there and fearing for their lives. And in the garage, a savage troll was there to squash the ones who retreated to their cars.

From the outside banquet hall, the Havocs stood with their rifles in hand listening to the madness inside. They could hear the thunderous roars from the creatures, the horrifying screams from the terrified men, and the gunfire from those who tried to fight back. Cain stood among his men, and when things started to grow silent, he gave a nod to one of his henchmen. The man knew this was the signal to stop the animals. The man brought a walkie-talkie up to his face saying, "Play the music."

The message was sent to a man at a radio station. The DJ at the station then pushed an eight-track tape into the player and started to play the sound over a radio station. The Havocs outside the banquet building stood next to very large speakers as they played the sound from the radio station. The three creatures inside the building all had these headphones strapped to their ears, and the radio station was playing for them as well. Once the creatures heard the sounds, their nonstop-thirst-for-blood attitude suddenly turned into a pleasant, calm, genial presence.

The sound playing over the radio was a recording of the sounds from the garden. The river flowing, the wind blowing through the trees, little things that made the creatures feel as if they had returned to the garden. It was a trigger that Ray discovered to keep the animals calm. Just the idea of them being back in the garden made them act as if they were. The Havocs entered the building. Furniture was broken and scattered in every corner of the room, and blood was splashed everywhere. Cain saw the creatures rambling around the place as if they were lost puppies. Cain said he would bring the creatures back to the trucks while the others could collect their payment.

Cain was able to keep money in his men's pockets by having them steal the cash from the victims. This attack was a major payment for Cain; for years, a client kept saying they would pay a million if the Havocs would take out the competition. Cain told the competition about this, and they asked for the same request but for double the amount of money. Cain never made the deal; the mob family was too strong for his men. But with the garden creatures at his command, he was able to eliminate the entire family all at once without losing any of his men. The men found a fortune among the dead bodies as they looted for cash, jewelry, and guns—a very successful night for the Havocs.

As the trucks were transporting the creatures back to the prison, or *the zoo* as the men liked to call it, they had to deliver sedatives to the animals to knock them out because they were getting too far from the radio signal. The trucks passed a warning sign that talked about a deadly chemical spill ahead, which indicated that they were getting close. Ray posted the signs around the prison to help lead people away from the location. It was a trick he had used from time to time. The animals now were so heavily asleep that the men had to carry and drag them to the cages. While the Havocs were doing that, Cain went upstairs to see if Ray was in.

Cain walked into Ray's lab on the second floor carrying a couple beers with him. "Saw the light was on from outside, so I figured you were here," Cain stated as he walked past the open door. Ray had his eye in a microscope like he always did; he lifted his eyes up to greet his friend.

"Did the attack go well?" Ray asked as he took one of the beers.

"Didn't even need to get my hands dirty," Cain replied with delightful grin.

"And here I thought that was your favorite part," Ray said, pulling off the bottle cap. Cain informed Ray that his idea of using the radio station plan worked like a charm. Ray was a little worried that the headphones would fall off the animal's heads during the attack. Cain assured him that all three headphones managed to stay strapped to their heads just fine.

A while back, Ray opened a new chemical plant nearby. Cain even installed a jail cell that was strong enough to hold a creature inside. Ray would sometimes bring an animal to the plant for further study. Ray said the hardest one to study was the phoenix; the thing kept setting the room on fire and melting the walls. But it was worth it, for Ray was able to find out the way the bird was able to make its own flames. It was a chemical in its body, and Ray was able to recreate that chemical. *The Phoenix Flame* he named it. If it burns too bright, it could make you go blind. Ray was even able to build a fireproof jacket from the feathers shed from the bird.

Ray learned a lot from these special creatures. They were able to live without the need to eat, drink, or even defecate. They had organs and blood, so it was possible to kill them by beating them to death or having them bleed out. But given how strong the beasts were, that would be a highly difficult thing to accomplish. Ray had a theory of how the creatures could live without food or water. He believed that the creatures were made for the garden only. They were created to make the garden look more mystical, he guessed. Since they were made for decoration only, they didn't carry any animal or human instincts. Ray believed that this was the explanation for the animals' out-of-control behavior after they were removed from the garden. Being outside their natural habitat placed their minds in a malicious state. The animals seemed to kill everything in sight. If they didn't get tamed, they would have to be put down; otherwise, their rampage would never come to an end.

As Cain and Ray enjoyed their beers, Cain asked why Ray was working in the prison and not the plant. Ray was tired of the plant, so he chose to work at the prison. Cain found that hard to believe. The animals were all locked up in the basement of the prison; all they did was sleep inside their cages. But they would let out nightmarish growls and howls from time to time. The Havocs were always uncomfortable during their time at the prison. Cain told Ray that if he was looking for a free room, the Renshaw Mansion was always open to him. Ray never thought about taking a room at the mansion, but once the offer was issued, he saw no reason not to take it.

December 16, 1970

The next day, Ray returned to his home to get some supplies for his room at the mansion. He thought a lot about his father, thinking that his father would be happy that he found friendship with his friend's son. Ray thought that maybe he'd bring his father's coat along with him. Thinking that the jacket was just collecting dust for years, it would be nice for someone to wear it again. Ray opened his closet and knelt to a chest on the floor. He carefully opened it and looked inside. Inside was some of his father's worldly possessions. He picked up a pocket watch and opened it up to admire it. Then he removed the jacket, the last thing his father would ever put on. This was the jacket his father was wearing the day he was killed.

Ray looked at this jacket a hundred times but never once put it on. Ray put on the jacket and was delighted to see that it was a perfect fit. Ray put his hands in the pockets, and his right hand felt something. It felt to be a book of some sort. He removed the object and saw that it was a journal. Ray thought he read all his father's journals, so finding a new one was truly shocking. Ray lost his ambition to find the one who murdered his father; he hadn't found any new evidence in such a long time. So maybe reading his father's last journal, his last words, could lead him closer to his murderer. Ray plopped down onto a chair and started to read through the pages.

The journal read as if Ray's father was paranoid about something. The journal went into detail about the murder of the other travelers from the garden. With the pattern of the killer coming at the end of the month, Ray's father feared that he was next to be killed. The journal said that Ray's father went to one of his fellow travelers' house and spotted the killer there. The last page written in the journal said that he believed that Logan was the one causing the murders. Knowing that Logan was the only person he knew that could teleport made him look like a real suspect. It said that he was going to confront Logan. Ray checked the date of when that was written; it was written on the day of his father's death.

Ray loosened his grip on the book, and it suddenly dropped to the floor. Ray knew that Logan was the magic man, so he must have the power to vanish out of thin air. If his father was on the way to see Logan to confront him as the murderer, then Logan must have killed him as well. It all was coming together for Ray now. Ray became a new man; a new hate was born inside him. The man who killed his father was the father of his best friend. Ray marched to his car and made his way back to the Renshaw Mansion.

The drive was long, but Ray made it to the mansion with great haste. Ray went over a million different ways his talk with Cain could go. When he arrived at the door, he was greeted with a warm welcome by Cain's men. They treated him with the same respect as they did their leader. Ray was informed that Cain was in the library, so Ray made his way there. Ray didn't have his usual attitude that he normally brought to the house. He didn't seem happy to be there. He didn't crack any jokes or even smile. He just had a blank stare and little to no words. It was as if he was processing so much that his motor skills had a slight delay.

Ray made it to the library where he found Cain sitting in a chair reading a book. Ray stood in the doorway of the room looking at Cain. Cain brought down his book when he heard Ray breathing in the doorway.

"You all settled in?" Cain asked with a friendly tone.

Ray had a slight delay before saying, "Yep." Ray then sat in the chair across from Cain.

Cain put the book down on a small coffee table in front of his chair and picked up two glasses of scotch that were sitting on the same table. Cain handed a scotch over to Ray, for he had one of his own. "Thought this caused for the fancy stuff." Cain smiled.

Ray only held the glass in his hand as Cain took a sip from his own glass. Cain found it odd that Ray wasn't drinking along with him. Cain assured Ray that this was top-shelf liquid. Ray put the glass down on the table in front of his chair, finally ready to speak.

"You said your father ran out on you a few years before he died, right?" Ray said with his fast tone of voice.

Cain found it weird that Ray would bring something like that up, but he humored Ray by telling the truth. "Well, I'm not sure when he died. He could be alive, for all I know."

"But you made me think he was dead all this time," Ray replied.

"He's dead to me, so I tell myself and everyone else!" Cain said, his voice raising in anger.

"Your father ran off the same day my father was killed!" Ray stated.

Cain gulped down the rest of his drink and placed the glass back on the table. "What's your point?" he asked with an angry grunt.

"I found my father's last writing. He said there was a man out there killing the men he entered the garden with. He said that he spotted the murderer, a man who could teleport, vanish into thin air. He said the only person who could do that was Logan, your father! His last sentence was him saying that he was on his way to confront Logan. AND YOUR FATHER MURDERED HIM!" Ray shouted as he stood up tall. "I'm sorry, Cain. I must have vengeance for my father!" Ray said as he removed a handgun from his holster and aimed it at Cain. "And since his murderer is gone, you'll have to do!"

Before Ray could pull the trigger, Cain flipped the coffee table that sat between the two up in the air, hitting Ray's hand. When the table slammed into Ray's hand, Ray's shot missed, causing the gun to fly out of his hand. Cain shoved his forearm into Ray, pushing him hard back against a wall.

"You come into my own house and try to kill me!" Cain howled.

Ray placed his hand onto Cain's arm that had him pinned to the wall and was able to twist it around, breaking Cain's wrist. Ray was now free from the wall. Ray hopped up and shoved both his feet into Cain's chest, kicking him hard.

Cain lost his balance and tumbled backward. Ray jumped over to his gun and fired it three times at Cain. Cain had been shot before, so he was familiar with the impact of a handgun at this close of a range. Cain just powered through the shots and sprinted at Ray to make another attack. Ray ducked and rolled away from Cain. Cain was stronger than Ray due to basic muscle build that would be in effect even without their advanced strength, but Ray was much quicker. As long as Ray kept his distance, he had an advantage. Ray rolled to the opposite side of the room.

By this time, the rest of the Havocs in the building had arrived in the room to help Cain. Ray had to think fast; he was way outnumbered and stood no chance on taking them all on. Then Ray jumped out of the window behind him and landed in the yard. Once outside, he took off running into the woods, quickly disappearing out of sight.

"Should we go after him, sir?" one of the Havocs asked Cain.

Cain didn't speak at first. The man was impatient to receive his orders, so he asked again.

"No, let him run," Cain said. Cain couldn't believe how much could happen within a few short seconds. His friend turned into an enemy over a simple drink. Cain would miss his friend, which is why he let him run. "Ray wants a war, then we'll give him a war!" Cain then said that he required medical attention as he needed to stop the bleeding from the bullet wounds before he bled out.

Ray ran and ran and ran. *What have I done?* he thought to himself. His whole life he had searched for his father's killer and wanted revenge. Now he found a way, and if it meant killing his friend, he would. Friends no longer mattered to him. Now the thing that mattered most was vengeance for his father.

CHAPTER 12

A War between Friends

Years passed, and several assassination attempts on Cain's life had been made by Ray. Cain was heavily guarded by his Havocs, so he was well protected. Ray knew that he would need to gain help in order to get past Cain's guards. It wasn't hard to find people who wanted to attack Cain; he had made tons of enemies over the years. The word on the street was "If you don't like Cain and the Havocs, they're always hiring at Saltwater Chemicals." Now that Ray had an army at his command, he had a fighting chance to defeat the Havocs. Neither side ever used the garden creatures on one another, for both sides knew how to tame the animals.

Deep in the woods that surrounded the Renshaw Mansion, tree houses were placed all around the mansion within a mile radius. Tree houses were installed to serve as a lookout for any threatening attackers heading toward the mansion. Ray and his men had tried to attack the mansion in the past, but the Havocs had the numbers to chase off the intruders. Ray learned that he couldn't attack Cain on his turf, as it was always well guarded. Cain may have been stronger with the larger army, but Ray had his intellect.

Ray was able to make attacks on Cain's life a few times. Ray invented new chemicals that could harm Cain. Once, Cain was splashed with one of Ray's chemicals during a battle, and he found himself very ill; he was sick for weeks from this attack. Cain was fearless, but Ray's intelligence was the only thing that he was truly afraid of. Cain sent spies into the chemical plant business to learn Ray's secrets and possible weaknesses.

April 12, 1979

Cain was loading his handgun that rested in his shoulder holster. Then he loaded another gun that was placed in his ankle holster. Cain exited his room and marched down the steps to the main floor. As he made it to the bottom of the steps, he saw some of his men getting ready to take off.

"Cain, I thought you were sitting this one out?" said one of his men.

The Havocs had a business meeting with some people trying to hire them for their services—the Sweden Brothers, to be exact. Even with this war against Ray, Cain still managed to keep his business running. This was a simple deal meeting, so Cain wasn't going to go.

Cain said that he was simply going out for a night drive. The man could sense that Cain was not up for small talk, so they headed off to the meeting. Cain had a few meetings of his own to attend that night. One was set up at the beginning of the day and could not be rescheduled. The second meeting's notice just arrived a few hours earlier. This one also could not be rescheduled. Cain had a busy night and was anxious to arrive to the second meeting.

Cain drove at dangerous speeds but was very focused on his destination. There was an old run-down gas station just outside of town. There was one parking light still working that lit over a still-working pay phone. In that dim light were two men waiting for Cain. Cain drove the car up to them, got out of the car in a hurry, and rushed up to the two men.

"What do you have for me?" Cain asked the two men, getting straight to the point.

The men felt uneasy as if they did something wrong. So they seemed to shout out their information.

"The meeting with the Sweden Brothers tonight is a setup, a trap for the Havocs!" one of the men said. These two men were Cain's spies.

They had this meeting set up earlier in the day so they could warn Cain about the surprise attack on the Havocs. The other man informed Cain that Ray was sending most of his army out for this attack.

"If Ray is sending most of his army on us, then we will send our entire army on him. Hit his surprise attack with one of our own!" Cain responded.

"Sir, if we send the entire army, your house will be unprotected," one of the spies sheepishly stated.

"If our men are successful, any future attacks from Ray will be delayed. He may even give up. That victory is worth letting the mansion's guard down!" Cain spoke so loudly that he made his men shake in fear. Cain calmed down, saying he'd make the order. Cain, with a calm tone, asked if there was anything else.

"We stole one of his weapons," one of the spies stated.

The other slowly took out a small red box. The mentioning of one of Ray's weapons made everyone feel uneasy, as if they spoke of a ghost. The very presence of the weapon made the men have chills. The man carefully handed the box over to Cain. Cain slowly removed the lip of the box to see the weapon. Inside, he saw a ball-like black object.

"According to Ray's writings, after studying the unicorn, he was able to create a chemical that could alter one's personality…so much that you would become a different person. The chemical is so thick that it hardened into a sphere shape. It would only affect people who have something called Loomation inside them. A simple touch would cause it to sink under your skin and start its effect."

"Loomation?" wondered Cain.

"According to Ray, he says it's what gives him and you your powers. You were born with it, and it was passed down from your father," one of the spies explained.

Cain looked back at the weapon; hard to believe that such a small object could change him into a completely new person, messing with his personality like it was a toy. Cain could understand why Ray would make such a tool. Ray knew that he and Cain were at their best when they were fearless, confident, and driven. If this weapon could change his personality, he could end up being a person who feared easily and become an outright coward. With emotions like that, Ray would be the stronger one and defeat him easily. Cain placed the lid back onto the box and handed it over to one of the guys.

"Place it into the storage locker with the rest of the stuff. Now, is that everything?" asked Cain. The men nodded; Cain told them to take off.

As they walked away, Cain pulled one of them back. He pulled him aside so he could talk without the other hearing. "Ray is going to notice something like that is missing. Ray is going to suspect a spy. I need you to turn in Erin." Cain said this with no concern for his follower; he took this order as simply business. Ray would go on a manhunt for a spy, and instead of hiding, Cain would expose one. Once he knew who the spy was, he wouldn't go looking for another, making the second spy safe. The man was going to obey his leader's command; he was just happy that he was the one to be spared. He may have been honored to be picked, but the truth was…he was just closer to Cain when he gave his order. If Erin would have been standing closer, he would have received this order.

Cain turned to the pay phone and used it to make a call. He called the mansion; he told them that Ray's men were planning an attack during the meeting the other Havocs had gone to. Cain ordered all his men to arrive at that meeting and to join in the fight when it started. Cain told the man on the phone to make sure that every available member was out on this fight. Cain then hung up the phone and rushed to his car. Cain had another person to meet up with that night. Cain was so excited to meet up with this person he ran to his car and drove at high speeds once again.

CHAPTER 13

Cain's Promise

A woman was in a hospital parking lot smoking a cigarette. Since it was her first cigarette in a long time, she was enjoying every bit of it. She thought the man she was waiting for would have arrived by now. The cigarette was almost burned out when she saw the man drive up to her. She flicked the cigarette butt aside and faced the car. The car turned off, and out came the driver, Cain.

"You're late!" the woman snapped at Cain. This woman spoke with no respect nor fear of Cain. They were not friends or rivals; their connection was two people who were completing a deal. Cain reminded her that he already made plans to see some people that he could not reschedule, which was why he was late. He wasn't expecting this meeting with the woman this week, but things changed, so he had to show up that night.

"Where is she?" Cain asked with force.

"She's in the car," the woman said, giving a nod to the back seat of the car she was leaning on. Cain tried to walk toward the car. "Money first!" she demanded.

Cain emitted a cruel gaze, but she was right. She kept her part of the deal, and Cain was a man of his word. Cain reached into his trench coat pocket, grabbed a very thick envelope, and placed it in her hands.

The woman looked inside and saw a huge wad of cash. Before she could touch it, Cain assured her that the agreed-upon amount was all there.

"My mother taught me to never trust a criminal master," she stated as a joke. She took out the money and started counting it to herself. Once she was done counting, she stepped away from the car to let Cain get to the door. Cain looked in the car window, and for the first time, he saw his daughter. She was sleeping peacefully in a car seat. Cain paused and admired the child's beauty. The woman looked at Cain; she had never seen Cain like this before. He looked vulnerable.

"Cain, are you sure you're ready for this? With your war against Ray, it may not be safe," she uttered.

"She will be safe," Cain replied.

"I was talking about you," the woman stated as Cain faced her. "She will make you weak, she'll make you worry, and she'll make you fall."

"I appreciate your concern, but my child and I are no longer your problem," Cain said as he opened the car door. He picked up the car seat and carried her over to his car. Once the baby was settled in the seat, Cain turned to the woman. "Part of the deal was that you leave town," he brought up.

"Don't worry, I'm moving back to my hometown to be closer to my mother—far away from your business," she explained.

Cain wanted the woman as far away from him as possible, for she was the only one who knew that Cain had a daughter. If any of his enemies knew this, his daughter would be a target. Cain was now a father, and his daughter's safety was all he could think of.

Cain drove home at the speed limit for the first time ever. When he approached his home, he was happy to see all the cars in the driveway were gone. This must have meant that the house was empty. Cain carried his daughter inside the house; he was amazed that she was still sleeping after all this time. There was no one in sight in the house, which was good. Everyone must have gone to the battle just as he ordered. Cain was not ready to tell his followers about the newborn, so this gave him more time to prepare to tell them.

Cain didn't realize it, but this was the first time he came to an empty house since his mother passed. He didn't have that blank feeling as he did the last time he came to an unoccupied house. This time he wasn't alone coming into the house, as this time he had his family with him. Then he heard someone coming out of the bathroom. The person was tightening his belt as he walked into the room Cain was standing in. The man looked up and saw Cain holding a gun at him.

The man was more confused by Cain holding a baby than him holding a gun to his head. The man was named Jason, and he was a longtime member of the Havocs. Jason put his hands up slowly, saying that he surrendered,

"What are you doing here? I ordered everyone to the battle!" Cain said, still holding up his gun.

"Well, I thought that since I'm just the accountant, I didn't have to go," Jason stated, hoping his excuse would be a good-enough reason. Jason wasn't a fighter. He had never seen action. He was the one who handled the paperwork, which gave him the nickname of the accountant. Cain finally lowered the gun and marched upstairs.

"Cain…," Jason said, following Cain up the steps. "Can I ask you a question?" Jason had a good relationship with Cain, so he spoke more as a friend.

"No," Cain replied.

"Well, I'm going to ask it anyway…whose baby is that?" Jason had no idea where this baby came from and was a little nervous about the answer.

Cain didn't say anything; he just walked up to a door. Jason grew silent when he saw Cain stop at this door, for this was the room of Cain's mother. One of the biggest rules of the house was that no one was allowed to step foot inside Cain's mother's room. Cain opened the door and walked in, turning on the room's light.

Jason walked in after Cain, expecting to see a bunch of cobwebs all over, but instead, he saw that it was turned to a nursery. "Cain…is that your baby?" Jason asked, still not believing what he was seeing.

Cain placed his daughter down in the crib he built for her. As she slept, he told Jason the story. "It was nine months ago when I got the call. 'Cain, what are we going to do?' she asked after telling me she was pregnant. She was terrified, and I was on the other end of the call trying to remember her name. She knew of my powers, so she worried about carrying the baby inside her. She didn't want to raise the child either,"

Cain said, never taking his eyes off his baby. "When I thought about being a father, I made a deal with her. I would raise the child alone. In exchange, I would pay for all the medical bills, and finally, when I came for the baby, I would pay her to leave the city and to never mention the child or me again."

"Congrats on the baby, but, Cain, this isn't the best place to raise a child. The hot water never works, the heater is always broken, and the lights flicker because the wiring is one hundred years old. The floor, doors, and steps creak, sounding like they're all going to break soon, and not to mention, it's always full of wanted thieves and murderers!" Jason stated with a heavy concern. "And if Ray ever finds out about her, then things will get a lot more complicated."

Cain then turned to Jason. "I'm putting you on nanny duty."

This made Jason uneasy; he walked over and spoke in a worried tone. "Cain, I can't. I don't know a thing about babies. I never even changed a diaper!"

Jason then took a look down at the baby. She looked so peaceful, resting in her crib that his worries started to calm down.

"She'll be strong like me. Her strength will protect her from the harsh environment of the house. That and it would give me more motivation to fix up the place again," Cain added.

Jason said he'll take the job, only if he never has to go into battle. Cain thought this was an easy deal, for he knows Jason wouldn't last long in battle anyway. Besides, Jason is the only one whom he trusted enough for this job, so he was glad that Jason took the job willingly.

Cain then told Jason to leave the house for the night. Cain explained that for the first time, the mansion was unguarded, for all the men were at a battle Ray had set up. Cain believed that if the Havocs were successful, then an attack from Ray would be pushed back for a long time, maybe forever. Having Ray's attacks pushed back would give Cain time to spend with his newborn, which was part of the reason Cain put all his men in this battle. If the Havocs failed, then Ray would come to the mansion. So Cain sat next to the front door with a shotgun in his hand, preparing to defend himself, his home, and his family.

April 13, 1979

Cain managed to stay up all night, and just before sunrise, he heard cars pulling in the driveway. Cain stood up from his chair and opened the door just a crack to see who was coming. He was happy to see that it was members of the Havocs, drunk off their success of a battle well-won. Cain then heard from down the stairs his daughter cry. He temporarily lost interest in his followers, put down his gun, and attended to her. Things would never be the same for Cain now; he now lived with this never-ending fear for his child's safety. He promised her that he would do whatever was needed to keep her safe, and he was sorry that she had to live with this constant threat from his enemies. Cain was hoping that this child would fill a hole in his heart and give him a chance to be a better father than his own.

CHAPTER 14

Ray's New Invention

Alone in Ray's office, Ray watched the news channel. The reporter said, "Another act of gang violence has risen last night, leaving many hurt or killed." Before the newscaster could go on, Ray turned off the television. Ray leaned back in his chair and stretched. Ray was at that fight last night leading the charge, but he failed to lead his army to victory. Ray had this anger inside; not only didn't he win the battle, but Cain didn't even need to show up to assure his men of victory. If Ray couldn't even beat the Havocs without their leader, then he knew he could never win. Then a knock at the door sounded.

"It's open!" Ray shouted. The door opened a crack, and in popped a head.

"You wanted to see me?" the man at the door said. This man was Erin, one of Cain's spies. Erin didn't know it, but his partner had turned him in to Ray on orders from Cain. Ray invited Erin in to have a seat. Erin sat down across from Ray with his desk between them.

"Hard night last night," Ray said as he opened one of his desk drawers. He removed a bottle of booze and a couple of glasses. He filled up the glasses from the bottle and offered one to Erin while he took the other.

"Yeah…hard night," Erin replied, taking the glass.

"I had the plan all sorted out, a simple trap for Cain's men. Just a small meeting, talking about hiring some Havocs for a job," Ray said before his first sip from his glass. "I knew this wouldn't bring Cain out from his well-protected *castle*. So Cain would send a few men to attend the meeting. I expected three, maybe four guys. Take out his men in small numbers at a time…weaken his army over time instead of taking them all on at once. But on the small chance Cain would come to the meeting, I sent my entire flock." Ray took another sip. "Everything was going well. There were only four men at the meeting and no sign of Cain. I knew him being there was a long shot. I led the charge, thinking I could take out four Havocs easy. Then I get bombarded from Cain's entire army!" Ray then threw his empty glass against the wall, shattering it.

"I know it was you who tipped off Cain. I know it was you who made my newly built weapon for Cain get *mysteriously* misplaced. I know that you have been working for Cain this whole time!" Ray shouted.

Erin jumped out of his seat and rushed to the door as fast as he could. Ray hurled the bottle at the back of Erin's head. Erin fell hard, face-first, to the ground, with shards of glass digging into the back of his head. Ray got up from his chair, picked up Erin's drink, and took a quick sip from it. Ray walked up to Erin who was so hurt that he couldn't even move.

"See, I had my suspicions that Cain had someone in my plant. Why do you think I left my latest weapon out in the open? It was the easiest way to get the weapon to Cain. I knew his spy would bring it to him. All Cain had to do was touch it! I'm guessing that didn't work either." Ray then used his foot to turn Erin's body to make him face him. "I guess finding his spy is a victory for me. I could use a win. It's not healthy to lose so many times in a row." Ray then smashed Erin's chest with his foot mercilessly until Erin took his last breath and died. Ray then walked back to his chair and put his feet up onto the desk.

Ray finished the glass and chucked it away. He then looked at the books and notes on his desk. One of the books was called *The Power of Loomation*. A very rare book, he was lucky enough to find it at an auction while he was on a business trip. Also on his desk was a notebook with the recipes of how to build his weapons. Another notebook consisted of all the studies conducted on all the creatures from the prison. The last book was his father's notebook from when he and the others found the garden. Ray read them all over and over, hoping to find a way to learn more about his powers and how to make something that could help him with his war.

While in thought, he was thinking about the attack last night. Ray only lost because Cain's army was larger. *Strength in numbers* the saying is. But Ray knew it wouldn't take large numbers to defeat Cain's Havocs. It just took the *strength* part. Ray knew that he and just five other guys at the same level of strength as he could defeat the Havocs with no problem. Then an idea sparked in his head. According to his father's journal, he and the others got their powers from a blast from the diamond in the garden.

Ray knew that without Cain, it would be impossible to return to the garden to cause another blast from the diamond. But maybe he didn't need to go back to the garden. The journal said that they took a piece of the diamond out of the garden and sold it to the highest bidder. Ray thought that if he could get his hands on that diamond, maybe it could release the same type of blast. With that, he could get a hundred men at the same strength level as he. Ray started writing these ideas down, saying he must find that diamond.

It took Ray a while to locate the diamond. It was up for sale a few times over the years and ended up in the hands of a millionaire who lived in England. The owner of the rock wouldn't dare sell it, no matter the sales pitch. The man had it on display. Owning the world's largest diamond gave him something to show off to the ladies, for he was married six times. The security was strong surrounding the diamond, so Ray had to come up with a solid plan on how to pilfer the diamond and return to America without being caught.

This challenge was a tough one for him, but Ray was a mastermind at this kind of stuff. It took years of planning; but in time, he managed to steal the diamond, carry it overseas, and bring it to his chemical plant. Ray studied the diamond very closely, trying to see if it could do anything. In his father's journal, it said after Logan cut off the piece of the diamond, all the energy was released. The energy didn't come back until after the diamond healed over the slivered-off part. Ray looked at the diamond and figured it out. If he could do something about the slivered-off side of his diamond, then maybe the energy would return.

Ray measured the rock. He drew up blueprints on how to alter the shape of the object so that there would be no bladelike teeth remaining in the diamond. He designed a cube, a flawless design that made the object smooth with no cut-off ends. Drawing up the blueprints was easy, but the process of designing the diamond into a cube seemed impossible. Nothing Ray had could cut the surfaces. Ray read that the piece was cut off by a sword that was found in the garden.

Ray was frustrated, as there was yet another thing for him to find. He didn't want to waste time looking for the sword. It took him years to find the diamond. Then Ray stood up, for something had just occurred to him. In one of his father's journals, he mentioned where he got the ring for his wife. There was a chipped-off piece of the diamond from the garden on Ray's mother's ring. His mother left the ring to him in her will, so it didn't take long for Ray to get his hands on it. Ray held the ring in his hand. "Thanks, Mom," Ray said, sentimental for a moment. Then Ray took the diamond from the ring and attached it to a drill and started sculpting his cube.

Ray was very careful, knowing that he couldn't mess up even a little; everything had to be perfect and exact. The patience he took to make everything right took a very long time. Making this cube was Ray's passionate project, with only a minor educated guess that all the work would pay off. Ray didn't feel safe working on this project at one place for too long, so he kept relocating his work area. He was off the grid for a long time to keep his work secret.

Ray carved the diamond into 121 pieces. He placed the pieces all together within a cube that consisted of six faces, twelve edges, and eight vertices. Each side of the cube was ten centimeters. He used tweezers to carefully connect each piece, as one would do to build a ship in a bottle. Each piece looked to be a random shape. But once they were all lined up, it merged into a flawless cube shape. Tension rose high just before he placed the final piece into place. This was the last piece needed to seal off the entire cube, completing the shape containing no shattered-off edges. The moment of Ray's hypothesis's conclusion was at hand. Ray put the final piece into place and held his breath. The cube illuminated a white glow like a lava lamp, or a type of night-light. The cube was shining similar to the North Star, just as the diamond in the Garden of Eden did. Ray had done it; he created his own Loomation power source. The Loomation was being contained within the cube just as the Loomation that powered the garden was contained in the diamond. This power was what gave Ray's father and the other travelers their powers, the same type of power that was passed down to him and Cain. With the power of Loomation in the palm of Ray's hand, he could make an army of advanced-strength soldiers.

Ray had to find a way to release the Loomation from the cube so that it could be absorbed into his men. Ray felt that simply removing just one piece of the cube would release the Loomation. Ray picked up his tweezers and very carefully grabbed hold of a corner piece. Once he removed the piece, the Loomation inside blasted out in a heavy shock wave. The wave struck down Ray, knocking him on the ground. The entire 120 remaining pieces scattered like explosive shrapnel. Ray was lucky that he was on the ground, as the shrapnel pieces sprayed all over the walls. If Ray would have been standing, the pieces would have torn right through him, killing him. Ray was awestruck with amazement; he had to write this down.

When Ray was hit with the blast, he was full of energy, as if he just took a shot of adrenaline. He felt wide awake, as if he could run an entire marathon and still have enough energy to do one thousand push-ups. Ray just spent hours and hours of working without sleep, so he was exhausted, and slightly disoriented, but after getting hit by that blast, he felt like all his senses were cranked up to eleven. Ray thought this blast would be nice to have, if he ever needed to recharge himself during a battle. All of this was written within his notes.

Ray had a problem. He couldn't be picking up all 121 pieces of the cube and then rebuild it every time he wanted to send off a blast. Not to mention, anyone who got hit by the scattering shrapnel recoil would surely die. Ray needed a way to keep the cube contained into one solid object after every use. Ray managed to come up with a solution. He was going to use the power of magnets to keep the cube from scattering after it released a blast.

It took some time, but Ray was able to hold all the pieces into place by wrapping the cube in special magnets. Each side of the cube had ten rows and ten columns, all able to rotate up and down. He rotated the cube up, down, side to side, lining all the edges of each piece together until the cube was one solid shape. Once the cube was completed, Ray had to slightly crunch down on the cube to have all the lined-up pieces touch one another. Once this action was done, the cube illuminated the same glow as it did last time. This glow meant that the cube now contained Loomation. As soon as Ray would release the pressure on the cube in its crunched position, the Loomation would be released. Ray took a deep breath and then took his hand off the cube. The cube released the Loomation in a white shock wave blast just like last time. The blast struck down Ray just as it did before, giving him that full-energy feeling once more. The cube flew across the room, but thanks to the magnets built into it, the cube remained intact. The columns of the cube rotated like crazy, causing the alignment of the pieces to be shifted from its placement. Ray stood up, grabbed the cube, and was grateful that it was still in one solid piece. Ray grinned and let out a cheerful victory yell, shouting, "IT WORKS!"

CHAPTER 15

The Calm before the Storm

April 23, 1985

It's been six years; and Kate, the daughter of Cain, had already turned six. With her father's power running through her veins, she was blessed with advanced strength and the mystical aging process. While Kate may have been six, her physical appearance looked that of a three-year-old, just like her father had before her. She grew up in the Renshaw Mansion surrounded by wanted criminals and her loving father. Kate was in the library, kneeling at a small coffee table trying to complete an assignment. Hovering over her shoulder were a few men who worked for her father.

"Benjamin Franklin, I think, was the second," said one of the men standing behind Kate.

"No, I think he was the third president," said another also behind Kate.

"He was never president!" shouted a third guy behind Kate. These three men were attempting to help the young girl with her history homework. The question was to name five presidents. Kate was homeschooled and was provided with books and assignments by her caretaker and teacher, Jason. Most of the men who worked and lived in the mansion loved Kate. The men loved having her around. She was such a sweetheart and a true delight. A child's innocence around the place warmed up the men's hearts, which was nice after a long day of performing their less-than-legal activities. Kate growing up with the house full of these men was something she had grown used to, so she never knew of a time when the house wasn't like this. She saw them as her pets in a way. Whenever she wanted something, she would simply go up to one of them, ask for it, and, in time, receive her request from any of the willing housemates. It was mainly food she would ask for, but she would come to ask for the newspaper from time to time.

Kate grew sad whenever one of the usual guys would not return to the house. She was never told what happened to them, but she knew there was a chance that they had died. She never worried about her father leaving the house, for she knew that he would always return. The men always praised her father, saying that he was the best out there and that no one could defeat him. Kate really didn't fully understand what her father and his employees did, as that was one of the rules when it came to Kate: no one could tell her what the Havocs did for a living.

"Okay, I got it! George Washington, John Adams, Thomas Jefferson, Teddy Roosevelt, and Zachary Taylor! And I even know that Benjamin Franklin was never president," Kate said with a silly smile. The three men who attempted to help Kate got in an argument with each other, saying how could Benjamin Franklin be one of the Founding Fathers and not ever be president? One pointed out how a person who wasn't even president end up on the hundred-dollar bill. Kate giggled at the men's argument. A young man in the kitchen overheard the conversation in the other room and yelled out to the three men.

"Don't you three have anything better to do than help a three-year-old with her homework?" This man was named Reed. He was new to the job and lived in the mansion. Reed always hated kids and thought it was embarrassing to have one in a place like this. It was even more embarrassing to see all the guys treat her with such an overcaring attitude.

"I'm six!" Kate said, politely correcting the gentleman. "And I don't really need their help. I just like the company."

"Yeah, Reed, she's really smart," said one of the guys.

"I assume it doesn't take much to outsmart you three," Reed said as he took a bite of his sandwich.

"For my last birthday, my dad arranged a spelling bee for me against these guys. I beat them with the winning word of *princess*!" Kate said with such pride and honor.

"How fitting," Reed said as he walked away. Kate felt slightly sad; this Reed guy didn't seem to enjoy her company. Her father always told her to never feel sad, gloomy, or scared. Her father told her to always stay strong and brave, for anything else would make her feel weak. Cain knew his daughter wasn't old enough to understand how her advanced strength worked; she had no idea that it was connected to her emotions, which was why he always told her to never be afraid.

Kate could tell her father that this Reed guy wasn't being nice to her, but she didn't want these guys to be kind to her because they worked for her dad. She wanted to earn her friendship with the men who lived with her. From the way Reed felt about her, it looked like they would never get along, but she didn't want to get him in trouble over this, so she never told her dad.

Just then, Kate heard the front door open. Kate jumped to her feet and ran to the door. Her father walked in with several men accompanying him. Kate ran into her father's arms and was lifted off the ground. It had been a few days since Cain was home; he was on a *business trip* out of state. Cain set his daughter on her feet and bent over to make eye contact.

"You do all your schoolwork Jason provided for you?" Cain asked. Kate smiled and nodded her head up and down. "Did you eat all your meals?"

"Yes, and I didn't forget to brush my teeth afterwards either!" Kate replied joyfully. Cain was happy to hear this as he stood straight up. "Dad...," Kate whispered. Cain looked down to her this time.

"You said that when you got back...we could go outside...together," Kate said, keeping her head down as if she was too shy to talk. Kate rarely left the mansion; and when she did, her caretaker, Jason, took her. She and Jason went to the zoo once, and she loved it. She was told that the Havocs had their own zoo, containing creatures that the world believed to be only mythical. She hoped her father could one day take her, but she was told that this zoo was not exactly a tourist attraction.

The reason for such a high degree of isolation was to keep her safe. Ray hadn't been seen in years, but Cain had other enemies besides Ray out there. It wouldn't be hard to figure out that Cain had a daughter if anyone saw them together, which was why they never left the house together. Before Cain left on his weeklong *business* trip, he told Kate that they would talk about going on a trip together, so Kate was very anxious to see him again. Cain looked at Kate without saying a word. Ignoring what Kate said, he asked where Jason was. Kate said that he was upstairs. Cain took another look at Kate. "It's good to see you, kid," he said before heading upstairs.

Kate didn't really have her hopes high on her father keeping his word. She knew that he loved her and would do anything to keep her safe, but Cain wasn't very good at opening up to his daughter. In the past, her caretaker, Jason, informed her about her grandfather and how he left his wife and Cain when Cain was just a baby. Kate was told how devastated Cain was when his mother passed and that Cain's one and only friend ended up being his greatest enemy. A lot in Cain's past kept him from being the heartwarming, open-to-his-feelings dad she wished he could one day be.

Cain made it upstairs and found Jason, and they had a meeting in Cain's office. Cain had a lockbox with him; he placed it on the desk. Jason was aware of this box and was thrilled to see it. "You're finally going to do it?" Jason exclaimed.

"She can't spend her whole life trapped within these walls," Cain replied. For a long time now, Cain had started an operation called *Better Life*. Within the lockbox were fake IDs, fake passports, uncashed checks, wads of hundred-dollar bills, and mapped-out living arrangements. Everything needed to start a new life for two people in hiding. Cain had a twenty-year plan; he and his daughter would rotate from town to town and change their names every time. They couldn't stay in a place for too long due to their aging process, and they would move to another town before anyone could notice. Cain wasn't really worried about most of his enemies. The Havocs were the ones the enemies wanted; and their leader, Cain, seemed more of a fairy-tale character than a real person. Cain needed to store up enough money so that he and his daughter would be settled nice for all this time.

"What about Ray?" Jason asked.

Ray was the only man Cain feared hiding from. Ray wasn't like most of his enemies. For one thing, Ray knew Cain was real, and he knew how to hurt him. Ray hadn't been seen in years; Cain's spy didn't even know where he was. Cain was hoping that his old friend had given up this foolish desire of getting revenge for his father. Jason asked Cain if he believed that to be true. Cain, looking down in deep thought, replied, "I wish it were true, but when Ray puts his mind to something, he'll never let it go." Cain took a moment of silence before admitting something.

"To be honest, I liked the fight." Cain turned his head toward the window to gather the words for his confession. "When you're as strong as I am, how Ray and I are, we try to look for thrills in life. We're looking for something to hurt us. I became a leader of a gain of mercenaries. Getting shot at and attacked was my idea of a fun day. Ray liked to challenge his mind. He found his thrill by making chemicals that could explode in his face if his research was false. When we started our war, I finally found an opponent who could be a true threat. And I know Ray loves trying to figure out a way to kill an unbeatable opponent such as myself. I think we kept this war going for so long because…we found it entertaining. There might have been times when I could have killed Ray. But I think I let it slide so that we could keep this going." Cain then turned his head back to his desk, where his eyes settled on a photo of Kate. "I'm ready to call it quits on this rival. But I know Ray will only end this if I'm dead. So I must kill him first."

Just then, a knock at the door sounded. "Come in," Cain replied.

The door creaked open, and a man stated that there was a phone call for Cain. Cain asked who was on the phone. The man on the phone was Baron. This shocked Cain, for Baron was Cain's spy for Ray. Cain rose from his chair and walked to the phone in the upstairs hallway. Cain put the phone to his head. "What is it?"

At a pay phone in a small town, Baron stood in the heavy rain with urgent news. As the rain slammed onto the top of the pay phone roof, Baron leaned in close for shelter from the rain and to speak loud enough for Cain to hear him over the line.

"He's surfaced, sir! Ray has returned, and he has gotten in touch with his old followers!" Baron hollered over the phone, yelling over the thunderous sound of the rain.

"Where has he been all this time?" Cain asked.

"He didn't say, but it sounded like he's got something big to reveal. He sounded very excited about it over the phone!"

"What is it, a new weapon?" wondered Cain.

"That's my guess. He's bringing in a lot of people for this. He's having us meet somewhere in southeastern Ohio in a cabin nestled in the hills," Barons reported. Baron delivered the address and informed Cain that he was going to head to the cabin much sooner than Ray was expecting; maybe he could learn what it was Ray had been doing during his absence. Cain ordered him to deliver him the news as soon as he found out. Baron hung up the phone, pulled the hood of the raincoat over his head, and hustled to his car.

Cain hung up the phone and stood still for a moment, lost in his thoughts. *The man hasn't shown his face in six years, and he waits until I'm ready to get out of the business to return.* Cain stopped one of his men walking in the hallway and ordered him to stand by this phone, saying that if anyone besides Baron was on the other line, he should hang up right away. If Baron called, he must find Cain immediately. Cain was uneasy, fearing what invention Ray had made up now.

Cain checked Kate's room and found it empty. Cain walked into her bedroom and walked to the open window. He looked out and saw her sitting on a branch of a nearby tree. "I remember the first time you fell out of this tree," Cain said to his daughter.

"You weren't too scared about it," she replied. Kate was pouting in a way, and the tree was where she liked to be when she felt this way. She wasn't allowed to leave the house, so climbing out to this tree from her room was her secret escape.

"Well, you're my daughter. I knew the fall wouldn't hurt you," he said.

"The fear of falling was more annoying than the impact," Kate uttered. There was an uncomfortable silence between the two.

"I know you had your heart set on seeing the world but—"

"It's more than that! I want to go and hang out with kids my own age, or at least people my own height. Be nice to have a friend who isn't one of the characters in the books from the library, or a grown man who works for my dad. I want to go to a real school, with real kids!"

Before Cain could say anything, both Kate and her father turned their heads to the sound of thunder from the distance. Kate looked over to her father. He reached out his hand to her to help her back in because a storm was coming. She took his hand and crawled back in the window. Once she was back in the room, Cain put his hands on her shoulders and knelt to meet her at eye level.

"I promise you, you'll live a life outside these walls. But something has come up…Ray has returned." The mere mentioning of Ray startled Kate. She knew of Ray as the only person her mighty father feared. If her father was mentioning him, then that must mean there was a serious threat at hand. Kate knew there was a crate in the basement that she was not allowed to open, for inside were a few stolen weapons from Ray's arsenal. Outside, the rain started to come down hard. Cain closed the widow and told her to stay in her room for the rest of the night. Kate nodded and understood. She then walked over to her nightstand by her bed. She picked up a book and offered it to her dad.

"I haven't read any more of the book during your time gone. I was hoping we could continue it together like we used to," Kate said to her dad with her eyes displaying a hopeful glance. A comfortable nostalgic feeling came to Cain's mind upon seeing this book. This was the same book his mother used to read to him as a kid. Cain wanted to continue the tradition with his daughter. Cain smiled and said he could spare some time to read a chapter or two to her. He tucked her in her bed and started reading from the book.

CHAPTER 16

The Night of the Great Flood

Baron drove out of town. After ascending a high incline with long winding, curvy roads, he approached the cabin up high in the gaps of the trees. The rain was pouring down hard, making the road almost impossible to see. Baron pulled the car to the side when he grew close to the cabin's location. He turned off the car and jogged through the woods to arrive at the cabin undetected. There were no cars parked out front of the cabin, so Baron was hoping that Ray was out. Baron checked his watch and saw that he still had a few hours until the meetup time was scheduled. Baron took out his lockpick and started to unlock the door.

With a delighted, relaxing feeling, the knob turned; and Baron was able to push open the door. He kept the lights inside the cabin off. Before closing the door, Baron removed his raincoat, folded it up, and placed it just outside the door. Baron then slipped off his shoes and placed them on the floor next to the door. Baron couldn't mar the room with evidence of dripping water from his wet jacket and footwear; otherwise, Ray would have known someone was in the cabin.

Baron tiptoed throughout the house using a flashlight for his guide. Upstairs, Baron found the room where Ray had his belongings. Baron shone his flashlight on a briefcase that sat on the top of a dresser. The sound of the thunder roared when the light shone onto the case. Baron opened the case and started digging though the files. Under the files was Ray's recipe book for weapons. It was a handwritten notebook containing some of Ray's most powerful devices.

"Jackpot!" Baron lightly cheered, still trying to keep himself quiet. Baron closed the case and made his way back to the front door with the notebook in hand. Baron took the notebook downstairs and carefully wrapped it in his raincoat to keep it dry in the rain. The book was more important than him when it came to being dry from the rain. Baron sprinted through the woods as if he was running for his life. He was relieved to reach his car. After getting in the driver's seat and slamming the door, he turned on the car's dome light. He removed the notebook from his jacket and looked inside.

His fingers flew through the book, quickly eyeing each page. There was the formula on how to make the Phoenix Flame gas. Also discovered in the pages was the formula that caused Cain to grow very sick and the formula to make the black spear that could change Cain's personality. In the back of the book were all the notes on the cube. Baron knew that this must have been the new weapon that Ray was ready to show off tonight. As Baron was reading the notes of the cube, he was fascinated by the achievements Ray has accomplished.

The blast from the cube could give Loomation to whomever is struck by it. This could give ordinary people advanced strength or possibly the ability to create magical spells. Being struck by the shock wave blast could even have healing side effects for whoever bears Loomation. A rush of adrenaline came to Ray every time he was hit with the blast, saying it turned him from a dead-tired mood to one with an astonishing amount of force. Baron knew Ray's plan now. He was going to use this cube on his men to give them the same powers he possessed. With an army of people that strong, Ray could eliminate the entire Havocs organization.

Baron chucked the notebook over to the passenger side, turned on the car, and drove back to that pay phone as fast as he could. Heading down the roads circling the massive hill almost caused the car to tip due to slippery roads caused by the rain. Baron had to remain cautious driving in this weather. Baron made it to the pay phone. He didn't even bother putting on his raincoat as he exited the driver's seat. He pushed the coins into the slot with heavy force, followed by pushing the numbers and making sure he got the right ones.

Over at the Renshaw Mansion, the phone rang; the man posted by the phone immediately answered it. After the man said hello, he heard the words "It's Baron. Get Cain now!"

The man on the phone rushed over to Cain's room. He didn't even bother knocking; he opened the door to announce to Cain that Baron was on the phone. Cain marched to the phone, picked it up, and asked for his report.

"The new device Ray has made is a cube. I managed to steal his notebook without him knowing. It said that the cube can give people Loomation powers, meaning they can have advanced strength or even create spells."

"How on earth did Ray create such a thing?" asked Cain.

"It says that he used some kind of diamond. There wasn't much detail on the diamond in his notes," Baron reported.

Cain knew exactly what diamond Ray used to make this cube. He knew it was the one from the garden, the one that their fathers sold many years ago. Cain couldn't believe how clever Ray had become. He now could give people powers just like theirs. Something about people getting their powers in an unnatural way had Cain feeling uneasy. He felt that if you were not born with this power, then you shouldn't have it. Not to mention the fact that with this power, Ray could easily defeat his Havocs. This frightened Cain very much, so he knew he had to act fast.

"Has he used this on anyone yet?" asked Cain.

"I'm guessing that's what his meeting tonight is going to be about. He's probably going to give us all this Loomation power tonight. Who knows? He's probably going to have us come barging down the Renshaw Mansion doors by sunrise."

"This has to be his final play, meaning if we destroy this cube, Ray would have to surrender." Cain's voice rose as if he knew that he would be going into battle soon. A battle that, if successful, could mean the end of the war. Baron informed Cain that he'd have to return to the cabin again at the requested time by Ray in order to keep his cover. Cain said that if he hurried, he could gather a group of Havocs out there to make an attack on the cabin. Cain had to get there before Ray could use the cube on his men. If they were too late, they may not win the fight.

"You want me to secure the cube like I did with the other weapons?" asked Baron. Cain didn't want that device to ever be used on a human. He wanted it destroyed. Cain instructed Baron to meet up with him before he went to the cabin; he had one more mission for him. Baron gave Cain a location on where to meet up before he returned to the cabin, and Cain said he would hurry. Cain hung up the phone and rushed downstairs. He found Reed and ordered him to round up some men, get them armed, and get to the van; they were attacking Ray tonight.

As Reed took off as instructed, Cain went down to the basement. Down there was a wooden crate with the words painted on the side saying, "FLAMMABLE!!!" This crate was meant to be taken to the storage unit where the other weapons that were stolen from Ray went. But the Havocs kept this one at the mansion; they felt that not all of Ray's weapons should be stashed away to never be used. Cain allowed this one crate to remain at the mansion; he was happy that he did, for what was inside could be the only thing that could destroy the cube. Cain very carefully opened the crate. Inside were several glass bottles, all filled with a gas that Ray invented called the Phoenix Flame. Ray said that if the Phoenix Flame burned hot enough, you could go blind from the sight of it.

A dozen Havocs were loading up in a black base camper van parked just next to the front porch of the mansion. They were all heavily armed with bulletproof vests on. Cain told the men he'd be taking his own car, a brown Mustang, parked in the yard. Cain got into his car and led the way. The harsh rain falling nonstop made the driving difficult, but they managed.

Baron was in his car waiting at the meetup spot for a while. He checked his watch and started to worry. Baron was worried that he'd be late to Ray's get-together. He looked in the rearview mirror and saw the headlights of Cain's car pulling up behind him. Cain got out of the car; the pounding rain didn't bother him one bit. Cain walked up to Baron's driver's side window. Baron cranked down the window.

"How was the drive?" Baron asked, trying to make small talk.

"I have one last job for you. If you live through it, you'll be second-in-command of the Havocs and get your well-deserved cash reward," Cain stated.

These were the words Baron had been waiting to hear for years now. Finally hearing them from his boss felt like a huge accomplishment. "What do you need me to do?"

Cain handed over the jar of gas; Baron knew exactly what this was and how dangerous it was. Cain told him that the cube must be destroyed, and this flame was their best shot at making that happen. Cain told Baron that he had a dozen Havocs with him; they were going to attack from the outside of the cabin. Cain informed Baron of the plan to attack, even getting their watches synchronized to the very second. Cain pounded on the car door and ended the conversation saying, "Don't mess this up!"

Baron couldn't believe the task he was given; there was no way he could achieve this and manage to get out alive. This was a suicide mission. Baron couldn't give up now as he was in too deep. He knew he couldn't switch sides and warn Ray that Cain was coming. Ray would surely kill him for working for Cain this whole time. The only way Baron could get out of this alive was to outsmart, and outskill, a genius, superstrength mastermind. He was going to need a miracle.

Baron arrived at the cabin just a few minutes before the time requested. He wasn't the first, for he saw other cars in the parking area. He walked into the cabin and saw six other men sitting around waiting for Ray to arrive. Time moved fast, and in no time, eight other men arrived at the cabin. The guys were talking about their excitement at finally taking down Cain and his Havocs. These guys had all been in battle with members of the Havocs in the past. For years, they felt that the group was untouchable due to their leader. But when word got out that this Ray guy was able to find ways to hurt Cain, they felt that they had a fighting chance. In Ray they trusted might as well have been the slogan for these men. The men were all called by Ray who said he had something that would change their lives forever. They didn't understand what he meant by that, but they were excited.

Just then, the back door opened. This startled the men, and some stood up from the living room furniture, while others were touching the guns in their holsters. It was Ray, and he welcomed the men with open arms.

"Gentlemen, it is so wonderful to have you all here tonight! For tonight is the beginning of a new era, the beginning of an all-new breed of life!" Ray said, sounding like some kind of preacher. The men were eating all this up, cheering like fans at a rock concert.

"I promise everyone in this room that their lives are about to be changed for the better! The time of living in fear, of the dangerous injuries, and breaking bones will be a thing of the past after tonight!"

The men cheered once more. Ray then placed a heavy steel box onto a table and flipped open the top lid, revealing the cube that was stored inside. "This is the way to a new breed of humans." Ray was overwhelmed by his own words. The men all huddled around the table to look at the cube.

The men didn't understand the importance of the cube, nor did they see how fascinating it was. But Baron knew exactly what this object could do. The temptation of having it used on him was huge. For a second, Baron felt that he could get the powers from the cube; and when the attack started, all he would have to do is duck, hide, and just go with the side still standing in the end. He felt like he couldn't lose. Baron did fear that Cain would out his cover to Ray, and he already knew that if Ray was aware of Baron being a spy, he would be killed by him. After running over every scenario in his head, he knew that fulfilling his mission from Cain was his best chance of living to see another day. Unfortunately, this mission had a high chance of him being killed.

Ray was telling the men about how this cube would change their lives. He said the cube could send out a shock wave of Loomation, and anyone who was hit with it would be granted advanced strength or possibly the ability to create spells. It was all very exciting for Ray to conduct test subjects for his experiment. The men asked if they would go after Cain once they received the power.

Ray explained that he wasn't sure how long it would take for their new abilities to kick in after getting hit with the shock wave. He also wasn't sure how their bodies would react to their newfound strength. He didn't want to march them into the Renshaw Mansion inexperienced with their new abilities. No, Ray wanted to do a test run first. He told the men that first thing tomorrow, they would head to the prison, the one containing the creatures that Ray and Cain gathered up from the garden. Ray assured his followers that after they took on any one of these animals without dying, they would have such confidence that there would be nothing they couldn't face and defeat.

Ray had everything needed to transport one of the garden creatures to a battleground. Behind the cabin was a reinforced truck able to carry the animal along with three strong tranquilizers made by Ray himself.

Baron checked his watch; the clock said 11:59 p.m. Baron knew that Cain had his Havocs covering the entire front side of the cabin. Right at midnight, Cain was going to order the attack to spray the place up with bullets. Baron's and Cain's watches were synchronized to the second, so as Baron looked at the ticking hand of his watch, he knew that he only had seconds to make his move.

"Are you guys ready?" Ray asked, anticipating their desire to get started.

The guys were getting inpatient, and frankly, so was Ray. Ray started to reach down for the cube on the table. Baron, who was standing just across from him, yelled at him to wait. Ray paused for a moment, frozen with his hand midway to the cube.

"What is it?" Ray confusedly asked.

Baron checked his watch and was now ready to fulfill his mission. Baron removed his gun from his holster and managed to shoot Ray with three shots to the chest. Ray fell backward, landing on his back in pain, but not dead due to his advanced strength stopping the bullets from causing mortal damage. The rest of the men in the room had the ability to kill Baron in seconds. Just before anyone could aim a gun at Baron, the planned attack from Cain started. Bullets came flying in all over the front side of the cabin like a war zone. Baron jumped over the table, landing in the kitchen and grabbing the cube in midjump. He landed on the floor hard and heard the bullets fly just inches over his head, nearly killing him.

The rest of the men inside the cabin were now fully occupied with the madness going on outside, returning fire at every chance they felt safe enough to pop their heads off the ground. Baron was low enough behind a counter to avoid the gunfire. With nervous hands, he placed the cube down on the ground next to him. Baron then removed the jar of gas from his jacket pocket, thanking God that none of the stray bullets had struck it.

With the jar in his hand, he just now realized that he had no idea how to ignite the gas to burn the cube. Baron then saw something that made this terrifying event even more deadly. In the corner of his eye, he saw Ray crawling toward him with eyes highly expressing his anger. Baron knew that the cube was more important to Ray than anything, so Baron knew how to get Ray away from him. Baron slid the cube across the kitchen floor. The cube slid right past Ray. Baron then rolled the bottle across the floor in the same direction. Ray recognized the bottle right away; he knew it was one of his own inventions.

"NO!" Ray shouted as he started to crawl as fast as he could toward the cube. Baron had to take his chances of getting shot by standing up and jumping out the window that was located just above the kitchen sink behind him. Baron quickly managed to get half his body out of the window unharmed. Baron then aimed his gun right at the gas bottle rolling right toward the cube. Once the bottle was right next to the cube, Baron fired his gun, shooting the bottle and causing the gas inside to ignite and set off a bright, burning, hot flame.

The flames scattered throughout the floor of the cabin reaching up to the height of the counters. The men who were busy returning fire on the Havocs, keeling so close to the ground due to gunfire, were quickly engulfed by the flames. Ray was the only one spared from the flames, for he wore a jacket made from the phoenix's feathers. The jacket was fireproof, and the flames seemed to hover right around him as if the feathers provided some sort of invisible fire shield protecting him from the oncoming blaze.

The heat was extraordinary, the fire was bright, and it felt as if all the air inside was sucked out of the room instantly. Ray knew he had to get out before he suffocated or died from the heat. But he saw the cube sitting right in front of him covered in the burning hot flames. Ray had no time to protect his hand, so he just grabbed the cube with his bare hand, fully knowing the pain would be exquisite. Ray did this quickly; he reached out for the cube with his right hand. Sinking his hand into the flame and gripping the hot cube, Ray hollered in horrible pain. Once he had a strong grip on the cube, he rolled to his side, crashing into an outside wall and landing in the backyard.

Ray managed to roll himself right through the burning wall to make it outside and landed in a puddle caused by the rain behind the cabin. He took in a much-needed breath of air, and the rain provided a way for him to cool down his body temperature. Ray's hand was hurting so much; he felt that the fire burned all the way down to the bone. While lying on the ground in the puddle of water, Ray was so thankful that he aligned the cube's pieces up beforehand; all he had to do was crunch down on the cube and release. The cube released out its shock wave of Loomation hitting Ray. This got Ray back to full energy, and the excruciating pain in his hand had even settled down to a minor pain. The wounds from the bullets were miraculously healed. The cube flew out of Ray's hand after it released its blast. Baron heard the blast and rushed behind the cabin to see what it was. Baron saw Ray pick up the cube and run to his truck.

On the front side of the cabin, the Havocs stopped shooting after they saw the flames. There was no return fire, so it may have been safe to think that everyone inside was dead. Cain was the first to start walking toward the cabin to get a closer look. When he was right in front of the cabin, his body was sweating, and his eyes were burning from looking at the fire. Cain saw from the shattered windows that the entire floor was covered with flames and that everyone inside lay motionless and was being consumed by the licking flames. Cain heard someone approaching from the right side of the cabin; he pointed his gun but was relieved to see that it was only Baron.

Baron was coughing from the smoke. He attempted to say something, but Cain did not understand his words. "He's got the cube," he managed to utter. At this point, the sound of a truck was heard driving down a driveway that led to a back road behind the cabin. Cain raced to his car and drove through the plants and logs around the cabin to head off Ray. He got himself on the back road that Ray was driving on and sped up as he chased Ray.

Ray was driving the truck he was planning on using to transport one of the garden animals. The truck wasn't fast, but since the road was all downhill, he was hoping he could get away from Cain. Cain was not slowing down for anything on the road; he managed to get his car right next to Ray's vehicle. Just then, a road sign popped up indicating a hard-right curve. Ray, with all his might, turned the wheel of the truck to the right in order to avoid driving right off the cliff. With the high speeds and the wet roads from the rain, the truck tipped onto its side and slid down the road right up to the edge.

During the crash, the cube was bounced around and landed on the side of the truck that was facing the road. When the truck reached the edge of the road and hovered over the cliff, the cube fell out of the shattered window and rolled helplessly down the hill. Ray, still buckled in the driver's seat, was devastated as he watched the cube tumbling down the hill. But his mood changed when he heard Cain's car come to a complete halt. The headlights of his car were gazing right at the tipped-over truck.

Ray heard Cain get out of his car and close the driver's side door. Ray heard no words from Cain or footsteps; he only heard the rain on the side of the truck. Ray must have thought that Cain was trying to figure out if he survived the crash or not. Ray knew that this hesitation from Cain would only last a moment, so he had to hurry up and find something with which to attack Cain.

Over by the passenger side of the tuck was a crossbow. The crossbow was loaded up with one of Ray's tranquilizers he was planning to use on the animal at the prison. He struggled to reach for it, fearing that too much movement would case the truck to tip over the edge. Just then, the truck was tipped over right side up by Cain. The crossbow landed in Ray's reach. As fast as Ray could, he grabbed the crossbow just in time.

Cain pulled the driver's side door clean off its hinges and yanked Ray's body out of the buckled seat, chucking him out of the truck. Ray was hurled out of the truck; he flew through the air with the crossbow in hand and landed hard on his back. Ray lifted his upper torso and saw Cain charging at him as if he was some wild animal. Ray acted fast to load up the tranquilizer; once loaded, he pulled the trigger aiming right at Cain's chest.

The impact of the dart arrow caused Cain to come to an almost-complete stop. Cain quickly removed the dart form his chest but found it hard to keep his balance. He struggled to stay up but powered through the disorderly feelings and continued to approach Ray with threatening actions. By this time, Ray managed to load another dart, firing it at Cain's chest once more. Cain now was standing still in a bent-over shape, doing all he could to remain standing.

There were four darts attached to this crossbow. Ray loaded up the third dart and pointed it at Cain. Ray managed to fire off the next dart. This dart struck Cain once more in the chest, causing him to fall backward onto the road.

Ray grabbed the final dart and smashed it on the ground. He then turned his head and saw a van approaching. Ray figured that this was the rest of the Havocs. Not wanting to stick around to find out, Ray got to his feet and ran to the edge of the cliff. Ray jumped up and took a dive down the edge, knowing that the cliff led to a large hill where he could roll down safely away from the Havocs. Once Ray hit the ground, he found himself covered in a water stream caused by the rain. The stream caused a sensation of being on a water slide, and it brought him to a flooded river. The current carried him downriver.

Ray was greatly devastated to discover this as he was hoping to find solid ground where the cube could have ended up. But the whole area was flooded, and the water was moving fast. The cube could be a mile or more away by now. Ray drifted in the water and yelled in anger at losing the cube; he was so loud that you could hear him from the top of the hill.

On top of the hill, the Havocs saw the crash site. They found their leader on the ground unconscious. He had a pulse, but barely.

"What happened here?" Reed asked Baron. Baron looked around and saw the crossbow. He ran his hand through his hair in a stress action, for he knew what had happened.

"This is Ray's tranquilizer crossbow. Ray was working on a special chemical that could put the animals from the garden so asleep that it would take a specially made chemical in order to wake them up," Baron explained. "Ray must have used it on Cain before he got away."

"Okay then, let's just find the chemical that wakes him up," Reed replied confidently, thinking that this would be an easy fix.

"No need to…it's right here," Baron stated. The guys all huddled over to what Baron was pointing at. It turned out there was only one dart containing the wake-up chemical, and Ray smashed it, destroying it before he left. The rain had already poured over the chemical, washing it away.

"So he's just going to sleep forever then?" asked one of the guys.

"I doubt we can get Ray to make another wake-up antidote chemical," replied one of the other guys.

"I have Ray's recipe book on all his weapons, but it didn't have anything on his tranquilizers," Baron added.

"Oh, come on, he can't sleep forever! He'll be up in no time!" Reed shouted.

"The creatures of the garden had this thing called Loomation inside them…Cain has it inside him too. This tranquilizer can recharge its effect with the Loomation inside him over and over, creating an endless cycle of sleep!" Baron yelled, frustrated. The guys just stood in the rain having no idea what to do next. But then Baron remembered the cube. He read that the cube could give such an adrenaline rush to anyone who was hit by the cube's blast. Baron said that if they could get their hands on that cube, they could use it on Cain to wake him up.

The Havocs searched all night for the cube, as did Ray, but neither found it. It rained hard the whole night and flooded the river. The water reached the city, flooding the streets and causing major water damage to many houses. The cube was light, probably carried with the current of the water for hours. It could have ended up anywhere; it could still be floating away in the river for all they knew.

The next day, Ray went off the grid again, going into hiding feeling slightly satisfied with his latest attack on his enemy. With Cain being asleep for who knew how long, Ray initiated a cease-fire until Cain awakened. The Havocs kept their leader in his room of the Renshaw Mansion. Jason took Cain's lockbox and started the *Better Life* mission for Kate, taking the place of her father for the trip. With Cain asleep, he could no longer protect her. They figured the Better Life mission was the best way to keep her out of harm's way.

The Havocs never stopped looking for the cube; they hung posters, offered rewards, and went out from time to time to check the hill to see if they missed something. The cube was out there, and they believed that one day, someone would find it.

CHAPTER 17

The Hang Out Group

Saturday, May 1, 2010

A small town in southeast Ohio called Maze was home to a little more than seventeen thousand people. The town was surrounded by what seemed to be endless cornfields. You would spot mountains if you headed east. Maze was a calm, pleasant little city, mainly surrounded by other small towns or even smaller villages.

A basement door in a small house in this town opened, and down came an older lady in her early seventies, followed by a younger male kid at the age of seventeen. The lady turned on the basement lights, brightening the room. The young man's eyes widened when he saw the large number of boxes scattered all over the basement floor. The small job he signed up for looked more like an all-day project. This old lady was moving out and was looking for help with packing up her boxes. The boy's mom worked with the old lady, so he was volunteered to help her that Saturday. His mom told him that it shouldn't take too long, but she was wrong. The kid worked until it got very late into the night, not the way he wanted to spend his Saturday.

The kid was keeping his grouchy attitude under his breath, always saying friendly things such as "No problem, I don't mind." The kid did have pride in helping the elderly. He may have disliked the work but knew she appreciated the help. The old lady seemed to be a hoarder, or at least her deceased husband was. After a long day, the kid loaded the last box at the last open spot on the loading trailer that was attached to the back of the woman's blue pickup.

"Is that everything?" the woman asked the young kid.

"Yep, the last box fit perfectly. Good thing too, any more crammed in and the door wouldn't be able to close," the kid said, pulling down on the handle of the trailer and locking the door in place.

"Did you check for any boxes under the steps?" the woman asked as if she just remembered to remind him about the storage under the steps of the basement. The boy wanted to roll his eyes in annoyance; all this kid wanted to do was go and hang out with his friends. He meant to meet up with them hours ago. But as polite as a Boy Scout, he told the lady he'd run down to check. The kid went down to the basement; seeing the place empty made him feel like he was in a completely different house. You could really see how big the place was with all the boxes out of it; a pool table would fit nicely down there. It would be a nice place to have hangouts, he thought to himself. On the floor of the basement, he saw a small door on the side of the steps. He pulled on the handle, and inside was a dusty box.

The kid brought up the old box to the lady. "There was only one box under the steps!" the boy shouted as he rushed over to the truck. The woman brought a hand to her mouth; her eyes squinted as if she was about to let out a tear.

"Oh, wow…I forgot all about this." She now spoke with a charm that she didn't have before. The woman asked the boy if he was familiar with the great town flood that occurred twenty-five years ago. The kid said he was aware of the story about the flood. The woman then opened the box, while it was still in the boy's hands.

"Many houses were horribly water damaged, but not ours," said the woman, referring to her and her late husband. "It was a miracle. See, the rain was flooding. Furthermore, the river and water were rising everywhere. But the next morning, my husband and I walked out, and the water surrounding our house was crystal clear. There was no mud, and none of the house was damaged by the floodwater. My husband and I found tons of debris that washed up against our house, and we put it in this box, thinking that one of them had to be good luck or something.

We figured, finders keepers, as it was on our lawn, so we claimed all the objects to be ours." The woman smiled, enjoying sharing this fond memory with the young man who helped her move her stuff.

"Why don't you keep it?" she said.

"No, I couldn't do that. This is your box of good-luck charms," he said, being nice. The boy had already looked inside the box as he was going up the stairs and saw that it was just a bunch of junk that he didn't want. But the lady insisted, saying that there was no more room for it on the truck anyway. The kid smiled and pretended to be very grateful for the gift. The woman got in her tuck and took off. The kid then headed over to his silver 1988 Jeep and placed the box in the passenger seat. It was just a little after nine, and he was very late on meeting his friends. The kid got into the driver's seat and drove toward his friend's house out on the country road.

The house was about four miles out of town, a small home in a grass field. Acres of cornfield across the street, and miles of woods deep behind the backyard. About two hundred meters within the backyard of the one-story house was a pop-up camper, a small shed, and a fire ring burning tall and bright. Three boys were sitting around the fire waiting for the kid in the Jeep. One of the three around the fire finished cooking a hot dog over the flames with a hot dog stick. He wrapped the dog in a bun and put down the stick, and just before he took a bite of the hot dog, he checked his watch.

"Man, where the heck is he? It's been almost four hours!" Hayden yelled impatiently. Hayden was the one who lived at this house. He spent most of his days out in the woods that were located behind his backyard, chopping up firewood. He also went into those woods during deer hunting season. Most of the time when he hosted hangouts at his place, he had a fire out back. The fire ring used to be closer to the house, but he was too loud, so his parents told him to move the fire ring farther away from the house. Hayden liked being at the fire ring. He spent his weekend nights sleeping in the pop-up camper.

"He just texted me and said he's on his way," Will said calmly as he stared at his laptop screen.

"I'm going to end up eating all the hot dogs before he gets here!" Hayden shouted as he was chomping down on his hot dog.

One of the kids sitting around the fire let out a tired grunt and said he wanted to go to bed. This person went by the nickname Timber. Timber received this nickname back in grade school. He was a part of the school play, playing the tree. He never went to rehearsal thinking how hard it could be to play a tree. On the day of the play, he learned that he had to dance and skip around the stage. Since Timber never practiced doing those actions while wearing the tree suit, he tripped while skipping; and as he was falling onto his classmates, he shouted out the word *timber*! And the nickname stuck ever since.

Timber was so tired because he wasn't used to staying up this late, as he was the only kid among his friends with an after-school job. He was used to going to bed early and getting to work early during weekends. He had this weekend off, so his friends begged him to come out to Hayden's to spend the night.

Hayden felt insulted that Timber wanted to go to bed so early. Hayden pointed out that it wasn't even ten yet and that Timber couldn't go to sleep until after Juice showed up. At this time, headlights came driving down the grass driveway from Hayden's house.

"Juice is here," Will stated, looking at the car arriving. The silver Jeep parked next to Will's car, and out came Juice. Before closing the car door, Juice pulled out the box he got from helping the old lady and started walking toward the fire with the box in his hands when he heard Will shout out to him, "You left your lights on!"

Juice turned and ran back to the Jeep to turn off the headlights. "Thanks, Will!" Juice said, feeling stupid for having to be reminded. Juice was another kid who went by his nickname so much that even his teachers and coaches called him that. He never understood how he got the nickname Juice. It could have been because he brought a quart of chocolate milk to first class all freshman year, but that was milk and not juice. Juice didn't even like juice, but he did love the nickname. Juice walked around the fire to find an empty chair. The fire area had plenty of room for sitting; lawn chairs, bag chairs, and even a small old bench huddled around the ring. All of them had small holes in them due to the falling embers from the fire.

"What took you so long?" Hayden asked like a nagging parent as he chucked a log into the fire.

"Yeah, so that *small* job my mom made me do for one of her coworkers took all day! I tell you, guys, this woman has never thrown away anything in her life! I found boxes full of calendars dating all the way back to the '80s!" Juice explained.

"Well, at least it sounds like she kept everything organized," Will uttered as Juice sat next to him. Will sat up with his legs rested on a log playing music on his laptop.

"What's in the box?" asked Timber. Just then, a bright spark from the fire emerged, letting out a loud sound. Everyone sitting hopped out of their seats. Timber even jumped behind the bench he was sitting on. Hayden started to giggle in an almost-evil laugh.

"HAYDEN!" Timber howled.

"What?" Hayden asked, doing a terrible job at playing innocent.

"I thought he was out of firecrackers!" Juice asked Will as he tried to calm himself down from the shock.

"I thought he used them all up last weekend!" Will responded.

"I was saving one for Timber!" Hayden screamed in a hilarious fashion. "Okay, okay, now I'm truly out!" Hayden said, taking in some deep breaths. Hayden was sitting with that firecracker in his pocket the whole night and wanted to wait until Juice arrived before putting it in the fire. He hid it in the log that he just chucked in when Juice sat down. This was a common thing for Hayden to do, a mystery fire, he liked to call it. He did that a lot last weekend when his friends came over. Timber was working last weekend, so he never got to experience the chaos.

The four guys sitting around the fire were all close friends for a very long time. They were all seniors about to graduate high school soon. Their class was small, which was to be expected when you lived in a small town and attended a small school. The class had their social groups: the jocks, the nerds, and the shy ones. This group of kids was a combination of people from all those social groups. Over the years, they would talk during class, asking who's *having the hangout this weekend*, meaning which house were they planning on meeting up at. They were pretty good at spreading out the hangout locations. Juice had his basement, Will had his man cave on the second floor of his house, and Hayden had his massive backyard.

Over time, the group started calling themselves the Hang Out Group, referring to themselves as the Hogs in text messages. That's why they spelled the word *hangout* with a space between *hang* and *out*. The first letters of the group name spelled out *HOG*. These four were not all the members, just the ones who were free that weekend. The other members were named Eric, Gard (short for Beauregard), and Miles. Eric and Gard were visiting Miles at the hospital in Columbus. Miles had been battling an illness for a long time now, so the group made plans on spreading their time to go see him while he was still in the hospital.

"So what's up with the box, Juice?" Will brought up after the Hogs returned to their seats.

"Oh, it's just a dinosaur. There was no more room on the ark, so it got carried off in the flood," Juice said with a straight face. Then he heard Will say *really*, acting like he believed his story. "No, but weirdly not too far from the truth," Juice said as he picked up the box and placed it on his lap. "It was the last box in the old lady's basement. There was no more room on the truck, so she just gave it to me. I know how much Hayden loves burning random things, so I thought he may have fun with it," Juice said as he opened the box, removing one of the objects. The object looked to be an old plastic dog bowl. Hayden snatched it from Juice's hands and tossed it into the fire.

"Everything burns" was Hayden's famous motto.

"She said she found all this stuff after that big flood that happened forever ago," Juice explained.

"My dad stills talks about that flood all the time. To this day, he still complains about having to tear out the carpet from his parents' house," Timber added.

Then Juice pulled out a light steel gray cube. The cube was ten centimeters long on all six sides. The cube was pretty cool looking to the Hogs. The cube had different pieces in ten rows of ten. Juice tried to see if the columns could turn in the same way a Rubik's cube functioned. All columns were able to move up, down, left, and right just like a Rubik's cube puzzle.

"Looks like the colors faded off," Timber said to Juice about the cube.

"Yeah, I can see that, Timber!" Juice replied with a smirk as he became frustrated that he couldn't solve it. After a few rotations, Juice cheered for himself, claiming that he solved it. "Look at that, I got all the colors to match up right away! I bet it's a world record!" Juice was about to chuck the cube into the fire, but Will told him to hold up. Will asked if he could see it. Juice passed it over to Will who took a closer look at the cube.

"I think you're meant to line up the pieces," Will said and then held the cube up to Juice. "See how the little squares on the cube line up with others. I think you have to rotate all the squares until it all lines up to be one solid piece." Will then felt that the cube could be crunched down in a way, thinking that when all the pieces are aligned correctly, you could crunch the cube down on all sides. This looked like a fun puzzle for Will to solve, so he was going to work on solving it.

As Will was rotating away, Hayden offered Juice a hot dog. Juice was starving, so he was happy to get some food. The group talked for a bit longer that night, and Will kept his nose close to the cube trying to see if there was a trick of some kind in order to solve it.

With graduation coming up and the members all going to different colleges, they had this big camping trip planned for right after graduation. Plans for this trip were on hold due to Miles's condition. Miles had given the group permission to go on the trip without him, saying they all shouldn't miss out on going just because he couldn't. The other members of the group weren't sure how they would feel about going without him, so the talk about going on the trip or not was a big topic of the night.

Some time passed, and Timber asked for permission to go into the pop-up camper for bed. Hayden said that even he was growing tired, so he agreed that it was time for sleep. Will told everyone to hang on because he found something on his laptop. Will used his laptop to check the internet to see if there were any instructions to solve the cube, and what he found was something pretty big.

"Juice, you said that the lady found the cube after the night of the big flood, right?" Will asked. Juice yawned out the word *yeah* while trying to stand up out of his chair.

"Why?" Juice wondered.

"Because I just found out that there is a reward on whoever finds it," Will stated. Will started reading the information on the website. "Lost cube shape object, a rare puzzle with a diamond color look to it. Once found please contact us, and you will receive a cash reward!" Will read with excitement. Juice, now with a newfound energy, jumped out of his seat, snatched the cube from Will's hand, and held it close to his chest, hugging it.

"Oh, Mrs. *I forgot your name*, you just paid for my college!" Juice happily cheered, talking about the lady who gave him that box that contained the cube.

"How much does it say?" Hayden asked with wonder. Will said that the site didn't mention the amount.

"Well, contact them. Tell them I want a hundred and fifty billion! Forget college. We're going to Mars, gentlemen!" Juice said with wild excitement.

"Juice, I think the money should go to the woman who had the cube," Will said.

"Hey, I worked almost an entire Saturday for that lady. I see this as my payment!" Juice replied.

"Yeah, plus she had her chance to turn in the cube. When things arrive on your yard, you do the work on finding who it belongs to," Hayden said calmly.

"Hayden, you take stuff that's not yours all the time," Timber added.

"This isn't about me, Timber," Hayden replied in a snapping way.

"How about this. We use the reward to help us pay for our camping trip. That way we can get our own money we put into the trip back so in a way we all get a reward. Sound fair?" Will offered. The guys loved that idea, saying it was fair for everyone. Will sent an e-mail to the address given on the web page. It wasn't long until they got a response. The response came with a time and location to meet up with them.

The location wasn't far, and the date was tomorrow evening. Hayden said he could take everyone in his car come morning. The four were feeling too excited to sleep. The mystery of how much the cube was worth made them wonder all night.

Sunday, May 2, 2010

The Hogs woke up early that Sunday morning. Hayden's mom had a platter of breakfast food for her son and his friends. The free all-you-can-eat breakfast service was arguably the best thing about spending the night at Hayden's. As the friends munched down at the kitchen table, Hayden's mother asked the boys what their plans for the day were. The boys paused their eating to pass wondering looks to one another. Should they tell her about the cube and the reward that came with it? Hayden said they were taking a drive out of town. It was now clear to the boys that they were going to keep the cube a secret.

Juice added that they were going to do some bird watching. Juice had a school project during his freshman year tracking bird migration patterns. He hated it at the time, but for some reason, he now found birding kind of enjoyable. It made the long hikes in the woods more interesting. The mother didn't ask any more questions and took the boys' word for it. The boys cleaned up their area and washed their dishes. Afterward, they all loaded up in Hayden's car and headed out to get their reward. They didn't go to the destination right away; they stopped at a place for lunch and went to a store just to pass time. The boys had to be at the destination at a certain time, so they were trying their best to wait it out. After stalling for a long boring time, they just chose to head to the place now. They thought, *What's the harm of showing up early?*

When they merged onto the road that led them to their destination, they found themselves driving deep into the woods. It was a creepy atmosphere because the sunshine through the tree branches didn't give much light. Will, with his face inside a map, informed Hayden that his final turn had arrived. Hayden turned the car to the left side of the road and went down a bumpy driveway. Hayden parked his car, and the four boys exited the vehicle.

Their eyes saw a very large, very old run-down mansion in front of them. The tree branches were growing up to the side of the building, causing scratches to the side of house. The boys heard loud creaks from the front steps of the porch as they went up the stairs. Timber looked up and saw a worn-down sign above the front door with the word *Renshaw* carved into it. With all four at the front door, Will knocked with his fist.

The knock wasn't too loud, so Hayden smashed his fist against the door. "It's a big place, Will. You need to knock louder," Hayden rudely stated.

"This place gives me the creeps," Timber whispered to the others. Hayden once again gave another loud knock at the door.

"We are an hour early. Maybe they're not home," Will speculated.

The Hogs were hoping to get in, make the transaction, and be on their way home by now. But given the fact that they still had an hour before they had to meet up with the owner of the cube, they decided to wait on the front porch. The front porch had a few rocking chairs; so Will, Hayden, and Timber took a seat on them. Juice just sat on the floor, resting against a support beam.

Will took the cube out from his pocket and attempted to complete the puzzle, while the others just clicked away on their cell phones. The sky was a muggy gray, the sun was setting faster and faster, and the Hogs were afraid no one would show. But they agreed that they would wait the hour and leave if no one showed up by then.

Hayden was playing with his Zippo lighter, lighting it up over and over due to boredom. Will turned his head to look at Hayden. Hayden, knowing that Will was looking at him, turned to him with an innocent look.

"What?" Hayden said, trying not to laugh.

"It's an old place, Hayden. Let's not burn it down by accident," Will uttered, so Hayden painfully put his lighter back in his pocket.

"Can we go now?" Timber loudly asked. Tensions were running high with the four because being still for so long was torturing them. Juice checked his watch and said that the hour was almost up. At this point, the boys no longer cared for the reward; they just wanted to go home. They continued to wait, thinking nothing was going to happen.

Nighttime had settled in, and all they could hear were the crickets chatting and the sound of Will trying to solve the cube. The sound of the cube rotating was getting on Hayden's nerves, so he shouted at Will and told him to stop because he couldn't take it anymore.

"Hold on, I think I got it," Will said as he made two more turns of the cube. All the pieces of the cube now lined up perfectly, and Will was able to crunch down on the cube connecting all the pieces into one. "I did it!" Will said, hopping out of his seat with joy. Juice, Hayden, and

Timber got to their feet and huddled around Will to see the cube. The cube was now illuminating a strange white light inside the cube.

"Wow, that's pretty cool the way it glows like that," Will pointed out.

"How did you do that?" wondered Timber.

"Well, when I crunched down on the cube, it started to glow," Will explained.

"Great. We have a fancy night-light," Hayden said, not impressed.

"Let me try," Juice said.

Will released the pressure he kept onto the cube to keep it in the crunched position in order to hand it over to Juice. As soon as Will let the cube ease back to its regular position, the glowing white light inside blasted out from the cube, causing a shock wave that struck down the four Hogs. All of this happened within the blink of an eye. The blast knocked all four of them off their feet and onto their backs. Juice smashed over the railing of the porch, tumbling onto the driveway. Will and Hayden fell back onto the porch opposite of each other. Timber crashed through the window and landed inside the house.

All four were just on their backs overwhelmed with this surprised event. Their entire bodies felt heavy, as if gravity was pushing them down hard.

"What was that!" Hayden shouted as he remained motionless on the porch.

"Will, I crashed through the window...I crashed through the window, Will!" Timber shouted, being the most startled from the blast.

Juice let out some coughing sounds as he shook his head. Staring up at the night sky, Juice was befuddled on how he fell off the porch so fast. Then a face came into his line of view. Juice had never seen this face before, so he had no idea who this was. The man wasn't alone; three cars arrived down the driveway just seconds ago. The men in the cars were the ones living at the mansion. The men felt that the boys were here for robbery or an attack of some kind. The men saw the blast out from the car window, so it was easy to believe this.

There were eight men who arrived, all pointing guns at the boys. The Hogs were never more scared in their lives. As they were still dizzy and still reeling from the shock of the blast, there was no resistance made to stop the men from dragging the four helpless teens into the house and tying them to chairs. Timber was on the far left, Will was to Timber's right, next to him was Hayden, and Juice was on the right end. The Hogs didn't want to say a word; they just passed apprehensive looks to one another.

The eight men were the remaining members of the vicious group called the Havocs. The once-proud and mighty group of mercenaries was now broke, struggling for work, and hounded by the police. Most of them had nowhere else to go while others still had hope for their leader to rise and take them to the top once again. Cain, the leader of the Havocs, had been stuck in a coma for years now; and in the meantime, a man named Baron had been running the group.

Baron was talking to his right-hand man, Reed. The two were debating whether the kids were hostile. Baron said that they must be the ones who found the cube. Reed said that they checked the boys, and none of them had the cube on them. Baron couldn't believe that four young boys could be sent to attack them. Reed stated that he was that young when he started doing things like that. The shattered window was a big sign that these boys could have been a threat. The Havocs had kept the mansion unprotected for so long due to their archrival announcing a cease-fire.

"They could be working for Ray…He may have sent them to kill Cain once and for all," Reed suggested.

Baron still wasn't convinced on Reed's thoughts but felt they should interrogate the boys just to be safe. Both Baron and Reed approached the Hogs.

"We're sorry about the window," Will said.

"Yeah…I'll pay for a new one and everything," Timber added.

"Who sent you here?" Baron asked, ignoring the talk about the window. The Hogs were caught off guard by that question; they thought the eight men already knew the answer to that question.

"We're the ones who found the cube…We came here to deliver it to you," Will stated.

"So where is it then?" Baron replied.

"We've already checked you and your car, so where are you hiding it!" Reed shouted.

The Hogs were sweating heavily. They grew silent as a mouse, and they were all looking at each other, hoping someone had the answer. If they gave them the cube, maybe they would be set free, they believed.

"WELL!" Reed yelled impatiently.

"Will, just tell him what you did with it," Hayden whispered to Will.

"I don't have it. Juice wanted it last," Will whispered back.

"I don't have it. I never got a chance to touch it," Juice replied in the same volume as the others.

"For crying out loud, someone just tell them where the dumb cube is!" Timber whispered as loudly as he could.

"Look, I dropped it on the porch just before you guys showed up. Not sure what happened after that," Will said to the guys. Reed didn't believe the boys; he left the room to find a way to get the truth out of them.

Baron asked the boys how they got the cube in the first place. Timber, Will, and Hayden all turned their heads to the left and looked at Juice, expecting him to say something. Juice felt like he was on the spot and reported that he found it in a box. Baron shouted that he needed more information than that. Juice said he got it from an old lady's house. For the life of Juice, he could not remember the woman's name, so Juice said that the woman looked like a Sally, but he felt that her name might have started with a *P*. He went into detail that she was moving to a new house, and he got her box of the stuff she found during some flood.

"The great flood of the southeastern Ohio area twenty-five years ago?" Baron asked.

"Yeah, not too far from here," Juice replied. Baron and the others could not believe that the cube was finally located. This information instilled a sudden silence in the room.

Juice broke that silence by simply saying, "The website mentioned a reward for whoever found it…" Once again, all Juice's friends' heads turned to him, but this time they displayed angry mug faces. By this time, Reed returned to the room carrying a flaming fire poker.

"Woo fire," Hayden uttered. This was another one of Hayden's famous catchphrases. Whenever he would see a simple spark, or a candle lit in a room, his natural response would to say *woo fire*. It would always give him a slight pleasure in his mood. Hayden didn't mean to say what he did at this time; it just slipped out. When Juice heard Hayden say his famous catchphrase at a time like this, he couldn't help but let out a small giggle.

"Maybe this will get you to tell us where the cube is!" Reed threatened while holding the hot fire poker. Reed extended the red-hot metal close to Hayden. Hayden did not flinch or struggle to get away from the coming torch. Juice turned his head away from the metal rod; the heat coming off it was uncomfortable. Will stared at the fire poker as it grew closer to Hayden's chest.

"Hold it! The cube was in my hands last. I lost possession of it after it set off a blast that knocked all of us off our feet. It even sent Timber through the window. I'm telling you the truth that we don't have it anymore!" Will pleaded, hoping they would spare Hayden from getting hurt.

Reed didn't believe him and felt that Hayden would tell a different story after searing him with the rod. Reed pressed down the fire poker hard onto Hayden's chest. Hayden's face and entire body remained still, as if he felt no pain at all. The sizzling rod burned through Hayden's shirt, touching his skin, and yet Hayden still didn't even flinch.

Everyone in the room was astonished as they looked at this. Everyone was expecting a scream in pain or at least a discomforting struggle or outburst. Everyone was speechless at this spectacle. It was hard to tell who was shocked more, the Havocs or the Hogs. Reed couldn't believe what he was seeing, but he maintained the pressure of the fire poker on Hayden's chest, waiting to see if Hayden would break his fearless act after allowing the heat to seek deeper. The Hogs' jaws dropped, all except for Hayden. Hayden was good at putting on this emotionless face; he put it on whenever he was playing cards and whenever someone took a photograph of him.

Will couldn't take this anymore, and with all his might, he tore the rope that kept his hands behind the chair he was sitting on. Once the rope was torn, Will was free from the chair and jumped up to tackle Reed. After Reed was hit by Will, he lost his grip on the fire poker, and it flew through the room. Will rolled off Reed and swung his foot across Hayden's back chair leg. With the chair leg broken off, Hayden was able to stand up; and with a mighty stretch, he was able to tear the rope that kept his hands bound together. Hayden rushed over to Timber to set him free, while Will got over to Juice's seat to set him free.

A loud shotgun fired off to the ceiling. "Enough!" Baron shouted to calm the room down again.

The Hogs froze with their hands in the air. The excitement of escaping had come and gone so fast that the Hogs felt helpless and weak once again. Having a gun pointed at them put the fear of God back into them.

Reed, still on the ground, looked over to the other room and saw the curtains on fire. The fire poker had caught onto the curtains and had spread like wildfire. The place was very old and not well taken care of for years, so a fire was bound to happen sometime. The fire was growing by the second, and the location of the fire was in a very bad position. Baron ordered three men to escort the Hogs into the walk-in cooler in the kitchen while the others tried to put out the fire.

The men struggled to quickly put out the flames but were losing the battle. Baron yelled out that this wildfire was burning right above the box of weapons in the basement. If just one single ember fell to the basement and landed onto the box of weapons, the gas bottle stored inside could ignite, setting the whole place in a blaze. Baron ordered someone to get down to the basement to move the box of weapons. Reed howled that it was too late. The floor was cracking, and the fire could fall into the basement at any second. Baron had to make a hard decision; unfortunately, he had almost no time to make it.

Baron said they had to abandon the mansion. The men dropped what they were doing and ran upstairs together. The flames falling to the basement were drawing closer and closer to the crate of weapons. The crate had huge words on the side saying, "FLAMMABLE!!!"

In the walk-in cooler, the Hogs had their ears to the door. "What's going on out there?" asked Timber.

"I think they're leaving," Will reported.

"They're going to take us with them, right? They didn't just forget about us, right?" wondered Timber.

"You want to go with them?" Hayden asked with a snarl.

"I don't want to be trapped in a burning building!" Timber replied with panic in his voice.

"I always knew I would go out like this," Hayden uttered.

"I'm sure the fire wouldn't harm you, Hayden. How did that fire poker not burn you anyway?" asked Juice.

"Dude, I don't even know. Check it, I don't even have a burn mark!" Hayden said with a newfound joy.

Juice looked at the torn threads of Hayden's shirt and saw no burn or any damaged skin whatsoever. The two were so amazed by this they forgot the situation they were in at the moment.

"This is a conversation we can table for another time. Right now, we need to get out of here!" Will stated loudly.

"It's a big, metal, locked door, Will. We're pretty well trapped," Juice reported.

"Plus, if they see us get out, they would take us with them," Hayden added.

"Again, I would rather be anywhere but here!" Timber shouted with big hand gestures.

On the stairsteps, the Havocs were carrying a stretcher holding their leader. They knew they only had minutes, maybe less, until the flames reached the flammable gas in the crate in the basement. One of the men asked what they should do about the boys trapped in the cooler. Reed stated that there was no reason to risk their lives for the boys. They all agreed and left the boys trapped. The men made it to their van, loaded up their leader, and took off down the dirt driveway that led out to the country road.

Inside the cooler, Will was pretty sure that they were now alone inside the house. Timber could not believe that they just left them behind. Hayden sat on a box, ready to accept his fate. Juice was bouncing off the walls like a bouncing ball and yelling his head off. Juice took a full charge at the metal door; Juice shoved his shoulder into the door and then fell back onto the ground hard.

Will felt the whole room shake when Juice hit the door. He even saw the door budge a little. Will had a gut feeling that they could push down the door together. Will said that if they all rushed at the door together, they could get it to open. Timber was up for any idea that could get them free. Juice was mad that Will couldn't have said that before he tried doing it alone. Hayden got up, and together they all stood back away from the door. Will said that they would all charge on three. The countdown was fast. Will could hear the ceiling start to crack, so it was just a matter of time until it collapses on top of them.

When Will shouted three, the Hogs all charged at the door together. They were screaming at the top of their lungs, as they got closer to the door. Within this moment, the group was full of confidence that the door was going down. Four athletic boys together could surely take out a locked cooler door. The Hogs slammed into the door with all their might. The door popped off its hinges and was stripped from the wall. The boys just kept running, pushing the door in front of them. The door had a huge dent in the middle, right where the boys' forearms drove into it. The Hogs ran the door uncontrollably all the way across the kitchen floor and crashed hard into the sink.

The Hogs came to a full stop after the crash, feeling a slight whiplash. Ignoring the amazing action they just performed, their survival instincts kicked in. All the rooms around them were ablaze with hot fire. Hayden pointed the way to the front door. Timber didn't bother walking anywhere in the house; instead, he climbed up onto the crashed door and jumped out the window sitting above the sink. Seeing that was the safest way out of the place, the others did the same. Juice slipped down on the door in his attempt to climb up it. Will gripped Juice's shirt and tossed him over the door. Will put way too much strength into that action because Juice was chucked way over the door and through the window with great force. Kind of humorous in a way. The sound of Juice's yell almost made Will laugh.

Will turned to Hayden; Hayden was taking one last look at the burning house. Only Hayden would find joy at being inside a burning house.

"HAYDEN!" Will shouted.

Hayden turned, and together they climbed up the door and got out from the window. Will and Hayden met up with Timber who was standing just outside the house.

"Where's Juice?" asked Hayden.

Timber, too busy coughing, just pointed over to where Juice landed when he was chucked out of the window. Juice was lying on the ground; before he got up, he spotted something in the corner of his eye. He turned to get a better look and saw that it was the cube. Juice looked around and could spot the front porch to his left. The cube must have been knocked off the porch after the blast. Juice picked up the cube. Will, Hayden, and Timber all ran up next to Juice who showed off that he had the cube. Will took the cube from Juice's hand and put it in his pocket. They all started to move away from the burning mansion. Standing so close to the flames was unbearable.

Inside the mansion, the fire finally reached the flammable crate in the basement and ignited the gas inside. A large explosion went off, sending flames everywhere. The Hogs heard the explosion go off and heard chips of wood from the mansion fly in their direction. The four Hogs sprinted away from the house like their lives depended on it. The fire grew so intense that they could feel the hair on the back of their necks sizzle, and their entire skin facing the mansion felt that it was covered in a hot sunburn. The Hogs reached a point where it was bearable to stand, turned, and faced the burning mansion.

"What just happened!" Timber yelled as loudly as he could.

"That was the coolest thing that has ever happened to me!" Hayden stated with a happy attitude.

"Yeah, I can cross *running from an explosion* off my bucket list now!" Juice joyfully added.

Juice and Hayden seemed to forget how they got into this situation and seemed to be looking at the bright side of things. While Timber was trying to calm himself down on the life-threatening events that he had faced in a matter of minutes, Juice and Hayden gave each other high fives, still hyped on this thrilling event.

"How do we get home now?" Juice asked Hayden.

"My car," Hayden stated, thinking that was a dumb question.

"Didn't they take your keys?" Juice elaborated.

"Yeah, but I got one of those spare magnets that you put on the outside of your car," Hayden added while emitting a surprisingly calm smile.

Juice gave Hayden another high five, complimenting him on a good job of thinking ahead. Timber couldn't believe how Juice and Hayden were acting; they acted like they just got off a roller coaster or something. Will was the only one smart enough to check the road. He wanted to see if the men who left them for dead earlier were long gone. He came back to his friends and told them they should go before the authorities arrived.

Will knew that someone could have heard the explosion, or someone would see the flames. The four boys rushed to the car; Hayden retrieved the spare key from its hiding place and got into the driver's seat.

Hayden drove down the driveway and turned onto the country road; Timber and Juice sat in the back and kept repeating the words *go, go, go!* Timber was worried, while Juice was just caught up in the heat of the moment. Hayden was having a good time giving off a slight evil laugh, yelling, "I'm going, I'm going!" The intense feelings brushed off after a while, and Joe brought the car back to the speed limit.

It was a pitch-black sky, and the four didn't see another car out on the road for miles. Not much longer to go before they reached their hometown. Timber looked over and saw Juice asleep.

"Juice is asleep," Timber stated.

"Boy can sleep through anything," Hayden replied as Timber leaned up to the front seat.

"It's all his fault that this happened to us," Timber added. "He's the one who found that cube in the first place."

"I'm the one who discovered the reward for it," Will added.

"I'm the one who drove us out there," Hayden uttered.

"So you're all to blame…great," Timber said, leaning back in his seat.

Will removed the cube from his pocket. He saw that all the pieces have shifted out of place. Will knew that there was something different about him—about all of them. He knew that this cube was the source of that change. He didn't think it would be safe to let it fall in the hands of the men who lived at the mansion. Hayden asked what they should do with it. Will felt that until they know more about it, they should try to keep it safe.

Hayden asked whom they could trust with this information. Will said that parents would just worry, and the police would ask too many questions. Hayden asked about the other members of the Hang Out Group and if they should know about the cube. Will said that they were going to have to let them know. They were the only ones they could trust.

No words were said after that. Later, Hayden found a bump on the road that he purposely ran over. The shake in the car caused Juice to wake up suddenly.

"Are we there yet?" Juice asked.

Will uttered, "We're almost home."

CHAPTER 18

In This Together

Thursday, May 6, 2010, Just after Midnight

It was a dark, rainy night as a car drove past an old worn-out warning sign saying, "WARNING: deadly chemical leak ahead. Please turn back now!" The men in the car knew that this sign was bogus, for there was never any dangerous chemical leak in the area. The men in the car were Havocs members heading to their new temporary headquarters. Skinny wooden trees covered the view on both sides of the road as they approached the building. The car reached a rusty metal fence. The man in the passenger seat exited the car and tossed his hood up over his head to keep dry from the raindrops, while the driver kept the engine running. The man outside ran up to the gate of the fence; he placed a key into its lock and removed the chains keeping the gate in place. The gate rolled to the side, opening a path leading toward the building. The driver pulled through, and the man closed and locked the gate.

This building hadn't been occupied for years now. Well, not occupied by humans, that is. After parking the car, the two men pushed on the intercom button just next to the front door of the building. They were waiting for someone inside to *buzz* them in. Eager to get out of the rain, one of the men pushed the button a second time. The buzz sound came on, and they pushed open the door. The two men walked down a long, poorly lit hallway. As they walked toward the stairs, they heard a sound that made their skin crawl. The Havocs had been staying at this building for a few days now, and that sound still made them shiver.

The building was well isolated from society. Due to the warning chemical signs that were placed all around the location, most people stayed clear of the building. Others stayed clear of the building for different reasons. Mostly teenagers and some adults fully believed that the building was haunted. Over the years of teens playing truth or dare, people looking for a thrill, or people who wanted to explore places that they had no business being in, intruders had come close to the building; but no one had ever made it past the chain fence that sealed it off.

Many said that some nights, you could hear sounds from inside the building. Not like normal human sounds; these were sounds of some undiscovered bizarre monsters. The Havocs knew the truth of what lived in the building, and the people who believed that it was a monster were right. Not just one monster—several monsters, which were locked up in the basement floor of the building. This old building was once a prison to hold criminals; now it held vicious creatures.

The Renshaw Mansion was the home of the Havocs since the beginning. After it burned down, they became homeless for a while. Three members left the group, leaving only five members. Over the years, the Havocs had lost more and more members; these people no longer believed in the rise of their leader and the restoration of the Havocs to their former, powerful glory.

The prison wasn't the Havocs' first choice of living quarters. Unfortunately, there were not many choices. The people they thought were allies didn't care to take them in for free. The Havocs learned that just because mob bosses hired them in the past didn't make them friends. The Havocs also had to find a location that could support their leader, Cain. Cain was in a coma and needed IV injections and machines to help him to breathe and monitor his heartbeat. These were all things they had to steal during that week due to their former supplies getting lost in the fire.

The prison was the only place where these people could stay. The place was well hidden, and there was enough room there to take care of their leader. The fact that it caged terrifying creatures in its basement was the only negative thing about the place. The creatures stayed in a type of hypersleep stage, during their time inside the cages. But at times, mostly at night, they would start to snore and make awful grunting noises. Nightmares may have been the reason that the creatures would lash out and holler from time to time.

The two men made it to the second floor to meet up with Baron. Baron sat at a round table with Reed on his right side and another Havocs member on his left. The two men sat and helped themselves to pizza from the pizza box that was in the center of the table. This large-size pizza was the supper for these five men.

The two men had returned from a mission to find the fire department information on the burned-down Renshaw Mansion. After the Havocs fled their former home, the fire trucks showed up. The brave firemen managed to keep the fire from spreading through the woods, but the mansion had burned to the ground. The report said no casualties. With this information, the men knew that the four boys managed to escape the burning building.

"How did they manage to escape?" Reed wondered. Baron felt that he knew the answer. But to tell it would give away his secret. Baron was told by Cain before he fell into his coma not to tell anyone the true power of what the cube could do. But Baron had sat on this secret for so long, it was time to share it with the remaining members of the group.

"The boys said they were hit with a blast of light after solving the cube."

The men could tell by the tone of his voice that Baron was about to share some important information, so they stopped eating and put down their pizza.

"The blast from the cube can wake Cain up. It also has the power to emit Loomation, giving advanced strength to whoever gets hit by the blast."

Reed leaned in closer to the table. "You're telling us this now?" he said angrily.

"What's Loomation?" asked Mitch who was sitting to Baron's left.

"It's a mystic element that Cain was born with. It's what makes him so strong and what slows down his aging," Baron explained.

"So we all can be as strong as Cain?" asked another man at the table.

"Why didn't you tell us this sooner?" Reed demanded an answer.

"What difference would it have made? We didn't even know where the cube was until now!" Baron replied.

"You think the boys have it?" asked a man at the table.

"Well, of course they have it! Once they found out what it could do, they probably wanted to keep it for themselves!" Reed said, standing up.

The men all wanted the cube now more than ever. The problem was that none of the men knew who the kids were or how to find them. Then Mitch remembered taking the keys from one of the boys in order to search their car for the cube. He checked his jacket pocket and found that he still had the keys.

The man tossed the keys over to Baron. There were a few keys on the key chain, along with a tag. The tag was an ID tag for a local gym. On the tag was a photo of Hayden. Baron turned the tag around and let out a huge laugh because on the back it said, "If found, please return to" and Hayden's address was hand scribbled in under that. The Havocs now knew where to go, but they felt that they should come up with a plan before going. If these four boys truly possessed the same strength as Cain, then taking them down wouldn't be easy.

Baron knew that the answer on how to attack the Hogs lay just below their feet. Back in the group's prime, when there were thirty or more members, the Havocs were able to transport the creatures in the basement and use them to attack their enemies. The Havocs haven't used them for a mission in years.

The Havocs were petrified to go anywhere near those creatures, especially without Cain. The creatures were strong, fast, and very hard to control. Baron knew that there were tranquilizer guns in the basement. They were used on the creatures when they were being transported. The plan to attack the Hogs would be a simple kidnapping. They would capture them by using some of the tranquilizer darts. They would need one, maybe two kids, then offer a trade for the cube and be done with them.

They didn't want to risk the chance of the kids calling the police. Though they had been inactive for a long time, the Havocs were still wanted criminals. There was a time when they didn't fear anyone, but times had changed. The team was very weak and afraid that they would soon be extinct. The Havocs decided to keep this fight between themselves and the Hogs, thinking the kids would not call the cops if they only went after them. They felt that if they went after their family members, then they feared that the kids would call the cops. The Havocs felt good about this plan: go in, get the kids, and offer a trade. Something they were hired to do many times in the past.

Friday, May 7, 2010

The Hogs had a very long week. Juice thought Wednesday was Friday due to how long the week felt. After getting the days mixed up, the weekend took even longer to arrive. Will, Juice, Hayden, and Timber no longer felt safe anywhere, not at school or even at their own homes. The boys were praying that the criminals believed them to have died in the fire. If this were the case, they shouldn't worry and maybe they could stop looking over their shoulders every time they left the house. Other members of the Hang Out Group, Eric and Gard, could tell that there was something unpleasant on their friends' mind. Hayden had a hangout at his backyard that Friday, his third weekend in a row. His parents were out of town, so he knew that they wouldn't mind. Will and Timber were unable to make it that Friday night; Timber had to work, while Will was going to visit his aunt with his family. Juice and Hayden were going to inform Eric and Gard about what happened last weekend during that hangout.

It was a little after five, and Hayden already had the fire going and the pop-up camper set up. Juice parked his Jeep and removed a bag of groceries from his vehicle. "Pie irons!" Juice shouted with excitement. A pie iron was a cooked pizza sandwich done over fire. Juice had the ingredients in the bag: mozzarella cheese, pepperoni, butter, and bread. Juice set up the cooking area on a foldout table next to the camper.

"Did you ever make it to the weight room?" asked Hayden as he fed the fire with logs.

"*Did you?*" Juice reasoned, lifting his eyes up from the table.

"No," Hayden said, sounding like it was obvious. "I can't find my gym pass anyway." Hayden hadn't been to the weight room at the local gym since the fall during football season.

"I did go on a six-mile run the other day. I broke my personal record, and I didn't even break a sweat!" Juice bragged. Juice ran cross-country and track, so he loved running long distances.

Will knew that when they told the others about their new strength, they would have a ton of questions. So Will wanted them all to find out how much they could lift and how fast they could run.

Down the grass driveway, Gard's car approached. After Gard parked his car, he got out, opened his arms wide, and yelled, "I have arrived!" Gard was so overwhelmed to be hanging out with his friends again. Gard was on the track team with Juice and the football team with some of the other members.

"You break up with her yet?" Hayden asked Gard as he drew closer to the fire.

"No, not yet. We may have a lot of problems as a couple, but she's already my prom date, so there is time for things to get better, I guess," Gard stated. Gard had been talking about breaking up with his current girlfriend for weeks now. She had been taking up too much of his time, and the two were growing apart with their different ideas of entertainment. When Gard brought her to Hayden's birthday celebration the other week, she didn't have a good time nor cared to be there.

Gard said he was sorry for having to leave Hayden's birthday celebration early, but he was happy that he was here all night. Hayden told Gard that his parents were in Pennsylvania visiting his brother. Gard knew that this meant that there would be no all-you-can-eat breakfast in the morning. He was upset that the weekend he could spend the night was when there was no breakfast.

Just then, Eric's car came driving down the driveway. When he got out and walked up to the chairs, Gard jokingly said, "Who invited this kid?" Eric was the captain of the quiz bowl team, and he played soccer all throughout high school. He, therefore, was used to doing physical activity and mental activity.

"I was thinking the same thing," Eric replied to Gard's comment as he sat down around the fire.

"Does anyone want a sandwich? I promise I won't burn them this time!" Juice shouted. They all said yes, and Juice made sandwiches for everyone.

As they ate, Juice and Hayden finally informed Eric and Gard about what happened to them last weekend. They told them about the cube, the mansion, getting tied up and locked up in the cooler, their new advanced strength that they now had, and Hayden's fireproof skin. This story came off as some sort of fairy tale to the two.

"I don't buy it," Eric stated. Hayden removed his lighter from his pocket; he flicked the switch to create the flame and rested his hand on the fire. Hayden showed no sign of unpleasantness from his hand touching the flame. Eric and Gard were unimpressed because he did stuff like this all the time. Hayden stood up and grabbed hold of a burning log from the fire, exhibiting not even the slightest scar from the burning wood. This was selling the story a little bit more now.

"My turn," Juice stated. Juice got up and walked over to the camper, rubbed his hands together, and started to stretch. Juice really took his time stretching to a point where it grew annoying; he was building the suspense, or so he felt.

"Just do something already!" Hayden shouted, getting agitated.

"Okay, okay…watch this!" Juice then, with one hand, lifted the camper, tipping it on an angle. Juice carefully placed the camper back down and gloated in his performance. Eric and Gard felt that they had their proof now; they were blown away with amazement.

"How much can you guys lift? Has this affected your appetite, your sleeping needs, or even your weight?" Eric was a guy who wanted to know all the facts, as he didn't like mysteries.

Juice and Hayden did their best to answer all the questions, but to be honest, they were still figuring things out themselves. Juice did point out that he was much stronger but was a little upset that his body didn't show it in any way. He didn't have rock-hard abs or huge biceps; he was just as weak looking as he had always been. Eric asked if Juice was also fireproof. The answer was no, which also went for Will and Timber.

"What makes you so special, Hayden?" Gard asked.

"I don't know. Fire just loves me so much that it doesn't want to harm me," Hayden said, giving a silly explanation.

"I bet the feeling is mutual," Juice added with a nod.

"What about scalding hot water? Could that damage the skin? And could the fire still burn off your hair? What's the feeling you get when you touch the flame?" Eric inquired.

"So far anything hot has no effect on me. My hair is also fireproof," Hayden stated. "And when I touch the fire, it's just a mild warm feeling. It still causes me to sweat, and the heat of the flame does make it unpleasant to be near to when it gets too hot," Hayden replied.

"Gard, guess how fast I can run a mile?" Juice said, trying to gain some attention. "Within three minutes. I'm not even a sprinter, and I can win the gold medal!" he bragged.

"Where was that speed this track season? We could have gone to state!" Gard shouted.

"Is there any way to reverse this?" Eric wondered.

Both Juice and Hayden were unsure of that; it seemed that whatever happened to them was permanent. Eric wanted to see the cube, which caused Juice and Hayden to look at each other.

"Show it to them," Hayden said.

"I don't have it," Juice responded.

"Yeah, you do. Remember when Will said he wasn't going to make it tonight and that you should bring it to the hangout," Hayden insisted.

"Oh yeah, you're right. I do have it," Juice uttered to himself. Juice ran to his Jeep to retrieve the cube and showed it to the guys.

Eric looked at it and asked how it worked. Juice simply said, "You just rotate the pieces left, right, up, down until they all line up. After that, you crunch down and release."

Eric put the cube in his hands to take a closer look at it. He made a few rotations and felt confident that he could solve the puzzle easily. Juice shouted at him not to solve it for fear that the white blast would fire out again. Eric wanted to examine the blast and see what it looked like. Gard was also curious about how it would look like. Hayden said that if Eric could solve it, he could find a way to create the blast without anyone getting hit by it.

As the Hogs were hanging out in the backyard, they had no idea that one of the Havocs members was in the cornfield across from Hayden's house. He got a phone call from Baron. The man informed Baron that he was standing out front of Hayden's house, hidden within the cornfield and the night sky. The man reported that he hadn't seen anyone inside the house. He did confirm that Hayden was in the backyard having a bonfire of some sort. Baron asked if the other kids were in the backyard with Hayden. The man stated that there were four kids there. Counting Hayden, only two of the kids were the ones at the mansion, while the other two seemed to be friends. Baron said that this could work. That all they needed was to retrieve two of the kids, and they could deliver the ransom orders to the other two. Baron and the other Havocs were on their way with the van and a car saying they'd move in soon. The orders were to tranquilize the ones with the advanced strength so that they wouldn't be able to fight back. The ransom orders would be delivered to the other kids.

It didn't take Eric long to line up all the pieces; he said the formula of solving it was like that of a Rubik's cube. After it was solved, he was very careful not to crunch down on it. The boys walked deeper into the backyard toward the woods. Juice, Eric, and Gard stood just where the trees met the grass while Hayden carried the cube into the woods. Hayden got a good distance away from the yard while still staying in view of his friends. He placed the cube down in the dirt and then placed a rock on top of it. The rock was attached to a fishing line Hayden had tied it to earlier. The rock was heavy enough to crunch down on the cube to connect all the pieces. Once the cube was in the crunched position, it immediately emitted the white glow. Hayden turned to his friends and asked, "You guys see it?"

"Yeah, now get back here," Eric replied.

Hayden walked backward, letting out slack of the fishing line as he went. Juice said that he had his video camera in his car; Eric thought it would be a good idea to get footage of the blast, so Juice ran over to his Jeep to get his camera. The space to the Jeep and tree line was about seventy-five meters, up an incline, so Juice jogged over to his car.

Juice made it to his car door; but before he opened the door, he saw an unexpected vehicle approaching down the grass driveway, followed by a large van.

Who's this? Juice thought to himself. Juice didn't recognize the vehicles, so he was very confused. The car came to a stop, and out came

one of the members of the Havocs. Juice recognized the face right away—
the thing he and his friends feared the most had now arrived.

Headlights on Juice put him right in the spotlight for the five Havocs
who were now all out of their vehicles. Juice gave a friendly, nervous smile
and said politely, "Hi…let's talk this out," as he put his hands up.

The Havocs member, who was the driver of the car, pulled out a
tranquilizer gun and aimed it at Juice. Juice, on impulse, turned toward
the woods and started to make a run for it.

"GUYS, THEY'RE HERE!" Hayden, Eric, and Gard heard Juice
from the incline. They all turned their heads fast and saw Juice taking a
shot in the back in midrun.

The Hogs by the trees were scared to death at that moment; they
couldn't believe that they were literally under attack. Baron shot Juice
with the tranquilizer dart, and he started to load up the gun with another
dart. Juice stopped running after he got shot as he was having trouble
keeping his balance. A Havocs member came to Juice's left side to pull
him into the van. Juice, with all his might, managed to shake the man off
him, pushing him a far distance away.

"Wait until the fluid fully settles in!" Baron shouted to his members.

Hayden, Eric, and Gard all sprinted toward Juice's aid. Hayden,
having the fastest speed due to his advanced strength, was almost to
Juice, while Eric and Gard were still behind a bit. Baron shuffled in closer
to his target and with precise aim fired the dart right at Hayden. Hayden
suddenly lost his balance, began to feel woozy and light-headed, and fell
to his left knee.

Reed took a few steps up toward Eric and Gard. He pulled out his
handgun from his holster and aimed it at the two. Eric and Gard came
to a frightened stop. Neither ever had a gun pointed at them before.
This was an uncomfortable, disturbing feeling, causing them to freeze
with fear. By this time, Juice was out cold and carried into the van. With
Reed's gun being pointed at Eric and Gard, they were helpless. Baron got
in close to Hayden who was fighting his urge to pass out.

"Where's the cube?" Baron asked.

"It's not here," Hayden grunted. Eric and Gard shared concerned
looks as to why Hayden would lie about the cube being here.

"That's a shame," Baron uttered. "Load him up in the van too," Baron ordered his men. Eric and Gard felt so weak and pathetic. They watched their friends being kidnapped right before their eyes, and there was nothing they could do about it. As Hayden was loaded in the van, Reed relayed information to Eric and Gard.

"Now don't worry, your friends are just tranquilized. Last weekend they, along with two others, showed up to our home, burned it down, and ran off with something we want, a cube. So this is just your standard kidnapping: the cube for your friends." Reed then took out a folded-up piece of paper from his pocket. This paper had the address of the burned-down mansion written on it. He told them to bring the cube to where it once stood by sunrise. Reed chucked the paper at them and started walking backward toward the car with his gun held high.

Reed assured the two that their friends would be unharmed if they followed up with the exchange and didn't call the police, which was Baron's final request. He did threaten to kill their friends if they got the police involved, and they would come back for the cube themselves in a more aggressive way. Reed put the gun down to his side and got into the car. The van and car both backed out of the driveway; the van quickly left their sight, speeding down the country road with the car following it.

"They turned right," Gard said to himself. He then turned and ran into the woods.

"Gard, what do you think we should do?" Eric said as he followed Gard into the woods. "Should we go to the police? Should we tell Will and Timber what happened?" Eric talked with uncharacteristic fear in his voice. He was nervous and scared; so was Gard, but he kept his cool. Gard and Eric ran up to the cube in the woods. If only the Havocs had looked into the woods, they would have seen the brightly glowing cube in the distance.

"We're going to give them the cube?" asked Eric as they both looked down on it.

"No. When they get the cube, they'll just kill all of us," Gard reasoned.

"That's why Hayden said the cube wasn't here. If they knew it was here, they would have bailed on the kidnapping plan and just shot us dead right here," Eric said, starting to think more clearly. "So what are we going to do?" wondered Eric.

"Right now, they're heading down the road that curves around the cornfield, which means that they are going to be right across the cornfield any second now," Gard explained.

"What's your point?" questioned Eric.

"I'm going to cut them off by going through the cornfield and save our friends!" Gard retorted.

"There is no way you can drive your car through the cornfield in time—" Eric didn't have to finish his sentence, for he knew Gard's plan. They both looked down at the glowing cube. Eric tried to talk Gard out of receiving the blast from the cube, telling him they had no idea the lasting side effects of getting powers from that thing.

"Look, we don't have too many winning options. If we don't give them the cube, they kill our friends. We give them the cube, and they kill all of us! My plan gives us a fighting chance, which is the option I want!"

The window of success in Gard's plan was shrinking by the second. If the van made it too far away, the plan would be a failure. Eric let out a deep breath. He could tell that Gard wasn't going to be talked out of this, and every second was just wasting time.

"I'm not letting you do this alone," Eric stated.

Gard grinned and picked up the cube and the rock, holding it down in the crunched position. Gard looked at Eric just before releasing the rock and wondered if he was ready for the blast.

Eric nodded. "Let's do this."

Gard took the rock away from the cube, and the cube released the same white blast as it did for the other Hogs. The blast knocked the two off their feet and on their backs. Both Eric and Gard felt heavy, as if their bodies were too sore to move. Gard yelled out to Eric and asked if he was all right. Eric said he felt like the wind was knocked out of him. Gard told him that he better get it back in him because they needed to get moving now. After the two managed to pull themselves up to their feet, they started to feel more stable and started to make their run. They ran out of the woods, past the camper, past Hayden's house, across the street, and into the cornfield. Gard, being faster, was leading the way with Eric doing his best to keep up.

As Gard felt himself going faster and faster, reaching speeds he could only dream of, he never felt more alive in his life. The wind in his face, legs, and arms felt exhilarating. Eric, behind him, was just hoping that he could keep Gard in sight.

The van and car had already made it past the curve in the road and were about to line up across Hayden's house opposite side of the cornfield. In Baron's car, Reed sat in the passenger seat next to him. "So are the kids going to be asleep forever like Cain?" Reed asked.

"No, the tranquilizer that Ray used on Cain was a more updated design. Ours would only keep them out for a few hours, enough time to get them to one of the open cells at the prison," Baron explained.

In the cornfield, Eric grew worried that they missed their opportunity to catch up with the van. He shouted out to Gard and asked if they were getting close to the road. Gard said that he wasn't sure.

"Wait, can you even see where you're going?" Eric shouted out to Gard.

"Not at all!" Gard replied. Just then, Gard was no longer running through the cornfield and was now steps away from the road. Gard was moving so fast he didn't have time to slow himself down. The timing was perfect. Gard uncontrollably ran right into the side of the van, colliding his shoulder onto the side of the vehicle, which caused the van to be shoved into the ditch on the side of the road. Gard bounced off the van and slammed onto the road. Gard's shoulder was in a lot of pain, as it felt dislocated. But Gard had played football and run races with injuries before in the past, so pain was something he grew to tolerate.

The car behind the van slammed on its brakes, and Baron and Reed exited out of the front seats. Baron moved his hands with great speed to reload the tranquilizer gun. With the dart in place, he pointed the gun at Gard.

"SHOOT HIM!" shouted Reed with a frightened voice. Just before Baron could pull the trigger, Eric emerged out of the cornfield and charged straight toward Baron. Eric slammed himself against Baron, pinning him hard against the car. Baron fell to the ground while Reed drew out his gun. Reed fired his gun at Eric from across the top of the car. Eric was able to duck just before the bullet was fired. Eric saw the tranquilizer gun next to Baron, snatched it up, moved up straight above the top of the car, and fired the dart at Reed. Reed was passed out before he even hit the ground.

Gard hustled over to the side of the van. Three Havocs members were stuck in the van, badly bruised from the crash. They were too sore to fight back. Gard opened the side door and yelled out to Eric to come over. Gard picked Juice up and threw him over Eric's shoulder. "You take the lighter one!" Gard yelled and then tossed Hayden over his own shoulder,

"Wrong shoulder!" Gard shouted in pain as he put Hayden over his injured shoulder. Gard switched Hayden to his other shoulder to carry him much easier. Both Eric and Gard faced Baron before running back into the field. They saw the men in the van struggling to get out. With them looking like they needed medical attention, they knew that these men wouldn't come back to them anytime soon. The boys ran back into the field. When they arrived back at Hayden's house, they picked up the cube and relocated to Gard's house in town. They didn't feel safe at Hayden's place for the night.

At Gard's place, Eric and Gard put Juice and Hayden onto the couches so they could sleep off their tranquilized state. A knock at the door came, which gave Eric and Gard an uneasy fright. They saw Will at the front door through the glass window. Gard yelled out to him that the door was unlocked.

"You guys were attacked by criminals an hour ago, and you still leave the front door unlocked?" Will said with a smirk. "How are they?" Will asked as he came in close to Juice and Hayden.

Eric said that they seemed fine. Will was relieved and then asked how the ones awake were doing.

"I got hit by a van going 60, and the van was in far worse shape than me!" Gard stated with excitement and laughter in his tone.

Will let out a small laugh and then turned to Eric to check on him. Eric was still shaken by the incident. He was shot at and close to getting hit.

Will put his hand on Eric's shoulders, saying he was sorry for not being there. Before Will could put his other hand on Gard's shoulder, Gard stopped him, saying that his shoulder was in a lot of pain, so he shouldn't touch it. The three sat down. Will apologized that they had to get hit with the blast from the cube. Gard believed that when Juice and Hayden come to, they would be very grateful that they did.

Gard told Will that he now understood why Will and the others had been acting so weird during the week. He could tell that having this newfound strength was going to be something that would take time to get used to. On top of that, there were people out there wanting to hurt them. Eric then brought up the importance of protecting the cube. Eric said that if guys like the ones who attacked them tonight had powers like they did, then the world would be a more dangerous place.

The three boys felt this high responsibility leveled upon them. The constant threat of the next attack and the fear of what may come to them now that they had these powers was a real concern. They, however, felt confident that they would be all right because they didn't have to go through this alone.

CHAPTER 19

Sick

Wednesday, May 12, 2010, Before Dawn

Two men walked up to a garage door within a garage storage unit. The two men were Baron and Reed. "It's about time," Reed stated, annoyed that it took them so long to find the storage unit.

"Sorry, it's been years since I've been here," Baron replied. "Besides, it was my partner who usually dropped off the stolen goods here."

"Well, where is he?" Reed asked.

"He's dead," Baron said as he removed the lock from the door and pulled up on the garage door. Reed suddenly grew silent, as did Baron.

Baron's early days with the Havocs were spent spying on their greatest enemy, Ray. Baron remembered it like it was yesterday. Cain, the leader of the Havocs, asked for…well, still to this day he didn't know if Cain asked for Erin or Baron. Because their names sounded so similar, they both came when Cain called out a name. Cain said he originally just wanted one spy, but since they both were offering, he assigned them both to the job. There were promised large rewards, money, and power within the group.

Baron and Erin's job was to inform Cain about upcoming attacks from Ray and to keep an eye on whatever he was working on. One day, Baron and Erin stole something from Ray, a weapon with mystical powers. This was why Baron and Reed came to the locker. The weapon was designed to affect people with Loomation inside them. Their plan was to use it against the Hogs.

"What am I looking for exactly?" asked Reed as he sorted through the junk on the tables placed all over the inside of the garage.

"It'll be a small red box," Baron described. That description didn't settle well for Reed. He found it hard to believe that something that could fit inside a small box could do so much *damage* to someone with advanced strength. Reed saw Gard overpower a speeding van, so he knew how powerful the Hogs were.

Baron informed Reed that the weapon they were searching for attacked the person mentally, not physically. Baron spoke very highly of Ray's intelligence and knew not to underestimate Ray's inventions.

Then Baron found the box. He paused because being in the presence of one of Ray's weapons made him uncomfortable. "Found it," he said to Reed as he picked up the box. Baron carefully opened the box by lifting the lid just a crack. Inside the small box was a ball-like black spear object. Reed glimpsed at the weapon by looking over Baron's shoulder. Baron told Reed that the weapon was supposedly harmless to anyone without Loomation. But just one human touch from someone who did have it and the weapon would penetrate under the skin and start to affect the mind. Baron closed the box, put it in his pocket, and exited the garage. He and Reed closed and locked the garage door of the storage unit and took off in their car into the country.

Later That Day

Will walked down an alley leading up to the side of Juice's house. Juice's neighborhood was on a one-way street with alleys between some of the houses. Juice had a side door on the side of the house facing the alley. Whenever Juice had his friends over, they would enter through the side door. Will opened the side door and headed down the basement steps that were located right next to the door. Juice was sitting on a worn-out, faded old couch playing an old video game from the 1990s, struggling to defeat the final levels of the game.

"Hey, Will!" Juice shouted without taking his eyes off the TV.

Will eyed the basement, and it was clear that he was the first to arrive. He saw a necktie resting on the armrest of the couch.

"Need help with your tie?" Will uttered.

"Yeah, I figured one of you guys could tie it for me," Juice said, pushing the buttons on the controller harder and harder. As Will started to work on getting the tie tied, other Hang Out Group members started to show up. Hayden and Eric met at the door and walked down the basement. All the Hogs had their nice clothes on, for tonight was their last high school awards night. Eric was in a full suit, jacket, and tie, while Hayden found the cleanest button-down shirt he owned and threw a clip-on tie on his shirt.

Will finished the tie and chucked it over to Juice, saying all he needed to do was tighten it. Eric sat down at the foldout card table and placed a folder down on the surface of the table. Hayden and Will joined him while Juice stayed on the couch, still occupied with the video game.

"Okay, one game of cards," Hayden said, hoping that was the reason they were sitting at the table.

"We don't have time for cards, Hayden," Eric stated.

Eric opened the folder and showed off some documents he was able to dig up on the Havocs. Eric was eager to get started on sharing the information that he and the others had discovered, but they waited patiently for Timber and Gard to show. The wait wasn't long; they arrived just a few minutes later.

Once everyone was present, Eric was ready to share what he learned about the men who attacked them last weekend. "Juice, do you want to join us?" Eric asked since everyone was sitting around the table but Juice.

"I'm listening!" Juice shouted as he continued to play his game.

Eric said that he checked a lot of old newspapers from the library, did interviews with senior police officers, and even looked up town legends in order to learn everything he could about the men who attacked them.

Eric started by saying the men who attacked them were believed to be a part of a group of mercenaries called the Havocs. Eric stated that there was once a time when the Havocs were the most feared group of criminals on this side of the Mississippi. The police could never find the location of their secret base. Word on the street was that the Havocs stayed in a large mansion with the word *Renshaw* written over the front door.

Timber was able to confirm that he saw the word *Renshaw* written on top of the front door when he was at the mansion. Gard asked how the Havocs became so feared. Eric responded that the Havocs were led by a mighty leader.

"*Cain the Animal* people called him. They said that Cain had unheard-of strength unmatched by anyone," Eric replied.

"Well, I think we can all guess where he got that kind of power," Will stated as he placed the cube down onto the center of the table.

"There was a time when the Havocs were able to take out entire armies, leaving no survivors. The crime scenes showed dead bodies that looked to be ripped to shreds," Eric added.

The Hogs sitting at the table took a hard look at the cube. They were able to come up with an educated guess. The leader of the Havocs, Cain, must have used this cube to give him and possibly other Havocs members the power of advanced strength; and they used that power to be the most powerful group of mercenaries. As the Hogs didn't have all the facts, their guesses fell short of the actual events.

Eric then added that the reports of Havocs' attacks had been almost nonexistent for about twenty years. Their reign of terror seemed to come to an end. Will believed that once the Havocs lost the cube, their empire started to grow weaker and weaker, which explained why they were so desperate to get the cube back.

"Makes you wonder how we will turn out in the future now that we have these powers inside us. We may end up criminals like them," Hayden theorized.

"That's bull!" Juice shouted out loud. The group all faced toward Juice and saw that Juice was talking about his video game. "I swore I had another life!" Juice added, sounding frustrated. The final level of the game Juice was playing had him lose his last life while facing four powerful foes. Juice thought he would get another chance to finish the game, thinking he had one more life, but he was wrong on the number of lives his video game character had left.

"Juice, did you hear any of this?" wondered Will.

"Something about an animal?" Juice guessed.

"This is why you get Ds and Cs at school," Eric said, pointing out Juice's lack of paying attention.

"Juice, this isn't some big test we're trying to study for. These are real criminals trying to kill us," Timber stated. The room grew deathly silent after Timber said that, as if they suddenly realized how much danger they were in.

"In all honesty, if this was a big test we were studying for, you should still have been paying attention," Gard mentioned. Getting back on topic, Gard asked Eric if he was able to learn anything about the cube.

"Unfortunately, I did not. The thing is a complete mystery. I have no idea what the white blast that comes out of it is or how it was able to make us so strong," Eric replied. "There was a quote from a famous scientist: 'When you come across a problem that neither sciences nor logic can give an answer, start to seek out the supernatural for answers.'"

This information was frightening to the Hogs; they were entering new territory in a way. Mystic artifacts and superstrength-like powers were a lot to take in. The Hogs wondered what else was out there that was real. What they feared most was the Havocs' next attack.

Will checked his watch and said that it was time to leave or they would be late. The boys rose out of their chairs and headed out the door. Juice lived the closest to the school where the award ceremony was being held, which was why they all met up there before the event.

During the event, both Eric and Will earned some high-profile scholarships. They also received the highest honors for grades along with Timber and Gard. Juice and Hayden received a perfect attendance reward.

Outside the school, Baron and Reed sat in their car patiently waiting for their chance to make their move against the Hogs after the night's ceremony's events ended. The Havocs were able to learn a lot about the Hogs since they last met. They knew where they all lived and even where they went to school. The reason why the Havocs didn't attack the Hogs was because they were leery. Last weekend, five of the Havocs took on the Hogs. They failed in their mission and even lost their van. The criminals knew they couldn't beat the Hogs, especially now that six of them had advanced strength.

The Havocs knew that if they had that cube, their riches and respect would return to them. However, going up against the Hogs was too risky; the Hogs had the strength to kill them. The Havocs were also afraid of the police. The police were on the lookout for them after the mansion burned down. The mansion's location was hidden from the police for years, and after it burned down, the police knew the Havocs were vulnerable and easy to take down at this time. The fear of the police was why the Havocs didn't go after the Hogs' loved ones; they felt that the Hogs would get the police involved if their loved ones were attacked.

"How much longer?" wondered Reed impatiently.

"I don't know, and quit asking," Baron retorted. The two men's mission was an easy one. After getting the weapon from the storage unit earlier, their plan was to simply throw it at the Hogs. Once the weapon touched the skin of just one of the Hogs, it would activate.

"How is this going to help us again?" wondered Reed.

"Well, if the kid's powers work the same as Cain's power, their strength performance relies on their emotions. Ray invented this ball to change Cain's entire personality with hopes to turn him into a coward. If Cain grew to be a frightened scaredy-cat, his strength would perform poorly," Baron explained.

"Yeah, but he never got a chance to test it. Who knows if it'll even work? And if you haven't noticed, we only have one…and there are six of them," Reed added.

Baron said it was the only weapon they had left from Ray's stolen arsenal. He believed that if they had a chance to depower just one of them, then it would be worth it. Plus, the Hogs might lose confidence and even fear the Havocs if this plan worked. Reed went along with the plan even if he didn't see its full potential.

The award show was now over, and people were exiting. The Hogs were all leaving together to make the short walk back to Juice's place. This was perfect for Baron and Reed because the Hogs were all walking alone on the sidewalk of a one-way street. There was a lot of traffic leaving the parking lot, so Baron kept the car in park and waited for things to calm down. Most cars went down the intersection where the streetlight was posted.

After most of the cars were out of sight, Baron put the car in drive. The car went down the one-way street that curved around the front of the school, which was the road where the Hogs were seen last. By this time, the Hogs were a decent distance away from the school. Baron drove the car on the one-way street, creeping up right behind them. The car drove past the Hogs who were walking together on the sidewalk on their right. After the car passed the kids, the driver drove a little farther and then slammed on the brakes. Reed acted swiftly, getting out of the passenger seat. He opened the door, turned toward the Hogs, and chucked the ball right at the center of the group. "Catch!" he shouted.

The Hogs didn't know how to react. Before they recognized that the person standing next to the car was Reed, they thought this to be a classmate saying that they left something behind at the school or something or maybe this was a classmate pulling a prank or doing a silly hello gesture. By the time they saw that it was Reed, the ball was already thrusting toward them. Their first instinct was to duck for cover from a possibly deadly attack. Most of them did jump to the side for cover, but some stood their ground. Call it being brave by standing tall, or in Juice's case, he was more of a deer in the headlights.

Juice reached out and caught the ball. By this time, Gard tackled Juice to his side. Will and Hayden charged after Reed, but Reed was already in the car and quickly drove off. Will and Hayden stopped and went back to check on Juice.

"Juice, drop it!" Gard demanded. Juice looked at his hand and saw a large black ink-like stain on the palm of the hand that caught the ball. Juice rubbed his hand on the grass, trying to get whatever was on his hand off.

"Juice, when someone who has tried to kill you twice chucks something at you…YOU DON'T CATCH IT!" Timber shouted.

"We don't fully know the type of arsenal these guys have, so we must be cautious about everything, meaning you don't catch something they throw at us!" Eric explained to Juice.

Juice and Gard were now standing. Gard checked Juice's hand and saw the black spot on it. Gard tried to clean it off Juice's hand but grew aggravated in being unsuccessful.

"Why isn't this coming off?" Gard said in a loud annoying voice.

"What was it anyway?" Will asked, taking a closer look at Juice's hand.

"Some kind of ball-looking thing," Juice replied. The black spot quickly faded away, and Juice's hand went back to looking normal. Juice then felt some tingling feeling; he described it to his friends as if a centipede crawled up his arm and up to his head. Juice was then hit with a powerful headache, as if someone just hit him in the head with a bat.

The Hogs didn't know if they should take Juice to a doctor or not. The Hogs were nervous, thinking whatever Reed hit Juice with could be deadly. Then suddenly, Juice said he was feeling better and the strong headache was now gone.

"Are you sure?" Will asked concerned. Juice was honest; he felt perfectly fine. They felt that whatever weapon the Havocs used on Juice just seemed to malfunction. They told Juice to call them if anything strange happened until they saw him again at school tomorrow. The Hogs finished the walk back to Juice's house, loaded up in their cars, and headed home. Juice went right to bed, but the unexpected thrill that just happened made it hard to fall asleep.

Thursday, May 13, 2010

That night, Juice had a nightmare about being chased by something. He felt like he was being chased by a black river. He ran past his house, his Jeep, and his school. The river just kept flowing his way as if Juice was a target. He ran downtown, something he'd done many times while preparing for the latest cross-country season, when he tripped and fell. While on the ground, he turned his head back to see how close the river was. There was no time to move; the river reached him and swiftly engulfed him.

Awaking from the dream, Juice's eyes opened wide. He sat up and looked around the room in a strange way, as if he was looking at it for the first time. He rested his head back down on the pillow and fell back to sleep.

Later that morning, the bell of the high school rang, ending the first class of the day. As Will headed to his next class, he spotted Juice in the hall.

"Juice, where have you been? We didn't see you this morning before school," Will mentioned.

Juice was late for class that day. He told Will that when his alarm clock went off, he just chose to go back to sleep. Will understood, thinking that after what happened last night, he might have lost some sleep. Will asked Juice if he was feeling any different. Juice, annoyed from all these questions, walked past Will and stated that he was fine. Will could tell something was wrong with Juice, for he was not acting himself.

Juice's attitude grew crueler, meaner, and more vicious as the day went on. He felt annoyed by his daily duties, as if his simple life was beneath him. He felt that with the new power he had, his life was worth more than your average high school student. He didn't even stay until the end of school. After school, the Hogs were talking about Juice's odd behavior. They felt that maybe they should give him his space for the night and check on him tomorrow.

That night, Juice found himself eating at a bar; he gambled on some games of pool and even thought of picking a fight with a few people. But Juice didn't see the point of trying to start a fight with these people, as they were slow, beer-belly drunks. If he was going to get into a fight, then he should work up a sweat out of it at least; otherwise, it wasn't worth it. As Juice was on his walk home for the night, he stopped at an ATM. He checked around and saw that he was alone. Juice then slammed his fist into the machine and cracked it open. Juice then scooped out the cash flowing out of the machine, greedily stuffing it into his pockets. He went home with a few thousand bucks in his pockets that night.

Friday, May 14, 2010

The next day, Juice wasn't at school, nor was he picking up his phone or answering text. Will told the school that Juice was sick, and Will started to believe that it was true. During lunch, Will asked Eric about his thoughts on the attack the Havocs made the other night.

"There's something about that attack Wednesday night that doesn't add up," Will stated before he took a bite of his burger.

"You know, I've been thinking the same thing. Last time they attacked us, they had a plan: kidnap us and make a trade for the cube," Eric replied.

"You think there was more to their latest attack than we know?" questioned Will.

"I think we shouldn't underestimate these guys," Eric said as he took a sip from his drink.

Will said that Juice had been acting unlike himself after he caught that ball. Will claimed that Juice hadn't had any care or morality in his behavior for the past two days. Eric added that he too had noticed a mild change of behavior with Juice.

"What do you think that ball the Havocs threw at Juice was?" Will asked.

"Well, after seeing what the cube could do, who knows what that ball could have done. We're now in a world of advanced strength and mystical artifacts, and we're just trying to play catchup."

"Best guess on what the ball could be," Will requested.

"Well, there are real types of medication to alter one's personality. Antidepression pills, for example. With our advanced strength, who knows how our basic health system works. Our digestive, nervous, and immune systems could all dramatically change with extreme chemicals. So maybe Juice is just suffering from a strong case of a dual personality. His mind could be heavily affected from whatever the Havocs attacked him with," Eric explained with his best guess.

Will didn't like that answer, mostly because he felt that it was the most logical explanation. He wondered if the side effects would wear off. Eric feared that the effects would just grow worse over time. The Hogs thought they should talk to Juice, so they made plans to go out for pizza that night. Will said he'd pick up Juice and bring him.

Later that night, Will opened the side door of Juice's house and walked down to the basement where he saw Juice standing over his card table filling a duffel bag with cash. Will felt that they were too late, that Juice's mind had been fully corrupted.

"Juice, what is all this?" Will asked with shock.

"I'm leaving Maze, Will. This small town is too boring," Juice said as he continued to stuff the bag.

"Where did you get all this?" Will asked.

"You know when you kick the vending machine with hopes of getting a free candy bar…you should really try that with an ATM, much better rewards," Juice replied.

"You stole all this?"

"Those Havocs guys had the right idea with the life of crime. It's thrilling, exciting, and when you have these powers, you feel like you're playing with a huge advantage!" Juice added.

"Juice, this isn't you…We think you're sick. Whatever the Havocs hit you with the other night, we think it's changing you, giving you a dual personality of some kind," Will explained.

Juice didn't respond; he just zipped up the bag and started to head to the door.

"Juice, did you hear me? We need to fix this!" Will yelled as he blocked Juice's way to the door.

"Get out of my way, Will!" Juice demanded.

"No, I'll force you here if I have to," Will said as he took a strong, intimidating step toward Juice.

Juice let out a small laugh. "Maybe that's what I want you to do," Juice replied. "See, people want challenge in life. They are so desperate to push themselves to the fullest. After I got this advanced strength, I don't seem to fear anymore. What makes a daredevil so brave is when they go on dangerous stunts while having consequences of receiving broken bones or even death if they mess up the stunt. I look at one of their stunts thinking, *What's so scary about that?* I crave the sensation of pain because I know it'll take a mighty force to cause it. I now enter a room knowing that the biggest, strongest guy in the room could fall over from just one of my punches. What a boring life this is. That's why I'm leaving. I'm going to find a way to satisfy my desires. So if you want to try to stop me, go right ahead."

With that said, Juice walked around Will. After passing him, Will placed his hand on Juice's shoulder to stop him from going any further. Juice paused and turned to face his friend. Will looked at Juice and saw his eyes turn gray with his forehead veins bulging up through the skin. This look only lasted a second, for his eyes and veins quickly went back to normal. Will looked worried seeing this and let his guard down. Juice then delivered a mighty punch at Will's chest. Will was flung across the room and hit the floor. Will gasped for air; he couldn't get to his feet because the shock and pain of the attack had him motionless. Juice smirked and left the basement.

It took a few minutes for Will to get to his feet. He struggled and stumbled while getting up the stairs. That punch really did a number on him. He exited the side door and looked down the alley. He couldn't see Juice's Jeep parked on the one-way street nor at the back of his house by the garage. He took out his phone to call Eric at the pizza place.

At a local pizza place, Eric was sitting with Hayden and Gard. Eric picked up his phone thinking Will was calling to say he was bringing Juice and that they could now order the pizza. Will spoke with a loud nervous tone over the phone.

"Eric, we were right. The ball had some type of dual-personality effect on Juice," Will stated.

"Has it gotten worse?" wondered Eric.

"Much worse! I even saw the whites of his eyes turn gray, just before he punched me across the room!" Will explained. "He's got a bag of cash he stole from an ATM, and he's on his way out of town!"

"Oh, wow, it's worse than I thought," Eric replied.

"Please tell me you know how to fix this!"

"I got a theory on that. I have the cube. It's all ready to be crunched down for a blast. I think, *well, hope*, that a shock from the cube will clean out whatever is inside Juice that's making him act this way," Eric explained. Will thought that idea may work, but they better hurry, for Juice was already driving on the road. Eric told Hayden and Gard that they need to leave now. He informed them about what was going on, and they all hurried out of the restaurant.

Hayden told them to load up in his car because the way Hayden drove, he'd catch up with Juice before he got out of town. Gard rode shotgun, and Eric was in the back. All were hoping they would spot Juice's car as they drove out of town. They were now out to the far edge of town limits.

"There's his Jeep!" Gard shouted and pointed.

This was the only car they saw on the road as not much traffic went out of town. Hayden sped past the Jeep and turned his car sideways, blocking the road. Juice stomped on the brakes and got out of the Jeep. The three Hogs in Hayden's car also got out and faced Juice. The only light for this dark night was Juice's headlights shining on the side of Hayden's car.

"Get out of my way, Hayden!" Juice demanded.

"We may have to hold him down," Eric whispered to Hayden. Gard walked around the hood of Hayden's car to get on Hayden's left side. The two nervously walked up close to Juice.

"Juice, you're not thinking clearly. You need to let us help you," Hayden said with a friendly tone as if he was trying to tame a wild animal.

Gard and Hayden drew in closer toward Juice. Juice let out a small smirk, and once again his eyes turned gray. This shocked the three Hogs.

"Get him!" Gard shouted.

Both Hayden and Gard dove in at Juice, going for his arms. Juice dodged the attack by simply twisting his body out of the way with great stealth. He took hold of Gard's arm, yanked it down, and with his free hand punched Gard in the jaw upward. He then swung Gard around and slammed him into Hayden, knocking them both to the ground. Eric sprinted in with the cube in hand; he got close to Juice and attempted to crunch down on the cube.

Juice swung his fist at Eric's face, punching him and knocking him down. The cube fell out of Eric's hand. Juice stepped over Eric to pick up the cube. Hayden rose to his feet and took a swing at Juice. Juice blocked the punch midway and slammed the cube at Hayden's forehead. Hayden fell backward onto the ground once again.

"Not that this isn't fun, but I have a lot of ground to cover, and since you're blocking my way, I'll have to make the way on foot," Juice said as his eyes eased back to their normal color. "Now that I have the cube, this changes everything." Juice looked at his friends on the ground and felt no guilt, regret, or concern for his onetime comrades. He put the cube in his pocket, faced the direction away from town, and took off running.

"Hayden, get up! We have to stop him!" Gard exclaimed as he was nursing his hurt jaw.

"Yeah, in a minute," Hayden said, still adjusting to the pain and agony he felt on his head from the attack. Eric helped Hayden to his feet, and they got to Hayden's car. Hayden drove the car down the road where Juice was last seen. The car came to a crossroads; there were three different directions and no Juice in sight. Gard got out of the car and said he'd run down the right road and call them if he caught up with Juice. Eric said he'd do the same for the road to the left. Hayden went forward with his car. But none of them caught up with Juice; he was long gone. He took shortcuts through the cornfields to help gain distance. He was simply gone.

Saturday, May 15, 2010, 12:23 a.m.

On a bench at a small rest stop slept a homeless man. He awoke with a jitter from a surprising sound. He immediately looked around, detecting a threat of some sort. But there was no danger; the sound that woke him was the glass of the vending machine shattering. The older man on the bench spotted a young man stealing from the vending machine.

This young man was Juice; he came to the rest stop to rest his legs and to grab a snack. As he munched down on the candy bars, the old man stepped over to him. Their eyes met, and the man asked if he could have some. Juice gestured his hands toward the free snacks and told him to help himself. The man grabbed a bag of chips. He opened it and took a few chips when he noticed that there were no cars in the parking lot.

"You ran out here?" asked the man.

"What's it to you?" replied Juice.

"Sorry, none of my business," stated the man. "It's just that we are in the middle of nowhere, and it's pretty late to be training for a marathon."

"You wouldn't believe me if I told you, so stop asking," Juice said with a mouthful of candy. Juice made his way to the vending machine containing drinks. The man was curious how Juice was going to manage to get a free drink from that machine. He figured a simple rock could smash the glass for the machine containing the snacks. Juice reached his hand to the side of the machine, and with his second hand, he stabilized the machine. He pulled open the door of the machine as easy as opening a standard fridge. Juice helped himself to a water bottle.

The man was amazed by this display of strength and couldn't believe his eyes. Juice wouldn't normally show off his advanced strength in front of someone like that, but he was still under the effects of the evil formula that the Havocs used on him. The man hesitantly walked over and grabbed a water.

"Pretty neat talent you got there," the man stated. "Say, how old are you?" wondered the man.

"Stop asking me questions. I'm not here to chat!" Juice yelled, annoyed by the stranger. Juice's eyes even turned gray once again when he lashed out at him. Undaunted by Juice's anger, the man looked into Juice's gray eyes and believed him to be sick.

"You know I can help you with that," the man said, referring to Juice's eyes.

Juice, now fully annoyed by this man, chose to leave but not without giving him a strong shoulder budge as he walked by him. The nudge was going to be strong enough to knock the old man down. But the man quickly placed his right palm onto Juice's head.

Just a second after the man's hand touched Juice's head, the gray in his eyes disappeared. Juice was fully healed and free from the formula that changed his personality. Juice looked around confused, as if he was looking at everything for the first time. He then felt the guilt of what he had done over the past two days. The weight of guilt he had felt as if an elephant just stepped on him. He almost started to cry. It felt that Juice's conscience was silenced for the past two days, and now it was really letting him have it.

"Are you okay?" asked the man.

"No...well, I am now...just not mentally," Juice said, feeling lost for words. The man now felt like he was talking to a different person. "You have any idea how far away Maze is?" Juice asked. The man shrugged, for he did not know. "That's fine...took a couple of hours to get out here, so I'll just go back the same way I came!" Juice stated. Juice then took off into the night, leaving the mysterious man behind.

The man walked back over to the bench and retrieved his backpack. He took out a notebook from the bag and took the pen out from his pocket. He opened it up from where he left off and started writing. He started by putting the date, time, and location. *After years of searching, I found another who carries Loomation. He seemed to have some disease, nothing like I've seen before. I gave him a heal spell, and I could sense the Loomation inside him. He said he was heading back to a town called Maze.*

That Morning

Will walked down the alley leading up to the side door of Juice's house. He and the other members of the Hang Out Group received a text message from Juice earlier saying, "I'm better now. Come on over for some free doughnuts." Will opened the door and walked down the steps leading to the basement.

"Hey, he's here!" Gard yelled out to Will as he reached the floor of the basement. "How did you end up being the last one here? You live right down the alley."

Will looked around and saw his friends happy and getting along. When Will came over, he wasn't sure how the mood would be; he thought he would see some sad or possibly angry faces. The group never faced a fight or even a heavy debate against one another. A real fight occurred, punches were thrown, and people got hurt. When Will knew they entered a war against the Havocs, he thought they would be fighting them, not each other. But seeing all his friends able to put the past behind them gave him more faith in his friends.

"Take a doughnut, Will," Juice pleaded.

Before Will could say no thank you, Hayden encouraged him too; he said Juice wouldn't feel better unless everyone took his *peace offering*. Will grinned and picked up a doughnut. Hayden then looked over and saw Timber about to eat one. Hayden snatched the doughnut out of Timber's hand.

"You don't need *an apology*. You didn't get attacked by Juice last night!" Hayden said with a mouthful of doughnut.

As everyone was eating, Juice took this moment to make a full apology. He first said thanks for the little thing, getting his Jeep back to his house after having abandoned it on the road last night. He thanked them for delivering the stolen money to the police.

"Yeah, could you imagine if we would have left your car on the side of the road with over $10,000 in the passenger seat," Hayden said.

Hayden wasn't a fan of returning so much money, but he and the others knew it was the ethical thing to do.

Juice once again apologized for his actions. Will chimed in saying that it wasn't really Juice doing those actions. The guys accepted Juice's apology.

"Thanks, guys. Not many friends would forgive someone so quickly for beating them up."

"It was a lucky punch. Let's leave it at that…but just know it won't happen again!" Gard said as he chewed his food.

"You were sick. We only wanted to help and get you back to your regular self," Eric stated.

"Well, I hope to be able to repay you guys," Juice replied.

"I want doughnuts every day from now on," Timber said as he picked up another doughnut from the box.

Gard slapped the doughnut out of Timber's hand and shouted, "You don't get one! You weren't there!"

This got the group to laugh, which was much needed to get them feeling relaxed. There was a small part of them that feared the Havocs even more now. But that wasn't on their minds at the moment. They were just happy to have their friend back to normal. Knowing that they had each other's back no matter what reassured them that they could handle whatever the Havocs would throw at them next.

CHAPTER 20

The Seventh Member

Thursday, May 20, 2010

The Hogs were at Eric's house, chilling in his basement. Normally the group wouldn't be hanging out on a weekday while school was still going on, but their fellow member Miles was out of the hospital, so they gathered to talk with him. Will, Hayden, Timber, Gard, and Miles were all over at Eric's that day.

Miles grew up with the group during their elementary school days. They all went to the same school until they reached high school; Miles was the only one who went to a different high school within the group.

Miles told his friends that the doctors said that the medication had been failing to do its job, and his sickness was taking over. His motor skills were failing more and more each day. Miles was suffering from muscular dystrophy, an inherited disease weakening his muscle strength and coordination. The Hogs were aware of this and had a group discussion about what they could do about it. The Hogs told Miles what had happened to them over the past few weeks. They told him about their powers, the cube, and how they were up against a dangerous group called the Havocs.

"Wow…I take a few sick days and miss out on all the excitement," Miles stated after hearing the story.

The story sounded very unreal, as if they were pulling a prank on him. The Hogs were able to show off some of their advanced strength by taking Miles to the garage to lift a car. Now fully believing their story, Miles grinned and asked how he could get his hands on some of that power. Will took the cube out from his pocket and showed it to Miles.

"Miles, we think that this can help you," Will said.

"It'll come at a price," Timber added, and Miles felt a heavy burden, for a life decision was at hand.

"After we got our powers, we found ourselves with this new advanced strength. After what happened to Juice last week, we all got a physical checkup with the doctor," Eric mentioned. "We are all extremely healthy. All organs are working better than normal, and with how strong we are, all our motor skills will never fail us…not until we grow old anyways," Eric explained.

"The needle was tough penetrating the skin, but all blood tests came back healthy," Hayden added.

Miles felt a warm proud feeling shine on him; after months of seeing different doctors and going on endless hospital visits, his friends were the ones who could provide a cure.

"Do you think it'll heal me?" Miles asked, highly curious.

The Hogs passed uncertain looks to each other.

"We're not sure," Gard stated.

"If it does work, you'll have this power inside you. It may look cool, but…," Will started to say. "You'll have a new view on everything. On yourself, other people, your actions, your desires. You won't ever be the same."

Things were quiet, as if the weight of the consequence of having these powers was taking its toll on them. They didn't want to scare Miles out of the cube's blast, but they felt that he should know all the facts before he made his decision. Timber said that he, Will, Juice, and Hayden received their powers by accident; and they didn't know what they were dealing with at the time. Gard said that Eric and he took the powers to save Juice and Hayden, it was an impulse choice, and they knew what they did was right.

Miles turned away from the Hogs, rubbed his hand through his hair, and weighed his thoughts in his head. The Hogs didn't say any more, as they felt Miles had all the important information. Miles faced his friends.

"I said I wanted to live life to the fullest…and after this disease hit me, I swore that I'd do whatever I could do to beat it. So whatever new type of life I must live after getting these powers, that's the one I choose," Miles said, fully embracing his decision. "Besides, if these Havocs are coming after my friends, I want to fight!" he added.

The Hogs could hear that Miles had no second thoughts on this, so they didn't bother asking him if he was sure. Will stepped up to Miles with the cube in hand, which was already set up for a blast. Hayden positioned himself behind Miles, informing him that the blast would push him off his feet, so Hayden wanted to catch him. All the Hogs took a few steps back from Miles.

Miles was nervous and afraid of the shock. He asked if it would hurt. Timber said the blast would happen in a flash, and Eric added that he'd have the wind knocked out of him at first. Will then crunched down on the cube. The cube once again started to give off its glowing light. Will then released the cube from its crunched-down placement. The white blast fired out of the cube in a wave of energy. The cube hopped out of Will's hand and dropped to the floor in a spinning movement as the pieces were mixing out of place.

Miles fell into Hayden's arms, and Hayden eased him to the ground. The Hogs all stood over Miles and waited for him to open his eyes. The blast of the cube had a different side effect on Miles, which was unlike any of the others. Miles was knocked out from the blast. While he was unconscious, he experienced a dream of some kind. Miles didn't see his body in this dream. He just saw a road fly by his view as if he was flying. On the side of the road were skinny trees as if he was deep into the woods. The visual was moving so fast, but he did spot a sign on the side of the road as he swiftly moved by. His visual slowed down when Miles spotted a building at the end of the road. Then in a quick motion, his dream entered the front window of the building. Inside, he saw several people standing around a body lying on a hospital bed. The man on the hospital bed opened his eyes wide. After that, Miles woke up from his dream with a large gasp.

"What was that?" Miles shouted as he squirmed around.

Will helped his friend to his feet and asked if Miles could elaborate.

"I saw something, a vision of some kind…It felt like I was looking thorough a powerful telescope," Miles explained.

The Hogs didn't know what Miles was talking about and had confused looks on their faces. They also found it weird that Miles was knocked out from the cube's blast; they feared that it hadn't worked and Miles hadn't received any powers.

"What did you see?" wondered Gard.

Miles first asked if anything like this happened to any of them. Will shook his head, saying no one had seen any intense visions like what Miles was claiming to have.

"I saw a road. It was leading me to a building," Miles stated. "Inside the building was a group of people all standing around a hospital patient."

"Miles, you passed out for a moment after getting hit by the cube. Maybe you just had a dream?" Timber replied.

"No, I felt like I was there, witnessing all of this in person," Miles uttered. Miles said he didn't recognize any of the people or the building.

Eric picked up his laptop and clicked open some of his files he had gathered when he was doing research on the Havocs. He had photos of some of the Havocs members saved into his computer and showed them to Miles.

"Any of the people in your dream look like these guys?" Eric asked as Miles looked at the photos.

"What makes you think Miles would have dreams about people he's never seen before?" Hayden asked, thinking that this was dumb thing to do.

Eric had a thought that since the cube came from the Havocs, then maybe it could show Miles where they were. It was a crazy theory, but oddly enough, Miles did recognize someone in the photo from his dream.

"That guy was in the building," Miles said, pointing to the photo of Reed. The other Hogs knew this man, for he was the one who threw the ball at Juice last week. He was the guy who tried to burn Hayden with a fire poker, and he was a part of the kidnapping mission. How Miles could have a dream about him was a mystery to the Hogs.

"Do you know where the building is? Do you remember what it looks like?" wondered Will.

"The building was old and abandoned looking. Kind of looked like a prison of some kind," Miles replied.

Eric was already looking up old abandoned prisons on his laptop. "What about the road, any specific details?" wondered Eric.

"Actually, there was a *warning* sign on the road. It was one of those chemical warning signs," Miles answered.

With that information, it didn't take Eric long to find a photo of the prison. He turned the laptop to Miles and asked if it was the building he saw in his dream. Miles saw the exact same view of the building in his vision. The Hogs now felt a taste of excitement rush through them. If this was indeed the Havocs' secret location, then maybe they could turn them in to the police and end this constant fear of their next retaliation.

"This is nuts, just waiting in here!" Timber shouted.

Having advanced strength was one thing, but having visions was just too much to take in at the time. This was strange and new to everyone for none of them had any vision like this before. They then asked Miles if he felt any stronger. Miles tried lifting the car but failed to do so. His strength was just as normal as before.

"Maybe the cube gave Miles different powers than the rest of us," Gard suggested.

"We did this in hopes to cure Miles of his disease. Maybe we should figure out if that worked before we do anything else," Timber stated.

"I actually feel great. Yeah, I failed to show off any new strength, but I feel healthier than ever," Miles answered.

"Good, now that you're better, I say we get revenge on the Havocs!" Hayden said forcefully.

"I second that!" Gard added enthusiastically.

"You guys are putting a lot of faith in something that may not even be real," Eric replied.

"If we have a chance to come in on a surprise attack against the Havocs, I say we take it. Just look at what happened to Juice. He's not with us anymore!" Hayden shouted.

"He's just grounded for ditching school last week…He's not dead," Timber explained.

"Well, I'm voting we start playing some offense for a change!" Hayden added.

"Hayden's right. We already lost Juice from an attack from the Havocs. It's our time to attack them!" Gard yelled out.

"Again, Juice isn't dead, just grounded!" Timber stated, finding it weird his friends were acting like Juice had been killed.

Will said that a simple anonymous call to the police giving away the Havocs' location could be all that it took. The group realized that perhaps a simple phone call could end this war between the two groups. Eric got directions to the prison and saw that it wasn't that far away. Hayden said he knew of that location. Hayden's elder brother told him that the prison was haunted; he was told stories of how the high school football team used to drive out there to hear the monster sounds that people claimed to hear.

"Miles, could you...I don't know...take another look at the building?" Gard asked.

Miles said that he could try and closed his eyes and concentrated hard on the inside of the building. He focused as hard as he could on that specific location. And in the blink of an eye, Miles disappeared into thin air. *Poof was* heard as Miles disappeared. The Hogs' jaws dropped in shock.

"Miles?" Timber uttered.

"Hey, where did you go?" shouted Gard. The Hogs all looked around the room, very confused and worried.

"Eric, if you're so smart...where did Miles go?" Hayden asked.

"I, I don't know," Eric said, sounding confused.

"He just imploded!" shouted Timber.

"Someone call his cell!" Will yelled out as he walked around the room.

"That won't work. His phone's right here," Hayden stated, picking up Miles's phone off the car.

The Hogs grew very worried, for they feared the worst.

"Maybe he went to the prison. It was the last place he was thinking of," Gard said.

"But that's not possible!" Timber replied.

"I say we go down there and check!" Gard shouted.

"And if he's not there?" Hayden wondered.

"We just tell Miles's parents that their son vanished into thin air," Timber uttered with a worried look on his face.

"Look, matter can't be created or destroyed. But it can be moved. Gard's idea of Miles being at the prison may be the best shot at finding him," Eric explained.

"Well, if he is at the prison, then he's in a room full of Havocs…if he's not dead…he may end up getting killed!" Will said in fear.

The Hogs took a moment to catch their breath. Then they charged to their cars in a hurry. Eric got into Gard's car, while Will and Timber got into Hayden's. Hayden knew the way to the prison from going there once before with his brother. He yelled out to Gard telling him to keep up. The cars spit out dirt as they sped out of the yard and onto the road.

Miles found himself standing inside the prison he saw in his vision. Miles recognized the room from his vision but was stumped on how he got there. He went from standing in Eric's garage to standing in the prison in the blink of an eye. The room was a wide-open space with a line of windows on the west side of the room. On the north and south sides of the room were exit doors; the door facing south led to a stairway, while the door on the north side led to another room. Miles turned around to the east side of the room and saw a hospital bed; he tiptoed his way to the bed and saw a large man lying there.

The man in the bed was hooked up to breathing tubes, IVs, and a heart monitor. Miles saw that the man seemed to be in a coma. When Miles had his vision, he saw this man open his eyes. Miles thought maybe the man would wake up, but it didn't look like that was going to happen. He remembered the room having more people in it, but the room was empty now; it was just him and the coma man. Miles didn't want to wait for the men to show up, so he tried to get out of there. He first tried the door facing the south side, but it was locked up tight. Miles started heading to the door on the north side, but he could hear people coming from the other side of the door. Feeling nervous and scared, Miles looked around and saw a utility closet on the east side of the room and dashed toward it. He closed the door after getting inside just before the Havocs entered the room.

The entire group of the Havocs entered the room; there were only five of them. One of the members named Mitch headed over to the man in the hospital bed with a medical bag. Baron and Reed stood by while Mitch hooked the patient up to an empty blood bag.

"So how long would this take?" asked Reed.

"I don't know. We're going to bleed him out slowly. It may be a short wait if we're lucky," Baron replied.

Reed found it laughable thinking that their luck would start changing for the better now.

The Havocs' plan to wake their leader from his coma involved using the cube. They did have a backup plan in case they never found the cube. The backup plan was too risky because it could kill him. But things had changed now that the Havocs knew where the cube was. The Havocs felt like they couldn't recover the cube from the Hogs, so they felt like they had no choice but to go to plan B.

Their leader Cain was hit with several doses of tranquilizer darts from his greatest enemy, Ray. Ray put a special chemical inside the tranquilizer. The chemical could keep the tranquilizer inside his bloodstream and never wear out if it could feed off Cain's Loomation inside him.

The Havocs' plan to wake Cain up was to drain his blood. The chemical flowed through Cain's blood; a man of Cain's size and weight took a certain amount of sedative to keep him asleep. The Havocs felt that if they could get him to bleed out enough of the chemical, then he'd wake up. They feared that Cain would die from blood loss during this procedure, so they had never attempted it. But today, they were going to wake him even if it killed him.

Miles was inside the utility closet listening in and was praying that they didn't need anything from the closet. He stayed focused on keeping himself quiet and not moving too much. His fear of being discovered made this easy for him. He hoped that his friends were out there and coming for him.

The Hogs arrived to one of the warning signs that bordered the prison. They drove their cars up onto the grass and hid them from the road by parking behind the trees. After the cars were parked, they continued on foot toward the prison. The five Hogs were moving in a hurry because they feared that their friend was in danger. They spotted the prison and took cover behind a rotting tree log lying on the ground.

Hayden had his eyes in binoculars looking at the prison. "No cars in the parking lot, but there are some garages where the Havocs could have parked," Hayden stated.

"Well, keeping your cars hidden is a smart thing to do when you want people to think you're not home," Timber replied.

"Any way in?" wondered Will.

The group could see the prison was surrounded by a chain-link fence.

"We could jump that fence," Gard said with confidence.

"Yeah, but if those security cameras work, then our element of surprise will be blown," Hayden said while keeping his eyes in the binoculars. Hayden then said that there were no cameras facing the south side door.

"That could be our way in," Will uttered.

"It's probably locked," Eric stated.

"Then I'll kick it down!" Gard shouted impatiently.

"We don't know what's in there. We don't even know if Miles is in there," Eric added.

The Hogs planned; Will, Hayden, and Gard would go in, while Timber and Eric kept watch. The Hogs inside would send a text to the Hogs outside if the Havocs were in there. After that, the Hogs outside would make an anonymous call to the police. If the Hogs found Miles inside, they would get him out. It was important for the Hogs to get out of the building before the police arrived. They didn't want to talk to the police about how they got involved with the Havocs.

Timber and Eric stayed by the log, while Will, Hayden, and Gard approached the prison from the south side. Gard jumped to the top of the fence, swung his leg around the top, and slipped down onto the other side followed by Will and Hayden.

So far so good, Will thought to himself as Gard checked the door, which was indeed locked.

"Can you force it open?" asked Will.

Gard got in close to the seal of the door and with a show of strength pulled open the door. Due to the forced entry, the door was torn up a bit at the seam, but Gard prepared for that by doing his best to keep the split wood from causing too much noise.

"All right, you guys ready?" Gard asked, looking at Will and Hayden.

The three were slightly hesitant because if the Havocs were indeed inside, their lives could be in danger. But if their friend Miles was inside, they felt that they had to do something. Eric was watching them with the binoculars and saw the three head inside.

"They're in," Eric reported to Timber.

"We're going to need another bag!" Mitch yelled as he removed the fourth bag of blood from Cain's tube. As Mitch carried the full bag over to the table to place it with the other three bags, he felt the bag slip out of his hand and helplessly watched it splatter onto the floor.

"I don't think we should drain any more. He's already completely pale," Barron stated while looking at Cain.

"His heart is still pumping. His superstrength has granted him a healthy heart to handle something like this," Reed replied in defense of continuing.

"He should be able to handle at least a half bag more," Mitch said.

"Maybe we drew out enough already. Maybe he's just not waking up due to the lack of blood now," Baron added.

"We have fresh blood ready to be transferred into him. I say, if he can take a half bag more, we push forward. That way we won't have to do this again, if you're wrong," Reed explained.

As much as Baron didn't like this idea, he knew Reed was right. He didn't want to bleed Cain out again. It was better to do all that they could now, so Baron hooked another bag up to Cain.

Will, Hayden, and Gard were on the south side of the room behind the locked door. They were looking through a small square-shaped window on the top of the door.

"Miles was right," Gard stated.

"I'll text Eric," Will reported and sent Eric a text telling him that the Havocs were indeed inside the prison and to call the police.

"I don't see Miles," Hayden uttered.

"Maybe he already got out, or maybe he was never here," Gard said.

"He has to be here. This is exactly what he described from his dream. That can't be a coincidence," Will mentioned and then checked his phone. Eric sent him a text saying he called the police, and the highway patrol would be there soon. The Hogs didn't have much time. They had to find Miles and get out of there fast.

Inside the utility closet, Miles had his eye up to the gap in the door's seal and was looking at the men. This was exactly what he saw in his vision, just from a different point of view. He knew that the men's plan of waking their leader up would be successful. He was just hoping that they would leave the room afterward so he could sneak his way out. Then he heard someone yell at Mitch, telling him to clean up the blood off the floor before it left a stain.

"I think there's a mop and bucket in the closet," Baron reported.

Miles's panicked heart skipped a beat, for his greatest fear at that moment had come true. He watched Mitch walk right toward the closet. Miles backed up against the wall, searching for any possible place to hide when the door was opened. It was a tiny closet, and Miles was a tall guy, so unless Mitch was blind, there was no way he could miss a high school kid inside.

The doors opened, and Miles was caught red-handed. Mitch was stunned at first but then grabbed Miles and pulled him out to the center of the room. "We got an intruder!" Mitch shouted as he pushed Miles to the floor. Miles saw himself being surrounded by the Havocs, all gazing at him with confused eyes.

Reed took a close look at Miles's shirt. Miles was wearing a T-shirt saying, "We're the Hang Out Group Hogs!"

"I've seen that shirt before. One of those kids who burned down our mansion had the same shirt on!" Baron stated. "He's with those high school kids!"

The Hogs on the other side of the door on the south side saw all of this.

"Guys, he's here," Hayden whispered loudly.

"We have to save him! If we don't, they could use him as a hostage for the police," Will added.

"I say we kill him!" Reed yelled out.

"Look, a ton of people have this shirt. The Hang Out Group is a pretty famous underground band. I was at a concert last summer with a ton of kids my age all buying the same shirt." Miles was shocked with his lying skills in the heat of the moment. "I'm here due to a dare from my older brothers and cousins. They said if I spent the whole day in here, they'd buy me a new dirt bike!"

Miles couldn't believe the silver tongue he grew in such a dramatic time. The lie provided some *insurance* in a way. The lie was well detailed but not overdone to look like a planned script. Miles was happy that he mentioned his brothers and cousins; if he told the Havocs that no one knew where he was, they would have just killed him.

"He's lying!" Reed yelled, not believing the story.

Fortunately for Miles, most of the Havocs were unsure if Miles was lying or not. They knew that the high school kids didn't know their secret location, and Miles was a kid they had never seen before. There was more evidence that Miles was telling the truth than lying.

Just then, the men heard a noise from the hospital bed. They all faced toward the bed and saw that Cain was able to move his hand. Baron, Reed and a few others rushed over to Cain's side. Cain opened his eyes, for he had finally awakened.

"Stop the blood drain!" Baron ordered.

Mitch acted fast and put an end to the blood draining. Baron then ordered someone to retrieve the fresh blood from the coolers to get ready to pump into Cain. As one of the men headed toward the cooler where the fresh blood was located, he spotted something from outside the window. It was a highway patrol car followed by three more police vehicles.

"The police are here!" the man shouted with fear as the others rushed to the window and saw that they had been discovered by the police.

"I knew it, he's a spy!" Reed shouted as he pointed a loaded handgun to Miles's head.

Just then, the door facing the south side was suddenly knocked off its hinges and slammed down to the floor. Gard ran in from the door and sprinted right toward Reed. Gard was fast enough to push Reed against the wall before Reed could aim his gun at him. Will and Hayden ran in the room to get in close to Miles.

"Miles, you all right?" asked Will.

"I'm fine," Miles replied as the three Hogs stood guard for Miles and stared down the Havocs.

"Shoot them!" shouted Baron.

"Sorry, Baron, the police are here. It's every man for himself!" Mitch said as he headed toward the north side door.

Mitch wasn't the only one running to the door. Two other Havocs hurried toward the door in an attempt to retreat. They felt like their only hope to avoid the police was to flee into the woods. Three Havocs took the north side exit and ran to the fence. Some were able to climb over the fence, while one dug under.

Inside, the Hogs just kept their intimidating stare on Baron. "You can fight us if you want," Hayden uttered.

"But you know you'll lose," Gard added.

Baron walked over to Reed to help him to his feet. "This isn't over," Baron said as he helped Reed walk out of the room.

Will then heard his phone ring. "Will, you need to get out of there!" Eric stated over the phone. "The police have the whole place surrounded. They already caught the Havocs who tried to make a run for it in the woods. They're sending in officers now to arrest whoever's inside!"

"Thanks for the update," Will replied before hanging up his phone. "We better bail before they arrest us next," Will said to his friends.

"If the police see us running, they're going to think we're with them," said Hayden.

"I say we stay inside, act like we were hostages," Gard replied.

"We can't tell them the truth. The police won't believe it. If we try to lie in any way, the Havocs could call us out on it," Will explained.

"What if I can get us out of here?" Miles uttered.

The three Hogs looked at Miles with confused glances. "I got myself here just by concentrating too hard on this room. I think I can get us back to Eric's garage by doing the same thing," Miles stated.

"Not the craziest thing I heard today. I'm in," Gard said with a degree of confidence.

"You sure about this?" wondered Will.

Miles reached out his arm, telling them to hang on. Will, Hayden, and Gard all took hold of Miles's arm. Miles closed his eyes and concentrated on Eric's garage. The Hogs grew worried because they could hear the police heading up the stairs. Then in the blink of an eye, the four Hogs were standing in Eric's garage. All they heard was the air whooshing around them upon their arrival. They looked around in disbelief.

"Did we just teleport?" wondered Hayden.

"I think we did," Will said, looking around the room.

"THAT'S AWESOME!" Gard shouted.

The guys started to laugh in disbelief and excitement. They were feeling quite joyful at escaping a bad situation with no trace of being there. Miles thanked the guys, saying that they saved his life back there. Hayden was mad that he didn't even get to punch anybody. Will took out his phone to call Timber and Eric. He told the two to get into the cars parked on the side of the road and get back to Eric's place. Gard then shouted over the phone, telling them to also bring a pizza.

Back at the prison, Baron and Reed didn't head to the exit. They headed down to the basement of the prison. In the basement, they found a control panel in front of a heavy door. Baron punched a secret code into the control panel, and the front door swung open. The two walked past the door and closed it behind them. They felt that this might be the safest place to stay because the police would be unable to open the door. It was a smart plan. As time went by, they heard no attempt by the police to open the door. They waited for hours, and when they finally got out, they were relieved to be out of their hiding place.

The place the two were hiding was in the hallway where all the creatures were locked up. They were normally quite during the daytime, but when nighttime came, they started to hear some growls and snores. They were lucky the police didn't hear any of that. The men walked around the empty prison; the police had taken everything: the guns, cars, and even Cain.

The Hogs all sat in Eric's basement eating pizza. In a way, they were celebrating. They believed that all the Havocs were arrested, and the nightmare was over. No more surprise attacks from people trying to kill them. With the Havocs locked up, there was also no one out there to try to steal the cube from them. They still felt that they should make sure it stayed safe, knowing that there were other bad people out there besides the Havocs.

"So…visions and teleporting," Eric said, looking at Miles. "Just when I think I've seen it all, and things couldn't get any stranger…you come and mess that all up!" he said humorously.

"It's weird that you didn't get advanced strength from the cube. You upset about that?" wondered Gard.

"I can teleport. I think that's way cooler!" Miles responded. "Not to mention, I've never felt healthier in my life. I think my next hospital visit I go on will be my last!"

"You know that you can't tell anyone about your powers," Will mentioned.

"Just tell them that you were saved by magic. No one will believe it. If you vanish out of the room after, then they might," Gard said, making everyone laugh.

The group felt that their transition into their powers had gone well. They did have this feeling of being different from everyone else, but that was a feeling that they always had way before the cube came into their lives. The Hogs always felt that they were a part of a special group, and now they knew that it was true.

CHAPTER 21

Prom Night

Saturday Morning, May 22, 2010

In a hospital, a man walked up to the nurses' station desk. The desk was crowded with a few nurses and two police officers.

"Excuse me, I'm the lawyer for the patient found during the Havocs' arrest. I was sent from the DA's office. I'm here to ask if he would like to press charges on the ones who kidnapped him and tried to steal his organs," stated the man.

"He's been resting, getting his strength back since we brought him in. He hasn't said much. Doctors say he's still in shock," said one of the officers.

"Well, I'll go check on him to see if he's awake," the lawyer said.

The officer then led the lawyer over to the victim's room. They both entered the room where the victim was wide awake in bed watching TV. The lawyer faced the officer and asked if he could leave the room. The officer turned and closed the door on his way out.

After the door was closed, the act of pretending to be a lawyer was dropped, and the man relaxed. "Anything good on the TV, Cain?" asked Baron, who had to pretend to be a lawyer in order to get in the same room as Cain. He even wore fake glasses to help hide his face from being recognized since the wanted posters of him were everywhere.

"I'm mainly in it for the commercials," Cain replied without taking his eyes off the screen. "It's amazing how much you can learn about all that you missed out on by watching the latest car, phone, and beer ads," Cain replied.

"Wait until you discover the internet. You'll be amazed by all the funny cat videos," Baron stated as he walked closer to Cain.

Cain clicked the mute button on the TV remote, turning off the sound to chat with Baron.

"Where's Kate?" Cain asked first, for his daughter's safety was most important to him.

Baron stated that after Cain fell into his coma, Jason kick-started Operation Better Life. It was a protection operation set up for her and Cain. Jason took Kate into hiding because her father could not protect her while he was in his coma.

"Where's Ray?" wondered Cain.

"Ray went off the grid the day after you fell into your coma. He left everything behind, and we were able to steal all his documents, books, and weapons. The word from his followers was that he was satisfied with the results from his last attack on you."

"Well, now that I'm awake, he'll be making a move against us soon. Are the rest of the Havocs at the mansion?" asked Cain.

"Yeah, about that...," Baron said with a worried hesitation.

"Don't tell me you let that place get worse while I was asleep," Cain replied.

"The Renshaw Mansion burned down. It's just a pile of burnt wood and ash now. As far as the rest of the Havocs go...counting you and I... there are only three of us left."

This information was shocking to Cain, especially since these actions were not even caused by Ray. Ray was the only one whom Cain knew who had the firepower to do something like all that. "How could you let this happen?" he said in a mean tone. Cain was more upset about his house burning down than anything. He was born in that house. It's where he lived his whole life, so knowing that it was gone made him very upset.

"Things took a turn for the worse when you took your *little nap*. Ray didn't need to intervene to take down the Havocs. We fell apart without you," Baron replied in a frustrated tone. "I struggled and tried to keep our numbers high, but as time went by, more and more people were leaving or getting arrested. We couldn't handle any of the big jobs anymore, so people stopped hiring us. Without the money, more men left." Baron hesitated before he brought up this next part. "Then we gained a new enemy."

Cain got a worried look on his face; a new enemy on top of Ray still being out there could be a big problem. Baron entered the room holding a folder. At this time, he handed it over to Cain. Cain looked through the notes and pages of information inside the folder as Baron gave him the sum of it all.

Baron said that a few weeks ago, the search for the cube ended when four high schoolers reported it found. Baron said that the four boys gained advanced strength from the cube, just as Ray designed it to do. Baron said a few attempts were made to retrieve the cube from the boys, but their numbers grew, and in the end, the boys were the one who turned in the remaining Havocs to the police. The pages in the file had the information of the high school boys' names and addresses of their homes.

"You let my empire fall due to a few kids," Cain said, embarrassed by that statement.

"Six kids with advanced strength. You should know better than any of us how hard it is to defeat someone with that kind of power," Baron replied.

"These kids have the cube still?" Cain asked.

Baron stated that yes, they still possessed the cube, and he started talking about how much stronger the Havocs would be if they had the cube. But Cain didn't want an army of superpowered people on his side. Cain was born with his powers and found it offensive that people could just receive those powers from a cube. He wanted the Hogs dead and the cube destroyed.

The news of Cain wanting the cube destroyed didn't sit right with Baron. Baron thought Cain to be a fool for ordering something as powerful as the cube to be destroyed. Baron knew the cube was the key to the Havocs' rise to power once again. But Cain gave his orders and wasn't going to be talked out of it.

"How do you plan on killing the Hogs?" asked Baron.

"Hogs?" questioned Cain.

Baron let out a small laugh under his breath. He explained that he had seen two of the kids wear a self-made T-shirt with the words *We're the Hang Out Group Hogs!*

Cain told Baron to use the creature in cell 108 at the prison to kill the Hogs. Baron was suddenly a little shocked and worried, for he feared the idea of getting anywhere near those creatures. Baron asked Cain if he would assist on this attack. Cain said he couldn't, as he wasn't up to full strength yet. The hospital was feeding him and providing a bed for him, so he was going to stay until he felt fully recovered. Baron said he had no idea how to handle any of the creatures.

"That's right, you joined the group after we stopped using the creatures," Cain said, thinking out loud and for the moment, free of any cloudy thoughts that might come from being in a coma. "In the basement of the prison, there is an audio system. Turn that on first. The sound coming out of the speakers would calm the animals down so much that you could reach out and touch them without any harm. In the cell, you'll find a Walkman. Take it and strap it to the head of the animal and start playing the cassette tape. The tape would play the same sounds coming from the speakers. The tape has an eight-hour playback track, so if the sound keeps playing into the creature's ears, it won't kill you," Cain explained like he had been through this process a dozen times.

Baron got his orders and left the room, leaving the folder with the Hogs' information with Cain. Baron made it to a car in the parking lot. The car was stolen and driven by Reed. Reed asked about Cain. He wanted to know what he wanted them to do.

"He wants us to kill the Hogs," Baron replied.

Later That Day

Hayden drove his pickup truck to the pond with Miles in the passenger seat. When the pond came into view, Hayden put the car into park. Both Hayden and Miles took in a deep sniff of that pond smell found in the presence of that great outdoor life. They got out of the truck and started unloading the small fishing boat from the back of the truck. After Miles untied the rope wrapped around the boat, Hayden simply lifted it with one hand, held it up to his shoulders, and carried it to the water.

"Wow," Miles said, amazed at seeing Hayden carry the boat by himself. Miles pointed out that it used to take them about ten minutes to get the boat off the truck and slide it to the water. Now it only took a few seconds. Hayden said that this whole new gifted strength felt common to him now, and he placed the boat into the water. Miles carried over some of the fishing supplies. Now that Miles was closer to the water, with one foot in the boat and one on the shore, he got a better view of the pond. An overwhelming feeling of joy came to him, for just last week he felt a fun day fishing at the pond would be something he would never be able to enjoy again. That cube was a real lifesaver for him.

Miles's last visit to the hospital made all the doctors speechless, as Miles's disease was now completely gone. The doctors ran tons of tests, and they all came back negative. Miles was relieved that the doctors didn't get any evidence whatsoever about Miles's new powers. Nothing on the x-rays, nothing on the CT scan, and even nothing on the blood work. Whatever Miles had inside him, humans hadn't invented anything to detect it. This was great because Miles feared that he would have become a government lab rat with scientists poking him with needles, trying to figure out what made him tick. So not only was Miles fully cured, he was free to live a normal life. Well, as normal as he could.

"You're sure that you're okay with missing your prom tonight?" Miles asked once again to his friend Hayden. Hayden said that a night out on the pond with his fishing buddy sounded way better than prom. Miles was happy to hear that. Hayden was in a long-term relationship that ended in late winter. This was part of the reason why Hayden had his buddies coming over most weekends; he didn't like spending his nonschool nights alone. With Hayden no longer in the mood to attend his prom and Miles being from a different school and unable to attend, they chose to go fishing together. They were the only two members who went fishing on a regular basis. This fishing trip was great because he was able to find a way to keep his mind off the prom. After weeks of hospitable beds, it was a relief for Miles to get out on the water.

Back at Juice's house, Will, Timber, and Eric were waiting for Juice to complete his tux attire. Will was once again tying Juice's tie for him. The small school that the boys attended shared their prom with the other small school from the nearby town. The schools would alternate hosting the dance and the after-prom party every other year. This year the Bay School was hosting the dance, while the school the Hogs attended hosted the after-prom party. There was a busy itinerary for the Hang Out Group that night. First, the four Hogs would drive to their school to meet up with their parents and their dates for the night. A limo, which they all chipped in for, would be waiting for them there. Once they got there, their parents took photos. At the school, the students could leave a bag of clothes in the locker room to change into for the after-prom party. After that, the limo would take them to their dinner, then to Bay for the dance. After the dance, the school would provide a school bus (for the students who showed up by limo) to take them from the dance to the after-prom party after they first stopped at the fast-food restaurant locations. At the after-prom party, the students would change in the locker rooms, enjoy the party, and take their dates home in their cars, which were left at the school's parking lot at the beginning of all of this.

Will had a special favor to ask his friends before they took off to the school. Will oversaw the cleanup crew Sunday morning. He and other students who were part of the student council had to clean up the dance the next morning every year. The other school's council, on the other hand, cleaned up the after-prom party. The special favor he asked his friends was their help on cleaning up after the prom was over. Will explained that he had permission from the Bay School to start cleanup right after the dance.

"Why do you want to start right after the dance?" asked Timber.

"Well…I thought that if we could get a head start right away, I wouldn't be wasting my whole Sunday morning," Will responded.

"Yeah, what about the after-party? We have to take the bus because the limo is dropping us off," Eric added

"We'll only clean up for about a half hour, and then Hayden's going to pick us up and take us to the party," Will answered.

"Yeah, but I was going to get some tacos when the bus takes us to the fast-food places," Juice whined.

"What's the point of working if it's only for a half hour?" questioned Timber.

"I think I got it," Eric stated. "You want to use your strength, don't you?"

Will admitted that Eric was right. He said that there was some stuff in that gym that took many people to move. Will knew that it could take a long time if the student council moved it. But if Will could use his advanced strength, he could have all the heavy stuff packed away in quick fashion. He couldn't use his advanced strength in front of the other students, but he could do so in front of the members of the Hang Out Group.

"If you can move all those things yourself, why do you need us?" asked Juice.

"For the story," Eric said, knowing the answer. It would be hard to explain how Will managed to move all the heavy things by himself to people, so if Will could say he had help from his friends, the story would be easier to believe. He would feel safer telling this story if his friends stayed behind as proof. Eric and Timber agreed, but Juice said only if they could stop for tacos afterward. Will agreed to the condition of tacos and even offered to pay. After that, the Hogs were all dressed and ready to go.

The Hang Out Group all had dates that night. The boys were sociable outside the group. Will's date was also on the student council. Juice asked one of the stars from the spring musical, whom he got to know during his time as a member of the stage crew. Timber asked a girl from his job at the supermarket, and Eric was taking the captain of the Bay quiz bowl team. Over their years of competing against each other at the quiz bowl meets, they had developed a friendship. Gard wasn't taking the limo with the others; he was taking his girlfriend to the dance in his car. He too was asked to help clean up after the prom with Will and the others, but he passed. He had plans on staying with his girlfriend for the night. Things between the two hadn't been going well, and he was hoping tonight would be a good night for them.

Out at the old prison where the Havocs were arrested earlier that week, Baron and Reed returned with a stolen moving truck. A new lock was now placed on the fence with a large "NO TRESPASSING" sign.

Reed used bolt cutters to cut the lock, and Baron drove the truck up to the front door. There was another lock on the front door, and Reed used his bolt cutters on that one also. Once inside, the two made it to the basement. They walked up to the locked door and entered the code into the lock control panel. The door swung open; the two could hear the snoring of the creatures inside. They didn't switch on the lights; they just used the lights from their flashlights to guide their way.

"All right, which one did Cain tell us to get?" whispered Reed.

"The one from cell 108," Baron replied.

Baron found a table that held a couple of record players. Both players had the same record placed on the machine; it was a record with the title "Sounds of the Garden." Baron searched the table and found many Walkmans and headphones also sitting on the table. There was a notebook that sat at the table. Baron opened it up and found it was instructions on how to remove the creatures. After Baron read the instructions, he pushed the power button on the record players. The records started to turn, and Baron placed the needle onto one of the discs. Once the needle touched the surface, the sound echoed throughout the basement. This startled both Baron and Reed. They shone their flashlights onto the walls of the basement and saw the large speakers that were scattered all over the basement. The scary chilling sound of the creatures' snoring grew silent.

Baron let out a small laugh, feeling all powerful at this moment. Reed told Baron that he found cell 108. Baron grabbed one of the Walkmans and headphones and headed to the cell. Another digital control panel controlled the lock of the cell door. Baron knew that the code to open any of the jail cell doors was the same code that opened the basement door. Before Baron could push any of the buttons, Reed stopped him.

"Are you sure about this?" Reed asked with fear in his voice.

Baron nodded and pushed in the code to open the door. The creature inside was terrifying, a large beast covered in dark-brown hair. The thing looked to have a similar build of a grizzly bear but with the body of a human. The thing was about eight feet tall with a twenty-two-foot size. There was a pale face buried within the hair of the skull; with sick-looking yellow eyes and dirty teeth, it was repulsive. Baron instructed Reed to place the headphones over the creature's ears, while he strapped the Walkman to the preplaced belt the creature wore around its waist. Reed moved very slowly placing the headphones onto the beast's head.

"Make sure you tighten it tightly. They should stay on if you do it right," Baron informed Reed.

Reed didn't realize that he hadn't properly tightened the head strap, but it held on, so he thought he did it right. Once the creature was prepared, the two gently woke the animal. Their hearts stopped when it woke. But the creature was as gentle as a common house cat. This relaxed the men a bit, but they were still petrified of the thing changing its mood. The tape in the Walkman was playing the same sounds heard from the record player. They walked the creature to the back of the truck outside the prison. The beast had zero resistance to the men; it was as if it was sleepwalking. The men turned off the record player in the basement, locked it back up, and made their way to the Hogs.

Baron asked Reed if he had any idea where the Hogs would be. Reed had been able to track down the social media pages of all the Hang Out Group members. Reed now knew all their names and where they all went to school. Reed knew the perfect time to attack the Hogs. According to the prom schedule posted on their school's website, tonight was prom night, and after prom was the after-prom party. The site also gave a positive shout-out to the head of the student council, Will, and his friends for volunteering a half hour after the dance to get a head start on cleaning up the gym. Baron said that would be a perfect time for them to stick the monster onto the Hogs.

After the dance, the boys' dates all took the school bus to the after-prom party event. The girls knew that the boys were staying behind for a short while to get a head start on cleaning up and had plans to meet up at the after-prom party. All the grown-ups and chaperones at the school headed to the after-prom to continue their duties there. The boys had their change of clothes with them and changed in the bathroom. Once the dance lights were off and the regular gym lights were turned back on, the place looked like a lot of work.

"Well, this looks like fun," Juice lied.

Juice headed over to the DJ table to play some songs while Will, Timber, and Eric helped move the heavy snack bar back into storage. Juice played some songs and just sat on a chair with his feet up on the DJ table. He said that he'd text Hayden to tell him to head over, claiming that they'd be done by the time he got there. Eric pointed out that they would get it done faster if Juice helped. Juice then pointed out that the wait for Hayden to arrive would feel longer if they got done sooner.

The parking lot was nearly empty; the only vehicle in the lot was a moving truck that Baron and Reed arrived in not too long ago. The men waited until the parking lot was empty before running up to the school building. From outside the school, they were able to see the gym lights on and spotted the Hogs inside. The two ran back to the truck because their plan of attack was now clear for a go.

"Help me get the creature out of the truck," Baron ordered Reed.

Baron pulled open the truck door, and inside the creature was sitting in the corner. The Walkman was still providing the meditating trance sounds into the headphones on the creature. Baron climbed into the back of the truck and helped the beast to his feet. Baron led the creature to the edge of the truck, and the two took a step down. Baron was on the animal's right side, and Reed was on its left. The two were walking it up to the school. The plan was to lead the monster into the school, and once Baron and Reed reached a safe distance, they would shoot the Walkman, causing the animal to lose its mellow mood and enter a wild rampage state.

"How are we going to get the beast back into the truck?" asked Reed.

"Oh, we can let this one go after it kills the Hogs," replied Baron. Baron told Reed that after the Hogs were dead, they'd find that cube.

"We meeting up with Cain after we get the cube?" wondered Reed.

"No, we're not taking the cube to Cain. If he gets it, he'll destroy it," Baron responded with a sense of urgency.

This news shocked Reed; he questioned why Cain would want to do such a thing. Baron wasn't fully sure about that. Baron explained that Cain ordered him to destroy the cube before he fell into his coma. At the time, Baron believed it was to keep Ray from making an army of superstrong people. But Baron thought Cain would have changed his mind now that Ray had disappeared and with the Havocs in such bad shape. But Cain still wanted the cube destroyed, and Baron wasn't going to let that happen.

"So what are we going to do after we get the cube?" asked Reed.

"We're going to rebuild the Havocs ourselves. Look at all the progress made by the group by just having one person with advanced strength. We'll have a whole army!" Baron stated.

"And if Cain tries to stop us?" wondered Reed.

"Cain's time for leadership is over. The man's a dinosaur. He won't be strong enough to take on an army of advanced soldiers!" Baron replied with determination in his voice.

The two were now very optimistic for the future and were excited for a much-needed change of direction for the Havocs. Reed pointed out that now that they knew how to control the creatures of the prison, they could pull more of them out of retirement.

"How much longer do we have on that cassette tape?" wondered Reed. The Walkman was playing a cassette tape of sounds of the garden on a loop. Reed got nervous that the tape would stop playing soon.

"Oh, don't worry, it's an eight-hour tape. We have plenty of time," Baron explained.

As the two laughed about their glorious plan to take over the group and to finally have a way to kill the Hogs and retrieve the cube, they failed to check one very important thing. The cassette tape had an eight-hour playback time, but the batteries on that Walkman were in dire need of a change. The batteries drained out right then and there in the school's parking lot. The sound coming out of the headphones strapped to the beast's ears stopped, and the beast seemed to wake up as if it was coming out of a hypnotic state. The two men were still laughing, having no idea there was anything wrong. The beast grew furious, wild, and deadly all within a second. The beast ripped the headphones off its head and let out a mighty growl. The men both screamed at the top of their lungs in fear; they were so terrified one of them even urinated in his pants.

Baron reached for his gun but was quickly grabbed by the beast before he could defend himself. The beast grabbed Baron and smashed him into Reed. The two were slammed into the ground hard; they couldn't get up. They were gasping for air and could feel that their bones were broken. The beast raised its very large foot above the two and smashed them both to death. The beast looked over at the school. He could hear the music inside the building; it incensed the beast even more, and it started to charge at the building.

Inside the school, the Hogs heard the monster's growl and were lost in thought trying to figure out what that was. Then they heard a noise from the front door. It sounded like someone came in. Will, Timber, and Eric, on the side of the gym closer to the front door, eased their eyes over to the entrance. The three saw a giant beast rushing right at them at full speed. They all scattered, running in different directions.

"IT'S BIGFOOT!" Timber shouted as loudly as he could as the monster chose to run after Timber, ignoring Will and Eric. The monster ran up behind Timber who could feel the air of the beast's breath on the back of his neck.

"You think that this is another Havocs attack?" Eric asked Will. He was speaking so fast it was hard for Will to hear.

"It must be," Will responded.

Timber ran toward the snack table and slid across the gym floor right under the table, landing on the other side. Once Bigfoot reached the table, he became motionless for a quick moment. The beast pounded the center of the table with one hand, making it collapse. When the beast was doing that, Will ran up to the monster to attack it. Once Will got in close enough, the beast swung his left arm at Will as if he was batting a fly away. Will flew back through the gym and landed hard on the floor.

Will felt the air get knocked out of him and lost sight for a few seconds. The hit hurt, but he was able to get back up to his feet. The beast grew confused when it saw Will stand back up. It seemed to be mad as it gave Will a hateful look. Eric saw the angry look on Bigfoot's face and was awestruck.

"This might sound crazy, but I think that it's mad that you didn't die from that attack, Will," Eric announced. The group all took a hard glance at the beast, studying its mood.

"For the record, I'm thrilled that you didn't die from that attack, Will!" Juice added.

The beast started charging at Will; everyone yelled out to him to run.

"We have to get this thing out of here before it does any more damage!" Will shouted as he was running for his life. Juice then threw a basketball at the monster's head and got its attention. Bigfoot stopped and turned to Juice. The beast then charged at Juice.

"There are acres of trees behind the school. We can lead it there!" shouted Juice in midsprint.

The monster got close to Juice, but before it could make an attack, Timber managed to charge up to the beast and shoved his right fist deep into the side of the Sasquatch. The beast turned to Timber and swung his arms at him. The beast's arms were so long he swung them like they were hockey sticks. The boys found out that the animal charged at the one who hit him last, so the Hogs felt like they could use this information to lead the best to the back door of the school.

Eric took out his phone to call Gard for help with this attack. Eric had no idea what to tell him, and it didn't help that he felt that he didn't have much time to deliver his message. When Gard picked up the phone, Eric sped through his announcement, hoping he left a clear message to his friend. As soon as Eric stopped talking, he saw Will charge at the monster once more. Eric hung up the phone and charged right with Will toward Bigfoot.

Timber managed to lead the animal out of the gym and into the hallway heading to the back door. But once they reached the hallway, the animal attacked Timber. Timber was slammed into the side wall by Bigfoot's swinging arm. Will and Eric attacked Bigfoot from behind, tackling the monster down to the floor. Both Will and Eric hurried to their feet, standing with the back door behind them and Bigfoot in front of them. The animal started to get up, eyeing Will and Eric, his next victims.

"I'll race you to the woods," Will said to Eric.

"You're on!" Eric shouted as he turned and took off running alongside Will.

The two boys ran down the hall, pushed open the doors, and sprinted toward the woods, all with Bigfoot on their tail.

Inside, Juice helped Timber to his feet. Timber didn't believe what just happened. "Just when I thought things were getting back to normal," Timber grunted as he got to his feet.

"Leading it to the woods still puts us in danger. The thing seems pretty determined on killing us. And after that, it'll just keep looking for its next hunt," Juice stated.

"To the woods then," Timber replied.

"Take a minute to catch your breath, just in case it's your last. Give Hayden a call. He'll want in on this too." Juice said as he looked at the woods in the distance. Juice took a deep breath and told Timber that he'd see him out there.

CHAPTER 22

The Beast's Last Howl

Gard was driving his car down the country road away from the dance with his girlfriend, Terra, in the passenger seat. They both had a fun night, but Gard thought the plan would be that they would go to the school's after-prom party. Terra made other plans for them because she wasn't interested in a party hosted by the school. She wanted to meet up with her friends who were having their own after-prom party. Gard knew that this other party would be mainly her friends, a few graduates, and a lot of alcoholic beverages. This was one of the disagreements that pierced Gard and Terra's relationship. Gard didn't care for the high school parties that included alcohol. He preferred hanging out with the Hang Out Group and setting off firecrackers within the fire ring. Gard always used the athletic sports he was involved in as an excuse not to drink when he was dragged to those parties hosted by his girlfriend's friends. But now that the sports were over, Terra was looking for a boyfriend who could be her drinking buddy and not a designated driver.

Gard knew that since the school year was ending and it was prom night, the party Terra wanted them to go to would likely be a keg party. This meant another night of passing on drinks from everyone, taking an annoying drunk girl home, lying to her parents, and saying she caught food poisoning or she was suffering from the day flu again. Before Gard could speak his mind on them going to the party tonight, his phone rang. Gard approached a four-way stop in the road. Once he stopped, he answered his phone. Gard didn't even get a chance to say hello after putting the phone up to his ear. Eric, yelling loudly, was on the line speaking quickly.

"We're under attack! We think it's from the Havocs, but to be honest, we've been so overwhelmed by this threat that we really haven't had time to discuss anything besides strategy tactics. We're leading it into the woods, and to be honest, you wouldn't believe me if I told you what it is! Get here fast! We need help!" Eric said over the phone before the call was ended.

"Eric...," Gard said, frightened. The phone was silent. Gard took a deep breath, for he was worried about his friends. Gard knew he had to get back to the school fast. He checked his rearview mirror and noticed that Terra's friends were in the car behind them.

"I need you to get out and get a ride from your friend behind us," Gard insisted in a calm manner. The calmness was challenging to perform due to Gard's anxiety hitting him hard because he was afraid for his friends.

"What, why?" Terra asked, disgusted by the request.

"I need to go back to the school. My friends need my help," Gard said, holding back the urge to raise his voice.

"No way, we're going to the party," Terra added.

"My friends need my help," Gard said, gripping the steering wheel tightly and growing impatient.

"Look, the time with your friends needs to end. They're a bunch of arsonists, pyros, and weirdos who live in this area. That's why I pushed you to go to that college far from here. The more time you stay away from them, the better!" Terra said, her voice raising.

"Get out of my car," Gard ordered, but Terra refused to move; she just glared at him with an angry stare. Gard shouted, "Get out of my car now!"

"You know what, Gard, we're done! Have a nice life with your dumb friends!" Terra shouted as she exited the car.

As soon as she slammed the passenger car door shut, Gard pushed down on the accelerator gas pedal and made a U-turn back toward the school. The mighty car engine roared like a beast down the road back to the school.

Out by the pond, Hayden and Miles finished up a nice, pleasant evening of some late-night fishing. The two were loading up the fishing gear in the trunk of Hayden's car when he got a phone call from Timber. Hayden picked up the phone and brought it to his ear.

"Hey, Timber, what's up?" Hayden asked.

"Hayden, you're not going to believe this, but Bigfoot is here!" Timber stated.

"Yeah, and Miles and I just caught the kraken during our fishing trip," Hayden replied sarcastically.

"I'm not kidding. It must be an attack from the Havocs or something. Will, Juice, and Eric are keeping it occupied in the woods back of the Bay School. Hayden, this thing is strong. It can push us around like we're throw pillows," Timber explained.

"We're on our way," Hayden said, believing Timber's story. Hayden hung up his phone and slipped it in his pocket. He told Miles that they needed to get to the Bay School fast. Hayden asked Miles if he could teleport them to the school.

"I've seen that place before. I think I can get us there," Miles replied.

Hayden had to grab a few things first. He picked up a duffel bag from the back seat under which was a hunting rifle along with his hunting knife. Once Hayden had both in hand, he told Miles that he was now ready to get to the fight. Miles placed his right hand on Hayden's shoulder, and then they both teleported away. They arrived at the front of the school in the blink of an eye. As they ran around the school, Hayden spotted the track marks from the school all the way back to the woods. These marks looked to be from a very large animal.

"You're going to need a bigger gun," Miles uttered once he saw the footprints in the grass.

Hayden just smirked because he was ready for a hunt. But before they could move forward into the woods, they spotted Gard's car driving right up to them. Hayden hid his gun behind his back in fear that this was an adult who could get him in trouble for carrying a gun so close to a school. It was a relief for Hayden to see that it was Gard's car.

"How did you guys get here so fast?" questioned Gard as he got out of the car.

"I can teleport, remember," Miles replied.

"Where are the others?" Gard said as he popped open the trunk of his car. Gard had his change of clothes in the trunk of the car; and he quickly took off his jacket, vest, and tie.

"They're in the woods," Hayden said while nodding in the direction.

Gard didn't need to hear any more; he just hurried to get his athletic shoes on and dashed off toward the woods. After Gard took off into the woods, Miles asked Hayden what his plan was. Hayden said that first he was going to load up his rifle, and then he was going to wait for his moment to sneak up on the beast. Miles said that he had an idea how to get the creature distracted. He said that he can sometimes feel the power inside him flowing through his body like warm water. He said that he might be able to turn it into an attack of some kind.

Will, Juice, Timber, Eric, and Gard were keeping the Sasquatch occupied. They felt like they were taking turns attacking the creature. Will and Gard charged up at the beast; the beast swung Will with his right arm. Will caught the monster's arm and pulled it back, which caused the monster to lean forward. With the creature's left side defenseless, Gard delivered a flurry of speed punches onto the creature's side. Left punch followed by right punch, over and over as fast as he could. The beast then kicked Gard away with his right foot and followed that by lifting Will up off the ground. The beast then repeatedly slammed Will into a tree with a speedy jerking motion. The bark of the tree flew off like wild shrapnel after each impact from Will slamming into the tree. Timber came running to Will's aid, but the beast just chucked Will right at him, knocking them both down to roll in the dirt.

"We're losing out here!" Juice said, panting heavily while standing next to Eric.

"We just need to weaken it somehow. That way we can get an advantage," Eric replied.

Juice was thinking fast about a solution; then he saw that the animal was standing on a path within the woods.

"Eric, keep it looking towards its left. I got a plan!" Juice shouted as he took off running quickly into the woods.

Eric had no idea what Juice's plan was but followed the plan keeping the Sasquatch looking left.

"Juice, you better not get me killed!" Eric shouted as he ran to the animal's left. He kept a small distance away from the animal, just out of arm's reach. The beast took a swing at Eric who shuffled back a bit to dodge the attack. The beast repeated his swings at Eric, while Eric continued to slide his way back. The beast managed to slash Eric's shirt as Eric nudged up to a log, lost his balance, and fell on his back. "Juice, whatever you're about to do, DO IT NOW!"

When Juice took off on his run, he ran on the path that went through the woods. Juice used to run cross-country meets at this school. The course went through the woods, which Juice knew like the back of his hand. Juice was building up speed as he ran on the path. He directed himself into a loop, and with great speed, he charged at the Sasquatch. Juice was now on the path and sneaking up on the animal. He then slid as if he was a baseball player sliding feetfirst into the home plate. With the force Juice gained from his run, he drove his leg right into the creature's right knee. There was a sound of something cracking on impact; the monster's leg twitched and bent in a painful way followed by a hellish howl from the creature.

Both Juice and Eric got to their feet during the creature's moment of weakness and regrouped with the other Hogs. Will, Juice, Timber, Eric, and Gard stood together as the beast continued its howl of pain.

"That should slow it down," Juice stated.

"Nice work, guys," Will replied.

The creature staggered its way toward the group; as it walked, it was favoring its left leg, so the Hogs could tell the beast's right knee was broken or dislocated. The beast was moving slowly and now had a weak spot that the Hogs could attack in the future. But this action came at a price because now the animal seemed more agitated. The Hogs stood their ground, waiting for the animal to come to them before their next attack.

As the beast grew closer, the Hogs saw a splash of violet light as it struck the creature's face. This was a shocking occurrence that brought an odd, confused feeling to the Hogs. The Hogs all turned their heads, and as they did, they saw another violet light fly across their sight as it struck the beast once again. The light looked like the northern lights; it even moved like the northern lights. When the Hogs saw the source of where the light was coming from, they saw Miles and Hayden. Hayden then charged at the Sasquatch with his gun aiming right at the beast's chest.

Hayden fired rapidly at the creature with every step growing closer to his target. Hayden was using one of his father's many hunting rifles, a .30-30 lever-action shotgun. The gunfire was loud, but so was the Hogs' cheering. The Hogs watched as Hayden moved fearlessly and headstrong, shooting his gun over and over. Bigfoot flinched from the bullets striking his body, but he kept standing tall, taking the attacks calmly. Hayden got right in front of the beast and fired the gun once more. But Hayden's gun was now empty; he must have miscounted his bullets.

Hayden saw the bloody Sasquatch with a cruel look on its face. "Can you give me a minute to reload?" Hayden kindly asked the angry giant.

The Sasquatch slapped the gun out of Hayden's hand with one hand, while the other hand lifted Hayden up by the neck, choking him.

While Hayden came in with his gun blazing and landing every shot, the Hogs were cheering like they were at a football game. But seeing Bigfoot still standing after that attack, all the excitement and hopeful feeling was replaced with more worry and dismay. Will, Juice, Timber, Eric, and Gard all sprinted over to Hayden to save him from being strangled. Juice was tugging on Bigfoot's right arm, while Will was pulling on the creature's left arm. Timber came up behind the Sasquatch and swung a wooden stick at the beast's back. The stick shattered, but Bigfoot was unaffected by the blow. Gard saw Hayden's large knife strapped to his belt behind him; Gard grabbed the knife and shoved it into Bigfoot's shoulder.

Will and Juice were working on their own plan. They both counted down from three together. "Three, two, one!" they both chanted. This was followed by them jumping up and using the Sasquatch's arms as support, and they managed to deliver a powerful kick right in the beast's face at the same time. The monster lost its grip on Hayden and dropped him to the ground, and the impact of the kick caused him to fall backward. Will and Juice were still hanging on to the animal and fell back along with it.

Hayden was on his knees coughing for air. Gard checked on him, happy that he was still breathing, and then handed the knife back to Hayden. Hayden slipped the knife back in his holster saying, "Next time aim for the throat." Hayden coughed as he was holding his neck with his free hand.

"I'll try to remember that next time," Gard replied.

"Thanks, by the way," Hayden added.

"No problem," Gard mumbled. As Hayden was catching his breath, Eric came to his side along with Miles. Miles was carrying Hayden's duffel bag.

"Miles, that light…was that you?" wondered Eric.

"I've been feeling this energy inside since the cube blasted me, and I felt that I could release some of it. I was hoping it would hurt the monster more than it did, though," Miles explained.

"It definitely got his attention," Gard stated.

"Well, this will definitely hurt it," Hayden said as he pulled a can of kerosene out of his bag. Gard grinned at the sight, for he knew they were going to set Bigfoot on fire.

Will, Juice, and Timber were running from Bigfoot while Gard and Hayden were about to execute their plan of attack. Gard jumped in front of the creature while pouring the canteen of kerosene all over the beast.

"Everyone, get clear!" Gard shouted as he dropped the can next to the beast, turned, and started sprinting away. Hayden then ran in, wrapped his arms around the Sasquatch's back, and lit his Zippo lighter. The creature's hair was set on fire, and its skin was burning, which was followed by yet another mighty howl of pain. Hayden pushed himself off the creature; his clothes were on fire, so he used his hands to pat out the flames. Hayden, being fireproof, felt no painful effect from the flames on his body.

"Hayden, are you crazy!" shouted Will.

"What? It worked, didn't it!" Hayden replied. Hayden knew that the flames wouldn't hurt him, and he didn't want to take the chance of tossing his one and only lighter at the creature, for he could have missed. Hayden was only upset that he lost his favorite lighter in the process.

The creature was burning bright; it tried to run away but tripped on its broken leg and fell to the ground. The Hogs all gathered around watching the beast roast, all hoping that it was over. The beast instinctually started to roll in the dirt, and the fire quickly burned out. The Hogs were hoping that the Sasquatch wouldn't get up. But the beast rose to its feet once again.

"Well, I'm out of ideas," Hayden stated.

"Hayden, your idea was shooting it and setting it on fire!" Eric replied.

"Maybe we can reason with it," Juice said.

"Juice, we just set it on fire. I think the chance of *reasoning with it* has passed!" Gard yelled.

"Well, maybe next time we should have a vote before we start setting fire to fictional animals!" Juice replied.

Timber pointed at the creature, yelling that it was coming right at them. As everyone ran away, Will, in a steady voice, stated that the creature was horribly wounded; and it shouldn't take much more of an attack to finish it off. Will said they'd attack one after the other, coming in from all different directions. Eric said that the creature could see them coming and would dodge their attacks.

"Miles, could you blast that light of yours in his eyes?" wondered Will.

Miles said that he was confident that he could make that shot. Will told everyone to spread out, and they'd attack after Miles made his move.

After everyone scattered, Miles turned and faced the creature. Miles pointed all his fingers on his right hand at the Sasquatch and sent a blast of violet light from the tip of his fingers toward the beast. Miles hit his target right in its eyes. Will yelled that their moment of attack was now. Gard, being the fastest, made his attack first; he slammed his fist into the creature's jaw on the right side hard. Gard's sprint never stopped, and when he was clear, Juice came in at the beast's back and punched him behind the right shoulder. Hayden then came in and delivered a kick at the animal's left side. Timber and Eric both came in front of the creature, stomping their feet onto the creature's knees. Then Will came in for the final blow, delivering a strong punch right in the chest of the monster. The beast hit the ground hard and died. It was over; the group had defeated Bigfoot, saving their lives in the process.

The group just wanted to catch their breath, for they were exhausted, sore, and bleeding. Congrats and good-job gestures were still something they were able to exchange. Hayden and Gard did have the power to give each other a high five, while Juice was able to give a pat on Will's back. Miles looked at his friends and asked if everyone was all right. Everyone, too exhausted to speak, shook their heads up and down, implying that they were fine.

"I'm going to check the area. If this was indeed a Havocs attack, there might be some of them around the school," Will said as he headed back to the school. Hayden picked up his rifle and said he would go with Will for backup. Eric stepped up next to Miles and complimented him on his shooting.

"Thanks. Wish I could have done more," Miles responded as he, Juice, Timber, Eric, and Gard all just stood still and stared at the body.

"We just killed Bigfoot," Gard said softly.

A heavy feeling of guilt dropped onto the Hogs at that moment. They felt that they had committed a very cruel act. Eric pointed out that the animal had murder in its eyes; if they wouldn't have put it down, it could have killed dozens of innocent people.

"Guys, over here quick!" shouted Hayden from a distance. The five Hogs ran as fast as they could, some of them with painful injuries that resulted in them walking forward with a limp. From the sound of Hayden's voice, it didn't sound like he was in danger, but they couldn't take that chance. Once out of the wooded area, they spotted Hayden and Will standing in the parking lot. When they got up to them, they saw two bodies in the parking lot.

"Are they dead?" Juice asked fearfully.

"They're dead," Will answered softly.

Some of the Hogs were very uncomfortable looking at the dead bodies. None of them had ever seen a dead body outside a funeral home before. It was hard to look at the bodies' faces, but when they did, they saw that they knew these people.

"These guys are Havocs members," Timber said, recognizing the men from previous attacks from them.

"*Were* Havocs members," Will corrected.

"Well, that confirms that Bigfoot was an attack initiated by the Havocs," Gard added.

"I thought the police arrested them all," Juice mentioned.

"Apparently not all of them," Hayden stated.

Things felt tense within the group. They were in the middle of the country road, standing in a school parking lot next to two dead bodies. They had a dead Bigfoot out in the woods they had to figure out what to do with, and it was getting late. If they didn't get to the after-prom party soon, people may start asking questions. Thinking about attending the after-prom party at a time like this felt childish in a way. Getting almost pummeled to death at one moment, followed by worrying about dead bodies the next, didn't give off the party attitude.

"I can move the bodies," Miles announced. Eyes were on Miles. Miles spoke as if he was shy. He said that he could teleport the bodies far from there so that there would be no trace back to the school or the Hogs. All this talk about moving dead bodies and the possibility of the police tracing back to them made them all feel numb. They were all dealing with this feeling differently. Juice was now taking in deep breaths and pushed himself at least six feet away from the dead bodies.

"Take the Sasquatch body to my backyard. We'll bury it in the woods behind my yard," Hayden replied.

"We going to bury the dead human bodies back there too?" Timber uttered.

"Hey, I know moving dead bodies is one of the sketchiest things to do," Gard said, raising his voice. "But let's not forget one big thing here. We didn't kill these two guys!" Gard worried that after all this talk about moving and hiding bodies, the Hogs were feeling a type of responsibility for the death of the two men dead in the parking lot. Gard, therefore, felt the need to remind his friends that they hadn't murdered the humans.

"According to Eric, the Havocs used to cause massive attacks on people which caused huge casualties with the aftermath being described as a bloodbath. Giving the evidence we now have, I bet the Havocs used Bigfoot to kill tons of people in the past. They must have planned on using the beast on us, but it seemed to backfire, and it ended up killing them instead," Gard explained.

It was clear to the Hogs that the two Havocs members were killed before Bigfoot went after them. This helped convince them that if they didn't kill Bigfoot, it would have kept on looking for its next prey.

"Juice, you okay back there?" Will asked his friend who was back away from the rest of the group leaning over face to the ground, breathing hard.

"Yep," Juice replied after lifting his head back up.

"We got to get these bodies out of here," Will ordered.

Hayden said that Miles should take the bodies to the highway road just outside town.

"The police are going to be confused on how they died," Eric stated. The bodies were clearly crushed, so Eric knew that this would be a big mystery for the news. Two dead smashed corpses lying on the side of the road with no explanation would get a lot of news coverage. The more press, the more detective work the police would put into the situation, which gave a possibility of the police tracing the story back to the Hogs. The Hogs knew that the Havocs must have had tons of information on them somewhere. How else would they know where their prom night was? If the police investigated their murders, they would learn that the Havocs were studying the Hogs, which could lead the cops to their doors.

"They have a moving truck. We could use that," Hayden added.

"Oh no," Timber said in a shocked tone.

"What, what's your idea?" asked Eric. Hayden explained that the road leading to Pennsylvania had a large ditch next to it. Hayden said that they could make it look like the two men parked next to the ditch to get out to pee or have a smoke or something, and the truck tipped over on them.

"No, absolutely not! Moving the bodies is one thing, but dropping a truck on them is crossing the line!" Timber said, shocked by the idea.

"We do have the strength to make a controlled tip, and the truck landing on them would give the police an explanation on how the bodies were crushed," Gard said, thinking out loud.

Timber once again expressed his dislike for this plan by calling everyone nuts for thinking about it. Will checked his watch and saw that he and the others were scheduled to arrive at the after-prom party by now. It was a matter of time before the Hogs' prom dates started texting them asking where they were. Will knew that this situation had to be resolved now.

The Hogs all gathered up and weighed the facts. Gard was right. They didn't kill the two men, so their conscience was clear on that. And they all fully believed that if they hadn't put an end to Bigfoot, it would never stop killing. Timber had a good point; setting up the bodies to make it look like they died by an accident didn't feel morally right. Eric reminded everyone that it was possible for the police to find the information on the Hogs found by Reed and Baron, then the Hogs would start getting questions from the police that they couldn't answer. In the end, they decided to go with Hayden's plan, for why should their lives get compromised due to two men who accidentally got killed by the thing they brought to kill them? They didn't like covering up the truth of the men's deaths, but they felt like it was the best plan. The Hogs were all worried; until now, they never felt like they could do something like this. They were afraid what would happen if someone died by their hands. What would they do then? They would now forever be people who had covered up a death. The only thing that kept them from feeling completely terrible was the fact that they hadn't killed the men, nor were they covering it up for someone else who did.

Gard told Will to take his car, as he wasn't going to the after-prom party. The four all crammed into Gard's car and drove to Juice's house. Once they got there, they changed out of their ripped and bloody clothes and into some fresh ones. They bandaged up any cuts they had from the fight with Bigfoot. They wore long sleeves to help cover the bandages. Back at the school, Miles teleported Bigfoot's body to the woods behind Hayden's backyard and grabbed some shovels from the shed. While Miles was doing all that, Hayden and Gard loaded up the dead bodies into the truck and drove the moving truck out to the highway. Once they reached a good place far enough from the school, Gard called Miles and told him to teleport to his location, saying it was just past the deer crossing sign on the road leading out of Maze. Miles was aware of that sign, so he was able to teleport there with no problem. Hayden and Gard got out of the truck and moved the bodies next to the ditch on the side of the road. Once they were in place, they moved to the side of the truck.

"Ready?" Hayden asked Gard.

Gard wasn't ready. Neither was Hayden. They both knew that this was going to be hard, but when the time came, it seemed to be much harder than they thought. Gard was very stiff now, as he just needed a minute to get ready. Miles was standing in front of the two, waiting patiently. Then the idea of another car driving by came to Gard. That thought freaked him out big-time, so he turned to face the truck, giving Hayden a pat on the back saying, "Let's hurry up and get this done."

The two tipped over the truck as gently as they could. Immediately after the truck was in place, Miles grabbed each of their shoulders and teleported them back to the fishing pond to return to Hayden's car. The sight of the pond reflecting the moon was a comfortable feeling. Hayden was about to enter the driver's side of the tuck, but Gard asked if they could spend a minute or two by the pond. Hayden and Miles agreed that taking a minute to relax after everything they just did would be nice.

The three sat on the shore of the pond and gazed out at the water. Gard chucked a rock at the pond, trying to skip it. "I have to tell you, dealing with Bigfoot was easier than dealing with those dead bodies," Gard said as he flicked another rock into the pond.

"Fighting that animal was terrifying, but covering up those bodies felt harder to do. So yeah, I know what you mean," Hayden replied. Hayden turned his head at Miles. "Hey, that light attack you did was pretty awesome!"

"You know, I didn't even know that was going to happen when I did it. I had this gut feeling that I could make attack with this power, and it turned out I was right," Miles stated. "Having these powers feels scary at times. You guys, you're just stronger, not much to figure out there. But me, I'm nervous, not always certain about what more I can do. I just feel like there is more to learn about this power."

"We'll figure it out together," Gard said.

"And we can handle whatever new thing that comes our way," Hayden added.

"With everything that has happened to us so far, I don't think this is going to end anytime soon. Yeah, the Havocs are gone, but we thought that before," Gard said.

"I'm keeping my gun with me everywhere I go from now on," Hayden mentioned.

"Didn't you always do that?" asked Miles.

"Yeah, but now I'll keep it loaded," Hayden said in a humorous way. This made the three let out a much-needed laugh. After the laugher ended, the three grew silent, allowing for nothing more than the sound of the crickets and the frogs. The Hogs felt at ease listening to the nature sounds, like how the creatures of the garden behaved when they heard their homeland. After a few minutes, Gard said something.

"So I got dumped today."

This made both Hayden and Miles crack up laughing hard. Gard delivered the news so casually that it came off as more humorous than upsetting. Hayden and Miles said, "Wow, you're having the worst day."

The two friends knew that Gard had wanted his relationship to end for quite some time now, so they didn't really feel bad. It was weird hearing regular high school news after everything that just happened. Gard bringing this incident up felt like it snapped them back to a normal reality in which getting dumped was the worst thing that could happen to a high school student. The three talked about it for a while. The two friends were happy that Gard was fine about it, and Gard was happy that he got to talk to someone about it. It was a good way to end such an overwhelming night.

CHAPTER 23

Kidnapped

Sunday, May 23, 2020, 2:00 a.m.

Some threatening men intruded in a house in a small neighborhood. The men were dressed in all black, complete with ski mask. They stuck to the shadows and moved quickly and quietly as if they were members of a SWAT team. These men were hired to sneak in and retrieve the girl, shooting her with a tranquilizer dart. There were three men, more than enough to handle a simple kidnapping of a sixteen-year-old girl. The men skillfully picked the many locks on the front door and entered the house, holding the guns in position ready to fire. The man who hired the three kidnappers informed them that there was only one person living in the house, and that was the girl.

The men checked the first floor fast and then headed up the stairs where there were two bedrooms. The first room that the men checked was empty. The men realized that the girl must be behind the other bedroom door. They slowly opened the door, and two walked in while the third held his position by the door. The two men in the room found the girl sleeping in her bed in the middle of the room. The man closest to the bed aimed the dart gun at her. Just then, the girl in the bed flicked a large knife right at the gunman's shoulder. This girl had been sleeping with a knife under her bed for years. She had trained herself to be the lightest sleeper ever so that even if she were attacked while in bed, she could still give herself a chance to fight. The man with the knife in his shoulder fell back to the ground.

The second gunman in the room drew his gun on the girl; she rolled out of bed, landing between the bed and her dresser. When the second gunman fired his dart at the girl, she managed to pull out a dresser drawer to block the dart from hitting her. She then chucked the drawer forward at the man, rushed right up to him, and delivered a mighty punch that sent the unsuspecting gunman across the room and crashing against the wall.

With both men in the room on the floor, one unconscious and the one with the knife wound squealing in pain, the girl walked to the hallway. As she passed the man who had the knife buried inside his shoulder, she pulled it out with her right hand. The knife removed felt even more painful than when it went in. The man just stayed on the floor, trying to keep blood from exiting his wound. Out in the hall, she saw the third man who backed away from her in terror when he saw her holding the knife.

The girl made eye contact with the man in the hall and could see his fear. She then surged toward him. The man fired off a dart with poor aim due to his shaking with fear. The girl leaned right, dodging the dart. She was lucky that these men were using darts because if that was a gunshot, she wouldn't have been fast enough to get out of the way. When the girl got right up to him, she didn't stop running; she just shoved her arms into the man.

The man fell out of the second-story window of the pleasant-looking house. At the window, the woman checked the area for more attackers. With her quick glance, she didn't see anyone; so she ran down the steps, entered the kitchen, and pulled the oven out of its place. Behind the oven was a backpack, an important item she would need. She swung the backpack onto her shoulders and grabbed the keys to her car on her way out. She ran to her car. She was in such a hurry that she didn't have time to put the key into the lock to get the front door unlocked, so she just smashed the window and unlocked the car from the inside. She opened the car door and then heard someone say her name from behind, "Renshaw!"

The girl turned and was immediately attacked. This man managed to sneak right up to her and with a fast motion reached out to grab her throat tightly. The girl knew this wasn't one of the men from inside the house. She didn't see his face at first. All she saw was the man's very, very burnt hand grabbing her before she could make a defensive move. When she finally drew her eyes to the man's face, she saw that she had never seen this man before but still knew who he was.

"You're Ray, aren't you?" she said like she had a frog in her throat due to the tight grip the man had on her neck.

"Yes…it's nice to finally meet you, Kate," Ray said, before shooting her with one of the tranquilizer darts. Kate quickly lost consciousness, and Ray carried her to his car. As he walked by the house, two of the hired thugs were exiting out of the house.

"Good show, men. I knew the daughter of Cain wouldn't be taken so easily." Ray wasn't completely sure if this girl had the advanced strength, so he needed to see her use her power in action for him to know for sure. Ray thought it was funny because he never told the hired men about the possibility of her being very strong. The men had no idea what they were walking into when they took the assignment. Ray loaded Kate in the back seat of his car, tossed the cash reward to the hired men, and drove off.

Early That Morning

Cain knew it was time to leave the hospital. They had been treating him like a victim of the Havocs this whole time, but Cain knew they would start asking questions that he wouldn't have answers for. It was, therefore, time to take off before breakfast. His clothes were in the hospital room closet, so he hurried up and got dressed. Before he got to the door, the room's phone rang. Cain found that odd as he paused to look at the phone. Cain didn't bother with it, as he exited the room. The floor was nearly empty with just the night shift finishing up their last half hour.

As Cain walked past the nurses' station, he found it empty. Then he heard the phone go off. This time the phone ringing didn't come off as odd as the one in his room did. Cain continued to walk to the elevator. Once inside, he closed the doors, and before he could push the ground-floor button, the elevator phone started to ring. This time Cain knew he was being watched; he eyed the corner of the elevator upper wall and saw a security camera.

Cain already knew Ray was teasing him. He picked up the phone, brought it up to his head, and said in a sinister voice, "Ray."

"Good morning, Cain! It's great to hear from you. It's been what, couple decades?" Ray said with a joyful tone.

"What do you want, Ray?" Cain said, getting straight to the point.

"I want to get paid for babysitting, Cain. Your life ought to do," Ray answered.

"What are you talking about?" Cain's voice resounded with anger, for he felt that he knew what Ray was talking about.

"I found your daughter, Cain. I kept my eyes on your little group of thieves after you started your little nap. I found it odd that the accountant skipped town so quickly. It took me a while to track him down as he moved around a lot. Figured he embezzled with the group, and there was a bounty on his head. But when I finally tracked him down, I saw that he was taking care of a young girl. And well, I'm smart, Cain. I had a pretty solid guess on who that girl was."

"If you hurt her…," Cain started to say.

"Don't worry, Cain, she's safe. She's at my factory. The place was a little dusty, but the cage still works fine," Ray responded.

"Let her go," Cain ordered.

"I will, but I want you to show up here, waving a big white flag. Don't worry, I'll make your death fast and painless. Then I'll let your daughter go and be out of her hair forever."

"If you think for one second that I'm just going to let you—" Cain was once again interrupted in midconversation.

"Dad?" said Kate's voice over the phone.

"Kate, how are you? Has he hurt you?" Cain shouted, frantic with worry.

Ray ended the phone call after that as Cain slammed his fist into the elevator wall, smashing through it. Cain was puzzled as he tried to figure out his next move. He checked his jacket pocket and looked at the folder containing the files of the Hang Out Group that Baron had left with him. He started to come up with a plan.

Ray was sitting in his old chemical plant in the break room. He was using his laptop computer on the table at the time. He was able to gain access to the security cameras at the hospital in order to spy on Cain. Ray sat at the head of the table; to his left was Kate, bound with chains. She was barely awake, due to the tranquilizer only now starting to wear off. She struggled in her chair, trying to find the power to stand up. The chains were bolted to the floor and were very heavy for her. The drug used on her that knocked her out had affected her strength now. Her whole body felt heavy; her muscles felt exhausted. After her first three attempts to overpower the chains, she collapsed in her chair with not even enough strength left to keep her head up. Kate was breathing heavily, doing everything she could just to catch her breath.

"Believe me, Kate, until the drugs completely wear off, you're not going anywhere. Besides, the chains were made to hold something stronger than you," Ray said as he rose up out of his chair and walked over to the stove. Ray was cooking some eggs before he made his call to Cain. He asked nicely how Kate liked her eggs cooked. Kate lifted her head slightly, made strong eye contact with Ray, and gave a spiteful look. Ray just shook it off and turned to the frying pan, pouring some scrambled eggs onto a plate. The toaster had already turned the bread into toast, so he snatched that up and placed it on the plate. He gently sat the plate and a fork in front of Kate. He then took his seat back at the head of the table, removing the morning paper from under the laptop to read.

Kate just looked at the food, having no desire to oblige. Ray, with his eyes on the paper, suggested she eat, saying that it would help her get her strength back.

She turned to him, aching at the mere sight of him. "Why are you feeding me?" she rudely asked.

"I want to be a gracious host. I may have forced you to come here and am holding you here against your will, but that doesn't mean I have to lose all my manners."

Kate looked at the food in front of her and could feel her stomach growl. Ray was right about the strong hunger brought on while the drugs in her system were wearing off. A small bite of the toast would be a true delight for her right now. Kate glimpsed over at Ray, this time keeping her head held down. He was just sitting there, reading the newspaper like some average Hayden at the breakfast table. Kate eyed the room while going through her memories, trying to figure out where she was.

The last thing she could remember was being ambushed by three intruders at her home. She remembered overpowering them and grabbing her book bag. Thinking of the bag put her into a panic state. She didn't feel it on her back nor the straps around her shoulders. She turned to the seat next to her. She checked the table and all around the room, searching for her bag. She became highly concerned when she failed to spot it. She was hoping the rest of her memories would cause her to remember what happened to her bag. But unfortunately, the rest of her memories after she retrieved her bag were of her getting captured by Ray, followed by waking up at the table. Once she came to, Ray put the phone next to her and told her to say *hi* to her dad.

"If you're worried about your bag, don't worry. It's in your cell," Ray stated.

"When did my dad wake up?" she asked her captor.

Ray, not taking his eyes off the newspaper, answered by saying, "Just a few days ago."

Kate didn't know how to feel now. On one hand, she was a prisoner, so she wanted to keep a strong-willed attitude in front of her kidnapper. But at the same time, she had mixed feelings knowing her father had been awake for a few days now. She was grateful that her father had finally awakened from his coma but also devastated that his biggest fear had come true. After Cain fell into his coma, Kate and her caretaker, Jason, went into hiding. They got fake IDS every five years and constantly changed their location. Due to Kate's slow aging process, she needed to keep playing the young school student.

Unfortunately, her caretaker didn't have that kind of luck. For Jason aged dramatically due to the constant stress of someone finding out about Kate's aging process or her advanced strength. This discovery would place a beacon right on them for Ray to come and attack or kidnap her. He died just a few months ago due to a heart attack. Kate was shattered by her loss. He was a father figure to her over the last twenty-five years and acted as a second father when she was still living at the mansion with

Cain. She never had a day without him being there before, and now she was all alone.

"Why do you want to kill my father?" she asked, as if she was weeping. Ray put the paper down away from his face and made eye contact with her.

"To be honest…I'm not sure," Ray stated. "At first it was just simple revenge. Then I felt that I owed it to my father to kill the son of his murderer. So it went from revenge to violent justice." Ray was very put off by this question. He felt like it should have been an easy answer, but since he hadn't really thought of his motive in so long, he felt like he forgot himself. "But if that was true, I would have ended his life years ago while he was in his coma. The Havocs were nowhere near as strong as they were when your dad was active. So he had a weakened army, and there was nothing he could do to stop me from placing a knife through his heart."

"So why didn't you?" Kate asked.

"I found satisfaction with putting Cain into a coma. I felt a type of victory in taking down the unbeatable, unstoppable *Cain the Animal.* I found pride in my successful actions, and at that time, I didn't care about the *why* I wanted to defeat your father. I couldn't have cared less for the justice for my own father in my victory…" Ray never spoke of this feeling before, so he was discovering these new emotions for the first time, and it made him grow quiet, causing him to slow down in his talking. "I guess the reason why I want your father dead doesn't drive me anymore. I think I just want another victory." Ray couldn't believe what he was saying. He didn't even know if it was true. He hadn't thought of the wanted justice for his father in so long he believed that it was no longer what mattered most to him.

When one had this advanced strength within, one tended to seek out strong challenges in one's life. Ray's favorite challenge was trying to find a way to take down Cain. With this motivation, he was able to build new weapons and even the cube itself. Ray was a sore loser, and since Cain was still alive, he felt like he hadn't fully won the war between the two. Killing Cain while he was in his coma wouldn't have been a challenging obstacle for Ray. Ray saw it as no fun. So he waited for his old friend to wake up so that he could continue to find another victory.

By the time Ray was finished talking, he saw that Kate had started to eat some of the toast. The hunger was too much for her to not take a bite out of the food. As Ray looked at her, he felt slightly guilty for keeping her chained up like this. But since Ray wasn't a man known for rethinking his actions, he refused to let emotions cloud his plans. He made a plan, and he intended to stick to it. He allowed her to get a few more bites in before he injected her with another tranquilizer shot and carried her back to her cell.

Later That Night

The Hogs were sitting around Hayden's fire ring. They spent the whole day together because they felt safe when they were together. When Will arrived at the school for prom cleanup, he was happy that there was no sign of Bigfoot or the two dead criminals. Hayden was paying close attention to the police scanner that morning and said that the two dead bodies were found by the police. The police called it an accident, claiming that the truck must have tipped over when they left it parked on the side of the ditch. The Hogs' plan worked just as they hoped it would, leaving them in the clear. They all felt a low level of guilt and hoped that they would never have to talk about this again.

Normally, the group wouldn't meet up this late on a school night, but everyone knew that the last Monday of the school year was senior skip day. The group talked about the big camping trip they wanted to take this summer. They said it was a much-needed vacation after the madness that was suddenly thrust upon them in the past few weeks. The fear of the next Havocs' attack should be over by now. The Hogs said the two guys that Bigfoot killed were the final members of the group, and the rest were all locked up in jail. But the Hogs felt that dropping their concern now would be premature; the last time they did that, they faced their greatest challenge. It was a good thing the Hogs were still on their toes regarding the Havocs because at just that moment, a strange car pulled into the driveway and made its way right at the Hogs.

Hayden was the first to get up, holding his rifle in his hand. Seeing Hayden on guard put them all on edge. They weren't emotionally ready for another fight, but they would fight if they needed to. The car stopped, and the engine turned off. Cain was the person in the car, and when he got out, all eyes were on him. Cain slammed the car door shut and walked up to the fire.

"That's far enough!" Hayden said, looking threatening as he held his gun toward Cain.

"Who are you?" asked Will.

"My name is Cain Renshaw. I was the leader of the Havocs."

The Hogs all passed shocked looks to one another. According to Eric's research, the leader of the Havocs was a man nicknamed *Cain the Animal*. History documents and word of mouth never confirmed Cain as real or just a myth. Seeing the look of this guy, he lived up to the name Cain the Animal. Large shoulders with strong arms could make anyone feel intimidated.

"You were the one in the prison, the one who they were draining blood from," Miles spoke up after recognizing the man. Cain explained that his men were draining him of his blood to remove a drug that was keeping him in a coma.

"If you're here for the cube, you can forget it. We're not giving it up without a fight," Gard threatened.

"I don't care about the cube. As long as you don't use it on anyone else, you can keep it," Cain replied.

"Then why are you here?" Eric asked, worried that the man was here for revenge.

"I want to make a deal with you," Cain announced. The Hogs weren't expecting that kind of request, nor did they like the idea of it. Will told Cain that he and his friends were not interested in making a deal with someone like him. Cain offered to pay them for their assistance.

"We're not going to become members of your Havocs gang, Cain," Will commented.

"Look, I can go and find people that'll work for me, no problem. I've been doing it my whole life. But I came to you because you are my only hope," Cain explained. His request turned into a type of unexpected plea.

"Only hope for what?" asked Juice, concerned.

"I have many enemies who all want me dead. The only one who I feared has become aware of my wakening and has kidnapped my daughter." Cain mentioning his kidnapped daughter seemed to have made him drop his tough attitude. Now he was talking like a worried parent. "My daughter is an innocent girl. She was never a part of my organization. And now her kidnapper, Ray, says I have to willingly surrender myself or he will kill her."

"Sounds like you can save her with no problem. Just give yourself up to the guy," Gard said. Cain didn't appreciate the back talk, but since this was a business offer, he remained civilized.

"I'm not going to turn myself in. Not when I have a chance to save her and myself," Cain stated.

"Why us?" asked Timber. "If you claim you can find new people to work for you, why choose us?"

"Ray would be expecting a rescue mission from me. If I send anybody in after her, he'll execute her immediately," Cain answered.

"So you're saying Ray wouldn't expect a rescue mission from a group of high school kids like us?" Eric said, figuring out Cain's motivation for recruiting them.

Cain gave a nod because Eric was right. Eric asked Cain what made him think that they could pull off this rescue mission. Cain brought up the fact that the boys defeated the Sasquatch, and surviving an attack like that showed real strength. Cain warned the boys that Ray carried the same advanced strength as most of the Hogs did. Along with that, Ray had a high IQ and was responsible for making the cube.

"I know it seems difficult, but I've had spies in Ray's company for years. I have tons of information on him and his factory. Ray does have his weaknesses. He relies on his confidence for everything. He never doubts himself, so he never looks over things twice. He doesn't like surprises or to lose his cool. So if you catch him off guard, he'll stumble and fall."

The Hogs wished they could discuss their decision in private, but it seemed that Cain wanted an answer now and wasn't going to leave without the one he wanted. The Hogs felt that if they gave Cain the answer he didn't want to hear, things could turn ugly.

"If we do this, then you and all your men leave us alone forever," Will requested. The Hogs were all unanimous with Will's deal to Cain.

Juice chimed in saying that saving the girl was the right thing to do. Eric said that they'd take all the information Cain had on Ray in order to prepare for the rescue. But beyond that, they didn't want any help from Cain on this. The Hogs didn't want to work for Cain because that would make them feel like Havocs. They just wanted to save the girl because they believed that would be the right thing to do.

Cain claimed to have a box of all the documents, papers, notebooks, and photos he stole from Ray over the years in the car with him. But the truth was that Cain had withheld one of Ray's notebooks he stole in this box. The notebook he didn't include inside the box was Ray's weapons recipes. He didn't want the Hogs to have a notebook containing ways to harm him, so he kept that in his storage unit. Cain took the box out from his car and handed it over to Gard. Cain also added his own notes of information the Hogs should know to the box. He then removed a piece of paper and took out a pen from the box. He wrote the location of where Kate was and even the room where she was being held. Cain said that they better work fast because Ray wouldn't wait much longer for his surrender. Cain then said that he'd be back there tomorrow when the sun went down. He said that they better have her there safe and sound by then. The Hogs watched the man return to his car and drive down the driveway, not saying a word. Once he was gone, the Hogs looked at the box and said they should head inside the house because they had a lot of work to get started on.

CHAPTER 24

The Rescue

The boys walked through the back door of Hayden's house and took a seat at the kitchen table. Gard plopped the box onto the table, and they all looked inside. Inside was a scrambled mess of papers, folded-up sheets, and notebooks. Nothing looked organized or neatly stacked. Gard thought it would be easier just to dump it all over the table.

"This is going to require snacks," Hayden said as he headed to the cabinets and searched for some junk food. The rest of the Hogs all took a seat at the table. Will asked Hayden if his parents were home. Hayden said that they wouldn't return from their weekend trip until tomorrow at noon. Juice said he'd play some music since there were no parents to avoid waking. Eric requested everyone stay focused on making a plan and not get sidetracked by treats and playing music.

"Well, I think this is all nuts, but who cares what I think?" Timber stated.

"Shut up, Timber," Gard replied as he ruffled though the papers.

"Is anyone up for some *French onion dip*?" Hayden asked in a French accent as he stood in front of the refrigerator. Gard asked if it was expired, and Hayden replied, "Kind of."

"*Kind of*, what does that even mean? You know what, I don't even care. I'll try some," said Gard as he was sold on the dip.

"So a highly wanted criminal shows up, wants us to rescue his daughter, and we just say yes?" Timber chimed in.

"Did you really want to see how he would have reacted if we would have said no?" Gard replied.

"I'm just saying we normally just react to stuff, only playing defense in a way. This is a whole change of pace for us," Timber retorted.

"Will told the man we'd do it, and I didn't hear any complaints at the time," Gard said as he was reading one of the documents.

"Why did you say yes to the deal, Will?" Eric questioned. Eric wasn't complaining; he was just wondering.

Will confessed to his friends that the death of the two Havocs by the Sasquatch was bothering him. The moving of the bodies to make it look as if they died of an accident was still weighing on their minds. But Will also felt responsible for them dying. The Hogs assured Will that the two men died by their own actions and that it had nothing to do with them.

"Since we had the cube, they felt forced to attack us with Bigfoot. We were the reason why they were with Bigfoot that night," Will explained. This was information that the Hogs knew but had never looked at that way before. If the men would have had the cube, they wouldn't have been killed by Bigfoot. Will said that this level of responsibility wasn't keeping him awake nor piling a heavy weight of guilt on him. But he figured that this Ray guy wouldn't have found out about Cain's waking if the Hogs hadn't turned in the Havocs that day at the prison. If Ray hadn't found out about Cain's rising, Cain's daughter may not have been kidnapped. Will didn't want any level of responsibility for the death of this girl. Cain said she was innocent, so she didn't deserve what had happened to her. Will looked at his friends and saw that his words had an impact on them. It now felt saving this girl was the responsible thing to do.

Gard said that before they planned anything, they should know if anyone wanted out of this. The Hogs all felt nervous about this whole situation, but after facing what they had faced the past few weeks, they were surprisingly comfortable with this challenge. They were kind of uneasy about how mellow they were about this, but right now, this was their lives, and they were growing evermore used to it. Everyone was in on this rescue mission. Hayden brought over a bag of chips and tried out the dip, which he said he found to be edible.

According to Cain's note, his daughter was named Kate Renshaw, and she was being held at a factory plant called Saltwater Chemicals. Will used Hayden's map to locate the place. Eric asked Hayden if he could get his hands on a vehicle from his dad's junkyard. When Hayden asked why, Eric said that he didn't want to bring any car that could be traced back to them at the plant. As Hayden stood up from the table, he said he was sure he could find a car that was still running and able to carry everybody. Hayden then requested a teleport ride from Miles to the junkyard. Miles said he'd join him on the search for the car as he placed himself next to Hayden. Once Miles had his hand on Hayden's shoulder, they both teleported away.

"I love that sound," Gard stated once Miles and Hayden were gone.

"The sound of the air closing in on the empty space after Miles disappears?" Eric assumed.

"Yep," replied Gard, grinning. Everyone at the table could relate to what Gard was saying. That noise was a cool sound effect that made Miles's power seem even more awesome.

"Too bad Miles will never hear it," Juice said, giving everyone a laugh. Eric pointed out that the ability to teleport would be a great exit plan. Will said that it would come in handy if they found themselves backed into a corner. Gard said they could purposely lead themselves into a corner because Ray wouldn't expect it nor think they could escape. If Ray thought they were trapped, he may back off. Juice leaned over to Timber, asking him to remind him to never enter a corner without Miles being with him.

Timber asked if Miles could just teleport his way inside the room, pick up Kate, and return with no problem. But unfortunately, Miles could only teleport to a place that he had seen before. Since there were no photos of the room or the halls of the factory, Miles couldn't arrive there by himself.

Gard then found the blueprints of the factory, claiming that it was a helpful find. According to Cain's notes, Kate was on the second floor, locked in the last room on the far east side. The blueprints showed she was in a small heavily concealed room with no windows and only one door. Will found information on the room's door. The door was the size of a bank vault and just as strong as one. The door had a digital lock that needed a six-digit code to open. They didn't find the code to open the door, but they did find the manual of the digital lock. Eric looked at it and said it was a very, very cheap security lock. The manual had Cain's notes written in it, which described the way to unlock the door without the code.

"This says all you have to do is take off the control panel and pull a few wires in order to get it unlocked," Eric stated.

"Why have such a strong door and then give it an easily hacked lock?" wondered Gard.

"I bet they had Bigfoot in there at one time. I mean, what else could a room like that be used for?" Will said, thinking out loud.

"Yeah, I bet if the room was occupied, no one wanted it unlocked," Juice added.

Eric said that he was confident that he could unlock the door. Timber was at ease, thinking that this wouldn't be as hard as he thought it would be. Unfortunately, there was a negative effect to unlocking the door without using the code. Unlocking the door by pulling the wires turned off the self-opening mechanism. Eric said the problem was that the door weighed over a ton, and it was going to be very difficult to open it, even with their advanced strength.

"Three of us should be able to get it open," Gard stated.

"Yeah, but since Miles doesn't have our strength, that means we need two more people with him and Eric when they get to the door," Will informed.

"I'll be part of the door opening crew," Juice volunteered. Will said he'd help with the door as well.

As Gard studied the blueprints, he discovered a concern that could ruin their rescue plan. Gard pointed at the room and said there was only one air vent that led into the room. Gard traced it back to its oxygen source. But the air vent had a second attachment to it that was blocked off. The second attachment led to the plant's chemical floor. Gard said that second vent could be attached to some poisonous gas of some kind.

The Hogs believed this theory, thinking this was how Ray kept his advantage in this kidnapping plan. With one remote control button, Ray could open the second vent and send his deadly gas into Kate's room, killing her instantly. They felt that if Ray ever felt a rescue attempt was under way, it would be the end of Kate with a simple push of a button. Gard said he'd feel better about Kate's safety if he was in the chemical room trying to find a way to keep the poison from going into Kate's room. Timber said that he'd head to the chemical room with him to assist Gard on that.

So the plan was to have Will, Juice, Eric, and Miles head to the door while Hayden, Timber, and Gard made it to the factory's chemical room. Eric requested Hayden to be with them at the door to have extra muscle at the door. Eric was nervous about getting caught and facing Ray. He reminded everyone what Cain said about Ray, that he was a highly intelligent mastermind who also had advanced strength. But then Will reminded the group that Cain mentioned Ray's negatives also. Will said that the guy wasn't expecting a rescue plan, so if they got caught, he'd have no time to prepare, and that could throw him off guard. Speaking of the word *guard*, the Hogs expected that the factory would have its share of guards.

At this time, Hayden and Miles returned to the kitchen. Hayden was successful in his mission of finding a working vehicle from the junkyard for their transportation. Once all seven were together, they started to break down their rescue mission into phases and making a checklist. Getting the car was the first thing checked off that list.

Monday, May 24, 2010

After a long night of planning, the Hogs were ready to set their plan into motion. They tried their best to get some rest before the event, but most of them had trouble keeping their eyes closed. When it was time to get up and leave, none of them really said anything. Miles took them to the junkyard, a place they had been to many times in the past to scrap cans for cash. Hayden showed them the vehicle; it was a dirty gray old van with very large windows on the side. Hayden lifted the hood up to install a smoke bomb within the car. When they got in, they detected the foul-smelling odor. The Hogs didn't say much. They just gathered inside and buckled up with Hayden in the driver's seat and Will in the front passenger seat. The Hogs were not fully awake yet, some still wishing that they could have hit the snooze button on this whole plan.

The ride was bumpy and the car was loud, but the sun rose out the east window, providing a nice sight. Eric just kept going over the plan in his mind, hoping he would find the courage to do his part. They were all nervous and worried about the possibility of something going wrong.

Juice leaned up to the front of the car to check the radio. He said the mood in this van was dead, so he wanted to give it some life. Juice turned the dial on the car radio, looking for a station that would fit the mood he was hoping to find. He found a country music station and quickly changed it before anyone requested that one. Then he found an upbeat '80s station and cranked up the volume. Juice started to nod his head, to get the groove going. He looked back and saw that no one was getting into the uplifting music. The fear of something going wrong was all that they could think about. The Hogs felt that they were risking more than just Kate's life in this mission; they feared that they could die from this experience as well.

"Come on, guys, we're not going to let Kate down! We're the Hogs! What's our motto?" Juice shouted.

"Everything burns?" Hayden uttered.

"That's your motto, Hayden," Juice responded.

"Juice, I don't know our motto. What is it?" Will delivered his question, more annoyed than excited.

"We…I guess we don't really have one. But when I was running cross-country, I always told my coach and teammates, 'Don't worry, I got this!'" Juice said, raising his fist in glory. "Come on, guys, we all need to have this attitude!"

"You know, he's right. I mean, we are pretty awesome," Gard stated, getting in the positive spirit. "We can't be beaten! We defeated the Havocs and kicked Bigfoot's hairy butt!" Gard said, now getting pumped up. The others started to let out a smile of excitement. The mood in the car was no longer low. They were now prepared and ready for their mission as if they were an undefeated team ready to take on another victory.

In time, the van grew close to their destination, which meant it was game time for the Hogs. Hayden reached for a string that he attached to the smoke bomb before they took off that morning. Hayden looked back at his friends; once he pulled the string, there was no going back. Hayden turned back to the road and spotted the factory in the distance. Hayden took a deep breath and pulled the string. The string ignited the smoke bomb under the hood, causing smoke to leak out of the car's hood.

"Oh no, you guys…I think there is something wrong with the car," Hayden said, making zero effort to sound convincing.

"Please tell me that you can act better than that," Will pleaded. Hayden emitted a small laugh and said he was praying that he could.

The smoke bomb was part of the plan, a trick to make it look like they were suffering from some small car trouble. This gave them a reason to pull over to the side of the road close to the factory. The Hogs all exited the car, and the fence that covered the factory was just a stone's throw away from them. They could see the empty parking lot of the factory and see the front doors of the building.

"No guards outside," Will whispered to his friends.

"We're in sight of the one security camera out front overlooking the parking lot," Hayden stated, which was exactly where they wanted to be.

"Miles, are you ready to go?" asked Eric, as their walking into the factory was the next step of the plan.

"Hey, now, I haven't even opened the hood yet," Hayden announced in a hurry before the two started moving. Hayden lifted the hood and reached in to retrieve the smoke bomb. He enclosed the smoke bomb in his fist to keep it hidden and to seal off the smoke leak. All the Hogs gathered around the hood of the car. Hayden informed Eric he should tell the people in the factory that the engine overheated, and they were giving it some time to cool off. Eric already knew the *script*, but it was nice being told it once again. This gave them time to stall for this to look legit. There was no more reason to hesitate, so Eric and Miles made their way to the factory.

The plan was for the two to go in, ask if they could use the restroom, and then sneak into the surveillance room. The two walked past the empty parking lot and made it to the front glass doors of the building. Miles attempted to pull open the doors but found them locked. Eric could see one guard inside sitting behind an oval-shaped desk.

The guard used his walkie-talkie to contact Ray who was on the second floor of the building in his own personal lab. When he received the message that there was someone at the front doors, Ray headed to the hall at the front of the building, which ran from west to east. To the west side was the fire exit staircase, and on the east side was the room Kate was locked in. The whole south side was encased by large bay windows. Ray looked out and saw the van with five teenagers standing around it. Ray didn't think anything of the group of kids, just some local teens whose van broke down. He replied over his walkie-talkie to the guard telling them to stand down, it was just some kids. He told them to make sure that they got back on their way because he was expecting Cain today. Back on the first floor of the building, the guard buzzed in Eric and Miles. The Hogs didn't know it, but their plan of not being suspected had worked.

Eric and Miles walked in thanking the guard for letting them in. They informed the guard that the van was simply overheating and needed to cool off, further mentioning that the owner of the van claimed that this happened all the time. The guard asked if they would be on their way soon. Miles said that it would only take a few minutes until they could get the van started again. He then asked if they could use their bathroom in the meantime. The guard told them it was down the west hall to the right.

Eric was grateful to Miles for doing all the talking because Miles could handle himself when lying better than he could. As they walked down the west hall of the first floor, they saw that they were out of sight of the guard. Once there, they walked up to the surveillance room on the south side of the hall, opposite of the restroom. Eric placed his hand on the handle and found it locked. Eric knew that he could use his strength to force open this door with one hand, but it wasn't the door he was worried about it. It was the guard inside that he feared. Eric knew that there must be someone watching the monitors of the security cameras. He knew he would have to throw a punch at the guard that was hard enough to knock him out right away.

Eric took a deep breath and turned the knob with force. The lock broke, and Eric softy pushed the door open and walked in. There was, indeed, a guard inside. The guard turned his head to Eric; and before he could say anything, Eric delivered a right hook to the man's head, knocking him out of his chair. The man, caught off guard, was knocked out with ease. Miles hopped into the room, quietly closing the door behind him. Eric checked on the guard to make sure he was indeed knocked out.

"Did you do it?" asked Miles.

"He's out," Eric stated. Eric first removed the man's cell phone and his walkie-talkie and then stood back from the guard because it was Miles's turn now. Miles touched the man's head, and they both teleported to a hospital miles and miles away from their location. Miles once went to this hospital during his prolonged illness. Once he was there, he put the guard where someone would spot him, then he teleported back to the surveillance room.

When Miles retuned, he felt very winded, as if he was gasping for air for a moment. Eric checked on him to see if he was okay. This moment of disconcert lasted only a few seconds, and he told Eric that he was fine. Miles had never had a problem teleporting before, so he wasn't sure what just happened to him at that moment. He couldn't have any problems with his powers right now, as the whole rescue plan was relying on him to get them all out of there.

Eric checked the monitors and saw that there was only one guard in the main entrance. Miles then asked where Ray was. Eric, who saw Ray in his lab on the second floor, let out a stressful grunt. If Ray was on the same floor as Kate's room, that meant they had to open Kate's door as quietly as they could in order to go undetected by Ray. Miles then asked if he could get a view of Kate's room. Eric said there was no camera in Kate's room, so there went the hopeful plan of Miles being able to just teleport inside her room. Eric then took out his phone to call Will.

Out by the van, Will's phone rang. Will saw that it was Eric and answered. "You guys in?" he asked.

"We're in, but we still have one more guard to take care of," Eric replied.

"Hold on now, look at this," Miles said. He was keeping his eyes on the main entrance monitor and saw the guard at the desk making his way out of the building. Eric checked the parking lot footage and saw that the guard was heading toward the van.

"Will, the last guard is heading your way. This is your chance," Eric informed him.

Will looked over and saw the guard walking up to the van. Will looked back at his friends, hoping that they were ready to join in on the mission. Everyone looked calm, for they were ready to act. The guard made it up to them asking if he could help them out in any way. Hayden just told the guy that they needed to give the car a few minutes to cool off. The guard was hoping for them to get on their way soon because his boss wished them to leave the area at once.

Gard asked Hayden if the engine had cooled off by now. Hayden went to start up the van to check. Hayden eased back to the driver's side door. Will still had the phone up to his ear and heard Eric's voice telling him that he was in the clear to make his move. The guard leaned into the hood of the van; and once he did, Will snuck up behind him and hit him in the back of the head, knocking him out. Hayden quickly moved to catch the falling body and carried the man over to the side door of the van.

"Okay, so we wait for Miles to teleport the guard, right?" Timber asked.

"That'll take too long," Hayden said as he opened the side door of the van. Hayden laid the body in the back seat of the van and started to tie him up with some fishing wire. "Any second now Ray is going to check in on this guard, and he's too unconscious to respond right now. At that moment, Ray will know that there is a rescue attempt in the works and will kill Kate right away," Hayden said as he removed the man's cell phone and walkie-talkie. "We need to get that door open ASAP, so we head to the door now, while Timber and Gard, get to the plant's chemical room," Hayden said as he finished tying the man up and slamming the van door closed.

Will told Eric that they were on their way in the building. Eric and Miles left the surveillance room and headed back to the main entrance. They saw their friends reach the glass door, so they buzzed them in. Once they were all inside, Eric informed everyone that Ray was the only threat they needed to worry about, saying that he's on the second floor right now. Gard tapped Timber's chest, saying that they needed to get moving. Gard and Timber ran over to the chemical floor located in the back of the office building on the first floor. Will, Juice, Hayden, Eric, and Miles headed off to the stairway. The Hogs studied the blueprints very well, so they all knew where to go. The boys going up the stairs moved quickly and quietly up the steps. There was no door separating the second-floor hall from the stairway. They came to a halt before entering the hallway.

"What are we doing?" asked Hayden, annoyed at their stopping.

"I'm checking if Timber and Gard made it to the second air vent's location yet," Eric said as he pulled out his phone to call Gard. Eric knew how important it was to disable that second vent because if they got caught, it would lead to Kate's death.

Over at the chemical and gas storage area, Timber and Gard arrived. Gard's phone rang, and he saw that it was Eric. He tossed his phone over to Timber, telling him that it was Eric and to pick it up. Timber answered and informed Eric that they were still looking for the vent when Gard suddenly yelled out that he found it. Timber ran over to Gard's side, and Gard pointed up to a black pipe that led into the air vent that ran to Kate's room. They followed the black pipe to a large gas-holding container. The container was all black, like a cauldron, with a glass window to see inside much like an oven window. The two looked up and told Eric over the phone that their theory on the deadly gas being pumped in Kate's room was true.

Looking inside, they could see that the gas was right now contained inside the container, but there was a closed door. If opened, the gas would draw into the pipe leading into the vent. Gard looked and saw that the pipe was attached to the celling before it reached the vent. Gard then snatched the phone out of Timber's hand and gave them the go-ahead on getting the door opened.

Eric hung up and said they were good to go on the door. Will, Juice, Hayden, Eric, and Miles tiptoed their way past Ray's lab and up to the door opposite the stairway on the other side of the hall. Eric looked at the control panel and hoped he could remember the right wires to pull as he removed the control panel and exposed the wires. Everyone was silent while Eric was in deep thought. Both Will and Hayden kept their eyes toward the hall and Ray's lab, praying that Ray wouldn't come out.

Eric had studied the notes Cain wrote on the manual for this security lock system so much that he knew it by heart. But he was still nervous as he pulled out the three wires needed to deactivate the lock. Once this was done, the Hogs heard the lock within the door move to the unlock position. This alerted the Hogs to two things: one, the door was now unlocked. And two: Ray had to have heard that sound.

All at once, the Hogs were digging their fingers on the side of the door, using all their might to peel it open wide. They were all thinking the same thing: *Get the door open, get the door open, get the door open!* Then a great fear rushed over them when they saw Ray step out of his lab into the hallway. Ray was stunned to see five kids there trying to open the door to get to Kate. The same kids he had brushed off for being a threat just a minute ago. This angered Ray, so he marched back into his lab to push the button that would send the gas into Kate's room.

In the chemical and gas storage area, an alarm went off by the cauldron. Timber and Gard investigated the storage unit and saw the door open, causing the gas to flow into the pipe. Timber screamed in panic. Gard, on the other hand, took a running start and with his strong legs jumped up to the pipe strapped to the ceiling. Once Gard was hanging on to the pipe on the ceiling, he pushed back against the ceiling with his feet, causing him to fall back to the ground, carrying the now-broken pipe with him. Gard hit the ground hard, as the green gas leaked out of the broken pipe and started to fill the room. Timber hurried over to his friend's side to help him up.

"Good job! Now let's get out of here!" Timber shouted as the two ran to the door.

Gard managed to keep the gas from seeping into Kate's air vent, but now his and Timber's lives were in danger. They had to exit that room as quickly as possible.

Back on the second floor, Ray retuned to the hallway. The teens still hadn't been able to open the door yet, and Ray marched up to them with a threatening gaze. The Hogs knew he was going to kill them, so Will went up to Ray to see if he could buy the others some time to get the door open. Will remembered the negatives Cain mentioned about Ray. Will knew that Ray was smug and always liked to come off as impressive. Will's theory was that since Ray didn't know Will was much stronger than he looked, Ray would let him take the first punch. Once Will and

Ray met up in the middle of the hall, Will pulled back his arm and sent a strong punch to Ray's chest.

Ray expected the punch to stop once it collided with his strong chest, not hurting him in the least. But that's not what happened. The punch hurt and caused Ray to lose his balance and take a step backward. This highly embarrassed Ray. Will then remembered the other thing Cain mentioned about Ray; he hated being caught off guard and hated surprises. Will could see that Ray was in shock, so he took that moment to throw more punches at Ray.

"Take him down, Will!" Juice shouted, cheering on his friends while his hands were still trying to pull open the heavy door.

"He needs backup!" Hayden shouted as he walked away from the door.

"No, Hayden, we really need you here!" Eric shouted at Hayden. Hayden ignored Eric as he pulled off one of the office doors in the hallway.

Ray managed to gather his thoughts and calmed himself down. He then saw one of Will's punches coming right at him, so he grabbed that arm, putting Will's attack to an abrupt halt.

"Now that's enough," Ray didn't even raise his voice when he said that, as he didn't like to run his emotion with rage when he could help it.

Will tried to pull his fist out of Ray's grip but failed. Ray looked into Will's eyes and said, "You boys found my cube, didn't you?" Then Ray swung Will across the room behind him toward the stairway. After he swung Will, he turned back to the other Hogs. At that moment, Hayden made his move with the office door; he ripped off its hinges. Hayden shoved the top of the door into Ray's stomach. The office door was between both Hayden and Ray, and since Ray was the one who had his end shoved into his stomach, he got the wind knocked out of him. Hayden pushed forward on the door, making Ray run backward to avoid falling. Will, being on the floor next to the stairway, curled up into a ball right into Ray's path. Ray tripped over Will when he ran into him. Ray fell backward down the stairs with the door falling and landing on top of him at the bottom of the steps. Hayden helped Will to his feet. They both looked down the steps and saw Ray on the ground.

"Did we kill him?" Will asked worriedly. Then they heard Ray grunt angrily as he started to get to his feet.

"We definitely didn't kill him!" Hayden shouted, panicked. Will and Hayden backed away from the stairway, getting ready for the fight to continue. Hayden really wished that he had his gun with him right now.

"You got that door open yet?" Hayden shouted.

"No!" Eric retorted, very annoyed that two of his helpers left him.

Will warned the Hogs at the door that Ray was coming back. Juice, thinking quickly, spotted a fire extinguisher on the side of the wall. "Hayden, grab it!" Juice yelled at Hayden while pointing at the fire extinguisher.

Hayden had no idea what Juice was talking about. Juice didn't want to use the words *fire extinguisher* because he thought it would make for a good surprise attack on Ray. Juice pointed again at the extinguisher with wide eyes.

"I don't understand!" Hayden shouted.

"Oh, do I have to do everything myself!" Juice yelled out as he walked away from the door.

"No, don't leave! We almost got it open!" Eric screamed because he was now the only one trying to open the door, and Juice had snatched the fire extinguisher off the wall and started running down the hall.

"Juice, he's coming!" Will warned Juice as Juice ran by him.

Juice then did a power slide down the hall up to the doorway. Ray returned to the second-floor hallway at this time, pointing his gun at Will. Since Juice was sliding on the floor, he wasn't spotted right away by Ray. When Ray noticed Juice sliding right up to him, it was too late; Juice started to spray the carbon dioxide out of the extinguisher canister right into Ray's face. The carbon dioxide was all over Ray, causing a gray cloud to surround his area. As Ray squirmed around in the gray cloud, Juice got to his feet and swung the fire extinguisher across his chest. He slammed it into Ray's gun and smashed it against the wall, bending the gun and causing it to be inoperable.

Ray, with a blind view, delivered a strong heavy punch at Juice's silhouette. The punch was mighty, and it launched Juice through the hallway and smacked him into the door they had been trying so hard to open this whole time. Juice was now on the door, feeling like his chest was just stomped on by a rhino.

"Oh man…I'm dead, aren't I?" Juice was only able to whisper out that sentence because of the crushing pain on his chest.

"Juice, I'm going to kill you! Your knocking into the door undid most of our work on getting it open!" Eric shouted.

Inside the room, Kate woke up from the drug-induced sleep she endured after each time she was taken out for a meal. The sound of Juice smacking into the door caused her to wake up. She could hear someone on the other side of the door trying to get it open. Kate felt that this was her chance to get free; so she grabbed her backpack, strapped it to her shoulders, and backed herself against the wall opposite the door. Outside the door, Will, Juice, Hayden, Eric, and Miles all started to pull hard on the door once again. Then Kate charged at the door with all her might, and with all their combined forces, the door flung open. Once the door was open, she got to see her rescuers, and she was shocked that she knew one of them.

"Tyler?" she said in a confused tone.

"Kate?" Juice replied in the same confused tone.

"You two know each other?" asked Hayden.

"Who cares! Miles, get us out of here!" Eric yelled. They all put a hand on Miles's shoulders, and he teleported them all out of the building. When Ray finally emerged from the carbon dioxide cloud, he saw no one and the vault door open with no Kate inside. He felt so lost and had no clue where they went.

Back outside, Gard and Timber were sprinting toward the van. Timber hopped in the passenger seat while Gard got in the driver's seat. The plan was that since they were not going to be around Miles for the exit strategy, they would take off in the van. Gard turned the key that had been left in the ignition, and the car started. Gard shoved his foot onto the accelerator, and the van took off fast. As Timber was yelling at Gard to drive faster, a disconcerting sound came from the van that had started to slow down on its own.

"What's going on?" asked Timber, panic in his voice.

"Dude, I think the car is dead!" Gard stated.

"No, that was the lie we told the bad guys! It should be fine!" Timber responded.

"Dude, this isn't a lie! It's really dead!" Gard shouted as he pulled the van over to put it in park.

"Screw this dumb junkyard van!" Timber shouted.

"I'm getting out of here!" Gard said very fast, as he opened the door and took off running down the country road. Timber really didn't want to run, but there was no way he was going to stay in the van. The tied-up unconscious guard started to wake up too, which made Timber get out of the van in a bigger hurry. Timber and Gard ran as fast as they could to the meetup spot; it wasn't far, just to the next intersection.

About two miles away at the meetup spot, the place where Miles teleported everyone else, the others waited for Timber and Gard. They were in the tree line next to the road. Kate was a little shaken from the rescue; then again, so was everyone else. The teleportation was a new experience for her. The Hogs promised her that they would explain that to her later. The Hogs told her that her dad was awake, and he was the one who sent them to come for her. They told her that she'd see him again tonight when he picked her up.

After they talked to her, they gave her space as she seemed to really need it at that time. As they waited for Timber and Gard, they asked Juice how he knew her. Juice said that he picked up some extra credit for working the stage crew. Last summer, he was asked to assist at a big musical where Kate was one of the leading roles.

"Where the heck are they? They should have been here by now," Eric stated.

"I'm going back for them," Will replied.

"No need...here they come," Hayden said as he looked down the road. Gard sprinted hard up to the tree line, while Timber was out of breath as he jogged up to them.

"We had some trouble with the car," Gard informed.

"Did you grab my gum on the car dashboard?" asked Hayden.

"No! I didn't grab your gum! We're fine, by the way!" Gard shouted.

"Can we go home now?" Timber asked, out of breath.

Later That Day, Just Before Nightfall

The Hogs returned to Hayden's backyard and waited for Cain to arrive. Will and Gard stood close to the driveway to spot his arrival. Eric brought out the box of the information they had on Ray that they had received from Cain the night before. Eric wanted it nearby in case Cain wanted it back. Miles peeked inside the box and saw a paperback book. The title of the book was *The Power of Loomation*. Miles picked it up and started to browse through the pages. Hayden, of course, started up the fire.

It was great that Juice had a preexisting friendship with Kate, so he handled the introductions, and she had someone whom she felt comfortable talking to. Kate found the nicknames to be funny. A very outgoing person, she didn't come off as shy to the rest of the Hogs at all. Juice was making some pie irons for his friends, starting with Kate. He handed over a plate with her sandwich on it, saying this was the sandwich he always bragged about back when they were both working on the musical last summer. When Juice was working on the musical as stage crew, he made sandwiches for the cast who were working all day. This was how Juice and Kate became friends; she was the only one who requested a peanut butter and jelly sandwich. Juice always said his best sandwich he made was a pie iron and that she would have to try it someday.

Hayden then offered her a root beer. She smiled, asking if he had any real beer. Hayden grinned and said that soda pop was all he had. Kate didn't care; she was so thirsty that any drink would do. She took a big bite out of her sandwich and felt her mouth burn from the food. She chugged her beverage straightway to cool off the burning sensation.

"It's still hot," Juice uttered.

"Yeah, but it's really good," Kate replied as she brought the sandwich back to her mouth and took another bite. This time the result was a calmer and more satisfying reaction from the meal. "So how do you guys know my dad?" Kate asked as she chewed.

The Hogs all passed stressful looks to one another because they didn't know what to say to that. Juice just stated that it was a long story.

Kate then asked if the boys were members of the Havocs. This relaxed the Hogs a bit because they were told that Kate was never a part of Cain's organization, so they didn't know if she was aware of the Havocs or not. But she brought it up first, so the Hogs felt free to talk about it. They informed her that they were not Havocs members nor hired employees paid by her father. They said that they had an agreement with Cain to rescue Kate.

"I'm truly grateful for the rescue, but I'm a little curious why my dad came to you for this mission," she stated.

"It's because we all have advanced strength," Juice replied.

"Except him, he has *magic powers*," Gard said, pointing at Miles.

"Actually, according to this book, it's called an active Loomation," Miles corrected.

Eric asked Miles where he got that book. Miles said he got it from the box, and Eric said he wanted to read it after him.

"That's..." Kate was lost for words at the moment. "That's really cool." Kate wished that she could have come up with something better to say than that. She then told them that she too had advanced strength. Eric claimed that he suspected that because he knew that the door she was trapped behind had to have had some heavy push on the inside when they got it open.

"And hey, I think my grandfather had an active Loomation too, so that's really cool." Kate's face presented a wide, almost-embarrassing smile. She couldn't help herself because she always thought her father and Ray were the only people out there like her. Being around people like her made her feelings of isolation vanish. She no longer felt like the different one of the group, and she could finally be her true self.

The Hogs, on the other hand, were a bit skeptical. When Cain told the Hogs that Ray was the inventor of the cube, the Hogs theorized that Ray was once a member of the Havocs, who invented the cube, went rogue, and wanted revenge on Cain. But when Kate mentioned that her grandfather had an active Loomation, they once again felt like the more answers they got, the more lost they became. Then Kate asked something that really caused them to stumble.

"How old are you guys?"

The Hogs were very confused by that question; they said that they were within the ages of seventeen and eighteen. Kate felt that she needed to elaborate more, so she asked them what year they were born in. The Hogs, again confused by the question, answered with the results making them seventeen and eighteen. Kate was a little stunned by that response.

"Kate, when were you born?" Eric asked politely.

"Nineteen seventy-nine," she stated. Once she gave her answer, Juice was midway in a sip of his drink and ended up spitting it out in response to the far-fetched reply. The other Hogs all acted like they just experienced a scare from that information. Kate was now the one who felt confused when she saw everyone's reaction.

"So you're saying that you're thirty-one years old?" Gard kind of shouted.

"Yeah," she replied like it was no big deal.

"But...how?" Timber said, trying to keep his voice low. This was such a shock, because Kate looked to be a fifteen-year-old girl.

"People who were born with this power inside them age slowly. It happened to me, my dad, and even Ray," Kate shed more light on the mystery. Kate said that she, just like her dad and Ray, had always looked half their age.

"So how old is your dad?" asked Gard.

"By now...eighty," she said. This made the Hogs physically shake as if an ice cube went down their shirt. They just saw Cain last night, and that guy looked to be in his early forties at least. They just couldn't wrap their heads around the idea that the man was eighty years old or that Kate was in her thirties. The Hogs were now very uneasy with the fact that they were going to age that slowly too.

"If you guys are truly the age you say, then why aren't you looking like you're nine?" she asked. Juice informed her that none of them were born with their powers; he said that they got them from the cube.

"What cube?" Kate wondered.

"She doesn't even know about the cube?" Timber said, stressing out.

Will showed Kate the cube, saying that they all got their powers from that. Kate confirmed that she had never seen that before and that this was the first time she learned about it. Timber frantically asked Kate if they were going to start aging slower like she did. Kate started to find the Hogs' freaking out about this to be kind of funny and chuckled out loud, stating that she honestly didn't know.

"Great. Now we could be even more abnormal," Timber said worriedly.

"Hey, come on now, be a little more respectful here," Juice said, standing up for his friend.

Timber immediately apologized, saying he didn't mean any disrespect toward Kate. Kate felt no disrespect from Timber. Frankly, watching him spaz out about this new information made her laugh for the first time in a long time. She was just so used to her aging process that she never really freaked out about it. Before anyone was able to talk again, headlights came glaring in their eyes from down the driveway. The overwhelming information the Hogs just learned about their powers had to be set aside because it was now tough-guy-attitude time. Hayden picked up his rifle, and Gard grabbed the fire poker for a feeling of safety.

Everyone knew it was Cain driving down the driveway. Kate was speechless and entered a frozen state of suspension. Kate hadn't seen her father since she was a kid, so this was a long-awaited reunion. The car came to a stop, the headlights turned off, and Cain emerged from the driver's side door. Once Kate saw her dad, her legs started to move fast. She rushed past the fire ring, making her way past the Hogs up to her dad. She hopped into her father's arms and embraced him with a big hug.

The Hogs were delighted to see Kate be reunited with her long-lost father. They felt a sense of pride for being responsible for this reunion. All the panic, all the worry from the next attack all washed away for the Hogs at that moment. They were happy that they were able to save Kate and that she was able to see her father again. The Hogs risked their lives going into Ray's factory to get her out, but it all seemed worth it just to see this moment.

Cain asked her if she was okay. She replied that she was fine. He asked if Ray hurt her. She said just some bruises on her wrist from the chains, that was all. Cain then asked if the boys hurt her. She said no; they were all really nice to her. Cain then faced the Hogs. The Hogs were speechless, as the heartwarming moment felt like it passed too quickly. Now Cain seemed to enter an all-business stage. Cain said that a deal was a deal; he announced that he'd stay out of the Hogs' way and that they could keep the cube. Cain turned to his daughter and told her that they were leaving now.

"Can I say goodbye first?" she kindly pleaded.

Cain didn't like that request, but he could tell that it was important for her to say goodbye, so he gave her one minute to say goodbye. Kate came to each Hog member individually, giving them all a heartfelt hug. She then returned to her father and got into the passenger seat of the car. Right before Cain entered the car, he gave one last glance at the Hogs. He nodded forcefully at them. No thank you was said, just a grateful nod, and the Hogs felt respected by this man's action. Cain left the Hogs, but he didn't bother picking up his box of information he had on Ray, as he felt that he didn't need it anymore.

Once the car was out of sight, Eric said that he was going home. The others said that they'd be heading home too, for they really missed their own beds and were ready for a much-needed good night's sleep.

CHAPTER 25

A New Threat

Tuesday, May 25, 2010

The next morning, Will drove himself to school. It was the final day for seniors, and graduation was soon. Most seniors were thrilled with their last day, but Will was hoping it would last as long as it possibly could. He felt this was the most normal part of his day. As Will took a few steps away from his car, a voice called out his name, and Will was once again reminded of how abnormal his life really was.

"Hello, Will," the voice said.

Will turned around slowly and saw Ray standing on the sidewalk. Because of Ray's location, Will should have seen him standing there when he parked his car. Ray must have been hiding between the houses on the side of the road or the bushes next to the sidewalk. Will worried that if Ray was hiding, waiting for him to show up, how did he know where he always parked his car for school every day? The answers were simple. Once Ray identified the people who rescued Kate after he captured her, he learned where they went to school. With his computer skills, he was easily able to access the school's security footage to find the location where Will parked his car every day at the same time. Ray hid on the porch of the house next to the road that Will parked on and waited until Will was out of the car to let him know of his presence.

"What do you want?" Will asked as he tried to hold back the fear he was suddenly feeling. Ray raised his hands up, indicating that he wasn't there to fight.

"I just want to talk," Ray said nicely.

Will turned his head to the left and then to the right, giving both sides a good glance, trying to see if Ray was alone.

"Don't worry, I didn't bring anyone with me. And I would like to say I came unarmed, but I want this to be an honest conversation," Ray said as he lifted his shirt to show off his gun placed in his holster strapped to his side. Will now regretted using his usual parking place. He knew why Ray picked him to have his chat with. Will parked on the one-way road behind the school as it was closer to his house, and he didn't have to deal with the crowd parking lot at the end of the day. It was also very empty; the student parking lot was in front of the school, and the staff parked on the side of the school. So there was no big crowd for Ray to avoid and only one security camera that Ray managed to disable during his little chat with Will.

"Make it fast. I got first period soon," Will responded, reminding Ray that someone was going to notice him missing soon.

"Don't worry, this won't take long. I'm a fast talker," Ray stated. "I just want to say how impressed I was with you and your friend's little rescue yesterday. Little sloppy, but hey, this was me you were dealing with, so you should be grateful that all of you got out alive."

"We don't know where Kate is," Will informed him with no hesitation.

"I assume that you returned her to her father. Knowing him, I bet he won't let her out of his sight right now. This is my guess why he hasn't made a counterattack on me yet. His babysitting is keeping him occupied, so he must pay others to do his searching for him. My educated guess is that Cain will have her leave the country any day now."

"Then what do you want with us?" asked Will.

"I want to know where your loyalties lie. Are you a part of Cain's merry band of thieves and murderers, or were you and your friends a hired job?" Ray questioned with a new striking tone.

"We don't serve Cain. We did what we did to save the girl, and that's it," Will retorted with a backlash.

"Well, then I would like to hire you. I will be willing to pay top dollar for a group with your strengths and skills."

"Not interested, so just leave us alone," Will said, unaffected by the lure of a big-time paycheck and wishing this conversation would end.

"Do you really think Cain is going to leave you guys alone?" These words from Ray made Will nervous. "I visited one of the prisons holding the remaining members of the once-proud Havocs group. The boys there spilled their guts and ratted out all that they knew about Cain and the members of the Hang Out Group for a very small fee."

Ray, knowing the title of Will's friends' group, made Will even more apprehensive. He was warned about Ray's intelligence, and now he knew why.

"You burned down Cain's home and got all his followers tossed in prison. See, Cain uses people. He knew he couldn't get his daughter himself, so he placed his revenge on you and your friends on hold, just until he could get you to do what he wanted. Now that you did what he wanted, he'll find time to get his revenge," Ray said in earnest.

Will was thinking about the deal the Hogs made with Cain. The deal was they returned his daughter alive, and he never bothered them again. But they didn't know Cain like Ray did. How could they be sure that Cain was a man of his word? The possibility of Cain turning on his deal caused much stress to Will; he even started to sweat thinking about it. Will wasn't feeling too strong now; he suddenly felt very weak in the legs and the arms. He tried his best not to show it in front of Ray.

"Join me, and together we'll take out Cain. He can't take us all on, and if we strike now, he'll be too weak to put up a good fight." Ray pitched his plan to Will, doing his best to persuade him.

Will did have to think about this. The idea of trusting the kidnapper started to sound safer than trusting Cain. It took a moment for Will to snap himself out of Ray's luring words. Ray was asking for Will and his friends to straight up kill a man all for their own personal safety. Will had faith in people, even Cain; so until Cain went back on his word, they were not at war with him.

"No," Will said, feeling the strength in his legs and arms return to him, and he was now able to lift his head high. "Cain is your problem, and you will not drag my friends and me into your war."

Ray didn't show any reaction to Will's refusal to join. He never liked to show any negative expressions. "Fine, but here's a quick question…is that your normal janitor?" Ray said as he pointed at the school.

Will turned around fast and saw that they were being watched by someone inside the school. In one of the windows, a man stood looking right in their direction. It felt very creepy, and to make things even more uncomfortable, that wasn't the school's janitor. This was a man whom Will had never seen before. Will turned back toward Ray, but Ray was already down the street turning on the curb.

The last thing Ray shouted out to Will sent chills down his spine: "I'll be back for my cube next time!"

Will was frozen with worry. He looked back at the school and caught the janitor walking away. Will remained motionless, just taking this all in. He believed that he did the right thing turning down Ray's offer, but he started to wonder if Cain had his men spying on him and the other Hogs. Will knew that the Havocs were all either arrested or killed by Bigfoot. Then Will remembered what Ray said about Cain paying people to spy for him. Cain was good at finding people to work for him. Heck, he was able to get the Hogs to do a job for him, so it was possible that Cain already had new workers spying on his enemies. Will just couldn't keep standing still; the bell was going to ring soon, so he made his way to the building to get to class on time. When he arrived, his friend Hayden was the first to see him.

"What is it?" Hayden asked Will.

Will looked flushed and was covered in sweat, so it was obvious that there was something wrong. Will said that he'd share it after school, saying that he didn't want everyone to carry his worry on their last day of school.

School provided a fun day for all the seniors, even Will. They were screaming in the classrooms and running up and down the halls. It was a wild place in the halls of the school that day. After the day was over, the Hogs all gathered up at the park at Will's request. The Hogs were all parked next to the park's basketball court—a place they went to many times before during the summers. Miles arrived by teleporting. This made Eric angry; he told Miles he just couldn't keep teleporting everywhere he wanted as the risk of being caught was too high. Miles said that he needed to keep practicing, and this saved on gas money.

Will informed the group of his little visit with Ray that morning. Will went into detail on what Ray wanted from the Hogs. They had a job offer from Ray, and they had to discuss that as a group. They hated the idea of doing a job for one mad criminal one day then getting hired by another the next. They didn't want a life working for thugs and criminals. The offer did feel tempting, which disturbed them.

They talked about when Juice was suffering from his dual personality and had an urge for that thrill life that came from breaking the law. The Hogs only knew three people who had the same powers they did, and two of the three turned to a life of crime. This felt like a slippery slope for the group, and taking another job from either Cain or Ray would find them in too deep of a life of crime, which they didn't want. They all agreed to not work for either one of them again.

Will brought up the new janitor that Ray pointed out. The fact that Ray knew the regular staff of their school was a sign that this guy did his research on people to a huge extent. Will was warned by Ray that Cain could have hired people to watch them.

"Why would Cain hire people to keep an eye on us?" Juice asked.

"Because he may be planning an attack on us?" Timber theorized.

"Or he does plan on coming back for the cube," Eric added.

"He said he didn't want the cube," Miles stated.

"He also would have said whatever it took for us to go save his daughter," Gard replied.

"Ray wants the cube...It was the last thing he said to me," Will announced.

The Hogs all felt very stressed out at this moment. They now felt like they were caught between a war between Cain and Ray, and they didn't want either side to have the cube.

"Look, Cain is headstrong on killing Ray. If he succeeds, then we should be fine," Hayden said.

"Yeah, but what about us in the meantime?" wondered Timber.

"Ray knows that Cain is on the hunt for him, so I bet he'll be trying to get that cube back as soon as he can because it could save him from Cain," Eric pointed out.

"So we don't let him take it then. We kept it away from the Havocs all this time," Juice mentioned.

"Yeah, that ended with them attacking us with Bigfoot!" Timber replied.

"Hey, now, we won that fight!" Gard stated.

"Timber's right. We can't keep fighting. It's going to get out of hand, and one of us could end up dead," Will chimed in.

"We could run and hide," Juice suggested.

Hayden and Gard didn't like that idea, but Will felt that he understood what Juice was pitching.

"We could go on our camping trip right away," Will told the others, selling Juice's idea. The Hogs had this big monthlong camping trip planned for the summer. The planning of it was on hold when Miles grew sick. Even after Miles was healed, the Hogs were too busy talking about the Havocs and the acquisition of the cube to worry about their camping trip. But the vacation would be the perfect cover for their run-and-hide situation.

The Hogs said that if they could find a place to hide, they could lay low for a month, hopefully enough time for Cain to kill Ray, and they would be in the clear. They figured that Cain had the better odds of winning, since Ray came to the Hogs seeking help to take on Cain. Cain was very confident that he could handle Ray on his own. And if Cain lived up to his word to leave the Hogs alone, this could be their best way to get all this behind them.

The Hogs did have to discuss the possibility of Ray winning the fight against Cain. They would need a deal with Ray to keep him away from them. The Hogs said that if Ray won and did come back for the cube, they would trade it to Ray for forever leaving them alone. The Hogs hated the idea of handing something so powerful to a criminal, but it was the only leverage they had. Besides, if the cube was out of their hands, a huge responsibility would be lifted. Some didn't see it that way. They believed that if Ray used the cube to do horrible things, that would be on them. It wasn't easy for everyone to agree on this trade, but they felt that they had no choice.

Sunday, May 30, 2010

The last days of the week were the longest for the Hogs. They all had to check in every morning and night with each other through text messages to make sure they were all fine. For all they knew, an attack on Ray or Cain could happen at any moment. They told their parents that they moved their camping trip to right after graduation. They would be gone for most of June. They were all packed up and ready to go; all they had to do was to attend graduation. Graduation was at noon, and it was a short but sweet ceremony. Afterward, they all took photos in the gym with their fellow graduates. Juice and Will ran into a surprising visitor, Kate.

"Congratulations, boys," Kate said to the two who were both very happy to see Kate safe and sound. She gave hugs to both.

"Is your dad here?" asked Juice.

"Yes, but he's keeping his distance," replied Kate.

"We appreciate that," Juice replied, trying to make it sound like it was a joke. But to be honest, knowing that Cain was close by made Juice very nervous, and his voice began to crack.

"Kate, how truthful is your father when it comes to his word?" Will asked.

"Don't worry, I talked to him, and he's going to honor his deal. He owes you guys my life, so it's the least he could do."

"Has he gone after Ray yet?" questioned Will.

"Not yet, but he's going to make a move on him soon," Kate answered.

"Is he spying on us?" Will felt that he had to ask.

Kate hesitated before answering. "Yes, but he's not interested in you," she said bashfully. "My father felt that Ray would come after you guys, so he hired some people to keep an eye on you to see if Ray would show up. One of his spies reported Ray at your school the other day."

"So Cain's having us watched. I don't like that. That goes against our deal," Will retorted angrily.

"He's only looking for Ray. And Cain was right. Ray did come to you, Will," Juice mentioned to Will. This would explain why Ray hadn't shown his face to the Hogs since he saw Will.

"We fear that Ray would make a move on us to get the cube," Juice informed Kate.

"I wouldn't doubt that. Expect a huge attack. When he came after me, he sent three men. I was easily able to handle myself against them, so Ray won't make that mistake again. And I was just one person. You guys are seven," warned Kate.

All this information made it clear that the Hogs had to leave town and find a place to hide. They didn't like Cain's spies watching them nor the fear of some big elaborate attack from Ray. At this moment, Hayden, Timber, Eric, Gard, and even Miles approached the three among the crowd, waving cheerfully.

Kate gave a friendly hug to the rest of the boys, and before she could walk away, one of the parents asked for a group photo with everyone. The Hogs all convinced Kate to stay for the group photo. She was honored to be included. She wore a large smile as she stood with her newly found friends. Her whole life she hadn't been able to tell anyone who she really was nor about her powers. But now being with people she could be honest with, a group who had the same powers she had, made her feel like she had a real group of friends. Kate took off after the photo, wishing the Hogs good luck on their journey.

CHAPTER 26

The Swamp

It was about 5:00 p.m., many hours after the graduation ceremony. Hayden was hooking his pop-up camper to the back of his truck. The inside of the pop-up camper was stuffed with luggage, while the truck was stuffed with camping supplies. Will and Hayden were in the front seat, and Juice and Timber were in the back, all loaded up and ready to take off. Hayden's mom wanted one more hug from Hayden through the driver's side window. She wanted a hug from all the boys as well. Being friends with someone for so long, you developed a kind relationship with their parents, which was the case with most of their parents. Will, Juice, and Timber already said their goodbyes to their parents before heading over to Hayden's.

Not too long after the truck left Hayden's house, Timber softly asked, "You think they'll be all right?" From the tone of Timber's voice, the boys knew exactly what Timber meant by that question.

"Safest thing we can do for them is to get as far away from them as possible," Will replied, feeling guilty for leaving their parents in the dark as to the real reason they were leaving. The Hogs were anticipating an ambush from Ray at any moment. They feared that their secret would be revealed during an attack or that their parents would get hurt in the cross fire. If Ray couldn't find the Hogs, then he couldn't negotiate any kind of ransom, thus keeping their families safe from kidnapping.

"So when are we meeting up with Gard and the others?" wondered Timber.

Gard had picked up Eric and Miles in his car already. They left town around the same time Hayden's truck did. Will said that they wouldn't be meeting up with them right away. The idea was to have both vehicles take off out of town from two different directions, both seeking a secure place to hide.

"So you're saying this is a competition then," Juice said, thrilled at the idea. Until Juice spoke up, the mood in the car was lifeless, as if the Hogs were heading to a funeral. Juice's excitement at finding a place to hide before the other car gave the boys a kind of fun game to play.

"Hayden, if anyone can get off the grid, it's you. Come on now, think. Where would you hide?" Juice questioned Hayden, trying to spark an idea in his mind.

Hayden just needed a minute with his thoughts to come up with a solution, and then he felt foolish for not thinking of it sooner. It's amazing how your brain works given the mood you're in. Now that Hayden was thinking this to be more of a competition rather than finding a place to hide, his mind opened to a fitting place. Hayden reached over to the passenger's side and opened the glove box. The glove box was a mess, full of fast-food wrappers and extra packs of gum, which poured out all over Will's legs.

"You need something, Hayden?" Will asked, annoyed that his legroom was now full of garbage.

"Yeah, I forget I had extra gum in there. Give me one," Hayden replied.

As Will was searching the gum packs trying to find one that wasn't empty, Hayden mentioned the map he had in the back of the glove box, which was what he originally wanted. Will gave up on the gum request and pulled out the map. Will unfolded the map and looked at it. Hayden's badly drawn doodles were all over it. He had a thing for drawing mushroom clouds on stuff, and this map was one of them.

"Hayden, are you a terrorist?" Juice asked in a friendly tone.

"If this was done by anyone else, I would be thinking the same thing," Will said with a chuckle.

"Last summer, I would take the fireworks I got from my brother and set them off in the middle of nowhere."

"You were blowing up fireworks and you never invited us!" Juice said, insulted.

"I was with my girlfriend!" Hayden shouted in the heat of the moment. "She, like me, had a love for seeing things being blown up. It was one of the ways we blew off steam…among other things."

"Nope, don't need to elaborate any further!" Timber shouted.

"Anyway, I had one rocket firework that I was told was barely legal due to its unusually loud *boom*. I knew I had to be as far away from civilization as possible and nowhere near an airport when I set it off. When I found the perfect place, I circled it on the map and called it *the dead zone*," Hayden explained. Hayden did his best to block any memories of him and his ex-girlfriend, which was why he never thought about bringing this location up before.

Will looked at the map and saw that the *dead zone* label on the map was in a swamp. "Hayden, the dead zone is a swamp?" he asked.

"Yeah, but I didn't call it the dead zone because of that…I called it the dead zone because there was absolutely no cell phone service within anywhere of that location," Hayden stated.

"Hayden, that's perfect! No service would help us keep off the grid!" Will said with excitement.

"Did you just hear him? He said it's a swamp!" Timber yelled, not wanting to stay in a swamp.

Despite it being a swamp, Will knew that this place was perfect. It was way out in the middle of nowhere. With no cell phone service, it was the place where you want to go when you want to disappear. Will read the map and navigated Hayden to the swamp.

A couple of hours later, the Hogs found themselves on the road next to the swamp. The stench of the area was miserable. Tall grass, all covered with flying insects, surrounded the area for miles. It was going to get dark soon, and there was no word from the other Hogs on their search. The Hogs, in turn, felt a little desperate to quickly find a place.

Will checked his phone and saw that it was giving him the *no signal* sign; this meant that they had arrived. Hayden had only been to this place once, and when he was there, it was nighttime. The Hogs were looking for a pathway into the swamp, a dirt or stone road of some kind. Hayden got tired of waiting, so he just drove his truck right into the tall grass. The ground was bumpy, which caused the truck to bounce up and down.

"Hayden, are you crazy?" Timber shouted.

"Oh, it hasn't rained in weeks. All the mud is dried up by now. Besides, I got four-wheel drive!" Hayden replied.

"Yeah, but isn't this illegal?" questioned Timber.

"We'll just tell the cops that the GPS told us to turn here!" Juice chuckled as he was enjoying the ride.

"I don't think that'll be very effective in court, Juice," Will uttered.

Just then, the high grass was gone, and the truck entered a muddy patch of land. After driving deep into the patch of land, Hayden slowed the vehicle to a stop. He put the truck in park and exited out the door. Will, Juice, and Timber also got out along with him.

"*Home sweet home?*" Juice questioned with his hand plugging his nose.

Hayden loved the outdoors, but this smell was a bit much even for him. Then Will saw something in the short distance.

"Hey, check it out!" Will yelled over to the others.

The three huddled around Will and looked in the direction he was pointing. They all saw a small cabin a short distance away.

"I knew it! We're on someone's property!" Timber said, growing even more disgusted for being on the grounds.

Hayden was the first one to march toward the cabin with Juice and Will following. Timber, not wanting to be the one who got left behind, hustled his way up to his friends. As the four got closer to the cabin, they saw a small pond just a short walk away from the cabin.

"Hey, a pond," Hayden pointed out. "Pond means fish…Fish means food," he said, sounding like a caveman.

Will was impressed with how clear the pond looked. He had seen dirty swamp water before, but this pond looked to be as clean as a swimming pool. As they got closer, they saw that the large tree next to the cabin looked mighty healthy, which seemed very odd given the area. Then they stepped on perfect green grass. Will put his hands on the grass and felt as if he had placed his hand onto a putting green found on a golf course.

This perfect, soft-looking grass went out a stretch. The cabin they were walking toward seemed to be right in the center of it all. The pond and the tree were both within this region of the lush green grass. Hayden then asked Juice if he could smell it. Juice said he didn't smell anything. Then they realized that when they were standing on this grass, that nasty odor of the swamp was somehow gone. Timber pointed out that the bugs even seemed to calm down. As soon as the four boys got out of the truck, they were swatting and batting at the bugs flying around their space. But the bugs here were not a problem on the green grass.

The Hogs all stood about six feet apart from each other on the soft green turf, while Will was still squatting with one hand on the ground. They were just looking at each other, puzzled by this place.

Juice smiled and said, "This place will work."

They all felt that Juice was right; all the problems of being in a swamp vanished as soon as they reached this miraculous area. Will had a great feeling about this place too; it felt like a blessing from the heavens.

The four Hogs walked deeper into the area and right up to the cabin. The cabin looked beautiful and brand-new. When the Hogs stood in front of the structure, they noticed the place had a porch. On the roof of the porch, there were words that read, "The Diamond in the Rough—1924." The Hogs thought that this title was fitting. They were so astonished at how such an old cabin could still look brand-new after all these years of damaging weather. Hayden went up to the front door with Juice behind him.

"Should we knock?" asked Juice as Hayden ignored Juice's question and simply turned the knob and pushed open the door.

"Knock, knock!" Hayden said after the door was open all the way.

There wasn't much in the cabin, just a hammock and a table. Above the table, a frame hung on the wall. The frame displayed an old newspaper from the year 1924. The place was so empty, and the only hint at the owner being there last was in the year 1924, so they just figured the place had been abandoned for decades.

They decided that this place would be their sanctuary. A place where they could stay hidden because no one would look in a swamp for them. And if anyone came looking for them, they wouldn't last long inside the swamp because of its cruel conditions. If they didn't travel deep enough into the swamp to find the Diamond in the Rough, no one would ever find them.

"Juice, help me set up the pop-up camper," Hayden requested. Hayden and Juice headed back to the truck to bring the camper to the grass, and Will said that he'd start finding some stones to build a fire ring.

"What you want me to do then?" Timber asked.

"Call Gard. Tell him we found a place to hide," Juice ordered as he walked away with Hayden toward the truck.

Timber took out his phone and saw that his cell was saying *no signal.* "How am I supposed to do that?" Timber complained.

"Just start walking in one direction until you find a signal!" Hayden shouted as he was now very far away from Timber.

Timber let out a big sigh and started to walk. Not too long after exiting the green grass, he hollered at his friends, "Does anyone have any bug spray?"

Hours passed, and the sun was about gone. The Hogs set the place up very nicely; the pop-up camper was up with all the beds made. They put up a steel frame canopy with a foldout table underneath to hold their food. They placed chairs all around the fire ring, which consisted of stones found within the swamp. Juice and Hayden used the truck to gather up tons of dead wood within the area to feed the fire for several nights. Will used an ax to chop the wood up into digestible bites to fit into the fire ring. The location was almost perfect—except the car that was carrying the food and drinks still hadn't shown up yet. The Hogs just sat by the fire waiting patiently.

Hayden was temporarily outside the comfort zone. When he came back, his friends saw him carrying a shovel. "The bathroom is all set up," Hayden said.

"Great. Now all we need is the food," Juice stated.

"They should have found us by now," Will said, starting to worry.

"I keep wanting to use my phone to simply call them, but I keep forgetting that we have no signal!" Juice said, becoming irritated.

When Timber was on his march to find a phone signal, he jogged for a long time until he was finally able to make a call. When Timber got all the way out there, he realized that he didn't have Hayden's map with him. So he had to tell Gard the coordinates from memory alone. Juice laughed saying that they found a place to hide that was so well hidden that people who knew where to find them still couldn't find them.

"You told them to drive through the tall grass, right?" Hayden asked as he tossed a few logs into the fire.

Timber told them what road they needed to be on when they arrive.

"So they could just be circling around the entire swamp right now, and we just don't know it," Will said, thinking out loud. To the north side of the comfort zone was a large hill, so the Hogs all headed up the hill. Once on top, they were looking for some headlights.

"Hayden, light off some of your fireworks to signal them," Juice requested.

"What do you mean? I don't have any fireworks with me," said Hayden who was a horrible liar when it came to things like this.

"You sure it's wise to be setting off fireworks when we're trying to keep a low profile?" Timber asked, thinking the idea was a dumb one that defeated the whole purpose of hiding.

Before they could continue the talk about the fireworks idea, Will spotted Gard's headlights out in the field. He was overwhelmed with joy to have been able to spot them. The rest of the Hogs looked in the direction Will was pointing and saw the car driving east. The four Hogs all started to yell and jumped up, trying to be spotted by the car.

In the moving car, Gard was having a blast driving at such high speeds that the car flew up in the air after running into some of the big bumps. Eric was very concerned about the beating his car was taking, but Gard said his car could handle the impact.

"Remind me to tell Timber he gives horrible directions," Eric said, angry by the extended long trip and annoying road conditions.

"We better hurry up and find them! Once the sun goes down, it'll be impossible," Miles stated.

"Knowing Hayden, I bet he already has a fire going. To be honest, that's what I'm really looking for," Gard replied. "We just have to keep our eyes open," he added. If the Hogs in the car had taken a long glance to their right, they would have seen their friends a half mile away, jumping up and down on the hill.

"WE'RE OVER HERE!" the group shouted, among other things. Just then, Juice took a mighty jump to reach a height high enough for the car to spot him. Once he launched himself up in the air, he screamed as loudly as he could. But Juice's body didn't return to the ground. In the middle of yelling, Will stopped and turned his head up toward Juice.

"What the heck, Juice?" Will yelled. This caused both Hayden and Timber to look up toward their friend. None of them could believe what they were seeing at that moment. Juice was just hanging in the air with nothing on him holding him up. He was clenching his muscles tightly as if he was hanging on to something, a natural reaction when one finds oneself up so high off the ground.

"Juice, get down!" ordered Timber as he gestured with his hands.

"I don't know how!" Juice yelled back.

"Are you stuck?" wondered Will.

"I'll go find a stick," Hayden said as he walked back down the hill.

"Juice, how did this happen?" Will asked.

"I just jumped up here…and I guess gravity just decided to stop working on me," Juice explained.

"Well, get it working again and come back to the ground!" Timber shouted, starting to stress out just as Hayden showed up with a tree branch.

"All right, Juice, grab hold of the stick!" Hayden said as he swung the tree branch over his shoulder. The branch waved beneath Juice's feet.

"Hey, take it easy! I'm not a piñata up here!" Juice yelled back.

"Wouldn't that be cool if you were now full of candy?" Hayden said, finding this whole situation hilarious.

Juice eyed the car in the distance; he felt that he could get to the car through the air. He told the guys he wanted to try it. Will told Juice to go with his gut feeling and try it. Timber chimed in and said he thought all of this was nuts. Juice flexed his muscles as if he was steering his body. Once his body was facing the car headfirst, he felt like he could push off from the air as if he was a bullet being fired out of a gun. He tried to perform that action and managed to launch himself like a dart soaring quickly through the air right at the car.

In the car, Eric noticed something coming their way. Gard slammed on the brakes hard and looked out the passenger-side window where Eric was pointing.

"What the heck is that?" asked Gard as he saw the object get closer.

"I think it's Juice," Miles guessed. The three didn't know what to think, but Eric believed that maybe Will threw him at them to get their attention.

"That is Juice," Gard said, sounding very confused.

The three got out of the car, and Juice flew right above their car yelling, "HEYYYY!"

"HOLY CRAP, JUICE!" Eric shouted as Juice flew right over their heads. He stopped in midair and turned to face the three.

"Juice, you're flying! That's awesome!" Gard shouted.

Miles was cheering with joy. Juice pointed to the campsite and said that was where the others were. Juice took off in the air back to the campsite to show them the way. The three boys returned to the car, and Gard drove his car following the flying man.

"Okay, he's coming back now," Will said with panic in his voice because it looked like Juice was trying to land. Will, Hayden, and Timber all scattered out of Juice's way as he came crashing into the side of the hill.

Juice lifted his head shouting, "WOO! That was incredible!"

"Yeah, that crash landing was really well executed!" Will said, laughing as he helped his friend to his feet.

"It was my first landing, Will. I'll get better at it," Juice replied.

The car came up with great speed. Hayden waved the car down the hill where Gard could see where Hayden parked his truck. Gard parked the car, and all three of them got out.

"Juice, when did you learn how to fly?" Gard said with great excitement in his voice.

"What was it like, flying through the air like that?" Miles asked, overwhelmed with this newly found discovery.

"Hold on, everyone!" Hayden shouted to get everyone to calm down for a moment. "We eat first!" he said, having his appetite speak for him.

Gard agreed, for he too was very hungry. When the Hogs were all together, the new arrivals had to take in the amazement of the *Diamond in the Rough* atmosphere. They were blown away at how nice this acre of land was given the fact that it was in the middle of a very large swamp. There was a lot to take in this day, in the new area they would call home for the next month as well as Juice's newly discovered ability. It was a very overwhelming night, and the Hogs loved it. They felt like a bunch of kids engulfed by the wonders of the world again. The Hogs roasted hot dogs over the fire and sat around drinking pop. They shared their thoughts regarding theories of how this land existed. And they wondered how Juice was able to fly now. They just added that to the unexplained topics list, along with the question of why Hayden was fireproof while the others were not or why Miles had the power to teleport. For now, the Hogs didn't really care about the unsolved mysteries. They had a great night that night. It was the first time in a long time they felt safe and free from worry.

CHAPTER 27

Homecoming

Getting Close to Midnight

An older gentleman made his way to a bar that lay within a small town in the south of Texas. He plopped onto a seat at the bar, close to the exit. A nice bartender stepped over, placed a coaster in front of him, and asked him what he would like. The man politely ordered a glass of scotch, as he dropped a $20 onto the table and told her to keep the change. As the lady poured the drink, the man checked his watch. He saw that the day was down to its final minutes. As he lifted his glass up, he suddenly observed his reflection in the mirror behind the bar.

"Really...you're having a drink tonight...tonight of all nights?" the man said to himself. This man was Logan, a man who'd been on the run for decades, always skipping town just before whatever was chasing him caught up to him. Logan had a history of talking to himself since being alone for so long would make a man do that. Logan would talk to himself in order to help him think; he believed thinking out loud would help him improve his ability to process information. There was a part of Logan that was shocked that he went to a bar to have a drink because the end of the month was at hand, and he had always made sure he had a sober mind during this time.

"I'm just feeling nervous," Logan said to himself. "I'm hoping a drink will calm me down," Logan said before taking his first sip from the glass. "I'm limiting myself to just one drink. I can still do my *thing* after one drink. I sure can't do my *thing* when I'm feeling this nervous!"

After Logan's second drink from his glass, he noticed an ashtray on the bar. He pulled it up close to him and stuffed some scraps of paper from his pocket inside it. Logan then took out a Zippo lighter from his other pocket and burned up the scraps of paper inside the ashtray. Logan learned a long time ago to burn his notes before leaving town. One time he left his journal behind, and that led to a massive incident that almost cost him his life. Written on one of the burning scraps of notebook paper was a list of what was causing Logan to be so uneasy. Logan liked to write down his thoughts in a notebook. The cursive writing was a soothing exercise for his fingers and hands. Writing helped him keep his mind focused on topics, a thing he was finding hard to do lately. Logan found himself forgetting things over the last few years. He feared that this was the early stages of Alzheimer's, which was one of the things that made him so unnerved.

Also, on that list of nerves was that the last day of the month was about to approach him, and he had yet been found by his terrifying foe. Logan had an active Loomation; among his powers were teleporting, firing off defense spells, and giving heal spells. Having Loomation inside him made him a target for his enemy who vowed to kill anyone who was more powerful than what God had intended. This vow was made by the devil, and he'd been hunting Logan for decades. Every time Logan would feel the atmosphere side effects of the devil's presence, he would teleport to a new place, and the devil would have to search for him all over again.

To this day, Logan never understood how the devil searched for him. He theorized on it but also had a lot of questions on that topic. Within the final four days of every month, the devil would find him and come after him, but the days were always random. This random timing made Logan fear that last week of the month, while he would mostly drink himself to sleep during the other three weeks.

Logan believed that the devil was using his powers to perform a tracking spell of some kind. The spell must take about a month to find the person the devil was hunting. That was one of Logan's theories on how the devil worked. The other was that the devil was keeping a constant eye on him. He reasoned that the devil was finding too much satisfaction playing mind games with him to ever actually kill him. He felt that the devil was just teasing him by only attacking at the end of the month. Logan had some information straight from the devil's mouth to back this theory up. The devil told Logan that he could only personally kill once a month; he said that it was a rule or something. The devil did have his loopholes; he could trick someone into killing another, or if someone gave the devil permission to kill them, he could oblige. With the fear of the devil keeping an eye on him at all times and in order to keep his son, Cain, safe from the devil's hit list, he never returned to his family.

Tonight, Logan felt that he was finally going to find out if the devil was keeping a constant eye on him or not. Earlier this month, Logan interacted with someone who had Loomation inside them. That was one of the reasons why Logan was so nervous. He followed that boy back to his house where he found the Hang Out Group. He learned that they all had the power of Loomation inside them.

Logan wasn't apprehensive about the devil coming to him; he was worried that the devil wouldn't come to him this month. If the devil was keeping a constant eye on him, then he must know about the boy and his friends he had discovered earlier in the month. Since the boys all had Loomation in them, they would become a target for the devil. The devil would surely go after one of the boys this month and leave Logan for another month.

After Logan discovered the Hang Out Group, he believed that they could be the ones to help him kill the devil. He wanted to talk to them right away, but he decided to think about it first. Logan went to his old cabin in the swamp after discovering the Hogs. He was happy to see some familiar sights. The cabin in the swamp looked just as it did when he left it all those years ago. Logan opened the door of the cabin and removed the flashlight from his backpack. He took a seat on the hammock inside the cabin. Once he raised his eyes up to the frame hanging onto the wall of the cabin, his eyes widened, and he beheld a great revelation.

In the frame was a newspaper clipping of him and the other seven travelers. He hadn't seen this photo since he left the cabin to go live in his mansion. He jumped out of the hammock to get a closer look at a spot on the photo. Logan was looking at the man named Derrick; he looked at what he was holding in his right hand. Derrick was holding the sword they took from the Garden of Eden. Logan could not believe that he completely forgot all about that sword. He blamed it on his newly found forgetfulness. But that didn't make up for all those years when his mind was young and more reliable.

Logan almost wept tears as he wished that he had remembered this sooner. He suddenly felt weak. He lost his strength to stand, and he leaned up against the corner and defenselessly sobbed as the sudden grief overwhelmed him. Logan did this about once a month, but the depressed feelings were hitting him hard this time. It was at moments like this when Logan felt the most powerless. He couldn't perform the easiest of spells at this stage. He just sat in the corner with his face buried in his knees and tears helplessly streaming down his face. He let this sad feeling overpower him for just a few minutes during times like this. After he would have his sad moment, he quickly brushed it off and returned to staying focused on what was important.

Logan looked at the photo and thought if anything in the world could stab that monster to death, it was that sword. Logan knew that if he managed to recruit the Hang Out Group in an attack to kill the devil, that sword would be vital to their attack. Logan didn't have much time to track down that sword, so he teleported to the last town he remembered Derrick had resided.

After days of searching, Logan did track down the sword in a museum. He couldn't steal it due to the museum being under renovation. All objects within the museum would be in a security vault until the museum reopened. Logan saw that it wouldn't open back up until June 1, so he teleported to the south of Texas. Since Logan never returned to a place where he'd once been found, he couldn't have been in the town with the museum the day the devil came for him, which brought him to now. Logan at the bar, just minutes until the last day of May arrived, ordered a drink to calm his nerves.

After Logan ran away from the devil one last time, his plan was to convince the Hang Out Group to fight with him against the devil. Logan had this feeling that the boys were the key to the devil's downfall. After he drafted the Hogs, he would go out and steal the sword from the museum, which would be open by then. But Logan wasn't going to find the Hogs first; he was going to find his son first. This was another item on Logan's list of things that was making him so uneasy.

Logan was not going to run at the end of June. He decided it was time to stand his ground and fight the devil to the death. If Logan was the one who would die, his son would end up on the devil's hit list at some point. The devil would discover that Cain had Loomation sooner or later. Logan had to warn Cain of the possible threat. Maybe Cain could even assist him in the fight against the devil.

Logan hadn't seen his son since he was a baby. He ran over the words he was planning to say to him but was stressed out about it. *What do you say to your son after not seeing him his entire life?* In addition to this, he needed to tell him that if he died, the devil may eventually find out about him and come kill him too. Logan had dealt with stress his entire life and had always found a way to deal with it. But everything right now felt piled on deep. To be honest, the side effects of the devil's presence would take some stress off him right now.

The devil's timing was perfect at that moment. The bar was now hit with a disturbing dry hot gust of wind. Logan knew this feeling all too well, so he downed his drink and headed to the exit. Once he exited the bar, the unmistakable stench of brimstone filled the area along with that arid heat. Logan started to run down the street. A mist of low-hanging fog shrouded the streetlights, which made them appear poorly lit. Logan knew this was caused by the devil's presence, and he tried to teleport away. He'd normally be out of there by now, but his nerves were getting the best of him. The drink failed to calm him down as much as he was hoping it would. He was too stressed out about seeing his son again. He was thinking about going back on his plan and just continuing the chase. But Logan knew he couldn't run forever; his mind was growing weaker by the years. He had faith in the Hang Out Group, and he felt like if he waited too long, it would be too late. He had to plan his attack on the devil now, and that meant teleporting away this one last time.

The fog lowered closer to the ground, and before Logan knew it, he couldn't see through the heavy cloud that was hovering over the ground. Logan ran right into a parked car on the street. He stopped at the car to catch his breath as he looked around. What Logan saw next made him jump toward the ground because a large bright fireball was torpedoing straight toward him. The devil was now in close range; it had been years since he'd gotten that close. Logan felt that his whole plan was about to end before it could even begin. He thought about his son; Logan's last wish was to see his son again. Knowing that he still had a chance to get to see his son gave him a small dash of joy and hope. And with that positive feeling, Logan was able to teleport away, once again avoiding another close call from the devil.

Monday, May 31, 2010

Logan was still on the ground when he arrived at the teleportation destination. The sight in front of him looked like a nightmare. The grand mansion he once lived in and housed his wife and child was burned to the ground. There was nothing left but burnt rubble and piles of scorched wood. A terrible hypothesis on how this happened came to Logan as he sadly gazed at the ruins. He feared that after all this time, the devil knew all along about his son, Cain. The devil must have come to the mansion and killed his son by burning down the house. This would have meant that Logan's entire reason for running had been for nothing.

"No," Logan said as he crawled to the wreckage. "It can't be," the disillusioned old man said in disbelief. "He was only chasing me. He never knew of my son!" Logan got to his feet and ran toward the burned-down house. Getting up close to the scraps of burnt wood sent a mighty force of anger down his spin. "NO!" Logan hollered.

Just then, Logan heard a car making its way down the driveway. He saw the headlights and quickly vanished into what he called *the spiritual realm*. The spiritual realm was a place out of the physical layer of reality. To enter this place required an active Loomation. Once there, you became invisible from everyone, as no one could feel you nor hear you. While in this realm, you could walk through anything as if you were a ghost. Only the objects within the spiritual realm could hurt you during your time in there, while no one outside could detect your existence. Once Logan was hidden safely in this realm, he stayed where he was standing to see who was in the car.

The car drove right up to the front of the burned-down house. The man who got out the driver's seat was Cain, and the person getting out of the passenger seat was Kate. Kate brought her hands to her face in shock at seeing her childhood home like this. Cain's feelings were more angry than sad.

"Come on, let's get what we came here to get," Cain said, sticking to his roots of never being vulnerable.

Cain could see that returning with Kate to this place upset her. Cain wanted to get her out of here as soon as possible. In the spiritual realm, Logan stared long and hard at Cain. He was standing right in front of him making eye contact. Cain had no idea that his own father was standing right in his presence. It was impossible for Cain to see him if Logan stayed inside the spiritual realm. Cain and Kate marched through the destroyed house and reached the backyard where there was a single grave marked by a tombstone labeled "Katherine Renshaw." The two paused in front of the memorial for a quick moment of remembrance and respect. After the moment was over, Cain squatted down in front of the stone and dug his hand into the dirt. He then pulled out a metal box.

"Remember when I told you that my mother was buried in the backyard?" Cain asked his daughter. Kate nodded. Cain told her that this information was a lie. He opened the metal box, and stacks of one-hundred-dollar bills were stuffed inside. Cain said that he scattered his mother's ashes within the woods during her funeral. He used her headstone in the backyard as a place to hide money in case of an emergency. Cain had a thing for stashing money in hidden locations, and this stash was the closest one he could get his hands on at the time. Cain tossed the box aside and gave half the pile of cash to Kate.

"This will cover you for a while," Cain stated. "I'll buy the ticket when we get to the airport and make sure you board the plane safely."

"We better hurry then if we want to make the flight," Kate requested. Being at the wreckage of her childhood home was too painful to be staying there, so Cain and Kate rushed back to the car and drove off into the night.

Logan then exited the spiritual realm, returning to the physical layer of reality. He watched from afar as the car drove out of the driveway and onto the street. Once they were gone, Logan turned back to the headstone honoring his beloved wife. He took a knee at the headstone. Logan heard that man call this person his mother. Logan was thrilled that his son was alive and well. Being next to the memorial of his wife caused him to tear up. The good memories came to him; the first time they met was in the woods that circled their home. The fact that she never saw him as an anomaly because of his active Loomation made her very special. The success of his mission keeping his son out of harm's way from the devil all this time brought a slight sense of satisfaction and a smile to his face. He couldn't be happier that all he did was indeed worth it. He was angry at himself for not speaking out to his son. Instead, he hid in the spiritual realm like a coward. He turned to the headstone and poured out his love, gratitude, and apologies. She was too good for him and didn't deserve what happened to her. He was about to take off to the airport because he knew his son was on his way there now. His last words to his wife were "I promise...we will be together again soon."

Later at the airport, Kate sat on a bench waiting for her father to purchase her plane ticket. As she sat and waited, she double-checked her belongings. In her front left pocket was her passport, along with her wallet, while in her right pocket was her MP3 player for her entertainment on the long plane ride. She then placed her backpack onto her lap and unzipped it. This backpack had been with her everywhere she'd been for as long as she could remember. When Ray and his hired men came for her, she still found time to retrieve this bag. The highlights of her life were inside this bag, so she couldn't just leave it behind. There were also hundreds of dollars cash in it at this time.

While peering into the bag, Kate took a moment to get a good look at all her nostalgic items. She pulled out an old novel book that she glanced at before setting it to her side. She pulled out a few pamphlets from her days of being in plays. Kate loved being a part of musicals and plays. She was a very lonely kid growing up because she was moving around a lot because of the fear of Ray discovering her. She also had to keep her slow aging a secret. Whenever she couldn't pull off her documented age, they would need to move and make new fake documents. Due to this, it was hard for her to make friends. She had to lie about who she was to everyone. Her advanced strength made her feel isolated from the others. She felt that no one could understand her and what she was going through. But when she was performing in the musicals and plays, she could pretend that she was someone else. She could be someone who was outgoing, someone who was well liked and friendly. She was very good at acting, for she spent her whole life convincing people of her pseudo lifestyle. This was why performing on stage felt like second nature to her. Some of her best childhood memories were of her time performing at the theater, so the pamphlets held a lot of sentimental value.

She then pulled out her photo album. Inside were photos of her at the zoo, water parks, and premiere nights of her at the plays in which she performed. A photo of her at her first day of school made her laugh. Kate couldn't believe how little she was in that photo. In the photo of her first day of school, she had the biggest smile. Before that day, she was always homeschooled at the mansion. She never thought she would get to go to a real school and be able to interact with other kids. It was a dream come true for her. Throughout the photo album, she saw photos of her birthdays. In the photos, she was standing next to her birthday cake. She laughed because her caretaker always put her real current age along with her fake age on the cake. She had so many twelve-year-old birthday cakes.

In the back of the album was a photo of her and her caretaker, Jason. This was the last photo she had of him before he died. Kate owed everything to Jason. After her dad fell into his coma, Jason took her under Cain's protection program. Cain was originally going to take her into this program, but he fell into a coma. Kate loved her father and was so grateful for this time with him. But after just a few days with him, she knew that Cain would have never had let her join any plays or even have photos of her taken, especially if Ray was still alive. When she was living in the mansion before her father's accident, Cain never let her be photographed nor liked her ever leaving the house. She might have lost massive time of being with her father, but Jason took risks that her father wouldn't have so that she could live a happier life.

Kate, suddenly brought back to the reality of the present, looked up and saw her father. He had her plane ticket and waved her to come on over. Kate loaded up all her belongings back into her backpack in a hurry and started to head over to her father.

"Excuse me, miss," a voice called out to Kate. Kate turned her head back and saw an older man holding her book. "You left this behind," the man said. Kate was dumbfounded, feeling so foolish for almost forgetting her book. She turned and walked up to the man.

"Thank you so much," Kate said joyfully. "This book means a lot to me, so I would have been devastated if I had lost it."

The man looked at the cover of the book, saw the title of the book, and was hit with a warmhearted memory. "You know, I gave my wife this book for an anniversary gift a long time ago," the man said.

"Awe, that's so sweet," Kate replied with a smile. "My dad used to read this book to me when I was just a kid. He said that his mother did the same when he was young, so he wanted to carry on the tradition."

The man browsed through the pages of the book and came across the words written on the first page. The words said *To Katherine Renshaw.* The old man's heart skipped a beat when he saw that. The realization that this was exactly the same book he gave to his wife came to him as a shock. This old man was Logan. He teleported to the airport after his time at the burned-down mansion because he knew that was where his son was heading. While at the airport, he watched both the girl and Cain. When he saw that Kate almost left her book behind, he felt that he needed to step in to hand it back to her. Until now, Logan never thought of the possibility of being a grandfather. But from the information the girl just gave him, he knew that this was indeed his granddaughter. When Logan looked back at Kate, he saw that she had a strong resemblance to his late wife. Logan was motionless, awed with his overwhelming discovery.

Before things grew too awkward, he handed the book over to her. "Here you go, Katherine." Logan didn't mean to say the name Katherine but felt that it wasn't too odd for her, given the fact that the name Katherine was written inside the book.

"Thanks," Kate said as she took back the book. "Everyone calls me Kate for short." Kate then turned around and headed to her father. With one last turn, she looked back at the old man, thanking him for finding the book once again. Logan just stood still and watched his granddaughter meet up with his son and watched them head toward their gate. Logan knew that his son had named his daughter after his mother, so that must have meant that there was love in the Renshaw house, even with him not being there. This was truly a wonderful moment for Logan as the old man walked away with his eyes welling up with tears of joy.

Cain and Kate made it to the gate. They were about to board the plane, so they had to say their goodbyes. They gave each other one long hug. Once they pulled away from each other, she said to him that it wasn't too late for him to come with her. She said they could go to England together. Cain brushed off the idea quickly. He believed that if Ray was still at large, she would never be truly safe. He believed that her being as far away from him as possible was the only way she would be safe.

Kate said that she wasn't sure if that was true. She knew that her father wanted her out of the cross fire between the two, and sending her away was the best way for that to happen. "Dad, be careful around Ray. I know you like to think of yourself as someone who can take care of any threat, but you have been out of the game for twenty-five years," Kate said, concerned for her father.

"I'll be fine," Cain assured her. Kate didn't expect any other kind of response from her dad. Classic old stubborn man her dad was, never admitting defeat. Cain then handed her a going-away gift, a cell phone. "For when it's safe," he said as she took the phone. The phone was a way for him to contact her when he was ready to reach out to her. After she took the phone, they hugged one last time.

"Dad...don't be afraid to surrender," Kate said in her father's arms. "I think all Ray wants is a victory. Maybe he'll accept your defeat if you feel like you have no choice."

Cain had no response to what she said, just gave it a heavy thought. She then boarded the plane. It was miserable for Cain to see her leave. For him, she was a little girl just a few weeks ago. So much absent time had passed between the two, and now she was once again out of his life. Cain had to keep reminding himself that she was safer being away from him.

Logan watched his son and granddaughter split up; he could see the depressed look on his son's face as he watched her leave. Logan was all too familiar with that look. He hopped back into the spiritual realm to follow his son back to his car. Cain drove out of the airport and headed out to find a place to sleep for the rest of the night. Cain had no idea that his father was in the back seat. He couldn't have, for Logan remained inside his hidden realm. Logan felt that he had his chance to speak to his son. He knew how his son was feeling; forcing himself to be away from his child was something he could relate to, but at the moment, Logan was too much of a coward to speak up.

Cain took out his cell phone and made calls to his hired men. He asked the men if any of them knew the whereabouts of Ray's location. Cain gave each person a specific location, including the prison, to keep an eye on. None of them had spotted Ray. Cain felt that it could be safer to return to the old prison since there was no sign of Ray there rather than spend another night at a hotel.

Out at the old prison, Ray hooked up wireless keys onto the digital locks on the cells that held the creatures of the garden. The man Cain hired to keep an eye on the prison came up to Ray and informed him that Cain called in. Ray asked the man what he said. The man said that it was all clear at the prison. Ray grinned, telling the man good job. Ray then paid the man and told him to return to his post. Ray knew that the men hired by Cain didn't carry the loyalty as the Havocs once had. Cain was so used to that loyalty that he never would have expected someone offering more money to betray him.

Ray knew that Cain was cheap; he knew he would use a different hotel every night while he had Kate with him. But after he sent her off, he knew he would find his own place to hide. Ray learned one of Cain's old catchphrases while they were good friends: *You can't afford to have millions stashed in hiding places all over if you don't live a cheap life.* Ray knew Cain would end up going back to the prison, and he was setting a trap.

Just Before Dawn

Cain arrived at the prison hoping to find a place to rest. He had barely gotten any sleep since he left the hospital. First, he was too worried about his daughter, and then he was staying alert to keep her safe. As much pain as it brought him sending her off, he also found great relief that she was somewhere safe. After Cain got out of the car, Logan remained in the back seat, hidden in the spiritual realm. Logan just needed a little more time to find the courage to speak to his son. Cain entered the front door. As he walked to the stairs, he could hear the monsters underneath making their fearful sounds. He never understood why they only made their sounds at night, but he didn't mind the noise.

Cain made it to the prison's old cafeteria, grateful that the lights were still turned on. He was happy to see his old coma bed still there. When the police took him from the Havocs the day the Hogs turned them in, the police put Cain onto a gurney and left the bed Cain rested in for twenty-five years. It was odd climbing back into it and a little scary as well. Cain was all settled in his bed and had just closed his eyes, when he heard the voice of Ray.

"Good to see you again, Cain," Ray said.

Cain opened his eyes wide and looked toward the sound of Ray's voice. What Cain saw first was a glass bottle soaring right at him. Cain rolled out of the bed, dodging the bottle that shattered on the bed. The bottle was full of one of Ray's personal chemical compounds, and it left the bed soaking wet. The liquid seemed to cause the sheets to deteriorate. Cain got to his feet and spotted Ray across the room.

"How did you get here?" Cain's voice was in a thunderous rage when he spoke to Ray.

"A lot has changed over the past two decades, Cain. People don't value honesty or trust anymore. All that matters is a solid-sized buck, and they'll sell their own grandma to get it!" Ray preached as he chucked another bottle at Cain.

Cain easily jumped out of the way of the coming bottle. After Cain landed, he reached for his gun in his shoulder holster, but by that time, Ray already armed himself with the twelve-gauge shotgun he had strapped to his back. Ray fired off two shots at Cain. Cain got low and tipped one of the metal tables over for coverage.

"You're getting slow in your old age, Cain! It never took you this long to draw out your gun before. Or perhaps you're just out of shape!" Ray shouted as he fired off two more shots at the table Cain was hiding behind. The shots went right through the metal table as if it was cardboard; luckily for Cain, Ray missed with both shots. Cain then shoved the table as hard as he could toward Ray. Ray saw the table tossed through the air and coming straight at him, and he dove out of the way. Once Ray hit the floor, Cain fired off a few rounds from his handgun at Ray. Ray crawled out of the way of the gunfire and managed to tip over one of the other metal tables between him and the bullets. The handgun didn't give off as strong of an impact on the table as the shotgun shells did. The bullets from the handgun ricocheted off the metal table, leaving only fist-sized dents on the table.

"You better be careful you don't kill me, Cain!" Ray shouted.

"Sorry, I thought that was the point!" Cain replied.

"I'm packing some insurance over here," Ray stated.

"What do you mean?" Cain shouted, trying not to sound too concerned.

"I got myself a dead man's switch attached to my chest. I rigged all the jail cells in the basement to it. If my heart stops beating, an alarm goes off, along with all the animals being set loose!" This was Ray's big master plan. He knew that if Cain managed to get the upper hand in this battle, Ray would still gain his vengeance on the Renshaw family. Ray knew that there would be no way that Cain could handle all the animals single-handedly. He knew once they were out, they would tear him to shreds. Cain knew that Ray had him in a fight-or-flight situation; this was the first time in a long time that Cain didn't want to kill Ray. Cain felt no choice but to make a run for it. Cain sprinted toward the door but was shot in the shoulder just before he reached it.

Cain hit the ground hard, and blood was flowing out of his shoulder from the wound. Ray cocked back the shotgun once more, walked up to Cain, stood next to his feet, and pointed the gun down at his face. Cain didn't try to move away nor fight back. He simply put his hands up calmly as he knew there was nothing more he could do. Ray was a little stunned by Cain's motions; he couldn't believe that he finally had won.

"Say it," Ray ordered Cain. "Say I won!" Ray demanded.

"I surrender," Cain replied, keeping his hands up. Ray could have ended Cain's life with one simple pull of the trigger. A shotgun blast from this close range would drive though his heart so fast he'd be dead before he heard the sound. Ray felt the trigger of the gun but wasn't sure if he wanted to pull it now.

"STOP!" This voice belonged to Logan. Once Logan heard the gunfire, he ran into the building, still in his spiritual realm state. When he saw the man about to kill his son, he had to reenter the physical level of reality for his demand to be heard. Ray saw a man appear straight out of nowhere within the room; he couldn't believe it.

"Please leave my son alone!" Logan pleaded.

"You're…you're him," Ray struggled to find his words. "You're Logan Renshaw!" Ray shouted, enraged, as he pointed his gun toward Logan. At that moment, Cain saw his opening to attack Ray. He shoved his feet at Ray's ankles, causing him to fall to his knees and making him miss his shot at Logan. Logan, with his surprisingly quick reflexes, fired off a special attack spell onto Ray. The spell that Logan fired off struck Ray with a green glow. This was the gravity spell, a spell that imposed a stronger grip of gravity pressure onto its victims. Ray just felt that he was being pushed down by an invisible force. Logan told Ray not to worry because the spell would wear off shortly but warned him that the more he tried to fight the force, the stronger it would grow.

Ray was brought to his knees and then tipped over, with his head gently crashing down to the floor. Logan now had both Cain and Ray lying in front of him, both in pain, one nursing a bleeding shoulder, while the other could hardly move.

"It's true, I am Logan Renshaw," he confessed.

"You monster…you killed my father!" Ray struggled to say.

Logan didn't know who this man was, nor did he even remember killing his father. Then a realization came to him. "Are you the son of a Parker Mantus?" he asked with a heavy heart.

"Yes, you killed my father eighty years ago. My father's last log in his book said that he and the other travelers were being hunted by a man who could teleport, which is you!"

"I'm truly sorry for what happened to your father. I may have been the one who ended his life, but I was tricked by a real monster."

"What real monster are you talking about?" wondered Ray.

"If you're the son of Parker, then your life is in the same danger as mine and Cain's," Logan stated. "That's why I left you and your mother, Cain. I couldn't let that monster find you, so I ran, making him chase only me for the last eight decades."

"What monster do you speak of?" Ray shouted as he attempted to lift his chest, but the spell forced him back down.

"Back in 1924, I traveled with six men, your father included. We discovered the Garden of Eden. But our entrance was the monster's exit. Years went by, and he discovered that the seven travelers all carried Loomation inside them. He found it to be a personal insult and vowed to kill all humans who carried it. Due to my teleporting power, I managed to keep the monster chasing me. I knew if it ever found out about my son, then it would surely go after him as well."

Cain always wondered why his father ran out on him, and now he knew. He always thought that the truth of his father's absence wouldn't have changed how he felt toward him, but he was wrong. Logan then explained how the monster was able to trick him into killing Ray's father. Logan admitted it was an awful thing to do, and he had lived with that guilt every day while he was on the run.

Ray then asked why Logan gave up now. Logan said that he was done running, and he just couldn't bring himself to do this anymore. He made his last run earlier that night, so they now had four weeks until the monster came for him once again. This time Logan planned on fighting to the death.

"Do you have a plan to defeat him?" asked his bewildered son.

"I discovered a group of boys. They too somehow carry the power of Loomation inside them. I believe they can destroy this monster," Logan stated.

"Don't tell me you're talking about the Hang Out Group! They're just a bunch of dumb kids!" Ray said, once again trying to lift himself up.

"You know them?" Logan questioned in a sense of disbelief.

"We've had our run-ins with them," Cain replied.

Just then, a beeping sound arose from Ray's chest. Ray's eyes widened, and he looked down onto his chest. His dead man's switch set to his beating heart was going off. The heavy force Ray was feeling from Logan's spell was causing his heartbeat to move so slowly that the device could no longer detect a regular heartbeat. Then the beeping on the device stopped, and an alarm started to go off from the basement. All at once, the jail cells popped open, and the alarm woke all the creatures from their deep sleep.

"We need to get out of here NOW!" Ray shouted. Logan then heard the terrifying howl of the creatures from the basement. It wasn't long after that when he felt the rumbling of an incoming stampede. Logan ran up close to the two men on the ground, and when he was close enough to lay a hand on both, he was able to teleport them out of there. But under the floor, the scorching-hot bird phoenix emerged, crashing through the surface and carrying its burning hot flame with it. The fire caught fast throughout the whole building.

Both Cain and Ray were tossed far apart from each other as the bird made its way up, crashing through the ceiling. From the stairs, a giant green ogre showed up about to smash Ray. On the other hand, Cain was dangerously close to the flames caused by the phoenix. Now, both men were about to die. Logan chose to save Ray first, as Ray had no chance of getting to safety away from the large ogre.

Ray saw Logan choose him over his own son, and when Logan reached Ray, he teleported him out of the building. Logan teleported Ray to a rest stop outside of Maze. Logan left him lying on a bench and teleported back to the burning prison. Ray couldn't believe that the man saved him over his own son. This act of kindness made Ray believe Logan's story that he was, indeed, tricked by this monster he warned them about.

Back at the prison, Logan spotted his son in mortal danger. The flames hadn't yet caught him, so there was still time, but the ogre was now closing in on him. Logan blasted a defense spell at the ogre, repelling him away from his son. Logan reached his son and teleported him away from the prison. Logan and his son returned to their once family home, the burned-down Renshaw Mansion. Logan didn't know where else to take him. The two weren't facing the rubble; they were facing the driveway, and they could see the sun start to rise.

Logan gave Cain a heal spell to instantly heal the gunshot wound. Cain felt fully healed after he was given the spell. This was awkward for the two at first. For years, Cain wondered if his father was still alive or not. He always wanted to express his anger to him for leaving him and his mother all those years ago. But now he knew the truth, he was not sure how to react.

"I know this is a lot to take in. Believe me, I'm just as overwhelmed as you are," Logan stated.

"I really need to get some rest. I've had a crazy couple of days…and today was the most insane…I just need time to process all this," Cain said.

"I understand. I have a few things to do myself. I was hoping to have more time to talk to you. We only have four weeks," Logan informed him with a sense of doom. "I'll give you your space for now…but just know I'll return here every day at sunrise until you're ready to talk." Logan and his wife had watched the sunrise from their front porch countless times. He wished to spend the rest of his mornings doing that again. Then Logan vanished, leaving Cain alone once again.

Back at the prison, the whole place was burning down. If you looked at the place from the outside, you would have seen all the monsters that were kept there for years all running and scattering about, while the burning bird left a trail of flames within the sky. The creatures were now loose out in the world.

CHAPTER 28

Heed His Warning

Morning came to the swamp, and Hayden was out in the woods area gathering up small sticks for the afternoon fire needed to cook lunch. Being outside the comfort zone, the disgusting odor brought the nasty stench back to his nostrils, but by now Hayden was used to it. Hayden loved being out in nature like this as he found beauty in all nature, even its deadliest aspects. He marched his way back to the campsite, carrying tons of twigs and sticks under his armpit. When Hayden stepped back into the comfort zone of the land, it was amazing how the smell dramatically changed. Even the breeze of this area seemed to be different. Although Hayden had been in many woodlands, had walked on many nature hikes, and had fished in a plethora of ponds, he had never seen any place like this pleasant location hidden away within the middle of a massive swamp. He had come across many new discoveries over the past few weeks, and this one was by far his favorite.

As Hayden walked up to the fire ring, he saw Will sitting at the table under the canopy. Hayden said good morning to his friend with a friendly wave. Will was eating a bowl of cereal at the time and waved back. It was early, and the rest of the Hogs were still asleep.

Hayden stacked up the kindling next to the fire ring and said, "We need to move the bug-net tent over to the toilet."

The Hogs had a pop-up camper on the campsite, a canopy over a table where the Hogs ate, a shower tent over by the pond, and a bug tent where a few air mattresses were scattered about. Hayden, Timber, Eric, and Miles slept in the pop-up camper while Will, Juice, and Gard slept in the bug tent on the air mattresses. It did seem a bit odd that Hayden didn't sleep outside given the fact that he loved the great outdoors more than anything. But since it was Hayden's camper, he got the best sleeping spot to himself, and he loved it.

"Why do we need to move the bug-net tent to the toilet?" asked Will.

"Trust me, you don't want be swatting off mosquitoes when you're trying to do your business," Hayden replied, speaking from experience. While in the comfort zone, there was no problem with the bugs. But outside the zone, where the toilet was located, the bugs were awful. Will was concerned about the morning dew because if they didn't sleep under the bug-net tent, they would wake up soaked. Hayden said to just sleep under the canopy and to move the table out from underneath of it at night. Will was fine with that plan and said that once Juice and Gard woke up, they'd move the bug-net tent out to the toilet.

Will was happy to discuss a simple camping problem. Simple talks such as this were what he was hoping to have while on this vacation. This trip was for him and the other Hogs to get away from all that drama they were facing. Here at the swamp, it was just the group, no Havocs, no Cain, no Ray. Being on the land did bring up a whole new topic last night. Eric was doing his best to unravel the secrets and mystery of this acre of land and was upset to be just as stumped as the others. Juice's new power of flight was also talked about. Juice couldn't do it again, so they didn't know if it was a onetime thing or not. They didn't know if everyone in the group could fly or not. They did have fun trying to find out last night; jumping off the top of the hill made them feel like young children again.

"How did you guys sleep last night?" asked Hayden as he sat in a chair at the table.

"Well, after Juice finally stopped talking, Gard and I were able to go to sleep. After that, it felt great. Didn't wake up once," Will stated.

"Not even when you got up this morning?" Hayden said as a joke as he reached for the cereal. Hayden was just pointing out the obvious, that Will did wake up at least once when he got up for the morning. Will laughed, explaining that he didn't wake up several times during the night like he had been doing. Hayden knew what Will was talking about and could easily relate, for he too had been having sleeping problems lately.

"What are you planning on doing this morning?" asked Hayden.

"Juice and I are going for a run later. We're going to see what else is in this swamp," Will said.

"Well, I got a head start on that. I got up early and did some hiking myself," Hayden replied. He reported nothing special stood out during his walk, but he did enjoy the peace and quiet. Both Will and Hayden were really happy that they found this place. It felt safe, and it felt like a home away from home.

A few hours later, far past lunch, Timber, Eric, Gard, and Miles were playing cornhole. Timber and Eric were standing on one side, tossing their bags to the board across them. The subject of their conversation was the mysterious land they were standing on.

"The grass here has obviously been mowed," Timber pointed out.

"Right, but does the grass here even grow?" Eric questioned.

"I feel like the owner of the cabin here has cut the grass recently and will be back soon," Timber replied. He was worried about being on someone's property, while Eric was more intrigued by the cryptic land. Timber was worried that the owner would call the cops on them once they were discovered. Eric had a theory that this land might have been used by the Havocs or even Ray. Eric said that the cube was the source of their powers, and that was made by Ray. And when they got attacked by the Sasquatch, it came from the Havocs. So he believed that all unnatural things came from those guys. They debated a lot this morning on leaving but were outvoted by the others.

"They're at it again," Miles stated to Gard over on the other side of the cornhole boards.

"They've been complaining about this place all morning. They probably would have started last night if it wasn't for Juice's flying surprise," Gard replied as he gathered up all eight bags. Gard then handed the four bags that belonged to Miles over to him.

"Yeah, that definitely was a shocking event," said Miles as he retrieved the bags. "What are your thoughts on that?" wondered Miles.

"I don't know," Gard said as he chucked a bag over to the board. "Juice isn't the first one to show off a different ability. Hayden is the only one of us who's fireproof. And your powers are in a whole different category." Gard waited for Miles to throw his bag before he asked, "How you been with that anyway? Any new skills pop up?"

"You mean am I blasting any more light attacks from my hands?" Miles asked as Gard threw his second bag.

"You said that night that you felt like there was more to learn about your powers," Gard said as Miles tossed another bag. "You also said you were scared from what more you could learn," Gard added as he tossed his third bag.

Miles paused before throwing his next bag. "You remember that book I found in the box Cain gave us. The one that told me my powers were called an active Loomation."

"Yeah, was that just some of Ray's theories or something?" wondered Gard.

"See, that's the scary thing. It wasn't written by Ray. The book talked about our powers like it was an encyclopedia. It talked about some ancient power energy called *Loomation*, claiming it's the power that God used to create everything," Miles explained just before he chucked his third bag.

"That's some heavy stuff," Gard uttered as he threw his final bag. Gard wasn't ready to believe the whole God-power idea quite yet.

"It said that Loomation wasn't made to be contained in humans. So when we receive it, it'll dry up and stick to our bones, muscles, and skin," Miles stated as he tossed his last bag.

"Which would explain our advanced strength," Gard theorized. "So since it obviously didn't dry up in you, the Loomation in you has become *active?* Did the book shine some light on what all you can do with it?"

"It talked about the teleporting ability. And that violet light attack I used on Bigfoot was called a defense spell," Miles said.

"Anything else?" asked Gard.

"Well, I came across something called the death spell." Miles's mood changed to something low-spirited when he brought this up. "The spell was so simple to perform it was scary. The spell will blast out of my hand and instantly kill any life that gets touched by it," said Miles who sounded a bit fearful as he talked. "I could end someone's life in a snap because of my powers."

"That's pretty scary," Gard said, feeling the same fear Miles was.

"That gave me a pretty fearful shock. Heck, the whole book I found is odd. So I did some digging into the history of this book," Miles said. Miles told Gard that the book publishing company was burned to the ground the same day they printed that book. They only printed a dozen or so copies; they loaded them up in a truck, and after that, the building was burned down. Following that fiasco, the company went bankrupt. The newspaper that reported the fire talked about a survivor of the fire. The survivor reported that there were two men within the burning building. The witness said he saw the two men vanish into thin air. Just one moment they were in the building, and then they were gone.

"That story made people think that the books called upon witchcraft. Some people believed that printing the explanation of the power caused the fire as if it was a curse. The books that were printed were mostly burned by superstitious people who feared the curse of the literature. The ones that weren't burned were eventually sold at auctions for a high price. The fact that the books came with this big backstory containing a curse has made the book very rare and very valuable. Miles saw that there was a receipt in the book and saw that it was purchased by Ray at an auction.

Miles told Gard that the curse scared him, which was why he didn't tell the others about the book's information. The fear of him being able to kill someone with such ease made him uncomfortable to use his powers any further than just a teleporting trip. He didn't want to use any more defense spells nor learn what more he could do with his powers. Gard understood but told Miles that if he ever changed his mind about learning more about his powers, the Hogs would support him.

Hayden was chopping up some logs with the ax when he heard his walkie-talkie go off. Will was reporting in to check to see how far the walkie-talkies could reach.

"Calling Hayden, come in, Hayden," Will said.

"This is Hayden. How far did you guys get?" replied Hayden.

"Juice and I ran out pretty far. We're still in the swamp. I'd say close to five miles away from camp," Will reported.

"Good, glad to know that these things have some long range," Hayden commented.

"You're coming in very clear too, which is great," Will added. The Hogs felt that they should get some walkie-talkies in order to be able to communicate within the swamp due to there being no cell phone service. They had only two walkie-talkies at the time, but Hayden was planning on buying some more later.

That afternoon, Logan woke up on a bench located at the park in the town of Maze. He didn't get to sleep until that morning, and after the long night he just experienced, he needed a long rest. Logan still had some cash in his pocket and ordered some food from a small diner. Now that he was well rested and full of food, he was ready to get started on the next part of his mission.

The first part of his mission was to escape the devil one last time, return to his son, and warn him of the devil's arrival. That didn't go as well as he wished. He felt that he just barely slipped the devil's grip—too close for comfort this time. Then he learned that his home was burned to the ground, and the unknown son of his best friend tried to kill him. Then he became responsible for all those creatures getting loose.

The escaped creatures were something he was planning on dealing with, but he had to put that on hold for now. The next step of his plan was to find the one called Juice and his friends. When Logan followed Juice back to his hometown of Maze, he saw that Juice had a group of friends all with dry Loomation inside them. He saw something special inside those boys, and he believed that they were the key to the devil's demise.

Logan searched all over the small town of Maze but failed to locate them. He only knew where Juice lived, so he went to the house and talked to his parents. Logan had to make up a lie to Juice's parents; he said he was recruiting for the army and asked if there were any young men looking for a future in the military. When they told him that their son wasn't home then, Logan asked when he would be home. He was crushed to find out that he and his friends had all taken off on a camping trip for the month. Logan just smiled at the nice people, thanked them for their time, and left the house.

Logan felt that his plan had now fully come apart and that he should just give up trying to kill the devil and return to his monthly game of hide-and-seek. Logan knew that his time of running would soon end. His Alzheimer's was getting worse by the year, and soon he'd be in no shape to fight or even keep himself alive. That fear always worried him. Anyone feeling early signs of this disease would become very stressed. Logan couldn't leave, not just yet. He had to track down all those creatures that he let out. Logan had a few ideas on how to track them down, but he had one more thing to do.

Logan's mission was to retrieve a sword after finding the Hogs. This would be the same sword that was found inside the garden and was used to slice off a piece of the diamond. Logan wanted to get it in May but couldn't at that time. The sword was inside a museum, which was currently under renovation. Everything inside that exhibit was locked away, so Logan didn't know where it was hidden. The renovation would be done by the end of May, and the museum would reopen on the first of June. Logan teleported to the museum in Toledo and looked inside. He was amazed as he discovered a freshly remodeled exhibit that contained the sword. The information presented about the weapon was far from the truth. The exhibit claimed it was from the Middle Ages used by knights. Logan had no idea where that information came from and was amused by the story that was generated from someone's imagination because he knew it to be a lie.

Looking at the sword bought back memories of the garden, his traveling comrades, and, of course, the diamond. The sword was responsible for his life changing. Who would have thought a strong swing of that blade would make his whole life different and send him down such a dark path? Now that same sword had a real chance to end this nightmare journey by slaying the beast. After Logan took a good look at the whole place, he headed to the exit and waited outside the building until business hours were over. His plan was to steal the sword once the place closed.

It took until nightfall, but once the museum was closed, he teleported into the building and appeared in the exhibit. He saw that the room was empty, so he acted fast before the guard came. He used a defense spell to shatter the window that separated the people from the objects. An alarm went off with this diversion, but Logan didn't care. Once the sword was in his hand, he'd be far away in a blink of an eye. Logan took hold of the handle, and once he did, a powerful stroke of a glorious, overwhelming feeling of power brushed over him. A real eye-opener it was to hold that handle again. The feeling comes and goes so fast, but it leaves a powerful residue of positive feelings on whomever holds it. Logan then teleported away to a place he once called home—a place where he knew he could stash the sword where no one would ever find it. A place he once named the Diamond in the Rough.

Logan teleported back to his cabin. Seeing the old place made him feel like he was at home once again, but before he could even move a muscle, he heard a sound from behind him. This sound resembled a crackling fire. Logan was deeply shocked because he expected the location to be deserted. Once he heard the fire, he turned his shoulders to face the sound. He saw that his once-safe place of solitude was now compromised.

Logan counted seven boys, all siting around a campfire. They seemed to be eating hot sandwiches on paper plates. The seven boys spotted Logan at the same time as he noticed them. Logan wasn't that close to the fire, so he was just a silhouette in the distance away from the seven boys. These seven boys were the Hang Out Group, and once they heard the air shift from behind them, they looked back and in no time spotted a man standing near the cabin. The Hogs all literally jumped out of their seats and put up their guard. Hayden pointed his .30-30 lever-action shotgun at the trespasser. Will lifted the ax above his head, and Gard snatched the fire poker for a weapon.

Once Logan saw all of them on their feet, he recognized them. His eyes widened in disbelief because he could not believe who he was looking at. At first, he thought that his eyes were playing tricks on him. How could it be possible that the group of kids he spent most of the day looking for were here at the last place he would have ever expected them or anyone, for that matter, to be? Logan had a feeling that there was something special within these boys, and now finding them here made him think that even more. This made him feel like he just received the ultimate sign from the heavens and that his theory on this group being the one to kill the devil was true.

It was clear to the Hogs that this mysterious person was carrying a sword. Hayden ordered him to drop it. Logan gave the sword a gentle toss away from him; this was followed by lifting his arms up to show them he meant them no harm. The Hogs stayed on their guard but were now more patient with the man due to his unanticipated cooperation. Will asked the man to step forward so they could see him. Logan lifted his foot, about to move forward.

"Slowly," Eric added.

Logan moved slowly with his arms up high as he stepped into the light from the fire. Once he reached the light, Juice recognized the man.

"I know you," Juice stated. All eyes were on Juice, for he was the only one who knew this person. Juice explained that this was the man he saw when he was at that rest stop while he was under the dual-personality curse. Juice said that that man was there when the curse wore off.

"I wouldn't call it a curse. It seemed to be more of an infection. I was able to cure you from it," Logan replied.

"How were you able to cure Juice?" Gard questioned.

"I have an active Loomation, and with it I can perform a heal spell. Something was in Juice, and it was affecting his brain. The heal spell brings a living human body back to full health by cleaning out any threatening infection, sealing over cuts and wounds, and restoring any lost blood," Logan informed them.

"So did you just follow me after that?" Juice asked, concerned.

"You asked directions to a city called Maze. I was aware of that town. By studying the cities of Ohio, I was able to teleport myself to the welcome sign. When you passed me on foot, you started to walk. You bought a box of doughnuts from a baker and returned to your house. Once there, you were visited by five of your friends. After listening to your conversation, I learned that you all have a dry Loomation," explained Logan.

"So you been following us ever since?" Will wondered.

"No, after that morning, I left you alone," Logan replied.

"Then how did you know we were here?" Hayden asked.

"I'm going to be honest. I was looking for you all day. I searched all of Maze and gave up. I came here, and here you were," Logan answered.

"Would your last name be Renshaw by any chance?" Eric was able to craft this theory from the information he learned from Kate because she said her grandfather had an active Loomation.

"Logan Renshaw is my name. I've heard that you've had *run-ins* with my son, Cain, in the past," Logan said sadly as he lowered his face to the ground. "Whatever conflict you have with him has nothing to do with me. Until last night, I hadn't seen nor even talked to my son since 1929."

"If you have nothing to do with your son, then why were you looking for us?" Gard said, asking the million-dollar question.

"Something is coming." Logan's statement sent a chill down the spines of the Hang Out Group. "I spent what feels like my entire life running from it, but my time of running is over. I'm going to make my stand and fight," Logan said as he lifted his head up. "This thing that's coming is pure evil, and it wants to kill any human who is more than what God intended."

The Hogs all had mixed reactions. Some didn't know whether to believe this man or not. Some thought that he was lying about not being involved with his son, Cain. And some were truly afraid of this evil the man said was coming.

"I once traveled with a group like this one. We didn't possess the same friendship as you all do for each other. Maybe if we did, we could have survived this evil..." Logan paused slightly before continuing. "It was my fault. I had to go to that crash site." Logan now seemed to be talking to himself and not the Hogs.

"What exactly is coming for us?" asked Will after Logan gave off another odd pause.

"When my group and I got our powers, I was the only one with an active Loomation. So after the monster killed the others, I fled...I teleported away like a coward." Logan thought he would have been stronger revisiting these memories, but the origin of his run was too painful to tell with a straight face. "This monster was able to locate me within four weeks. I have been able to set my calendar to his visits in a way. Every time he found me, I would run. If he was chasing me, he never bothered looking for any other humans who had Loomation inside them. Keeping my son safe from the monster's murdering wrath became my only concern. It wasn't until last night when I learned that my plan was successful." Logan took a moment to catch his breath and to reflect on the gratitude of his sacrifice. "Now, I must stand my ground and fight this monster. I want you all to join me in this fight because I believe that you have what it takes to defeat him!"

The Hogs felted very overwhelmed by this message. To them, all of this felt surreal. A mystery man literally appeared out of nowhere, told them a great evil was coming, and believed that they were the saviors to kill the beast.

"How are we supposed to kill something that is *pure evil*?" questioned Will.

"With the sword I came here with. I was going to keep it safe within my cabin until the time for battle arises," Logan replied. The Hogs all eyed the sword on the ground, not knowing where it came from nor how special it was. Logan was feeling relief, as he had now been able to explain to the Hogs his warning of the coming threat. The Hogs were puzzled, for they felt like they were missing some details.

"Why now?" asked Will. "Why wouldn't you just continue your retreat? It's been working since 1929."

"Yeah, speaking of that, how old are you?" asked Gard.

"One hundred ten years old," Logan said without the slightest hesitation. Logan's body looked like he was in his fifties. The Hogs were dumbfounded, not believing that a man could live that long. Logan then said that the Loomation inside him had slowed down his aging process.

"Since your Loomation is active, you don't have the advanced strength. So how could you be in such great shape for someone your age?" questioned Eric.

"The heal spell?" Miles said, giving out his theory.

"Yes…every morning I give myself a heal spell. By doing that, I have been able to maintain a fully healthy heart and regenerated organs. I never experienced those aging pains. Never had a bad back nor bad knees. I have the body of a man in his prime every day," Logan added.

"So you can never die?" Hayden asked.

"Of course, I can. I could be hurt so badly that I couldn't focus on giving myself a heal spell before I bleed out. An accident such as getting buried in an avalanche or cave-in could happen where I die instantly. And not to mention any way a regular person can get killed, like being shot in the head or stabbed in the heart."

"So as long as you avoid getting killed, you're immortal," Gard claimed.

"Death comes to every human, no matter what tricks you attempt to postpone it. No human can live forever," Logan said sadly. "See, I've been alive for a very long time. The heal spell makes my body feel like brand-new. But it doesn't do anything for your mind." Logan once again lowered his head. "The human mind wasn't meant to be this active for this long. And mine has been very active for far too long now." The Hogs could sense that this man was dying from the way he was speaking. "I'm suffering from Alzheimer's...I've been forgetting things, and it's been getting worse over the years. The mind can only hold so many memories, and over time, some of the memories need to be pushed out for new ones. Once the mind is trained to push out memories, it doesn't stop even if you don't need it to. After a while, the mind starts pushing out the recent memories too, and that's been happening more often." The Hogs felt sorry for the old man as he started to speak slower and slower. "This is why I'm making my stand against the monster now. If that thing kills me, I'm going out swinging, and I want my mind to be at its best when I do. I can't push it back any longer. If I keep running, one day I fear that I'll forget what day of the week it is and forget to teleport away. I may even forget how to teleport, something I do every day."

Hearing a man suffer from any stage of Alzheimer's would make a person appreciate their blessings, which the Hogs were doing at this moment. The Hogs were now more convinced that this man was facing the fight of his life at the end of this month and were afraid of him losing.

"If this thing coming to kill you is killing you because you have Loomation inside you...that means we're all in trouble, aren't we?" Will hesitantly asked.

Logan nodded and assured them that if the monster won the fight and he died, it would be a short matter of time until the monster learned about the other people who carried Loomation inside them. The Hogs felt that they were dealing with a whole new threat. Mercenaries, kidnapping scientist, and even Bigfoot felt like child's play compared to this great evil Logan was speaking of.

"We should think about this, guys," Eric said to his friends.

"Yeah. I mean, we don't even know what we're dealing with here," Timber added.

"Can you give us some time to think about this?" Will asked Logan.

"What's to think about! We're about to be on some monster's hit list, and we have full warning and guaranteed backup. We can't just ignore that!" Gard shouted.

"Yeah, this doesn't sound like something we can just brush under the carpet and be on our merry little way," Hayden added.

"You said we have a few weeks to think about this right?" Will asked the man.

"Four weeks," Logan answered. The Hogs didn't all seem to be on the same page at the moment. Logan could see that. He guessed that this would happen. It would have been too much for all of them to unite at once on this idea of killing the monster. Logan walked over to the sword and picked it up. He said he'd let them sleep on their options for now and would return.

"Where are you going to go?" asked Juice.

"I have something important I need to do. I'll stay in touch. Until then, stay safe," Logan said just before he vanished. The Hogs dropped back into their chairs, feeling very stressed out. Some of the Hogs felt that Logan was crazy because he had been on the run for so long. Others felt that they should be grateful to him for giving them a heads-up on a life-threatening attack. The threat felt real for everyone, which made them all nervous and scared about the coming weeks.

CHAPTER 29

The Phoenix's Flame

Tuesday, June 1, 2010

The next day, all morning long, the Hogs seemed to be in a stressful state. It was afternoon time, and Juice was standing on top of the hill that was located not too far from the campsite. He went up there to gather his thoughts. He wasn't the only one looking for solitude; all the Hogs were sitting alone by themselves doing the same thing. But Juice's mind wasn't on the mysterious man who warned them of a coming threat. He looked up to the sky, wishing he could join the birds. So far, he had only taken flight once; and by now, the others were calling it a fluke. There were other things to discuss now, and the power of flight seemed to be yesterday's news. The rest of the group all gathered for lunch, so Juice headed down the hill to join his friends. Lunch wasn't anything special, just cold meat sandwiches. Juice was the last to arrive at the table while the others were already sitting and eating.

"It's June!" shouted Juice in an upbeat way. The boys just grunted in annoyance. "Come on now, I thought we'd be happy to say goodbye to May."

"What would make June any better?" wondered Miles.

"Well, my birthday is this month…You guys planning anything special for me?" Juice said with a happy grin.

"We're going camping," Hayden said with a careless attitude.

"Well, we're kind of already camping," Juice replied. Juice saw all the low faces around the table, and for some reason, he wasn't feeling the same way. Juice hated being the only one having a good time while the others around him felt miserable. So he was hoping to turn everyone's mood around.

"Everything is a disaster, Juice!" Eric stated.

"Yeah, May started off bad when you ruined our lives by bringing that cube to one of our hangouts!" Timber added.

"Hey, now, I was going to toss that cube into the fire. Will was the one who wanted to look at it," Juice said, defending himself.

"Now we may be living our last month because some evil monster wants to kill humans who carry Loomation inside them," Gard argued.

It was now sadly clear that Juice's cheerful approach wasn't going to catch on. Juice decided to join them at the table for lunch even though he wasn't too hungry. He reached for a soda pop from one of the coolers. When Juice opened the cooler and pulled out a can, he felt that it was warm and wet. Juice felt sad he had to inform the rest of the group that they were now out of ice.

"I told you that four bags should have lasted us about a week," Hayden stated.

"Well, if it should have lasted us a week, then why did it last only three days?" Juice asked.

"Because you only bought one bag of ice, Juice," Hayden answered Juice calmly, his mind too wrapped up in other things so that he couldn't muster the anger to be mad at Juice's mistake or laziness. Juice just now remembered that he was the one in charge of buying ice and now realized that he clearly didn't buy enough. Adding this mistake to forgetting the hammer for the tent stakes, this was Juice's second mistake of the trip. After the Hogs just placed the blame for the situation they were in on Juice, he felt his smiling mood slip away. Juice said that he'd buy some ice if he could get a ride into town. Hayden offered to take Juice into town in his truck because he felt a nice car ride would be a soothing opportunity. Juice and Hayden took off in Hayden's truck, and the rest of the Hogs carried on with their lunch.

Later That Night

An old farmer took a brief peek outside the window above his kitchen sink and saw two of his cows standing in his field. He took a moment to look back at the sink to finish cleaning the last dirty dish. As he turned his head toward the sink, he heard a loud gust of wind from outside. He turned his eyes back to the window and saw only one cow standing in the field. The man believed it to be some sort of wild animal attack from a coyote or wolf. He moved in a hurry, snatching up his rifle and slipping on his old boots to go check it out.

The old man moved quickly, for he wanted to protect his cattle. When he got to the field, he saw something big out in the distance. It looked to be some kind of animal. As he approached what he believed to be an animal, he heard chewing. That thing was eating one of his cows. The man lifted the barrel of the gun upward and slowly moved forward. He had a small flashlight in his pocket, so he turned it on and shone it at the animal. The light was beaming on the creature's back, so the creature didn't know it was being watched.

The animal was taller than the farmer, over six feet tall, and was covered in large maroon feathers. The man believed that he was looking at a fully grown, feathered pterodactyl-type beast. He was now shaking in fear, and the light lingered over the dead cow that was being devoured by the bird. Once the light shone onto the cow, the creature eating it spotted the light and turned its head, looking at the farmer with vicious eyes. The man fired his gun at the animal several times as he backed away screaming. The bird shrieked hellishly, and flames started to ignite around its body.

The bird was glowing brightly in the steaming-hot flames surrounding him. The man dropped the gun and started to make a run for his life. The bird started to flap its wings hard and fast; and then, suspended in the air, it took flight toward the man, while spewing the hot flames it was giving off in its path. The bird flew at an incredible speed with a few flaps of its wings. It drove its mighty beak through the man's back and out of his chest, burning up the dead corpse with its wings as it flew past. The bird didn't stop there; it then flew right through the house, causing its flames to torch the entire place. The bird looped back to snatch the second cow with its heavy-duty talons and took off into the air.

Out on the country road around the old prison where the creatures escaped from, Logan was on the hunt for the creatures of the garden. Logan heard the alert of the house fire from the police scanner he had stolen earlier in the day. He was determined to locate the escaped creatures as he felt responsible for their untimely release. He knew having a police scanner would be a good way to hear other people report sightings of the animals. When he heard of a wildfire on a farmhouse, he sensed that it was a sign of the phoenix. Logan took out a smartphone that he had stolen from someone from the store. With the phone, he was able to find a photo of the farmhouse with the use of internet maps. Now that he knew what the house looked like, he was able to teleport himself there.

When he arrived, he saw the scorching house burning brightly. He saw that there was a line of fire within the field so followed the fiery trail. There, he found the farmer's gun, lying quiet and undisturbed on the ground. Then he found the top half of the farmer's body, roasting in flames. Then when he turned his head, he saw the bottom half of the disfigured corpse also lit in flames. Logan was devastated at seeing the death of this man, but there was nothing more he could do for him now. He had to find the bird. He looked out in the distance and saw something in the sky. Logan had a pair of binoculars around his neck, which he used to look at the object in the sky. He saw the phoenix in the air, hovering in place with its magnificent wings flapping effortlessly in the cloudless sky. Logan saw that there was a building near the bird, so he teleported to the top of the building and found himself standing on top of an abandoned used-car lot.

Logan saw that the bird was close and surrounded by an abandoned parking lot, so there was nothing that could catch on fire underneath it. He had the sword strapped to his back and thought about using it for battle, but he couldn't get close to that thing. Logan's defense spell wouldn't reach out that far. That spell only went the distance of half a football field, and the bird was out of reach. Logan saw that the bird was in the middle of eating, so the monster wouldn't stay in its position forever. He knew he needed help, and he knew just the people who could help.

Back at the swamp, Will, Timber, Eric, Gard, and Miles were all sitting around the fire while Juice and Hayden were heading back with the ice and a few extra walkie-talkies, along with other supplies. When Logan appeared to them, it made them jump out of their seats once again. They were not used to having a guest who just appeared out of nowhere whenever he wanted.

"I need your help," Logan said, getting straight to the point.

"I thought you said we had a month until the threat came," Eric said with a hint of uncertainty in his voice.

"It's not what I warned you about last night. It's something else," Logan replied in a hurry.

"What is it?" wondered Will.

Logan then explained to the Hogs about the escaped animals from the prison that night he came to visit his son. He said that his son and Ray had a whole prison full of these wild creatures, and thanks to his actions, they were set loose on the world.

"That prison must have been where they got the Sasquatch from!" Gard theorized.

"So you have fought creatures like them before?" Logan asked.

"Just one, and we barely made it out alive," Timber replied.

"I've located the phoenix. I can teleport you there. We need to kill it while we have the chance!" Logan spoke fast, for he didn't want the bird to fly off before they could get back to it.

"Wait, why do we have to go fight a phoenix? Maybe it's friendly and happy to be out of its cage," Eric stated.

"The bird has already killed a man and burned down his house," Logan replied.

The Hogs were shocked about that statement and were now frightened not of the animal, but of who else the animal could hurt. Will stepped up to Logan and said that he was willing to help him with the phoenix. The others followed Will's lead and were willing to do whatever they could to stop the bird. Logan then teleported the Hogs to the top of the abandoned car lot building. They all spotted the phoenix right away. It was shining so brightly with its dashing flames leaking from its wings. The beast looked like a giant prehistoric bird.

"Wow...birders would kill to see a sighting like this," Eric stated as everyone stared at the creature. Eric took a close look at the bird and was fascinated at how it was ingesting its meal. "You see how it's holding the cow with its talons and cooking it with the flames coming off its own body, while it uses its wings to stay suspended in the air."

"Yeah, lots of teeth in that long pointy beak too," Timber nervously added.

"I'm calling Juice and Hayden," Gard said. Since they were now out of the swamp, they were able to use their cell phones. Gard called Juice and informed them about what was going on. Gard told them that they were at the deserted car lot and to meet them there as fast as they could. Hayden said that they were not too far away and would be there soon. Gard told them to step on it and to meet him in the middle of the parking lot by the road.

"You got a plan, Gard?" Will asked.

"Yeah, we're going to have Hayden shoot that thing down," Gard explained.

"Shoot it, that's your big plan?" Eric asked, completely dumbfounded by that idea.

"That didn't work on Bigfoot, and I don't think setting this animal on fire is going to do any good this time," Timber added, and Eric also mentioned that setting Bigfoot on fire didn't work either.

"I'm guessing the farmer used his gun on the beast before he was killed by it. I found his gun resting close to his dead body," Logan informed the others.

"Well, that may explain why the bird is eating off the ground. It feels safer in a higher altitude," Eric observed.

"If the animal feels safer up there, then it won't come down. It'll flee if it sees us trying to bring it down to our level," Will said.

"How are we supposed to fight that thing anyway? It's covered in fire!" Timber shouted, pointing out the obvious problem.

"Will, Eric, and Miles, you guys stay up here and keep your eye on the bird in case it takes off," Gard said, taking charge of the situation. Gard felt an idea coming to him, so he went with it. Gard then asked Logan if he could teleport him and Timber to the middle of the parking lot by the road. Just before Logan placed his hands onto Timber and Gard to take them to the site, Gard had to make sure that Will was carrying his walkie-talkie. Will revealed his walkie-talkie, and Gard showed that he too had one on him. They switched them on the same channel before Logan teleported the boys to the middle of the parking lot. Once Timber, Gard, and Logan were on the road next to the parking lot, Timber asked Gard what the plan was. Gard said that they needed to wait for Juice and Hayden to show up.

The wait for Hayden's truck wasn't long; Hayden cut through a grass field to get to the location quicker. Hayden parked the truck on the side of the road, keeping the headlights on for some light. Juice and Hayden met up with the three by the parking lot. "Holy cow...is that thing eating a cow?" Juice asked as he stared up at the bird in the high distance.

"Yeah, and we're pretty sure that once it's done eating, it'll take off, and we may never find it again," Gard explained.

Hayden had his rifle in his hand and was ready to shoot it down "Hayden, I don't think that's going to work," Timber uttered.

"Oh yes, it will...It's phoenix season," Hayden said jokingly. In all honesty, Hayden had a feeling that the gun wouldn't work. He just really wanted an excuse to shoot his gun again.

"The farmer tried killing it with a gun before the bird killed him," Logan informed Hayden.

"This thing has already killed someone?" Juice said with shock as Gard said that it was very important that they take out the bird now before it had the chance to kill anyone else. "So what's the play here then?" asked Juice.

"We're going lure the bird into the building. Once it's in there, the flames it's carrying will set fire to the walls, and hopefully the structure will collapse while the bird is still inside," Gard explained.

"You do realize that our friends are still on the roof of that building, right?" Timber mentioned. Gard told Timber that he made sure that Miles was left up there so that he could teleport them to safety when the building came down.

"Gard, I've seen that bird in action when it flew out of its cage at the prison," Logan said, bringing up something important about the bird. "The bird flew straight up from the floorboards of the prison and crashed its way through the concrete roof."

"So there's no point of trying to seal it inside the office building then," Gard said, disappointed with this new information.

"Hey, now, I thought it was a good plan," Juice responded with positive charm.

"So we can't shoot at it because that won't work and will most likely make it fly away. We can't trap it inside a building because apparently it can crash through walls. And we can't bring it down here because it feels safer high in the sky. And even if we could bring it down here, the thing is on fire. So how are we going to attack it?" Gard said, adding to the list of problems.

"I wish we could just go up there and fight it," Juice uttered. Suddenly Gard had a new idea.

"Juice, you're right…you can go up there!" Gard shouted.

"What, I can't go up there!" Juice yelled.

"Of course, you can! You're the only one of us who can fly!" said Gard.

"I did that one time by accident, and I've failed every attempt of flying since! And besides, what am I supposed to do when I get up there, reason with it?" Juice asked in a panicked voice.

"He can stab it with this," Logan said as he removed the sword from his back and presented it to the boys. The Hogs were mesmerized by the beauty of the sword. Gard asked if the sword was strong enough to do the job. "Trust me, a person without a dried-up Loomation can slice through a diamond like bread with this blade," Logan insisted.

"There you go, Juice. You take that sword and stab that bird," Gard ordered.

Juice was so overwhelmed with panic that he couldn't move. He found the bird to be very intimidating, and knowing that he would have to fly in order to get to the bird made him very nervous. The thought of being up there by himself with no backup made him fear dying alone.

Gard could tell that Juice was feeling nervous, so he gave him a pep talk. "Juice, I've seen you climb and get stuck in so many tall trees when we were kids. I saw how you panicked when you joined the cross-country team because you didn't think you could complete running one mile let alone three, and you ended up being one of the fastest runners on the team. I've seen you break Bigfoot's knee, and when Kate was kidnapped, you managed to stall Ray long enough for the others to open the door!"

"Actually, Ray knocked me into the door, making me close it a bit," Juice admitted.

"What I'm saying is you're not scared of heights. You're stronger than you give yourself credit for. And when the time comes, you always find a way to contribute! Now what's that thing you've always said before you ran a race?" Gard said cheerfully.

"I GOT THIS!" Juice yelled, now feeling super driven and full of confidence.

"You got this!" Gard yelled back.

Juice then snatched the sword from Logan. Once he had a grip on the handle, he felt this new positive sensation being injected into him from the sword. Juice was already very motivated from Gard's speech, but now that he had the sword in his hand, he felt that there was no challenge he could lose. Juice gave a loud cheer and took off into the air, flying fast straight at the bird. Once Juice took off like a rocket, Hayden, Timber, Gard, and Logan all cheered in the heat of the moment.

"Look!" shouted Miles to Will and Eric. The three on the roof of the building spotted Juice soaring through the air, making a straight path toward the phoenix. Everyone on the roof, along with everyone in the parking lot, was all cheering for Juice who was moving headstrong at the bird, getting in close for the stab. As Juice got closer to the animal, he felt the heat radiating from the bird and was immediately covered in sweat. The heat was so distracting that Juice had to wipe the sweat off his face with his forearm. The creature had its back at Juice, so it didn't see him coming. But the bird did hear him coming and turned its head straight toward Juice and gave off a hellish roar as flames were released from its face. Juice screamed in terror, turned around, and retreated as fast as he could back to Gard and the others in the parking lot.

As the Hogs on the roof saw Juice's cowardly retreat, Eric simply said, "Well, that failed." When Juice returned to Gard and the others in the parking lot, they laughed at him for his little kid scream and the fact that he was covered in sweat.

"Yeah, it's hot up there!" Juice stated, not finding any of this funny. "The sweat kept getting in my eyes, and the heat was unbearable. Even if I could get a stab at the beast, it wouldn't be a good one due to me not wanting to burn my body to ashes from the flames of the bird!"

"The fire must be some sort of protection, such as a turtle going into its shell," Logan started.

"I like its style. That would be something I would do," Hayden added.

"Will, is the bird still eating?" Gard asked over the walkie-talkie.

"Yeah, but there's not much left to eat. We need a new plan fast," Will stated.

"Well, my first two ideas were both a bust, but we'll keep thinking down here," Gard replied.

"It's a shame that Hayden can't fly. With him being fireproof, this would have been no problem," Timber stated.

"Oh no, I'm terrified of heights. You wouldn't catch me dead up there," Hayden admitted.

"Terrified of heights, aren't you joining the air force? What do you think they'll have you do there, dig foxholes?" Juice shouted.

"For your information, there are plenty of jobs for the air force that are done on the ground, such as loading the planes up with artillery," Hayden explained.

"They're going to trust you with artillery weapons? I barely trust you carrying a lighter around!" Juice yelled, dehydrated and stressed. "I wouldn't be surprised if some of the missiles end up missing while you're on the job out there."

"Would you two shut up and let me think!" Gard demanded. "So Juice is the only one who can get near it…and Hayden is the only one who can attack it…," Gard said, thinking out loud. "Okay…I got another plan…This one is a little scary, Juice. You'll have to be the bait."

"I don't know if you ever went fishing before, Gard…but there is a grim reason why people use live bait only once!" Juice exclaimed.

"With my plan, you'll be more like the cheese in a mousetrap!" Gard replied.

A little time passed, and the Hogs on the roof spotted Hayden running to the center of the parking lot carrying a tarp and the sword. Over the walkie-talkie, Will heard Gard's voice talk to Hayden saying, "Hayden, stay low out there."

"I am!" Hayden, who was already in a hunched-over position in order to stay low, replied.

"I know. I just wanted to give you a hard time." Gard chuckled. Once Hayden made it to the middle of the parking lot, he put his stomach to the ground and covered himself with the tarp.

"Gard, what's going on down there?" asked Will.

"Right now, both Juice and Hayden have a walkie-talkie, so they're on the same channel listening in," Gard informed him.

"Hey, Will, did you see me flying earlier?" Juice said over the channel.

"Yep, also heard you scream," Will replied.

"Oh, you heard that, did you?" Juice embarrassingly asked.

Gard informed Juice over the walkie-talkie that since Hayden was now in position, Juice was good to go for his part of the plan. Juice then took off into the air to get the bird's attention. Once the Hogs on the roof saw Juice unarmed in the sky, Will again asked for the game plan from Gard. Will was holding the walkie-talkie facing up so that Eric and Miles could hear Gard's plan.

"Right now, Juice is going to trespass into the phoenix's territory. Since the bird feels safe in the air, it's going to feel forced to defend its airspace from intruders. Once the bird starts chasing Juice, he will lead the bird close to the ground over by Hayden. And since Hayden is hidden by the tarp from his truck, the bird won't see any human threats on the ground and will follow Juice down."

"That's a solid plan. Given the fact that Hayden is the only one able to get close to the beast without getting burned, he's our ace in the hole," Eric mentioned.

"Guys, Juice is now close to the bird," Miles stated. The three men on the roof, along with Timber, Gard, and Logan on the side of the road, watched the two in the sky. Juice was now facing the bird from a distance where the flames weren't so warm.

"Hey, Red," Juice said to the bird. The bird just ignored Juice as she was finishing off her meal. "Where are you from...originally?" Juice asked awkwardly, trying to make small talk. Nothing was happening; the bird just kept right on eating.

"Juice, you got to get your butt closer to that bird!" Gard shouted this so loud that he didn't have to say it over the walkie-talkie for Juice to hear it. Juice really didn't want to do that because he now started to wonder if he was fast enough to keep the bird away from him once it started chasing him. He was now very much regretting being a part of this plan. Juice slowly closed the space between him and the bird. He once again started to feel the heat and started to sweat again.

"Hey, you big dumb bird!" Juice said before making a loud clap with his hands. Once Juice clapped his hands, the phoenix dropped the dead cow carcass and looked straight toward Juice with an evil stare. Juice's heart was pounding, and he started to sweat from fear rather than the hot temperature. He now had the bird's attention. Step 2 was now to fly as fast as he could away from it. Juice turned and flew off fast with the bird restlessly chasing after him, flapping its large heavy set of wings with her hazardous flames shedding under its flight patch.

"Okay, it's chasing you. Now drop down to Hayden!" Will yelled. When Eric heard Will yell that, he snatched the walkie-talkie out of Will's hand.

"Negatory on that, Juice! The phoenix is too far away from you. If it sees you drop too low to the ground, it'll turn back. You need it to get so close to you that it won't notice how low it follows you. We may only have once chance at this!" Eric informed Juice.

"Yeah, no problem!" Juice said sarcastically. Juice turned his head and saw that the bird was closing in on him. He was nervous, and he didn't slow down at all; the bird was just getting faster. Juice then started talking to himself, "You didn't bring enough ice for the coolers, Juice. Everything is a disaster, Juice. You ruined our lives, Juice. You need to get closer to the scorching hot bird, Juice! You know what, I'm starting to think my friends don't like me very much."

"Juice, keep the bird over the parking lot. The short distance of the area will keep the bird from gaining any more speed, not to mention the fire droppings from it won't start a wildfire!" Eric said, coaching Juice.

Will took back the walkie-talkie from Eric to contact Gard. "So Juice is going to lead the phoenix over the tarp, and Hayden's going to pierce it from underneath?"

"No, I want Hayden to have eyes on target when he makes his swing. When I tell him *now*, he's going to jump out and immediately make his move so that the bird doesn't have a chance to get out of the way. Since Hayden has no experience with a sword, I told him to swing the weapon like it's a baseball bat!" Gard stated.

"So Juice is leading the animal into his strike zone?" Will asked.

"I can hit the high ones!" Hayden hollered over the walkie-talkie.

Over by the side of the road, Gard watched the phoenix start to close the gap between him and Juice who was leading it toward Hayden's swing zone. Gard looked over to Timber and asked, "Timber, you played baseball with Hayden. What was his batting average like?"

"Pretty good. He was just a slow runner, so he got tagged out on base a lot," Timber answered.

"I don't care about the number of runs he achieved. I want to know that he can hit his target!" Gard shouted. "I'm afraid that when I tell him *now*, he'll be swinging too late or too early. If he swings too late, he'll miss, and if he swings too early, he'll kill Juice!"

"You're just now bringing this up?" shouted Timber in panic.

"It just now occurred to me!" Gard yelled.

"So you're saying one of our best friends could be responsible for killing another one of our best friends?" Timber stated, panicked.

"I think it's now close enough!" Juice reported to Gard.

Gard and Timber turned their heads back to the sky and saw that the bird was now dangerously close to Juice. "If we don't go forward with this plan, the bird's going to be killing one of our best friends for sure!" Gard said nervously. Gard pulled the walkie-talkie up to his mouth and told Juice to start making his descent toward Hayden's strike zone.

Juice wiped some sweat off his forehead and told himself that he had this. He lowered himself down slowly in a slope motion. He flew right over the building where Will, Eric, and Miles were staying low to avoid being seen by the bird. Juice was now at the right altitude, and the bird was still right on his tail. Juice saw the tarp Hayden was hiding under in the parking lot—just a little to his right. Juice knew that Hayden would jump out and swing once he was clear. It all came down to Gard giving the signal.

Gard watched Juice and the animal chasing him draw closer to the tarp. He compared this situation to his time at the track meets. In the past, Gard would record the race times for his fellow track teammates by clicking the stopwatch as soon as he spotted the smoke from the starter gun. He grew very talented at clicking the button at the perfect time, which was not at the sound of the gun but at first site of the smoke.

Gard felt that he had this, and Hayden would hit the phoenix and not Juice. Juice was right about to pass the tarp, and Gard remembered what Timber said about Hayden's lack of speed, so he yelled in the walkie-talkie, "NOW!"

Hayden, as fast as he could, jumped up, tossed the tarp out of his way, and drew back the sword behind his right shoulder. By the time Hayden was in his ready-to-swing position, Juice had passed him, and so Hayden swung with all his might. The phoenix flew right into Hayden's swing patch and was sliced in two. A large ball of fire blew out of the cut bird and engulfed Hayden. The body of the bird left fire tracks past Hayden's position leading up close to where Juice had made his crash landing. The men were stunned as they looked blown away upon witnessing the event.

After the fireball had gradually disappeared, Juice was able to see Hayden standing with most of his shirt burned off. Hayden simply patted out the flames on his clothes with his free hand. Juice, ever grateful to have his feet back on solid ground, made eye contact with his friend Hayden. The distance between the two was about fifty meters with a fire line burning between them. The two cracked a huge smile and charged at each other, cheering. Once they united in the middle, they started saying how awesome that was.

"Once I saw you jump out of the tarp, I knew we had it!" Juice shouted.

"I was under the tarp the whole time it was flying around, so I never saw how fast it was. But when I was ready to swing, I was like…fast ball right down the center, I'll hit it every time!" Hayden cheered. By this time, the rest of the boys were rushing over to the two. Gard sprinted over to join them in on the celebration.

"That was so intense. My heart was pounding like a thousand beats per second watching that!" shouted Gard in on the hype. "Oh, wow, Hayden, your skin looks like a terrible sunburn!" Gard stated. Hayden never experienced that kind of heat so close before. The flames didn't cause any permanent skin damage, but it was letting off steam from the heat.

"Timber, bring over one of the bags of ice from the truck for me!" Hayden shouted, in need of assistance.

The rest of the Hogs showed up along with Logan. Timber tossed a large bag of ice at Hayden, and Hayden hugged it like it was a teddy bear. Juice jumped in on that hug for a way to cool himself down after having the phoenix so close to him. Eric asked what they should do with the dead bird.

"Which part? Hayden sliced it in two," asked Gard, making a joke.

"We should bring it back to the swamp," Will said, staying focused on the situation.

"Both parts?" Hayden asked, being funny.

"Guys, a bird is dead. Let's not act like savages," Eric pleaded.

Logan gathered up the bird and said he'd take them all back to the swamp. Hayden tossed the keys to the truck over to Timber, saying he could drive it back because he and Juice wanted to take the teleporting ride back. The Hogs took one last look at the parking lot as the flames on the pavement started to fade away. Seeing how reckless the animal was, who knew how many more people it could have hurt or killed if they didn't put a stop to it? Logan then took all but Timber back to the campsite within the swamp. Juice and Hayden took off to the pond to splash some water on them to help cool themselves off.

The others went back to their chairs around the still-burning fire. Will told Logan he did a good job finding the phoenix. Logan said that there were still a few other animals out there.

"So you just search for them all day? Where do you sleep? Do you sleep?" questioned Gard.

"I actually wanted to talk to you about that. When I originally came here, I was planning on spending my nights in my old cabin," Logan explained. Since the Hogs were already camping there, he felt that he had to ask permission from the Hogs to stay there now.

"Hey, this was your place first. We should be the ones asking for permission to stay here," Will said.

Logan said that he was greatly exhausted and that he had had enough excitement for one night. He went to bed in the cabin after he told them not to expect to see him come sunrise, as he had somewhere to be in the early morning.

After Logan went into his cabin, Eric asked Will if it was best to let him stay with them. Will said that the man seemed harmless. Eric reminded Will that Logan claimed to be hunted by some great evil, and they shouldn't be anywhere near him when he was found by his hunter.

"We have time to worry about that later. We still know next to nothing about this guy or his hunter. Plus, he's our best shot at finding the rest of the expected monsters from that prison. And if this guy is our enemy…well, keep your enemies close, right?" Will said to Eric. Will, in a weird way, felt safer having Logan there as he figured that someone who had survived for as long as he had could give some good advice.

Miles agreed with Will's decision to let Logan stay at the campsite. He felt that Logan could help him understand his active Loomation better. Miles feared the escaped monsters and didn't want to shy away from them because he was too scared to exercise his powers. And Miles knew that if something evil was coming at the end of the month to kill him and his friends, he would want to know how to fight.

CHAPTER 30

The One-Horn Horse

Wednesday, June 2, 2010

The next morning, Miles woke up early in hopes that he would have a chance to talk to Logan before he took off. Miles was sleeping on the couch that faced front to back within the pop-up camper. Timber was sleeping on the couch facing side to side in the camper. The camper had two queen-size beds on the ends of the camper. Hayden had the one on the back of the camper every night, while the other queen-size bed was rotated between Timber, Eric, and Miles. Miles carefully slipped on his shoes, trying not to wake up Timber or Eric. Hayden was already awake and out and about like most days. After Miles had his shoes on, he opened the front door and was slightly blinded by the morning light. Miles walked out of the camper, went around the campfire, and grew closer to Logan's cabin.

"He's not here!" Hayden yelled out to Miles. Miles jumped in fright at hearing Hayden's voice. He turned to Hayden and saw him sitting in the bed of the truck, holding a thick stick with his large knife. Miles was so focused on the cabin that his surroundings were a blur. If Hayden was sitting on a chair that was around the fire, Miles would have noticed him. Hayden, instead, decided to sit on the bed of his truck that morning.

"Did you see him leave?" asked Miles.

"He was gone before I woke up," Hayden replied. Miles, who was a little angry at himself for not waking up sooner, then walked over to Hayden to see exactly what he was doing. When Miles asked Hayden what was up with the spear he was carving, Hayden told him not to worry about it. Typical Hayden answer.

"What did you want with Renshaw?" Hayden wondered.

"Oh nothing, just wondering if he was still here, that's all," Miles lied.

Hayden knew Miles was lying, but he felt that it was none of his business, so he didn't press Miles on the topic any further. Hayden said that Renshaw now staying with them within the swamp made some of the members in the group uncomfortable. He knew that there was going to be an unavoidable discussion about what to do next. Some people wanted to leave the swamp; some wanted to ask Renshaw to no longer be around them. Miles asked Hayden what he would vote on if it came to that. Hayden said that Renshaw being in the swamp didn't bother him, and he definitely didn't want to relocate. Hayden asked Miles how he would vote, and Miles simply said, "I'm not sure yet."

A few hours later, Will was standing over a coal-powered grill cooking some burgers for lunch. Gard came over carrying a plate to put the burgers on as they were now cooked. Once Gard got up close to Will, Juice's shadow flew past them. Will looked up and saw that Juice was completing another lap around the area.

"Are you sure it's okay for him to be up there in broad daylight?" asked Will.

"We're a few miles away from a road, and those roads may get two cars on it during rush hour. He'll be fine as long as he doesn't go up too high," Gard stated.

"I'm going to call him down for lunch now," Will said as he slipped the burgers onto the plate.

After the plate was full, Will grabbed the walkie-talkie to inform Juice that it was now time for lunch. Gard then yelled over to the shower tent to let Hayden know the same information. Hayden had to take a shower because when he returned from his hike into the swamp earlier, he was covered in mud and dirt. Gard and Will sat at the table under the canopy with Timber, Eric, and Miles. Juice returned to the campsite for a soft landing right by the canopy. Around the same time, Hayden exited the shower tent and came to the table. Now that everyone was together at the table, they started eating.

Eric had a box next to him; it was the box they got from Cain when he recruited them to rescue Kate. He said that he fully went over everything he found inside it. Eric was hoping that some of the documents that were stolen from Ray would shed some light on Logan or maybe the great evil threat coming at the end of the month. He sadly informed them that there was no information concerning Logan. He was grateful to tell them that he found a notebook that gave out full details on the creatures from the prison who were now set loose.

"The notebook on the creatures revealed that there aren't many more out there. We already took out the Sasquatch, and now the phoenix is out of the picture. All that's left are the ogre, the troll, and the unicorn," Eric stated.

"Is there anything in that notebook that tells us where all these creatures came from?" asked Juice.

"Nothing specific. The only thing I found was a statement on the animal's attitude: 'The creatures grew into a huge murderous rage once they were removed from their *home*,'" Eric quoted from the notebook. "The notebook had two hypotheses on this: They don't belong here, so they went mad. Or they now see humans as their enemy since they were the ones who removed them from their home in the first place."

"So the Havocs found a way to aim that murderous rage onto their enemies? That's awful!" Will mentioned, disgusted with the Havocs and feeling a bit of compassion for the animals.

"Well, it turns out Ray was able to find other *uses* for the animals," Eric reported. "The hair from Bigfoot could be used to manufacture a powerful rope. Ray sold it to rich sailors for a high price." Eric went on to say that the feathers from the phoenix were fireproof and heat resistant, so Ray used them to design a trench coat. The fire department couldn't afford the price of Ray's superlight, very comfortable coats, so he sold them to wealthy fat cats who had a thing for real fur. Then Eric talked about the unicorn, saying that it had a chemical inside it that could change the color of its horn. Ray was able to copy it and used that chemical to make antidepressions, bipolar pills, and split-personality medication. Once the Hogs heard this information, they remembered when Juice had his split-personality infection and connected the dots.

"Any weaknesses on the animals?" asked Will.

"A sword cutting them in two seemed to be a weakness," Hayden uttered with a forced grin.

Eric said that these animals didn't work like anything living does. For example, they didn't need to eat to survive. "This explains how they were kept alive inside the prison for so long, as they didn't need anyone to feed them," Eric explained.

"Yeah, but the bird was eating last night," Gard mentioned.

"According to the book, all animals were offered food ten different times. The animals only ate when they felt like Ray theorized it," replied Eric. The notebook said that the phoenix ate the most, with her stats saying that it ate six out of ten times food was offered. Ray believed that the animals used the food to give their jaws a workout and to give their stomachs a stretch. The offering of the food stopped after a while, for the bowel movements were too annoying to clean.

After the talk of the animals was over, the big question was asked to Eric. Juice asked it, not knowing how big the topic was. "Anything on the *great evil* Logan warned us about?" Eric was sad to report that none of Ray's notes talked about some great evil that hunted down people who carried Loomation.

"Miles, I was hoping you could inform us about Loomation. You read that book, right?" Eric asked, giving Miles the spotlight. All eyes were on Miles, eager to hear what he had to say. Miles eyed Gard who was the only person he had shared the information with. Gard didn't want to push his friend to reveal what he knew, but Gard felt that this would be a better time than any to share it. Before Miles even said a word, Will said that he looked up the word *Loomation* online and didn't find anything that was related to their powers.

Miles said that any of the Loomation information wouldn't be found anywhere online because the book he found in the box was a first printing, and there was never a second. Due to the rareness of the book, none of the owners would post any of the writing on the internet because it would make the resale price go down. Miles told the ghost story of the publishing company: that not too long after a dozen of the first-print editions were made and shipped off, the whole company was burned to the ground as two obscure men disappeared from the flames.

This story did seem mysterious to the Hogs. Knowing that Logan was the only person who knew that the power inside them was called Loomation, and that he also had the power to teleport, made it seem clear that Logan was one of the cryptic men spotted hidden within the flames. The Hogs were guessing that the second man seen in the fire was this unknown evil. Miles talked about what he read in the book; he told them the differences between an active Loomation and a dry Loomation. Active means you can cast spells, while a dry one gives you advanced strength.

Miles mentioned that the writer had to go through old religious archives to find these terms. He read that the angels used their Loomation powers to perform their powerful attacks. Another mention of Loomation being used within religious archives was that the prophets were the only humans built to embody this unique power. This was why the chances of the Loomation drying up in a human were very high.

"Miles, could it be possible that you're a descendant of a prophet?" Will asked with enlightened wonder.

"The book did say it's a possibility, but it also could be total randomness on why the Loomation in me became active," Miles replied, feeling that the correct answer was the second one.

"So if humans were not made to contain Loomation, it sounds like angels were," Juice stated.

"Hold on now…are we really going to believe the whole angels route now?" Gard asked, finding the religious route being a little far-fetched for him.

"We literally just got done talking about Bigfoot, the phoenix, and a unicorn like they're annoying possums, and now we hear about angels and prophets. That's where you want to draw the reality line?" Timber ranted.

"Yeah, Gard, I mean, this would explain why there's no scientific evidence to support any of the craziness we have faced these past four weeks," Eric replied, being more of a believer.

"Did any of this get brought up in Ray's studies?" Gard asked Eric.

Eric said that Ray was a man of science. But he did reference a quote from the scientist Jerrod Jochovo from time to time, which was, "When you come across a problem that neither sciences nor logic can give an answer, start to seek out the supernatural for answers." Eric saying this showed that even Ray believed in some kind of higher presence in the world.

"Well, the book did have information on other non-angel people who carried Loomation. A few men with immense strengths in the biblical times and a woman who could control roots of trees in the 1600s were also mentioned," Miles added.

After that, the Hogs grew silent. They just sat around eating their lunch. Juice then brought up the Logan topic. This whole powwow was to discuss the Logan situation. The Hogs all said that they didn't feel like Logan was a threat, but he was very secretive, and the Hogs didn't care much for that. The biggest problem was that Logan claimed he was being hunted by some great evil, and if this thing found him, all the Hogs would be in danger. The Hogs knew that the threat wouldn't be a problem until the end of the month. They also felt that having Logan around gave them the chance to learn all they could from him and that he was the best shot at locating all the animals from the prison.

"Maybe if he opened up a bit more, we could warm up to him," Will stated.

"Well, we could be more open to him, maybe include him in a meal or something," Juice replied. The overall feel for Logan was that they were going to tolerate his presence, so there was no vote on kicking him out of the swamp or relocating themselves.

A few hours passed, and Miles was out on his own, hiking on the running path Will and Juice stomped out during their morning runs. Miles saw that he was now out of sight from the campsite, and he found a smooth rock to sit on. Once on the rock, he removed his backpack and took out a water bottle and the book about Loomation. Miles flipped through the pages to the spells section of the book. That was where he read about the defense spell, the one he really wanted to work on. Another one he wanted to learn how to perform was the heal spell, and the other one he wanted to avoid completely was the death spell. Miles also wanted to take a second look at the teleporting ability as he felt there was more he could learn about that.

Just moments into the reading, Miles heard a sound that made him shift his sight toward the field. At first, he thought it was an animal of some kind. But what he heard was Logan out in the distance simply walking back to the campsite in a calm matter. Logan didn't see Miles as he marched through the field. Miles saw that this was his chance to finally get some one-on-one time with him, so he hustled over to talk to Logan.

"Hey!" Miles shouted when he grew close to the man. Logan was caught off guard by Miles's presence. Miles asked Logan what he was doing there in the midst of the swamp. Logan told Miles that every time he teleported to the campsite, all his friends gave a look of fearful shock, so he thought he'd show up to the campsite the old-fashioned way this time.

"You're Will, right?" Logan asked.

"No, I'm Miles."

"Sorry, my memory isn't what it once was," Logan apologized. During this slow and awkward small talk, Logan saw the book Miles was holding in his hand. "Is that what I think it is?" Logan asked with a stunned look on his face. Miles held the book up to Logan and told him the title of the book. Logan couldn't believe that one of the Hang Out Group members was in possession of that book. "I thought all the copies burned up in the fire," Logan stated.

"So you're aware of the story behind this book?" asked Miles.

"You could say that," Logan replied.

"What all do you know about this book?" questioned Miles.

The first detail Logan revealed was that the book was written from stolen sources. Logan looked back the way he came, feeling that he had time to tell Miles the full story of the book's cursed background. Logan said that the source of the book was from his own personal journal.

There was a time when Logan was trying to find as much information on Loomation as he could. He studied stories of people who may have had this power in the past. He wrote it all down within his journal, the same journal that contained all his instructions on how to use his spells. When he discovered a publishing company that printed books on the strange and unexplained events, he went to the company to see if he could compare notes with the man in charge of the company. The man shared what he could, but Logan didn't share his studies, unless there was something that overlapped. The man knew that Logan was withholding some information and was eager to get a new book published.

The man offered Logan a place to stay at his house. Logan accepted because finding a place to sleep wasn't easy, so he took what he could get. Logan stayed in that town until the devil found him, then he hastily teleported away. A day passed, and Logan realized that his journal was now missing. He knew that the book publisher stole it because he hadn't used it since he was staying at the man's house. The guy could have had it for days for all he knew. Logan didn't feel safe returning to the town where he just escaped from the devil, but information about his son was in that book, so he had to get it back before the devil could get his hands on it.

When Logan returned to the warehouse where the book based off his stolen journal was being printed, he was unaware that a truck had already gone off with a dozen or so copies. Logan confronted the manager in a threatening rage. The man feared Logan's return, so he always kept the journal with him, hoping that returning the book would be an act of forgiveness. The man said that he didn't mention the writer of the book nor any of the personal information. The man only wanted the Loomation information for the books. Logan was a bit relieved that he managed to retrieve his journal and that his son's Loomation was still a secret. But then the signs of the devil's presence appeared, and Logan could tell that the devil was in the building. Logan demanded everyone leave the building right away; he led them to the door like a sheepdog leads its pack. But the door burst into flames because the devil was behind the door setting fire to the building.

Logan fired off some defense spells at the devil so the people could exit by way of the fire escape located behind them. Logan hadn't taken on the devil since the first time they met, but all he had to do was wait until everyone was clear and he could teleport away. The people were all in such a panic that to get them all to stand still for him to teleport them away to safety was out of the question. The last man who made it to the fire escape turned and saw Logan and another person whom he couldn't quite make out. Then Logan vanished, and not too long after that, so did the silhouette. The man on the fire escape couldn't believe his eyes.

Now that Miles fully knew the history of the book, he found that it all made sense that the author was Logan all along. He then felt that it was okay to tell Logan that he too had an active Loomation. Miles said that he was the only one of his friends who had it. Logan never thought of the idea of one of the Hogs having the power of an active Loomation. He never saw Miles perform any actions related to the power he had, so he just assumed that he had a dry Loomation like the others.

"Tell me...what did you see when it became active inside you?" Logan asked with a sense of wonder. Miles knew right away what Logan was talking about. He said that he saw a vison of Logan's son, Cain, waking from his coma in the old prison. Logan turned away from Miles to process that information. Thinking to himself, he wondered why would Miles see that, and was there a connection?

"What did you see?" asked Miles.

Logan turned back to Miles and told him what he saw. "I saw a great evil. The same great evil that would one day chase me for decades." When Logan told Miles what he saw in his vision, he told it as if he was making a confession. He could not remember if he had ever revealed his vision to anyone before.

"The book called it a prophet spell," Miles stated.

"Yes, I believed that prophets were humans who were made to contain Loomation. They would get their future visions from the heavens by a blast of light. Once inside the prophet, the energy would become active, and that would give them a glimpse into the future."

"Have you ever done it before...like on purpose?" wondered Miles.

"No...but I've tried. I never figured it out. I didn't waste time on trying to see the future. It was the past that I wanted to change," Logan replied. There was a slight awkward silence after that. Then Logan asked a question of Miles as if it was very important. "Have you been working on the defense spell?"

"Yeah, I was able to strike Bigfoot the other week," Miles answered.

"The color, what was the color?" Logan asked, anxious to know.

"Purple...a light violet," Miles said, now feeling overwhelmed.

"No, no, that's not good. You should be at green by now. It'll take weeks to get you to that level if we're lucky."

"What does the color mean?" asked Miles.

Logan explained that the color was the level of strength. He said that light violet would chase off some small critters, but it wouldn't do anything against something stronger. Logan entered a bit of a panic mode but started to calm himself down by reminding himself that there was still time to train. Logan, feeling calmer, asked Miles if he learned the heal spell.

"I want to learn that one, but there was a spell in the book that I'm afraid of," Miles replied. Miles talked about the death spell. Once he spoke of the death spell, he went on saying that he didn't want to kill anyone and was leery on how easy it was to do. He was afraid that he may set it off accidentally and kill someone he loved or anyone for that matter.

Logan grew silent at the mention of the death spell, and his mind was now brought back to the first days of his studying the power inside him. At first it was exciting, but he knew learning the death spell was one he never should have discovered. Logan, with a heavy heart, confessed to Miles that he had done just what Miles feared. Logan told Miles that by a misleading threat, Logan used the death spell on his best friend. The action of that was one he'd never forget. Time still hadn't erased that fateful date. It didn't matter how much he started to forget; that massive burden of guilt had never been eased.

"I'm sorry," Miles said, feeling guilty at reminding Logan of his tragic past.

"Don't worry about it. The memories haunt me every day," Logan stated. Before Logan forgot what he was originally going to do before Miles called out to him, he thought of a good chance to give Miles a training lesson. "Come with me, Miles. There's something I want you to see."

Miles blindly followed the man deep into the swamp. They didn't walk long, nor did either say a word. Logan stopped after reaching a stream. He looked worried and started to look around in fear.

"What is it?" Miles asked, confused by Logan's behavior.

"I found one of the creatures in the meadow. I was able to teleport it here and hit it with the gravity spell that should have kept it grounded long enough for me to return with you boys and the sword. But I must have taken too long, or the horse was stronger than I thought it would be."

"The horse…you mean the unicorn?" Miles shouted.

"Yeah, there were distress calls to the police about a wild horse attacking some hikers. Judging from the blood all over its fur, I feared the worse fate had come to those hikers. I was able to teleport the animal here in the swamp where it couldn't hurt anyone," Logan explained.

"Well, now the only people it can hurt are us," Miles said with a sense of apprehension.

Logan jumped across the stream and made it past some dead trees. There he spotted the horse a short distance away. Miles was right behind Logan, and when he saw the horse, he took off his backpack to receive his walkie-talkie to call in help. But Logan snatched the book bag from Miles's hands.

"You need to learn how to do the death spell. Trust me! Once you figure out how to achieve it, you won't fear it any longer. If you go your whole training fearing that you'll do it by accident, then you may end up doing it without trying. But once you find the trigger for it, you'll always know how to keep yourself from doing it!" Logan said as he wrapped the bag behind his back. Logan then faced the horse and yelled at it. The unicorn started rushing over to the two. Logan said that this was Miles's battle, but he'd stand guard and help if needed. When Miles asked Logan to elaborate on that, Logan disappeared into thin air. Miles assumed that Logan just teleported away to safety. Miles felt that he should get the heck out of there and teleport himself back to the campsite to get help from his friends.

But the mighty steed was charging at Miles in such a flurry that he was too overwhelmed with fear, and he couldn't concentrate. So Miles took off running as fast as he could. "I'm going to get killed…by a unicorn!" Miles cowardly yelled. He could hear the horse galloping right behind him with the noise growing louder. Miles ran back to the stream and squeezed himself through the dead trees bordering the water. He ran through the shallow stream and turned back to face the horse, which was too large to squeeze through the trees. Only its head was able to pop over to the other side of the trees.

The unicorn started to use its all-around sharp horn to slice the branches, carving a patch through the trees. Miles knew that he had to run but saw that the horse needed a few minutes to fully cut out a patch for its entire body to walk through. He saw an opportunity to attack, so he firmly placed his feet down in the dirt and stuck his chest up with his shoulders back. Miles then chucked his right arm in the direction of the unicorn. The tip of his fingers released a defense spell. The blast was light violet, and when it hit the horse, it created just a very minor annoyance for the creature. What Logan said to Miles about the defense spell only being a light violet was true; it wouldn't protect him from anything above a squirrel's might.

Miles then took off running, embarrassed that his attack was so pitiful. He then reached a muddy field when something caught his eye. It looked to be some man-made animal trap. Miles recognized some parts of the traps as it was the trunk that Hayden was carving into a spear just this morning. He saw two spear-shaped trunks slightly hidden in the ground.

Miles got close to the trap and noticed the trip wire. He saw that once the trip wire was triggered, the two sharp sticks would rise in a forty-five-degree angle, stabbing whoever was charging through the wire. Miles carefully stepped over the wire and placed himself between the two sticks. He was going to allow himself to be the bait and lure the unicorn to the trap. The unicorn had now crossed the stream and was charging straight toward Miles who was shaking with fear as he watched the horse get closer and closer. Miles saw that the two sticks were a little too far apart; at this time, he thought, *I think a third one between these two would work better.* Then Miles realized that Hayden must not have finished this trap because there was an empty placeholder for a third spear right where Miles was positioned.

It was too late to run now as the unicorn kicked the trip wire, and the two spears rose at the steed. The sides of the animal were pierced, casing the animal to come to a stop and holler in pain. The horse was wedged between the two spears, but it was still approaching Miles with its horn leading the way. Miles was also stuck between the two spears, and the horn was getting closer. The unicorn had to drive its body deeper into the two spears, stabbing it in order to grow closer to Miles.

Miles knew he had to kill that horse before it got any closer, so he focused on the death spell. He took a deep breath before firing it off. The attack came out of his hand in a dark-violet blast. The blast moved like lightning, but it didn't go far because the horse was so close to Miles. The spell struck the steed, and it became motionless. Miles was still filled with too much caution to start his celebration. He gave the horse a tap to see if it was truly dead. There was no response. The unicorn was wedged lifelessly between the stakes, and Miles was safe.

Logan appeared out of nowhere to congratulate him and to help him out of the trap. Miles asked where he went. Logan said that he never left and that he'd explain how he did that on another day. Logan took Miles's hand and pulled him out of the trap.

"The death spell...I did it. It didn't look like one of my defense spells. It looked more unstable," Miles said.

Logan explained that the spell had no solid way of aiming it. He said that it would wave around where you directed it and find something living to touch. He said that it was because the death spell was so unstable and not always predictable, it was something he shouldn't use for many reasons. Miles said that he no longer feared doing it. Logan was right. Now that Miles had done it, he wouldn't fear doing it by mistake ever again.

The two looked at the horse and said they had better get it back to the campsite and bury it with the other creature. Miles said that he'd do the honors. He placed one hand on the horse and his other hand on Logan and teleported them back to the campsite. When they arrived, they frightened the Hogs who were sitting casually around the firepit.

"Man, we really need to put a bell on you or something," Juice stated. The fact that Miles and Logan arrived together wasn't the focus of the group. Hogs gathered around the dead animal and noticed it was covered in blood. Will asked Miles and Logan if they were okay. Miles informed everyone that the fresh blood on the animal was its own. But the stained blood was from its victims.

"How many did this one kill?" Timber asked.

"I'm not sure. The distress call I heard over the police scanner said that some hikers were ambushed by some wild animal. By the time I located the beast, the blood was already dried on its fur," Logan stated. The Hogs felt a level of sadness for the victims who had been killed by these animals, wishing that they could have been there to save them. Miles told the story of how he ended up killing the beast. Some of the Hogs were upset about missing out on the fight. Hayden brought up the fact that he hadn't yet finished that trap but was glad that it had helped.

"What are you doing setting up traps in the swamp anyway?" Eric asked.

Hayden said that he felt safer setting up traps around the area. He took the threat Logan warned them about seriously and felt the need to protect his friends. Hayden was hoping that protecting the land from coming threats would make them feel safer. It saved Miles's life, so they were happy that Hayden's hunting actions helped save the day.

Eric requested the horse be moved because they were just about to eat, and the smell was making him lose his appetite. Gard said that he'd remove the dead animal from the site. After Gard took off, the rest of the Hogs headed to the table for their meal as Logan walked to the cabin.

"Hey, grab a chair, Logan!" Juice yelled out to Logan. Logan turned and saw that the table was set for eight. Logan grew still because he was touched by this kind gesture. He couldn't remember the last time he was invited to dinner.

"Yeah, we made enough for everyone," Will added as he brought over the plate of meat and cooked veggies. Logan stepped up behind the table and placed his hand on the back of the chair. On the table were paper plates, plastic silverware, a salad bowl, a fruit bowl, and condiments.

"What do you want to drink, Logan?" asked Juice, who was grabbing soda pop cans from the cooler.

"I would love a soft drink. Doesn't matter which one," Logan said as he anxiously sat down in his chair.

Will told Logan that they were finishing off the burgers from lunch that day. He used the heat from the campfire to reheat them. At this time, Gard came to the table drying his freshly washed hands; he felt that he needed to due to carrying the dead horse.

"So, Logan, you said the other day that you once traveled with a group like us...Any wild and crazy stories?" Juice asked. The Hogs were trying to find a friendly way of getting information out of Logan. They didn't like the idea of straight up demanding answers from him. Logan took a long sip from his soda can before he replied and said that his time with a group like this was many, many years ago. Before he had the Loomation inside him.

Just that little sentence set the Hogs off in a wave of curiosity. The Hogs knew that Kate was born with her dry Loomation; and since she said that her grandfather, Logan, had an active Loomation, the Hogs figured that Cain was also born with his powers. But knowing that there was a time when Logan was once a nonpowered human made them think that he was patient zero in a way.

"You know, I don't recall much about those days...," Logan said as he put his eating on hold. "There was Derrick...Zach...Jake. Ha, most of the time none of us could stand him. Ha-ha." Logan then talked more slowly. "I know there were more...I can't believe that I can't remember their names right now." Signs of Logan's Alzheimer's were popping up for him again. To be fair, it had been decades since they'd died. The Hogs were distraught by this; the idea of not being able to remember the names of their friends someday came to them, and they hoped that would never happen.

"And of course, there was Parker. Him I'll never forget. He was the first one to walk with me...He became my best friend," Logan stated sadly. Miles was told by Logan in private that Logan was tricked into killing his best friend, so he was the only one at the table who knew the true sorrow Logan had for his friend Parker.

"It was my fault...I'm the reason they all died," Logan added. "I pointed out the falling meteor...and of course I was the first one dashing toward the crash site, not even waiting for the others to slip on their boots." Logan was now holding back the urge to cry. "I led the way down the tunnel in the side of the mountain, leading us to paradise...a beautiful lie that turned out to be." The Hogs hung on every word Logan said, feeling bad that their one simple question was bringing back such harsh and sad memories.

"I was the one who used the sword that lies within my cabin to slice off a piece of the diamond, unknowingly releasing a blast of Loomation that sunk its way inside all of us. I was the reason this monster wanted us on his hit list. If I would have just closed my eyes and gone to bed when they did, none of us would have spotted that cursed meteor that night," Logan thought, speaking out loud. After that, Logan suddenly stopped talking, took a few bites of his hamburger, and grabbed his drink. The Hogs were searching for what to say next.

"I'm sorry to hear about your friends, Logan," Juice said.

"You shouldn't blame yourself. You had no idea any of that would happen," Will added. All the Hogs were saying the same thing, that they were sorry and that Logan shouldn't blame himself. Logan said he was all right; he normally broke down several times a month thinking about his past. The one good thing about his Alzheimer's was that he sometimes forgot to blame himself.

Eric then got up from the table to retrieve something from the pop-up camper. He came out and showed off the cube to Logan. Eric asked if the cube looked familiar to him.

Logan took a long look at the cube and said, "This is the piece of the diamond I chopped off. It wasn't in the shape of a cube, but trust me, I would never forget this rock as long as I live."

"This cube was what gave us our Loomation powers," Eric stated.

"That's amazing. I guess whoever had possession of the diamond was able to use it to recreate the same shock wave that gave me and the other travelers our Loomation powers all those years ago," Logan theorized. The Hogs could feel the missing pieces coming together. They learned how Logan got his powers and where the cube finally came from.

"Where did the tunnel on the side of the mountain lead you?" Will asked, realizing that Logan never fully gave an answer about the location.

Logan simply said, "The Garden of Eden."

Once Logan revealed the location, the Hogs felt like everything now made sense. In the notebook containing the information of the fantasy creatures, it said that they grew wild once they were taken away from their *home*. The Hogs now knew that their home must have been the garden. The source of the Loomation came from the garden, and the cube was made from a piece taken out of the garden. They all felt that they were creatures of the garden, for the power that bloomed in the land was now inside them.

"And this monster coming to kill you...came from the garden too, didn't it?" Will asked, feeling like he knew the answer.

"Our way in was the monster's way out. And it is fully set on killing any human who carries the Loomation powers," Logan replied.

"Does this monster have a name?" asked Hayden.

"I don't think so...but it does have a title. The beast is the one and only...true devil."

This was a lot of information to take in for the Hogs. None of them had any doubts that this information wasn't true, and that fully startled them more than anything they had ever faced. The conversation stopped after that; the chewing was the only noise emitted at the table. After a while, Will brought up the creatures that were still out there. He said that they needed to find the remaining ones before they could kill any more souls. Logan said that he planned on searching the entire area until they were all found. The group all agreed that they would help Logan find the monsters.

After dinner was over, Logan went to bed, reminding the group that he wouldn't be here come sunrise. Things between the Hogs and Logan became much better after that dinner. The Hogs no longer feared him and were happy that he was staying on the land with them. Making an alliance with him would help them find the creatures and be fully ready for when the devil made his next appearance.

CHAPTER 31

Trouble on the Back Nine

Wednesday, June 16, 2010

Miles was firing off some of his defense spells onto a thick tree within the swamp. He was feeling exhausted because he had been rapidly driving his force with all his might. Miles fired off three more discharges in order to complete his dozen. After that, he took a much-needed break. Logan was happy to see that Miles had now passed to the next level of strength for his defense spells; the color of the visual appearance was now blue. Miles had come a long way, training many hours of the day. Each day would see great progress. The defense spell emitted a gassy light. It moved like a liquid being carried by a stream, and when it hit its target, the light splashed in a way of striking the target like a solid.

In Logan's book, it said that the attack came from the active Loomation inside the body. The power was held in the center of one's chest, shining in multiple colors, flickering like a flame. It was unable to be seen by anything humans created such as x-ray or thermal vision. When Miles called on the defense spell, a dash of his powers traveled through his body, releasing it out of his fingertips, in much the same way the sun released solar storms that ended up being the northern lights. Having the power come out of his fingers gave him the best accuracy, and the Loomation traveling through the body gave it that speed in order to travel its distance. Logan's farthest strikes had measured up to about fifty yards while Miles was achieving some twenty yards.

The drawback of having the attack come out of his fingers was that the strength of the attack got powered down as it traveled through the body. For example, if Miles released his attack from his chest, right at the source of the Loomation, the attack would be much more powerful and would be the size of his torso. But that attack would only travel a little farther than his arm could reach, not to mention the recoil of that blast would knock him back hard.

Miles was not only working on the defense spell, but had fully learned the healing spell and knew how to fully avoid using the death spell. The last thing to learn for the day was how to improve his teleporting ability. Miles told Logan about a time he grew very out of breath after teleporting while he and the rest of the Hogs were saving Kate. After Logan was informed of the full details of the rescue, he realized what had caused Miles's shortage of breath.

"Teleporting from point A to point B…then within a short amount of time…under a minute I'd say, teleporting from point B back to point A…would make you feel winded and out of breath," Logan explained. Miles had completed a few teleporting rides before then, but he just now realized that he never did a quick there-and-back situation before like that time at the chemical plant. Logan then warned Miles that if Miles would teleport a very short distance, like shorter than one hundred meters, he would suffer from whiplash.

Miles was upset to hear about this because he was hoping to use the power of teleportation while in combat. Logan informed Miles that he could overpower these side effects by a few ways but insisted that he use teleporting as a retreat only while in combat. For no matter how much he trained, teleporting still required hard concentration on the destination, meaning if he was in battle, he should keep concentrating on his defense spells and heal spells so that he wouldn't need to retreat. Miles asked what the ways of improving his teleporting powers were.

Logan said, "Well, I think you're ready to enter *the spiritual realm*."

"What is that?" Miles wondered, for this was not mentioned in the book.

"Let me ask you something. When you teleport, where do you think you go?" Logan asked.

"I go where I'm aiming to go, the picture of the area in my head," Miles replied in a confused tone.

"No, I mean…do you know where you are when you're between point A and point B?" Logan cryptically asked. Miles never thought about that before. Now that the thought was in his head, he couldn't believe he never thought of it. Logan gave Miles a coaching request. "I want you to teleport. It's how you enter the spiritual realm."

"Where do you want me to go?" asked Miles.

"You'll figure that out later," Logan responded.

"That's not how it works. I can only teleport by thinking of my destination," Miles replied.

"Normally yes, but this time I want you to do it without the destination in mind," Logan said. Miles then closed his eyes and tried to do what Logan asked him to do. Nothing was happening; Miles still couldn't wrap his mind around what Logan was asking him to do. "Okay…I want you to try something different," Logan said as a new idea sparked in his head. "I want you to teleport right where you're standing."

"What?" Miles asked, now thinking the old man was off his rocker.

"Trust me, just do it," Logan ordered. Miles once again closed his eyes and tried to do what Logan asked of him.

When Miles opened his eyes, he saw that he was still standing right where he was. He felt a chill run through his body, the normal feeling after he teleported. Miles's vision looked a little blurry, as if he was viewing the world through some smudged goggles. He also felt very light, as if he suddenly became weightless.

"Miles, I can't see you now, so it must have worked," Logan stated.

"What do you mean you can't see me? I'm right in front of you," Miles said. Miles heard an echo in his voice. Now that he thought about it, he heard an echo in Logan's voice as well. "Logan, can you hear me?" Miles said, raising his voice. Logan didn't respond, for he could not hear Miles. Miles started to panic as he thought he had died and become a ghost of some kind. Logan then entered the spiritual realm. Miles now saw Logan as clear as day once he entered the same realm as Miles, and there was no echo when the two talked to each other.

"So this is the spiritual realm?" asked Miles.

"Yes, this is where you go every time you teleport. Once you enter here, you travel at the speed of light, so you don't ever notice any of it," Logan explained.

"So no one can see or hear us while we're in here?" Miles asked.

"Precisely," Logan stated. Miles was amazed by this. He now found a new way to gain privacy. Logan went on telling Miles about the other features of the realm. He said that they could phase through solid objects. Logan said that the mind had all the power, and since the mind had been living in the physical realm its whole life, it would take a lot of thought processing to convince it that you could travel through physical objects. Logan did put a warning on that ability. Because once the mind knows it can slide through physical objects, Logan said that if you entered the spiritual realm in an attic, you'd end up in the basement fast without doing it on purpose. So Logan said that it would be best to let his mind keep thinking that he couldn't go through physical objects.

"How do we get out of here then?" wondered Miles. Logan said that all they needed to do was complete the teleporting spell they used to get there. Miles then focused on teleporting right where he was standing once again. When Miles reentered the physical realm of the universe, he felt the entire weight of his body quickly overwhelm him as if there was no muscle system to hold him up. Miles fell to the ground feeling completely sore all over; it was even a struggle to open his eyes.

Logan returned to the physical realm and helped Miles lift his head up and said, "I should have warned you that the transition on the way back is a rough one."

Miles was too sore to reply. Logan said that it was a good thing he was only in there for a short while, as the longer you stayed in, the longer the recovery time was. Logan assured Miles that he was completely fine, which was why a heal spell wouldn't do any good for him now. Logan said that he stayed a half day in the realm once, and he was then stuck in bed for two days after that transition. But this was another thing that could improve the more you did it. Logan could now stay for hours within the boundaries of the spiritual realm with no transition aftereffects. Logan did say that the better you handled that transition, the better at teleporting he'd become with no more feeling winded from quick back-and-forth rides.

Logan helped Miles return to the camper. When the rest of the Hogs saw Miles in need of help walking, they asked what happened. Logan said he was fine, just worked too hard. Bed rest was what he needed right now. This type of ailment just needed to be slept off. Logan said that he was off to bed himself because he had a place to be by morning. The Hogs still didn't know anything about the mysterious event Logan went to every morning, but they respected his privacy.

"We may have a lead on one of the creatures. We were going to check it out," Will said to Logan.

"Well, I'm pretty tired myself…How about I just give you guys the sword, and you go without me," Logan offered. The Hogs felt that they could handle the creature, and there was a big chance that this lead was nothing at all. They grabbed the sword and took off in Hayden's truck.

The sun went down after the Hogs left, and dark clouds filled the night sky. Hayden was driving his truck out on the country road bordering an affluent golf course. On the right side of the car, you could see the putting greens and tee boxes, while on the left side of the car you could see the expensive big houses. Hayden felt out of place being next to these nice upscale houses. Everyone was crammed in the vehicle. Eric, not enjoying being stuck in the middle of the back seat, asked why they couldn't have had Miles just teleport them to the location.

"Miles has been working on improving his defense spell nonstop, and he needs his rest," Gard replied, keeping his eyes out the window facing the golf course. The Hogs had been keeping track of the missing-people reports over the past weeks, while Logan had kept his ears to the police scanner. A few places had been searched out, but no wild murderous animals had been spotted. There were two missing people in this area, so the Hogs did some investigating. Will said he knew the town; he had once played golf there when he was on the golf team his first year of high school.

The Hogs had an idea that the creatures were on the look for pride land of some sort. Wanting to live in a place that made them feel like they were at home could have been on their minds. After looking into the golf course, they found that they needed more groundkeepers, for maintenance seemed to be needed more and more. This was evidence of active wildlife trespassing on the greens.

Hayden drove past the entrance of the course. When Gard pointed it out, Hayden informed him that this wasn't a swamp or abandoned building. He said that a highly exclusive golf course would have security cameras in its parking lot. Gard knew that, but he was very anxious for the mission, so he wasn't thinking about the security cameras at the time.

"So what are we going to do then?" wondered Juice.

"When we reach the edge of the course, I'll pull over, and we can get out," Hayden answered.

"Having the truck parked on the side of the road is just as suspicious as pulling into the parking lot in the middle of the night," Eric pointed out. Hayden told Timber to stay in the truck and continue to drive around the area to avoid a suspicious parked car.

Hayden reached the edge of the course on the side of the highway. The boys got out, while Timber moved to the driver's seat. Hayden had his trusty rifle, and Gard had the sword gripped in his hand. Will made sure the four walkie-talkies were all working and on the same channel.

"Here you go, Juice," Will said as he handed one of the devices over to Juice.

"You want me in the air?" Juice asked who was ready to receive orders. Will informed Juice that he and the others would head to the creek out toward the back nine, believing that the animals must be staying within that location in order to stay hidden. Will wanted Juice to have a bird's-eye view of the rest of the course just so they would have a complete check of the entire area. Juice grabbed the walkie-talkie and took off to the air. Will then handed Timber the second walkie-talkie; they would contact him when they were ready for pickup. After Juice and Timber took off, the rest of the Hogs marched their way to the woods.

The boys felt uneasy being out in the open. They had trespassed before, but that was just to pull harmless pranks on their fellow neighbors. This was a high-class property, so if they got caught, there would be no angry grown-up yelling from his porch. Instead, they would see police lights for sure. Having Juice in the air as a spotter did give them some sense of alertness, but at the same time, they were alarmed someone might see him up there. Once the road was out of sight, the men on the ground turned on their flashlights.

"We'll split up in order to cover more ground. Make sure you stay in shouting distance, though," Will stated when they reached the woods.

None of the Hogs entered the woods. They opted instead to simply walk along the fairway, shining their lights through the trees. As they walked alongside the trees, the fear of being caught by the police or night security went away. The fear of finding what they came for was what made them shake with nervous sweat that was starting to grow more visible. Some were hoping to find a creature, while others were hoping that this was just a dead end like the other searching grounds.

Eric hadn't realized that he wandered off too far from the rest of the group. He just kept directing his flashlight at the gaps between the trees. Then he heard something within the woods close by. Eric froze with fear when he heard this sound; it sounded like a menacing growl. Eric then moved his eyes to his right and now saw how far away he was from the rest of the group. Eric knew that he should wait until his friends were closer to him to shine his light on whatever made that growling sound. But Eric felt the hand holding the flashlight move toward the sound. His passion to discover the answer of what caused this hideous growl took over his logical thinking.

Once the light reached its destination, Eric saw an ugly green face with green eyes and yellow teeth. He let out a terrifying scream, for he had found the ogre. Eric read all about the ogre in Ray's notebook; it was seven feet high with a belly that stood out four feet in front of its body. The ogre could lift a ton and move at great speed for a short burst. Once the light shone onto the creature's face, it charged straight at Eric. Eric took off running for his life because he knew that if this thing got within arm's reach of him, it could snap his neck with one hand.

"Shoot it!" Eric yelled out to Hayden with all his might. "Shoot it now, Hayden!" he screamed while in a raging panic. Hayden felt that this was his time to shine. He positioned his feet and raised his gun and aimed it. Hayden had the ogre in his sight and fired the gun. He accomplished a direct hit right onto the monster's forehead. Hayden was thrilled at being able to make that shot, but his moment of great glory turned out to be pointless, for all his attack did was knock the ogre's head back slightly. It didn't even slow the creature down.

"Why doesn't the gun ever work?" Hayden shouted to the heavens. He had gone hunting for years and had missed so many targets within that time. But now that he was finally making his shots dead-on, nothing happened. This aggravated Hayden because he just wanted his gun to come in handy at least once.

Since Gard was holding the sword, he felt that it was his turn to make a move. Gard positioned himself right in Eric's line of sight. Gard saw Eric coming right at him with the ogre right behind him. Gard took a deep breath and charged right at the ogre. Eric saw Gard running at him with the sword in hand. He knew that he would have to leap out of the way right when he met up with Gard. The wait wasn't long; both Eric and Gard were running full speed at each other.

Eric dove out of the way when Gard reached him. Gard, on a dead sprint, swung the blade across the beast's very large belly. Gard ran all the way past the ogre, carrying the sword all the way through the animal. Gard didn't slice the ogre in half but did manage to do enough damage to make it trip over and die. Gard stopped running, as his whole left side was covered in blood from the beast.

"Did I kill it?" Gard shouted out, standing motionless with his eyes closed tight. Gard kept his eyes closed because some of the blood from the animal was splattered all over his face after his attack.

"Yeah, it's dead," Will stated, checking on the creature and kneeling in close to see if he was able to hear it breathing. When the others gathered around the animal, they saw something that made them want to vomit.

"Oh my...I think I'm going to be sick," Eric said when he shone his flashlight onto the dead animal. What Eric saw was truly unbearable to witness, for a dead human body was visible from the sliced-open belly of the creature. Will threw a punch onto the grass in frustration; another human had died due to these creatures. The Hogs held a moment of silence; they then contacted Timber and told him to bring the truck back to the course because they would be loading the ogre in the truck.

The Hogs removed the dead body from the ogre on the side of the road and called in an anonymous tip for the police. After that, they loaded the dead ogre in the back of the truck, covered it with the tarp, and drove off. As they made their way back to the swamp, the Hogs at first didn't say a word. Part of it was shock from the event they just experienced. Along with the ogre attack, they had to deal with another dead body. It had been a while since they had to face that kind of action.

"We made pretty good time out there," Gard stated, breaking the long silence. He was sitting in the back, facing the left side door because all the ogre's blood was mostly splattered on his left side. Juice and Eric were sitting in the back with him, and they both looked confused. "I mean, we got in and out really quickly," Gard added.

"Yeah, we're getting pretty good at this," Juice commented.

"I think it's time to discuss if we're going to help Logan fight the devil when the time comes," Gard nervously brought up. The Hogs had postponed this discussion since Logan had fully moved into the swamp. They felt that they had time to sleep on it and thought it would be best to focus on the escaped creatures first. But since it was now the middle of June, Gard believed that they should see where everyone stood.

The Hogs went over all that they knew. The devil always located Logan the last week of the month, so they still had two weeks. Logan had already said that if the Hogs didn't wish to fight with him, he would take on the devil himself. There was no way of convincing Logan to just continue his teleporting retreat move. The best-case scenario was that Logan managed to kill the devil all on his own. If Logan died in the fight, then it was a matter of time until the devil learned about all the other people who carried Loomation in them.

"The devil could never learn about us," Eric stated. "The devil never learned about Cain, Ray, or even Kate over the past decades."

"Yeah, but that was because the devil only had eyes on getting Logan. Once Logan dies, the devil's eyes will wander around. We would live our whole lives with the fear of being discovered," Juice replied. Will mentioned that the devil learned of Logan and his friends who entered the garden just two years after they got their powers.

"Yeah, and this may be our only time we would have a warning of his arrival," Hayden added.

"I don't want to go through life with the fear that at any moment I could be killed by something," Timber said with fear in his voice.

All this talk about the possibility of being killed off at any moment made Gard open up with a personal story to his friends. He told them that his uncle died from a heart disease. The disease ran in the family, and it was possible that Gard could have it. Gard's uncle died in the middle of mowing the lawn. There were no warning signs, just a total collapse, and then a loss of life. Gard rarely had the fear of that same fate happening to him; he tried to never let it hold him down.

Most of the Hogs never knew this and were kind of shocked that Gard never brought it up before. These guys had spent so many weekends together; they all thought they knew everything about each other. But Gard opening up the way he did was part of the whole camping trip. The weekends together were coming to an end once college started. The Hogs planned out this monthlong camping trip at the end of the previous summer. They figured if they spent that much time together, they would get sick of each other, and some college time apart would be for the best. The camping trip was the big way to get to fully know each other before they left.

The Hogs knew why Gard brought this up. He was pretty much saying the fear of some heart disease killing him one day would be nothing compared to the devil coming for them. The Hogs felt that if they didn't fight now, they would surely lose on the inevitable day the devil came for them. The vote in the car was unanimous. They were going to fight the devil with Logan. Some felt bad discussing this without Miles. But Gard had already told Miles about his uncle when Miles was sick. With the amount of time Miles had been training with Logan, it seemed clear that Miles was on board with fighting as well.

CHAPTER 32

Making Amends

Thursday, June 24, 2010

Most of the Hogs had gone to bed by this time, but a few members were sitting around the campfire after a long day of searching for the last creature. The final creature released from the prison that was still at large was the troll. According to Ray's notebook, the troll's hostile attitude was still just as dangerous as the other creatures. The animal could run fast, but it was also a great swimmer. With all the bodies of water out there, the beast could have swum a great distance and be miles away from the prison by now. Logan and Miles were taking Hog members out in different locations, forming search parties and hoping to spot it. After a long day of searching, the Hogs retreated back to the swamp for the rest of the night. Logan was on his way to his cabin, but before he reached the door, he remembered something he wanted to tell Hayden.

"Hey, Howie!" Logan shouted out toward the campfire. "No, I mean Harold?" Logan said, not remembering the name of the kid he wanted to talk to. Hayden stood up from his chair and told Logan that his name was Hayden, not Howie or Harold. Logan apologized. Hayden thought about it for a second and said it was fine. The boys were now used to Logan's forgetfulness regarding their names. They just figured it was his Alzheimer's. Hayden hustled over to the cabin to see what Logan wanted.

"Hayden, the other day you asked me if there was anything you could shoot the devil with that would cause some damage," Logan said. In the past hunts against these creatures of the garden, Hayden was outraged that his gun hadn't harmed the prey. Hayden felt that he knew that his gun wouldn't do any good against the devil when the time to fight arrived. But Hayden was taking his weapon into battle anyway as he would feel naked without it. "Well, I think I have something that can help you with your bullets," Logan said as he opened the cabin door and invited Hayden in.

Inside, Logan tried to strike a match to light the lantern. But Hayden already had his lighter lit to provide a fire source for the candle in the lantern. The lantern lit up the cabin very well. It was a small living quarters with only a small table and a comfy hammock. Logan pointed to the newspaper clipping that was hanging on the wall. The paper showed a clip of Logan and his fellow travelers who entered the garden all those years ago. Logan already told the kids that the cube that gave them their powers came from the diamond that was shown in that same photo. Logan then told Hayden that after Logan chopped the diamond off the main source, there were chips of diamond parts that sprinkled onto the ground. Logan said that he retrieved those chips, brought them to the swamp, and buried them under the cabin.

"Wait a minute. Is that why this section of the swamp is so rich and well groomed?" asked Hayden.

Logan said yes; the chips that he snatched from the chopped-off diamond were able to bless this land with the same power that kept the garden so perfect. Hayden said that he and the others thought it was a spell Logan cast onto the land or something.

Logan then told Hayden to slam his foot through the floorboards. Hayden complied, and since he's very strong, he did it with ease. Once Hayden removed his foot, he saw the dirt underneath and a red X painted on the ground. Logan knelt to the floor and reached his hands over the red X. He started to dig out the dirt until he found a wool bag. Logan left the bag in the hole and carefully opened it. In the bag were the mystical diamond chips.

Hayden cracked a smile when he saw the objects. The beauty of the pieces was spectacular, and the way they reflected off the light from the lantern gave them a shiny fiery glow. Hayden knew right away what he could do with these pieces. "If I could lace my bullets with these shrapnel pieces, maybe we could gain a new advantage hurting this monster," Hayden said with excitement.

Logan warned Hayden that once he started to remove the shrapnel from the ground, the swamp would reclaim more and more of the blessed land. Hayden didn't care about the campsite; he figured the group would sacrifice some space in order to increase their chances of defeating the devil. Hayden picked out all that he thought might be useful for his plan while discarding the ones too small to work with in the ground. When Hayden stepped out of the cabin, he saw that the swampland started to reclaim some of the soft, lush green grass out in the distances. It was quite an interesting thing to witness. After Hayden left the cabin, Logan went to bed, since he must wake up before the sun rose.

Friday, June 25, 2010

When Logan woke up, he did what he did every morning; he teleported to his old home. He returned to the Renshaw Mansion. The place was nothing but rubble and destruction, but Logan didn't pay any attention to any of that. He came here every morning for two things. One was viewing the sunrise that he and his wife spent countless mornings sitting on the porch watching over the driveway between the trees. The second reason he came here every morning was because he told his son that he could visit him there at this time. Logan was hoping his son would return to talk to him, and every morning he made sure he gave him that chance. Today was just another morning Logan spent watching the sunrise alone.

When the Hogs woke up, they all noticed that their campsite was now smaller. The shiny, gentle green grass that once stretched out at least an acre over the swampland seemed to be cut down more than half its size. The Hogs were baffled by this discovery. Then they spotted Hayden sitting in the bed of his truck cleaning his gun. They asked Hayden if he knew what happened to the land, and Hayden explained to them about the diamond shrapnel that was buried under the ground. Hayden said that he left enough of the pieces in the ground that the pond, campsite, and pop-up camper remained within the borders of the blessed ground. That and there weren't enough pieces to fashion a third bullet.

Hayden then showed off the two bullets he spent all night crafting. He was able to weld the chipped chunks of diamond shrapnel to fully cover only two of his gun's bullets. Hayden also welded the remaining pieces into the tip of his hunting knight and within the blade's teeth. Hayden said that since these diamond particles came from the garden, there was a high possibility that they would hurt or even kill the devil.

"Two...you were only able to make two bullets?" Timber said, unimpressed.

"Last I checked, we were only getting attacked by one devil!" Hayden replied.

"What if you miss?" shouted Timber.

"I'm not going to miss!" yelled Hayden.

"You literally have room for one error," Gard cautiously stated.

"Well, it's a good thing I'll have two attempts then. Not to mention my knife," Hayden said. The doubtful questions continued to arise. Hayden believed the reason was due to the campsite being smaller. He said that he thought the plan was to have a long life, not a long lawn. Hayden said he finally had a bullet that could hurt something they were hunting, while the other Hogs would rather have had the ammo remain underground.

"Guys, this is a huge bonus for us!" Will called out. He could tell the Hogs were just nervous as the day of facing the great evil was coming. The search for the troll had kept their minds off it, but now that Hayden had built new weapons for the big fight, it just reminded everyone that they were almost out of time. "We've been practicing maneuvers for getting our opponent into a kill strike for days now. Now that Hayden has these new weapons, we don't have to rely on the sword alone," Will added. The Hogs knew Will was right; this should have put their troubled minds at ease, not make them worry more.

"I think they're cool," Juice mentioned.

"Thank you, Juice," Hayden said.

The rest of the Hogs all agreed with Will. They now felt a little better at having another way of causing some heavy damage to the devil. Miles pointed out that the cube was made from the same diamond and proposed the idea of using that for more bullets. The Hogs had a long discussion about that idea. One of the pros for the cube was that when it released, its shock wave drove a blast of energy inside whoever got hit by it. The Hogs said that a charge up like that may come in handy for a possible round 2 with the devil if they didn't get him in a kill strike right away. The cube would be taken with them whenever they left the swamp from now on, as it was now considered to be a vital part of their arsenal.

That afternoon, Cain walked right up to Ray's old hideout, the Saltwater Chemicals plant. When he reached the front entry, he delivered a heavy knock on the glass door. Cain then heard the security camera adjust to view him. When Cain looked up at the camera, he removed a white flag from his jacket pocket and waved it in front of the camera. There seemed to be no response, so Cain then raised the object in his right hand up at the camera. This object was a six-pack of beer, which Cain waved with a friendly smile. A moment passed, and Cain heard a buzzing from the front door. Cain, in turn, pulled the door open and walked in and made it up to Ray's office. Inside, Ray was just sitting at his desk.

"Is the beer for me?" Ray asked when Cain walked into the room.

"Half of it is," Cain replied as he sat down and peeled off two cans from the plastic holder.

"The white flag was a nice touch also," Ray said as he reached out for Cain's peace offering.

"Yeah, I thought you'd like it," Cain said as he popped open his can.

"You know, it's weird, us sitting down like we're friends again. Last I checked, we were enemies," Ray stated as he opened his can.

"What unites two enemies?" Cain asked Ray in a charming way.

"A common threat," Ray said as he leaned in, setting up a tapping of the cans. Cain complied with the tapping of the cans, for that was the right answer. The two took a long sip. "So you believe your father's warning then? That some great evil is coming to kill all Loomation carriers?" Ray asked.

"I do," Cain replied.

"And how's that make you feel?" wondered Ray.

"I'm going to sum it up by calling it…a *complicated* feeling," Cain uttered before taking another large sip of his beer. "I had so much hate for the man leaving my mother and I that I felt that there wouldn't be any solid reason that would overturn my feelings of hatred."

"Then you found out him leaving you was the only way to keep you safe," Ray added as he sipped his beer. "The guy could have written a letter or something," Ray then added.

"Well, I thought that too. But when I talked to him that night, I could tell that he didn't want to leave me. At that moment, all those loving stories of him that my mother told me all made sense. I'm betting it was killing him every day to not reach out to Mother and I." Cain tipped the can back for another sip, but the can was already empty after just a few sips. Cain removed another can from the holder and popped it open.

"Have you talked to him since that night?" wondered Ray. Cain just simply shook his head no, as he was taking his first drink from his second can. "How do you think I feel about all this? I spent so much time of my life thinking that your father was the one responsible for killing my father, and ever since I thought that, I tried to take my revenge out on you," Ray said as he finished off his first beer. Cain handed over Ray's second can.

"My father confessed that he was the one who killed your father," Cain mentioned.

"Yeah, but he admitted that he was tricked into it by the great evil," Ray said before he took a sip of his second can. "This makes sense, for my father spoke very highly of Logan in his journals. It never made sense to me that Logan would kill his only friend."

"Trying to kill your only friend is kind of the theme in this room," Cain said. This statement gave the two an awkward moment of silence.

"I'm sorry for all I've done to you, Cain," Ray said. "I'm sure I made life terrible for you ever since our friendship fell apart."

"Ray, you attacked the Havocs and me a few times a year when we were fighting. But trust me, I received way more attacks from tons of other thugs than you during that time. To be fair, you were the only one who I truly feared. But I could have ended it at any time. I had the numbers to defeat you, but I always requested to only play defense."

"Why did you do that?" asked Ray.

"I guess I found this war to be a little fun. It wasn't until after Kate was born that I was ready to end the feud once and for all," Cain answered.

"And here I was thinking that you just liked me," Ray said as he took another swig of his beer and smiled.

"I could say the same thing. When you put me in that coma, I was a sitting duck for years, but you chose to let me be," Cain replied.

"You know your daughter said the same thing to me. Smart kid that girl of yours. I'm still waiting for your payback for me kidnapping her," Ray said.

"I told you back at the prison that I surrendered. You were the one who didn't kill me when you had the chance," Cain said as he finished off his second beer.

"Your dad came in and stopped me," Ray uttered as he finished off his second beer.

"Oh no, don't blame him for your hesitation," Cain said as he shoved the last two beers still in the plastic holder over to Ray. Ray grabbed the remaining beers, and they both pulled back on their cans together in order to remove them from the holder. "You had plenty of time to pull that trigger before my father made his presence known."

"I guess the satisfaction of fully defeating you and hearing you verbally surrender was all I needed," Ray said as he opened his last can. Cain opened his can, and the two took a long sip.

"I came here a few days ago, but you weren't here," Cain stated after finishing his sip.

"I just got back to the States last night," Ray replied after his sip.

"This is kind of a weird time for you to take a vacation, isn't it?" Cain said.

"Well, your father said that the beast would come to kill us all at the end of the month. And you know how much I've always wanted to see the Greek temples."

"I figured that you would be preparing for when the monster comes," Cain said.

"I've always been the one to walk away from the casino when I'm ahead. I've started a very successful chemical business, always graduated top in all my classes, walked in the great Garden of Eden, and helped craft the most fascinating one-of-a-kind collection of creatures ever. When your father informed us about the coming threat, I saw the warning as a chance for me to get my affairs in order," Ray bragged.

"You never back off from a challenge, Ray! You love finding ways to overpower the overbearing threats!" Cain shouted.

"See, that's what I like about you, Cain, you know me all too well," Ray said with a grin.

"That's part of the reason why I'm here. I know you have a better plan than my father's plan," Cain replied.

"What, you don't think the Hogs can defeat the beast?" Ray asked, laughing. The two men thought it was ridiculous that Logan was putting his bet on those boys being able to kill the monster. Ray then explained that he had been traveling to places but not for vacation purposes. Ray had been exploring the world, searching out the world's deadliest objects. Ray found the most poisonous plants, reptiles, and insects and gathered up their venom for a master chemical of death.

Ray walked over to the in-wall safe, used his thumbprint to open the door, and removed the large jar that contained this chemical. Ray said that he added a lot of his own poison chemicals to the item as well. "And the grandest feature in this cocktail came from the west coast," Ray spoke very proudly. "In the west coast of Mexico, there is this dark-purple-stained rock by the cliffs hanging over the sea. The rock has been listed in a few strangest discovery title books over the years. Anyone who has touched this rock has died within seconds due to the unknown poison that has stained the stone. People have had to wait until the tide carried the dead bodies away before they could retrieve the corpses. Birds who have landed on it, sea creatures, and bugs who walked on it have all died. The townspeople call it the rock of death."

"What do you think it is?" asked Cain.

"According to myth and legend, the stain on the rock is the venomous blood of the Leviathans," Ray explained. "Now you and I both know all about mythic creatures," Ray said with a nod. "In the early 1800s, there had been reports of weird, unidentified sea skeletons washing up on the shore of that same coast. So I was convinced that the stain on that rock is indeed Leviathan venom."

Ray placed the jar onto the table. Ray said that he was able to take a huge sample of that stain by carving it out of the rock. Once the rock touched some of Ray's chemicals, the rock disintegrated, leaving only the Leviathan venom. Cain put his ear close to the jar, for he thought he heard the liquid swarming around within the jar.

"It sounds like—"

Before Cain could say any more, Ray spoke up. "Like it's bubbling?" Ray admitted that his invention scared him very much. He claimed that one drop of this would kill a fully grown whale before it could catch its next breath. Ray felt the need to constantly change the triple-thick bulletproof glass jar every eight hours so that the chemical didn't deteriorate the glass and start to leak. After hearing that part, Cain suddenly moved away from the jar.

"You think this will kill the monster?" Cain fearfully asked. He didn't want to meet a creature that could survive this poison.

"If this monster is as powerful as your father fears, then I honestly don't know," Ray said as he took the finishing gulp of his last beer. "All I know is that I'm not going to run from this monster. If it kills me, then I'm going down swinging, and this invention is my baseball bat!"

Cain said that he wished to help Ray out in any way he could. Cain also didn't wish to spend his life running in fear; he too would take a stand and fight. Ray said it would be a big help if he could learn more about the monster. He was hoping Cain could find out more information from his father. Cain told Ray that he knew where to find his father, as he'd known all month. Bringing up the idea of meeting Cain's father made Cain uneasy. Ray could tell that Cain wasn't ready to confront his father just quite yet.

"In the mood of us being *friends* again…I'm going to give you some friendly advice," Ray stated. "I would trade anything just for one day to get to know my father better. If I had the chance to go see him, I would go…But I will never have that option. There's still time for you, Cain."

The two men seemed to have buried the hatchet with a couple of beers. Things weren't perfect, mostly on Cain's side. Ray did apologize, but that didn't bring back the twenty-plus years that Cain lost while he was in a coma. Nor did it make Cain forgive Ray for trying to kill his daughter. But Cain was able to set that aside to help Ray kill this beast. They both agreed if they both survived this attack, they would forever part ways and let bygones be bygones. Cain stayed at the plant that night and even got to borrow one of Ray's cars before sunrise.

Saturday, June 26, 2010

Logan returned to the burned-down remains of the Renshaw Mansion to watch the morning sunrise. Today, he was at last joined by his long-lost son, Cain. Cain came in Ray's borrowed car, and he carried flowers with him. The flowers were for his mother's gravestone. Logan's face beamed in delight at the sight of his son. He was starting to lose hope that his son would ever come see him. There wasn't much talk when they first saw each other; they just walked up to the gravestone together. Cain placed the flowers down and just stared down at the grave.

"I miss her too," Logan stated. Cain didn't reply; he just kept looking down. Logan went on to say that he met her in these woods. Cain had heard this story countless times from his mother. "Son, I can't begin to express how sorry I am for leaving you. Just know the day you came into my life was the best day of my life."

Cain fully understood why his father left him, and there was a part of him that wanted to show his appreciation at the sacrifice he made. But as Cain looked at his mother's grave, his hatred for his father's absence was the only emotion on Cain's surface. Cain's mother never knew why her husband left her, and that was why Cain's rage was still coming to the surface. Cain remembered all the nights she stayed up on that porch waiting for his return. The woman died of a broken heart. So a way for Cain to hurt his father was by telling him everything.

He told Logan about the heartbreak both he and his mother dealt with. Cain told him about his criminal life, the bad things he'd done for money or for some sick thrill. Cain knew that none of this was what his father wanted to hear, but Cain felt the need to lay it all out because Logan's disapproval was the only way Cain was able to hurt his father. Cain had literally swallowed decades of rants for his father that he now finally got to release. After all was said, the hate dimmed, and Cain felt free in a way. Cain then gave his father a fully honest thank you. Cain then told his father about Kate. He only related that topic with warmhearted stories. A daughter who would have never been born if it wasn't for Logan's sacrifice.

The story of Kate did make Logan happy. Logan's memory of talking to her at the airport felt more heart lifting now that he knew more about her. Logan said that since she had the power of a dry Loomation inside her, she was in just as much danger as the rest. Cain informed Logan that she was still out of the country. Cain even called her last night to tell her everything. He told her about the return of his father and how he and Ray had officially ended their feud.

"Did you tell her about the monster?" Logan asked.

"If I did, she would have begged me to cross the seas to be with her, or worse, she would have wanted to come back to help fight it," Logan replied.

"She deserves to know. I can't protect her anymore," Logan stated. Logan then explained his reason for no longer running away from the devil. When the devil found Logan again, they would fight to the death.

"Why do you have such faith in the kids?" Cain asked about the Hogs. "And why do you believe they are the key to the monster's defeat?"

"I thought it was obvious…" Logan was keeping this reason close to the chest, not even telling the Hogs themselves. But Logan was able to indulge Cain with a few facts. "I have been praying for a hero to come and deliver me from this torture. I always felt that this was my curse for stealing from the garden or something. I figured with my luck I would find my hero right when was ready to call it quits. Then I found the one they call Juice. He and all his friends have the power of Loomation. One of them has an active Loomation, one is fireproof, and Juice can even fly. I once found a prophecy saying that the great ones fly!" Logan stated hopefully.

Cain didn't buy any of it; to him they were just a bunch of kids who were on a lucky streak. But Logan denied that, as Cain chose the Hogs to save Kate and was impressed by the rescue. Further, Cain knew they could handle the rescue because they beat the Sasquatch. Cain again just summed that up to them just being lucky. Cain then pulled out a small device from his jacket pocket and handed it to Logan. The device seemed to be a hi-tech garage door opener.

"When you want to trade luck for skill and intelligence, give that button on a push!" Cain said.

"Son, I didn't spend your whole life running from this monster just to have you get caught in the cross fire!" Logan replied.

"Oh, but you'll happily deliver those kids to the beast yourself!" Cain yelled.

"I believe in them," Logan said.

"BELIEVE IN ME!" Cain shouted. "I'm your own flesh and blood!" Cain kicked up some dirt in frustration. "What's the real reason why you don't want me fighting this thing? You say you don't want me in the cross fire to keep me safe, but when you explain why you want the Hogs to fight with you, it's because you *believe* in them. This makes it sound like you don't believe in me!" Cain shouted as he waved his fist. "I've won so many battles while being hugely outnumbered and outgunned. I was the most feared mercenary in human history!"

"All the fuel for that success came from your hatred towards me!" When Logan said that, Cain gave a mighty eye roll, finding it ridiculous that the absent father tried to take credit for his son's successes. "Then you indulged in a war with your only friend because you found some sick entertainment out of it. And when you finally had the moral, loving reason to fight in order to save someone you love, you passed the job off to someone else!" Logan explained with a heavy heart. "If you go up against the devil with that, you will lose. I've only seen one person lay a strong punch on the devil, and he was a better man than you or I will ever be!"

The family reunion now felt over. Cain was tired of hearing his father's voice. There was an awkward moment of silence after Logan finished his speech. Cain's attitude was now one of all business. One of the reasons Cain came to see his father was to learn all he could about the monster. Cain instructed his father to tell him everything he knew about the devil and everything the Hogs were planning for their attack. Logan complied with his son's request. Logan, to the best of his knowledge, told how strong the devil was, and all he had seen him do. Logan then told Cain all about the Hogs' weapons, along with their fighting strategies.

After that was completed, Cain left without even a goodbye. And Logan couldn't blame him; this long-awaited meeting with his son was one he wished had gone better.

That afternoon, Logan retuned to the swamp to talk to the Hogs. He said that now that they were within the final five days of the month, they best get moving to a new location. The Hogs didn't understand what location Logan was talking about. Plus, they thought they were going to stay and fight the devil; moving now felt like retreating in a way. Logan explained that it would take the devil four weeks to find him; it didn't matter if he spent three weeks in one location and the final days of the month in another. Logan wouldn't gain another four weeks until after the devil found him. Logan said the only time the devil found him earlier than four weeks was when he returned to a place he was already once found. Since the devil still hadn't found him, he was still under his four-week countdown.

"So when is he coming?" asked Juice.

"It's always been slightly random. All I know is that it takes a month, and he always shows up somewhere within the last four days of the month," Logan answered.

"The last four days start tomorrow," Eric pointed out.

"When we reach that period, he could literally show up at any time," Logan added. This made the Hogs very nervous; they couldn't believe how fast this month went by. They thought they had more time, and they felt that they hadn't prepared enough.

"Where is this place you want us to go?" Gard asked Logan.

Logan elaborated on how the devil took on his opponents and said the monster liked to give the impression of letting his victims have a fighting chance. So the devil would take a few hits. He did this so he could give the illusion of hope. The devil loved taking away hope from people when they needed it the most. Logan heard this from the monster himself, so he knew that this was true.

"The plan to kill the devil requires three things," Logan said to the Hogs. "First, I need all of you to fight at my side. Second, I need the sword as it may be the only thing that can kill him. And the third thing is the battleground." The Hogs all looked at one another, for none of them heard Logan mention the battleground as part of the plan before. Logan read the quizzical look on the boys' faces and then realized that his poor memory had failed him once again. "I know a place we can go where we can take an infinite number of punches from this beast and still be able to fight at full strength."

"The garden?" Will assumed. This made sense because the land gave a nonstop heal spell to all humans who were in the light of the land. Logan said that he could take them all to the garden now.

"We still have the troll out there to find," Hayden stated.

"We can find it after the battle with the devil," Eric replied.

"What if we die in this fight? Who will take care of the troll problem then?" Will mentioned.

"We just found a few possible locations where the troll could be. Give us two days to search out the places. If we find it, we'll take it out. If not, then we head to the garden," Gard offered. Logan re-explained that the devil would show up at a completely random time within the final four days. He may show up right away or on the final day, so it was possible to spare a few days in order to find the troll. As much as the Hogs would have loved to be safe and sound within the confines of the garden, they knew that the troll was a killing machine and must be put down. So they said if they didn't find it by Monday morning, they would head to the garden.

CHAPTER 33

The Final Monster

Sunday, June 27, 2010

The Hogs spent all Saturday checking their possible troll hiding locations. They did a thorough check, and all results came up negative. The Hogs were now checking the last location on their search list. The place was a long tourist attraction boardwalk by the lake. On the side of the boardwalk was a carnival-type atmosphere. The whole place was closed due to the high number of missing people who had mysteriously disappeared from the area. Operators of the rides and game booths had either gone missing or were interviewed about missing people. The Hogs saw these reports and believed that this was, indeed, the place to find the troll.

When the Hogs teleported to the city, they saw that it was a very foggy day as the mist from the lake gave off a soggy heavy feeling. The Hogs split out in groups; Will and Juice were going to check the closed-off section where all the carnival rides and booths were. Will took a quick look around to check for any security. Once he saw that the coast was clear, he hopped up onto the fence to climb over it. Juice just flew over the fence in a hurry.

"Juice, you just can't be flying in public in broad daylight like that!" Will whispered harshly as he swung his leg over to the other side of the chain-link fence.

"Fine, next time I'll just jump over it," Juiced replied.

"That's not what I meant," Will said as he jumped off the fence and landed on the other side. "We're not in the swamp right now, so we can't just be using our powers like they're normal."

"Yeah, I get that, but you said the coast was clear," Juice muttered. Will and Juice walked through the park. It felt creepy. The empty game booths and shut-down rides made the place look very eerie. Seeing the empty large Ferris wheel made the whole place feel like a ghost town.

Hayden, Timber, and Miles were walking down the beach toward the boardwalk, while Eric, Gard, and Logan were on the other side of the beach heading toward the same place as they planned on everyone meeting under the boardwalk. Hayden carried his gun in his large duffel bag. Will carried the sword inside the carnival location, also secured in a bag.

"We better find that troll," Timber stated.

"Logan won't let us search for it anywhere else if we don't find it here," Miles added.

"I just want to get to the garden," Timber said. The Hogs were on edge now that the inevitable attack from the devil could literally happen at any second. They just wanted to get this place searched and then be on their way. If they found the troll, that would be a plus. A call on Hayden's walkie-talkie alerted him. It was Gard on the other side of the beach asking if they had spotted any movement in the water yet. Hayden reported a big negatory; he also said that there was no sign of the troll on the beach either.

Gard then asked Juice if he or Will had spotted anything inside the carnival. Juice was about to say no, but he saw one of the tent booths shake. Juice, holding the walkie-talkie, told the group to stand by as he may have found something. Juice pulled the walkie-talkie away from his face and clipped it back to his pocket.

Before Juice investigated the tent, he got Will's attention by snapping his fingers. Juice didn't say anything. He used the hand signals the Hogs had been practicing over the past weeks. Once Will got the information that Juice believed the creature might be in that tent, Will removed the sword from his backpack and placed himself in an on-guard position. The plan was that Juice would flush out the animal while Will came in from behind for the stab.

Once Juice saw his buddy ready to make his move, he slowly walked into the tent. The tent was a game tent. Judging from the barrels and baseballs strewn on the floor, it looked like the simple balls in a barrel toss. There was a pile of stuffed animal prizes on the ground at the back of the tent. Juice found the stuffed animals to be kind of disturbing. With the gray skies and misty drafts, the colorful, smiling stuffed animals seemed lifeless and cold. Juice picked up one of the animals faster than he should have. He figured since he didn't see a giant troll in the tent by now, it was safe to put his guard down.

But Juice was wrong, for when he moved the stuffed animal, he saw the troll's face hiding under it. The whole animal was buried under the stuffed animals, and now that it saw Juice, it shook them off his body and got to his feet. Juice turned and ran out of the tent, yelling at Will that he had found it. The troll ran with great speed out of the tent, chasing right after Juice.

Juice still had one of the stuffed animals in his hand, so he chucked it at the troll in a last-ditch effort to defend himself. When Juice looked back in order to chuck the toy, he saw that the attack did absolutely nothing and that Will was having trouble catching up with the troll. Juice yelled out, "Screw this!" He wasn't going to let himself be chased by a big ugly creature. Juice then flew straight up, ignoring Will's request to not be out flying about in the public. He figured that the giant troll would more noticeable than his flying off the ground. Juice flew just out of the creature's mighty reach. Out on the beach, both search groups spotted the troll jumping up and down over and over trying to catch Juice who was easily avoiding the troll's desperate attempts to bring him down.

The creature was so determined to grab Juice that it never saw Will make his kill strike. Will came in fast, thrust the sword in a mighty swing, and killed the unsuspecting troll. Once the beast was killed, Juice softly landed next to Will to give him a pat on the back and say good job. Will told Juice good job too. The rest of the Hogs and Logan met up at the creature's body. The Hogs were impressed at how well they were able to handle the situation. When they first were attacked by one of these creatures, they panicked and got hurt a lot. Now that they were easily able to overcome these attacks, it turned into a good confidence booster, and they were ready to take on the devil. They didn't even feel like they needed the safety of fighting in the garden.

This was why they begged Logan for one more supply run. Since the last creature was taken care of, Logan wanted to head to the garden now. But the Hogs said that there was a small grocery store nearby; they could go get their stuff and be back in fifteen minutes. Logan agreed, saying he could get the troll back to the swamp and underground within that time. Logan gave them only fifteen minutes, and they would all get right back here to go straight to the garden. The Hogs agreed and took off to the store. They were excited about going to the garden even though they would never be able to tell anyone about it.

As they crossed the street heading to the store, Will spotted a church a little way down the road. Will called out to his friends that he'd meet up with them later because he was going to check out the church first. Since Will was already on his way over to the church, Gard had to yell out to him to be sure he got back to the carnival within the designated fifteen minutes; otherwise, Logan would get upset. Will marched up to the church feeling a little odd carrying a weapon in his backpack, but that didn't stop him from walking in.

Neither Will nor the other Hogs knew this, but they were being watched by two guys in a parked car on the street. The two men were Cain and Ray. Ray watched Will enter the church while Cain watched the rest of the group enter the store. Cain pointed out that Logan wasn't with them. Ray had a laptop on his lap and was able to track Logan's whereabouts. "He just went back to the swamp," Ray informed his friend. When Cain gave Logan that device yesterday, Logan had been carrying it with him everywhere he went. Ray had planted a high-power tracking device inside it. That was how the two knew where the Hogs were right then and there. They wanted to keep a close watch on Logan because they knew the devil would come to him first.

Will saw that the church was small, but it had its charm. The stained-glass windows showed the remaining sunlight fading away. Will wanted to take a knee to say a prayer, but before he could sit down, he heard someone from the confession box. The voice was the priest, asking Will if he was there for confession hours. Will didn't plan for that, but he had time to kill and felt like he should have a clean slate before he fought the devil. Will went into the confession box.

At the store, the Hogs were loading up the cart with all their favorite junk food. "Do you think campfires are allowed inside the Garden of Eden?" Hayden asked.

"Yeah, would the firewood from that place ever burn into ash or just keep going forever?" wondered Juice.

"You're planning on chopping down trees in this peaceful land?" asked Gard. At this moment, Gard spotted Juice putting bananas into the shopping cart. "I'm not wasting money on fruit. This is a junk-food-only cart!"

"I'm not going to eat the fruit there. You know what happened to the last people who ate fruit there? They died!" Juice replied.

"They were banished, Juice," Eric corrected.

"Well, eventually they died," Juice stated.

"You don't say," Hayden uttered.

"We could die. I mean, let's not forget why we're going there," Miles said.

"Yeah, knowing that makes this feel like we're picking out our last meal," Eric replied.

"We can handle the devil. You see how easily we took out that troll. Not to mention the ogre last week." Gard spoke with pride because he didn't want to let the idea of losing this fight be in anyone's head.

"Yeah, but they were all wild animals. We're going to be dealing with something else, something way more powerful," Eric stated.

"There's eight of us and one of him, and besides, we have the almighty powerful sword on our side," Gard said. Hayden then mentioned his two special bullets along with his knife that had the fused diamond chips on the blade. The Hogs felt so much confidence in their preparation and training that they had no doubt they would win this fight.

Back at the church, Will was giving his confession. He confessed how easily he and his friends had been breaking the laws lately. Will said that something had happened to him and his friends, and now they were different. He said that ever since they became different, they had been acting like they could do whatever they wanted. He further stated they had trespassed to a point that it didn't bother them anymore and had convinced themselves that the ends always justified the means. Will further mentioned that he and his friends had turned in stolen bank money without giving away the person who stole it. Will said that he believed two people were dead because of him and his friends. The Hogs may not have killed the two men, but they were the reason they had Bigfoot in the first place, and the Hogs had covered up their deaths.

The priest told Will that it sounded like he had been hanging out with a bad crowd. Will had to keep secret many of the details from the priest, so many of the positive outcomes from those good deeds were not mentioned. So much fighting, lying, and trespassing over the last fifty-eight days piled up all at once; and it all went by so fast. The priest asked how Will felt about all this. Will said that all his actions were to help his friends. He wanted them to be safe and out of trouble.

"So you look out for your friends then," the priest stated, trying to make sense out of all this.

"Yeah, and it's not just me. We all look out for each other. I know I felt like I just listed out all of our flaws, but we've done some great things over the past weeks as well." Will mentioned the fact that they rescued a girl and brought her back safely to her father. He brought up all the people who were now out of harm's way because they took care of that *pest* problem. Will said he guessed they were acting with good intentions, and that was why they got carried away by some of the illegal activities.

Getting this all off his chest, Will felt a sense of relief he had not experienced in a long time. He had always tried to keep the group on the right path. If they didn't have someone being their moral compass, who knew how the group could have turned out.

"There is a balance of good and evil out there," said the priest. "Some of the best intentions come complete with some shades of evil attached to it. Sometimes you just must look the devil in the face and say, 'I will not let you win.' His temptation into evil is only that. You can always find the light in yourself if you know you've found the right reason to act, and protecting your friends is all the strength you need."

Will felt the full impact of knowing the dark art of protecting others in life-threatening situations. Sometimes the one carrying the sword gets the deepest scars. Not everyone can live with these scars. And that's why it was important to keep your friends safe. You protect them, they protect you. Will's new enlightenment was a perfect lesson to receive before his big upcoming battle.

Back at the abandoned carnival, Logan returned to a now-night sky. Logan checked his watch and saw that there were about five minutes left before the boys were scheduled to return, so he patiently waited in silence. Over by the street parking area, Ray mentioned to Cain that Logan had returned to the town. Ray said that he was close, standing somewhere within the carnival location. Cain said that they should go scope the place out on foot. Cain hated waiting inside the car, and if something was going to happen, he would rather be there than have to run to it from the car. Ray agreed, and the two exited the vehicle and headed to the chain fences.

Not too long after that, the Hogs were making their way back to the meetup place. They had a few grocery bags in hand as they hopped over the fence. They were a little early, but if Logan wasn't back yet, they would wait. They had to wait for Will to return, so they were going to be waiting anyway.

Then Logan felt an all-too-familiar feeling as his stomach began to turn. First it was the air, for the misty cool wind was now replaced with a nauseous dry heat. The stench of brimstone started to permeate his surroundings. Logan knew that these were the calling cards of the devil. *No, not now!* Logan thought to himself in terror. Logan's first instinct was to run, teleport away; it had been his natural response for decades. He had to fight off this instinctual feeling. He had to remind himself to not disappear. Logan then turned his head and saw the Hogs walking toward him. Logan started running at them, yelling, "He's here!"

Juice, Hayden, Timber, Eric, Gard, and Miles saw Logan running toward them; and they heard his fearful warning. The Hogs knew that the devil was in the area as they too could feel something very ominous. The Hogs were never caught more off guard in their lives. They were hoping for another day before the devil's arrival so much that they even expected it. The Hogs felt that their plan was suddenly foiled as they were not at the garden, nor did they have the sword with them. Will had the sword back at the church, and he wasn't carrying a walkie-talkie.

"What do we do?" Juice asked in fear, as this was plainly not a drill.

"We get to Logan, and we all teleport over to the church to regroup with Will and the sword," Eric hastily instructed.

The Hogs all started to run to Logan to meet him in the middle, but as they grew close to each other, the devil appeared right in the middle of them. The devil delivered a fiery blast attack in the form of a circular wave, striking everyone in its path. Logan was blasted back away from the devil, while the Hogs were kind of scattered by the attack. Some landed in the empty tents and others between the tents. Each Hog present got a look at the beast. He was tall with dark-red charcoal skin, dark-yellow eyes, and two black horns on his head. He wore raggedy torn-up clothes that were the color of smoky gray on his body. His body and clothes resembled a torch blowing smoke. His hands had dark claws, as did his feet. And he still spoke in Parker's voice.

"I have to say, Logan, I'm very impressed!" The devil spoke very loudly. The voice of the devil sounded as if he was talking through an echoing speaker. The tone of his voice was ear piercing to everyone hearing him speak. "Here I thought you were the only one left, but you've been hiding a whole group of them!" Logan was on his back, looking up at the devil with an angry look. The devil then used the fire he was able to make from his hands to emblazon a symbol into the ground. "There is no way I'm leaving here without killing at least one of you!" the devil added while he burned out the symbol.

Logan noticed that the devil didn't seem to have his strong, silent attitude at this moment. Before, the beast seemed to only speak when needed. This new attitude made Logan even more nervous because now the devil seemed excited in a way.

"I'm the only one here you care about," Logan stated.

"Don't lie to me, Logan. I can feel the Loomation radiating off several humans here right now."

Over behind one of the tents, Eric crawled over to Miles. Too afraid to get to his feet, he felt safer staying low. All the Hogs were, at this moment, hiding from the devil within the maze formed by the sprawling carnival tents. It was amazing that a single sight of the devil and the sound of the monster's voice made them lose all the confidence they just had a moment ago.

"Miles, teleport us to Will so we can retrieve the sword," Eric said to his friend.

"I can't, Eric. I've been trying to, but something is keeping me from teleporting. I think it's that symbol the devil burned into the ground. It must be a roadblock from the spiritual realm or something," Miles explained.

"So we're stuck here then?" Eric said, panicked.

Timber and Hayden, who were hiding in another tent, were also too frozen with fear to move. Timber looked over to Hayden and pointed to Hayden's bag. Slowly regaining his composure, Hayden nodded, knowing what he could do. Hayden removed his gun from his duffel bag as quickly and quietly as he could. When he had his gun in hand, he reached into his pocket, trying to get his hands on the specially made bullets. When he got them out of his pocket, they rolled out of his shaking hands. Hayden, in a sudden panic, crawled after them.

Over by Logan and the devil, Logan fired off a defense spell at the monster. The color was dark yellow. The devil took the full hit of the blast and even flinched in slight pain from the attack. The devil was a little surprised to see how strong Logan had become. But the devil pointed out that it wasn't strong enough.

"Did you tell them all about me, Logan? Did you tell them that I killed all of your friends and then tricked you into killing one of your own friends?" When the devil said this, it was the confession that Ray needed to hear to fully clear Logan for his father's death.

Ray turned to Cain and said, "It's time for us to make our move!"

"Normally I would never trap you with an anti-teleporting symbol because I always enjoyed the chase. But there are two active Loomations in this area, and I'm not letting anyone get out of here alive!" The devil walked up close to Logan. "Since everyone is hiding, I'm going to go ahead and just kill you!"

Just then, the devil was hit by a powerful gunshot right in his heart. The devil was hit with a powerful sniper rifle fired by Cain from a short distance. The gunfire was heard by the townspeople. Will was exiting the church when he heard the gunfire. Will knew that was coming from the meetup spot. He knew there was something wrong, so he started to sprint over to the scene.

The bullet harmlessly hit the ground after ricocheting off the devil, as the skin of the monster was so thick that a close-range sniper attack couldn't pierce it. Cain started to march up to the devil from behind Logan, as he continued to fire his bullets right at the monster. The shots were causing some pain to the creature, for the impact knocked his shoulders back. Cain stopped marching when he reached his father. The Hogs were watching the situation, hoping that Cain and Logan could take care of this. Then they spotted Ray coming up from behind the devil.

Ray shoved the devil's shoulders to make the beast face him. Then he shoved a large syringe into the devil's heart, injecting him with the poison he made. The needle was made from Ray's mother's wedding ring because the diamond of that ring was also from the garden. A trick they wouldn't have thought of if Logan hadn't informed Cain of all the Hogs' attack plans and weapons. Ray injected all his poison right into the heart of the beast, hoping it would kill him from the inside. Ray then broke off the syringe, leaving the needle lodged in the devil's heart.

The poison worked fast; the devil was howling in pain. This sound was music to Logan's ears; he had never heard the beast make that kind of sound before. Ray was gloating about his attack for a moment. Then he wanted to back away from the monster, but the devil reached out to grab Ray. The devil moved so fast he dragged his feet through the ground, destroying the symbol he made. Ray was now screaming in pain for the devil had dug his right-hand fingers deep into Ray's chest. The only way Ray was getting free from this grip was if he left his chest behind.

The Hogs jumped, scared at seeing Ray grabbed; some had to turn away due to how terrifying this was. Hayden finally got to his bullets he dropped, but with his still-clumsy and unsteady hands, he couldn't get the bullets loaded.

Cain, seeing his friend in pain, sprinted toward the devil, firing off his gun until it was empty. The bullets were making the devil bleed; the pain from the poison had started to damage his tough skin. When Cain got next to the devil, he was about to use his gun as a club to hit the devil's head. But the devil released a flame from his body, striking down Cain.

The devil was still howling in great pain from the poison inside him. He was causing flames to emit from all over his body to expel the toxic liquid from within. The flames were so hot that it was hard to look at. Ray, being so close to the beast, was slowly being engulfed by the flames. He was being burned alive as the sound of the devil's pain was destroying his ears.

Will finally made it to the fences surrounding the abandoned carnival. With one swoop of the blade, Will managed to cut open the fence. Will followed the sight of the bright flame and hellish howls. The devil was starting to feel better, for the poison was almost all burned out of him. He ceased his bellowing in pain and pulled Ray in close to say something to him.

"I'm going to say something to you, something I never thought I would say to a human…You've impressed me!" The devil was blown away by how much a regular human was able to hurt him. These were the last words Ray heard before he died from the flames, and the compliment made him smile with satisfaction. He may not have killed the devil, but he felt proud of being able to impress him. Once Ray was dead, the devil chucked him aside as if he was now nothing.

The devil was still hurting from the poison, so he couldn't even stand up straight. He looked around and saw the shocked faces, then heard someone making their way to him. He turned and saw Will coming in fast. The devil saw the sword in Will's hand, but he was now too weak to fight. Will fearlessly swooped within swinging range of the devil and swung with all his might. As the blade got close to the devil, the whole sword started to glow with a bright golden light. The devil, shaken by this brazen and unexpected attack, teleported away just in time. Since the symbol the devil made earlier was destroyed by the same person who made it, the spiritual realm was back to normal.

The devil was now gone, and the Hogs slowly emerged from their hiding places. Juice walked up to Hayden who was still sitting on the ground. Juice placed his hand onto Hayden's shoulder, and Hayden looked up in shame. "It's safe now," Juice said softly.

"No…no, it's not," Hayden said as he got to his feet. Hayden was mortified as he shamefully held his gun, feeling that he had failed to carry that weapon. Gard hung his head low for hiding during the whole event. Will was the only one grateful to see all his friends were still okay. Though the blast they received from the devil no longer carried pain, they were far from okay. Timber gave Will a hug, for it seemed that Will's attack caused the devil to retreat.

"What happened?" asked Will. Everyone was too humiliated to speak. Cain was standing over his dead friend's body.

"Son," Logan said, standing behind Cian.

"Don't say anything. You're alive because of this man," Cain said with hate and anger. "Ray and I not only stood up and fought the monster, Ray was able to hurt it!" Cain shouted. Cain then faced his father, shoving his finger in his face. "Your choice of warriors to fight this monster was ridiculous. They were helpless, useless, PATHETIC FOOLS!" The Hogs knew everything Cain was shouting was 100 percent true. The Hogs couldn't believe they froze up like they did. Logan had no response; despite all the faith he put in the Hogs, he knew his son was right about them at this moment.

"You bet your money on the wrong horse, and now a man is dead because of it! Because of all of you!" Cain shouted out to everyone. The Hogs wallowed in self-pity for a moment. Then they heard the police sirens coming. Cain asked Logan if he knew how to get to Ray's chemical plant. Before Logan could say no, Miles stepped in, saying he could get everyone there. Cain ordered everyone to circle around Ray's body. Miles took hands that chained to all the other hands and teleported them away, with Ray's body included.

When the group arrived at the plant, Cain let everyone in as he carried Ray's body. Cain turned and faced the group. "I'll give you all ten minutes to get your heads on straight. After that, we'll gather up in the conference room so we can prepare to kill the devil once and for all!" Cain then carried Ray's corpse off to one of the office rooms. The Hogs just needed some time to process what just happened and know if they could indeed win the battle against the devil.

CHAPTER 34

After Shock

Cain brought the body of his friend to one of the empty offices of the building and gently placed the body onto a desk and removed Ray's jacket. Ray always had his phoenix feather jacket on whenever he went into battle. The fireproof jacket had helped him out a few times over the years of battling with Cain. Cain saw that the back of Ray's body was totally burnt free from the devil's fiery attack on him. *The fool should have had his jacket buttoned up,* Cain thought to himself as he put the jacket on because he felt a rematch with the devil was imminent.

"I'm sorry for your loss," Logan said as he stood quietly in the doorway. Cain had his back toward the door, so he didn't know he wasn't alone.

"You should be," Cain said, not finding it surprising that his father was there. The man had been out of his life his entire life, but now he wouldn't give him space when he wanted it. Cain didn't turn his head; he just kept looking at Ray's body. "You know, there was a moment there when I thought…hey, we can kill this beast. When I charged at the beast to stick him with my rifle, I was thinking, *If only my father would have trusted me with the golden sword.* It sure would have been a better weapon to hit him with!" Cain said as he slammed his fist onto the office desk. "But it wouldn't have mattered. The devil at his weakest state was still able to blast me away. Even if I did have the sword, we still wouldn't have won," Cain sadly confessed. Logan had no response, not a helpful one anyway. The two just sat there in a moment of silence for the fallen warrior.

In the bathroom, Juice was vomiting in one of the toilets. The memories of the attack were growing too unsettling, and with all the nervous tension he had built up, he knew he should have gotten to a toilet earlier. When Juice got out of the stall, he saw his friend Will standing by the door. "You okay?" asked Will.

"Nope," Juice said as he walked over to the sink, turned the nozzles, and started to clean his hands. "I always hated throwing up. You know, when I was a kid, whenever I had an upset stomach from eating something that didn't settle right with me...my parents would say, 'If you have to throw up, don't fight it. You'll feel better after it's out.' I would convince myself that being sick was better than throwing up." Juice then started to wash his face and rinse out his mouth. "Back on the cross-country team, a few of the guys threw up from nerves before a big race. I never did... Not to say I wasn't nervous. I just handled it differently."

Will then handed over a towel to Juice who grabbed the towel and started drying himself. "We're dealing with something completely different. This isn't some high school race. This is something that we have been told to be afraid of our entire lives. So it's okay to be scared," Will said kindly.

"It's not okay...A man is dead because we were scared," Juice replied, feeling very guilty.

Inside the surveillance room, Gard sat in the chair, blindly staring at the monitors. Eric was in the room with him, sitting on the ground and leaning his back against the wall.

"You know, last time I was in this room, I remember that I had to knock out the security guard," Eric said with an arm motion. "I had to do it in one punch so that he wouldn't be able to scream for help." Eric's attitude was upbeat when he talked about his past mission. "I remember being at the locked door, knowing that it was time for action. I remember thinking why didn't I change jobs with someone else at that moment?" Eric chuckled at that statement. Gard didn't reply, just stared at the screens feeling a heavy burden of guilt. Eric could see that the attack from the devil still had Gard shaken up. "But there was a job to do. We had a well-executed plan, and I wasn't going to be the one who messed up the whole plan by being afraid."

"We had a well-executed plan for the devil, and when the moment came, we were nothing more than a deer in the headlight!" Gard shouted.

"We were ambushed!" Eric stated. "Caught off guard. We received a shock from something truly terrifying. And when Cain and Ray interfered, it may have been for the best not to do anything. The two had the well-executed plan that almost worked!"

"Well, it didn't, and we all just sat and watched one of them die," Gard said as he stood up out of the chair. "The Renshaws are going to ask us to fight that thing again, and I can't give them a single reason why I'll be helpful."

"There's still a job to do, and we still have time to prove ourselves worthy," Eric said as he got to his feet.

Cain walked up to Ray's personal lab on the second floor. He trashed the place searching for any kind of helpful weapon. Cain was hoping that Ray had a second batch of that poison somewhere in the lab. Still, Cain doubted it; knowing Ray, he probably used all that he had on the monster. Logan followed Cain into the room.

"What are you doing now, son?" asked Logan.

"I'm making a mess!" Cain said as he tipped over a shelf full of glass jars. "That's what you do when you're frustrated, right!" Cain said as he started throwing some of the objects on the table at the wall. He was outraged, for there was no more of Ray's weapons to be found. Cain knew that he had Ray's journal that contained vital information on all the weapons he was able to create. He knew that none of them would be able to hurt the devil, nor did he want to waste time crafting them. Cain then left the lab and went over to Ray's office with Logan following.

Cain walked around the desk in the office and pulled open the drawers. He spotted an envelope with the words *last will and testament.* Cain put his frustration on hold when he laid eyes on that. He carefully picked the envelope up and opened it. Inside was nothing but statements and reports. Ray gave all his property and fortune to a Katherine R. Hart. Cain plopped down in the office chair with a stunned look on his face.

"Why didn't he tell me?" Cain uttered to himself.

"What is it?" asked Logan.

"Ray…it says here that he gave everything he has to Katherine Hart. That's my daughter's current identity. He even put her name down for his entire inheritance," Cain reported. "All she will have to do is show off two forms of ID and sign a few papers."

Cain knew that Kate's caretaker was well capable of getting his hands on birth certificates, fake social security cards, passports, and even a fake driver's license. They were all good enough to fool a lawyer, so Cain knew that she would have no problem claiming the gifts.

"Why would Ray donate his entire inheritance to her?" asked Logan.

"Probably to say sorry for trying to kill a member of the Renshaw family for all these years," Cain replied. Cain just felt so dumbfounded that his enemy would do something like that. "You know, I had no doubts about Ray and I losing the fight with the devil." Cain's tone changed to a reasonable volume. "That's how I've always been. Thinking failure was never a possibility. If I would have died, I would have left Kate orphaned, with nothing."

"When I left you and your mother, I knew you two would have each other and a strong sturdy house," Logan said.

"That house was not strong nor sturdy! Every other week there was something that needed fixed," Cain replied. "The roof was leaking, the gas line kept breaking, and the mice kept getting in, and yet Mom still refused to move."

"Why did you stay?" wondered Logan.

"It was home. It was all that my father left me," Cain said. The two were now only starting to reach a better relationship. Cain did appreciate his father not letting him alone right now, for he really didn't want to be by himself right now. His only friend did just get killed right in front of him, and he was now coming to grips that he was not as invincible as he thought he was. The reality of death being a possibility made him uneasy. "You left so that I could live," Cain said, looking at his father. "I'm going to do whatever I can to make sure this devil dies. If my father has taught me anything…you sacrifice everything for your child!" Cain said as he got to his feet and exited the room.

Logan stayed in the room. He thought that Ray had a good idea with leaving something behind for someone. Logan had nothing for anyone, but he did have a message for the Hogs. Logan sat down and wrote out a letter, stuffed it in an envelope, and labeled it with the words *For the Hogs.*

Will, Juice, Eric, and Gard were walking down the hall, heading to the conference room. They walked by the lobby where they saw Timber sitting on the couch by the front door and Miles sitting behind the front desk. Will called out to Timber to ask if he was ready to go, and Timber gave a nod and got up off the couch. Will asked Timber if he was okay, and Timber replied confidently that he was ready to go. Timber then told everyone that Hayden was outside in the parking lot. As Will was heading to the front door to get a hold of Hayden, Miles spoke up.

"I was sitting here thinking about our situation." Miles had everyone standing around the desk he was sitting at with all eyes on him. "I can teleport, meaning I can whisk us away every time the devil comes for us. We know how he works. When he finds us, we could just gather up, and I can easily take us to safety." Miles pitched his idea in such a lifeless voice, as if he knew it was the wrong choice. The Hogs didn't waste any time thinking about this idea. They all agreed that running wasn't what they were going to do.

"We all have lives to get back to," Eric said.

"I'm not living the rest of my life being on the run, and if that means we have to fight the devil, then that's what I'm going to do," Timber added. What Timber said made sense to everyone. There were times that one had to fight for what they wanted, and not even fear could keep them from trying. The Hogs felt ashamed for the fear that engulfed them all when they first saw the devil, but sometimes the bravest ran and hid. And there were times when the cowards show the most courage. The Hogs now felt more ready for another encounter with the devil. The option of having the chance to run seemed self-defeating in a way. The Hogs' option to stand and fight filled each of them with an unspoken pride and a sense of courage that they had never thought was in them. Just then, the Hogs heard gunshots from outside. They all sprinted outside to check on Hayden and found him shooting his gun repeatedly. He was shooting at a parked car in the parking lot.

"Hayden, what are you doing?" asked Will.

"I just had to make sure that I could still do it," Hayden answered as he admitted to his friends that he froze when the devil attacked. Hayden had his gun loaded with his special bullets, but he never aimed his weapon. Hayden said that he was shaken with so much fear, his accuracy would have made his only two shots pointless. Hayden said that he never backed away from a target, and since he did, he felt that he' never be able to pull the trigger again. He felt most responsible for Ray's death than the others. Hayden wanted to fire off a few rounds just to remind himself that he still could pull that trigger. Hayden promised that he wouldn't hesitate again, but he couldn't promise that he wouldn't miss.

Now that the Hogs were all together, they made their way to the conference room. When they got there, they saw Cain waiting for them. There were enough chairs for everyone at the oval table. Once everyone was in a chair, they just had to wait for Logan to show up. There were small chats between a few of the Hogs as they waited for Logan to make his presence. When Logan finally arrived, he grabbed a chair next to Cain. Since Cain was the one who set up this meeting, it felt right to wait for him to start talking first. But instead, Will stood up and asked for a moment to honor Ray, their fellow Loomation carrier. Logan thought this was a good idea and asked Cain if he could say a few words. Cain stood up to speak.

"Ray was the smartest person that I ever knew. He was the only one who I trusted to fight with against the devil. And now he's dead, and now I'm left with all of you!" declared Cain.

The Hogs and Logan were hoping for something a bit more touching or at least something not so negative toward them. Juice complimented Cain's speech because he was touched to see Cain say a few nice things about his enemy. Cain then sat back down; it was time to talk business. Cain got the already-known facts out of the way. They had now all seen the devil in person, so there was no more belief in him not being real (which never really was the case). It was better to point out how powerful he was and how intimidating he truly came off.

"So we have four weeks until he shows up again, right?" Eric questioned.

"Yes," Logan replied.

"Well, is there any way to speed up that progress?" asked Cain. The people at the table looked at Cain with shocked faces. The question was, why would he want to take away prep time? Cain said that the devil wasn't expecting to discover more Loomation carriers when he found Logan today. That was a surprise that they wouldn't get the next time he showed up. Cain believed that the only way to get the upper hand on the devil was to attack now, before the devil had time to prepare.

"There is a way to call out to him," Logan said, remembering something from a long time ago. "The first time I met the devil, he said that he could only kill once a month. He said he had rules or something."

"Rules?" questioned Eric.

"This guy has a manager or something?" wondered Gard.

"I don't know. I've been chased by the guy for decades, and I still barely know anything about him," Logan replied. "But he did tell me that he could kill me at any time if I first gave him permission."

"So he can only kill one person a month at a time, unless he has permission?" questioned Juice with a quizzical look.

"Well, that's why he ran away after he killed Ray. He had his kill of the month and then took off," Eric pointed out.

"So the next time we fight him, he could just flee whenever he takes one of us out," Hayden added.

"If we all give him permission, he might stick around to kill us all," Will theorized. This statement made the Hogs feel a little on edge. It was one thing to fight the devil to the death, but knowing that they had to give the monster permission to kill them first just felt odd. Juice pointed out that you really couldn't fight for your life unless you let it be in danger first. It would be a true fight to the death for everyone.

The people in the room then discussed their weapon inventory. The golden sword was put into account along with Hayden's two diamond bullets and the hunting knife with the diamond chip pieces lodged within it. The Hogs then said that they had been working on attack strategies for a while. Cain said that he was a fast learner when it came to combat, so he felt that he could be some help with that. Cain requested to have the sword. Some of the people in the room weren't too sure about that.

Logan said he voted to have it in the hands of one of the Hogs. The Hogs voted for Will to have it, since he was the only one who was able to run into battle when the devil showed up. Cain said he was the best fighter at the table and that if anyone was going to stab that monster, it was going to be him.

After that, everyone felt as ready as they would ever be to attack this monster. Logan requested a good night's rest first. Now that the countdown had started up again, there was no hurry to arrive at the garden. Cain didn't want to wait, but he was outvoted on this one. So a few hours of rest were agreed upon, but it seemed unnecessary as no one could really sleep given everything that had happened to them and what was about to befall the next morning.

Monday, June 28, 2010

Everyone tried their best to get some sleep, and surprisingly, they did get a few hours of rest. When they woke up, they were as ready as they would ever be. Logan teleported everyone to the mountain that contained the entrance to the Garden of Eden. Logan took them all to the same place where he and his fellow travelers had set up camp all those years ago. Logan had a very nostalgic feeling upon returning to this place. The others just saw a mountain landscape, but Logan was looking at one of his few memories that he could still remember of his old friends.

"Which way, Logan?" asked Gard. But it was Cain who knew this territory all too well, as he used to make trips back and forth to the garden all the time.

"This is where you and Ray got all those creatures that were locked up in your prison. What made you decide to do that?" Eric asked Cain as they marched up the mountain.

"Ray wanted to study them. I was looking for some kind of attack-dog purpose for them," Cain replied.

"That was a truly cruel act to do. We had to slaughter all of them due to their unrestrained attitudes. They've killed people," Eric rudely said.

"You don't know half of their victims," Cain said. Eric was reminded that even though they were fighting alongside this man, it didn't mean he had to like him.

In the back of the line, Juice started talking to Logan. "So this was where it all happened?" Juice asked Logan. Logan nodded, saying that this was the same way he took when he first saw the meteor crash into the ground back when he was young. Juice asked Logan what it was like being the first to discover such an ancient, hidden land. Logan said it was the most beautiful place he had ever seen. Juice grinned in excitement at being able to see this place. The travelers made it to the tunnel and made their way to the stone door. The walk down the dark tunnel was foreboding, as it felt more like the way to hell rather than a peaceful land.

"All right, open it," Cain ordered the Hogs.

"I don't know how to open the door," Hayden stated, dumfounded by the demand. Cain faced his father, frustrated that he didn't give them the instructions on how to move the rock. The Hogs were now questioning how to move the rock.

"It takes two people with Loomation inside them to move it. All you have to do is simply place your hand on the rock, while the other does the same," Logan explained.

"Yeah, and it feels like it's draining your life energy as it moves," Cain added. This frightened the Hogs, as they couldn't fathom how opening the door would take such a physical toll on them. Cain was already making it clear that he wasn't going to be one of the two to open the door.

"I'll do it," Juice spoke up.

"You sure, Juice?" asked Will.

"Hey, if getting weak in the knees by opening a door ends up being the worst thing that happens to me today, then I see that as a huge win," Juice said as he slapped his hand onto the rock. The wait for a second hand started. Logan volunteered, but Cain vetoed it, saying that Logan was an old man, and there might be a chance opening the door could kill him. It wasn't a high chance, but Cain didn't want to risk their most experienced fighter dying because of opening the door. Timber then stepped up to the rock, saying he'd do it. Timber took a deep breath before placing his hand on the stone. He was alerted that as soon as he touched it with Juice's hand already placed on it, the process would start immediately. Timber slowly placed his hand next to the rock and leaned in.

Both Juice and Timber fell to their knees, while their hands seemed glued to the rock. They were both wailing in agony. Cain shouted out that this was normal and that it happened every time to prevent the other Hogs from getting worried. The rock did start to move, and the radiant light from the garden started to beam into the tunnel. The shining of the light amazed the Hogs, temporarily blinding them. Believing in the garden was one thing, but now the reality of seeing it was beyond their dreams. They were dazed as this reality suddenly dawned on them, and they looked straight on with wondering, awestruck eyes.

The rock continued to slide out of the way with Juice and Timber's hands still pressed against it. Once the rock was fully moved, the boulder released its grip on the boys, and they fell to the ground. The Hogs checked on their friends as they were too weak to stand. Cain instructed them to bring them to the light, as he knew the healing factor that came from the land would start to make them feel better. Gard and Miles helped Juice, while Will and Hayden helped Timber. Everyone walked past the rock and into the edge of the tunnel that overlooked the garden.

The sight provided a panoramic view of the garden. The waterfall was to their left, the stream of crystal-clear water cascading down. They saw the fresh green grass and the bundle of trees scattered about. The sunlight felt nice on the weakened members, as if they were flowers now blooming in the light. Standing on the edge, the Hogs were all struck by the beauty of the place. Hayden commented that it kind of looked like the swamp. But his friends just laughed, saying not even close.

Logan remembered standing on this same edge eighty-six years ago with his group. He even saw the same rope he tied to the rock so they could climb down and back up. The rope was still just as he remembered it as it never aged a day. Logan thought he would have seen this place as nothing more than the birth of his curse. But charming memories of spending time with his fellow travelers were the first thoughts that came to his mind when he saw the beauty of the land. At that moment, Logan was able to remember all their names.

Cain had memories of him and Ray first entering this place. The wooden ramps from the ground to the tunnel were their first project together. Cain remembered all the joyous times he had with Ray when they came to this land, for they were never in this land as enemies. At this moment, Cain felt sad for his fallen friend. When Ray died, it happened so fast all Cain could do was blame everyone, which only led to hateful feelings. Cain wished that his friend could be standing there with him at this time.

Hayden was the first one to start walking down the ramp, saying that they didn't come all this way just to look at it. Juice and Timber were now feeling well enough to walk, and once their feet touched the grass, they felt completely fine.

"We should head inward and find a place that could help us stage an attack," Cain ordered.

"Agreed. It's too open right here," Will added.

"If we can find some trees clumped closer together, we can hide out in multiple locations," Hayden suggested.

"Lure him into a kill circle," said Eric, adding to the plan.

"Then act fast and get the sword into him as soon as possible," Gard stated.

"Then we go home," Juice mentioned.

Cain mentioned that there wasn't a forest-type area that he was aware of, but he knew of a place where they could find some cover. Cain led the warriors deep into the garden. The Hogs felt like they were getting a tour in a way, soaking up all the wonderful sights along the way. They walked a couple of miles deep into the garden. The amount of time that passed during their walk went by so fast, but the Hogs didn't feel like it did. The Hogs saw that the sun hadn't moved at all, which made the passing of time feel nonexistent. Eric started to ask questions. He wondered how the grass that was under the shade looked so alive and fresh. If the sun never moved, then the shaded grass would never get any sunlight. It was pointless to attempt to apply logic to this place. Hayden pointed out that since the sun neither rose nor set, it meant that there was no sense of direction. No west or east, meaning there was no north or south. With no sense of time or direction in the garden, the Hogs felt like they were walking in place and going nowhere.

"Have you ever gotten lost in here?" Hayden asked Cain. Cain said that the river was their compass in a way, for it led right back to the way out. The idea of getting lost within the garden hadn't come to the others until Hayden brought it up. They were happy that the way back was the simple task of following the river. When they looked back during their hike, the exit was long gone, out of sight.

As they walked, Miles talked to Logan about that symbol the devil burned into the ground when he attacked them. Miles said that when the symbol was branded onto the ground, Miles couldn't teleport, and he felt that it was because of the symbol. Logan said that he felt a stifling feeling when the symbol was made. Miles said that he felt that feeling too but didn't think anything of it. The two theorized that the symbol turned off the spiritual realm in that area, and after the devil dragged his feet through the symbol destroying the mark, it turned the realm back on.

"So he had the power to keep you from fleeing all this time?" Miles said.

"When he thought I was the last one, he was okay with the chase. It must have been his way of torturing me…It worked. Knowing that he could have killed me this whole time does make me outraged, but it was his loss. Him chasing me, keeping himself busy only with me, he never bothered looking for anyone else. My son and granddaughter remained safe because he kept letting me get away."

Miles now saw how mind numbing the never-ending chase could be. He was glad that none of his friends chose to do what Logan did, for in the long run, it wouldn't lead to a better life.

Cain stopped the hike and said that they had arrived. The Hogs looked around and saw four different trees in slightly close. Cain said with all the trees scattered out on this land, these four had the shortest distance to each other. Cain said that he and Ray used it as a place to set up camp when they were working there, and they could split up into different trees in the area and attack from different sides when the devil showed up.

"We'll need someone to be out in the open. I say that the flyer should do it," Cain reported.

"Hey, now, you don't make decisions for our group," Gard shouted, pointing his finger at Cain.

"Yeah, we may be working together, but that doesn't mean we're your Havocs members," Will added.

"Have you forgotten what we came here to do? This is an assassination mission! I think the person who has real experiences with that should be leading the pack!" Cain replied.

"We've handled missions like this by taking care of all your escaped creatures," Eric countered.

"All that practice didn't come in handy when the devil showed up the first time!" Cain retorted in a sudden rage, losing his temper.

"I'll do it," Juice stated. Everyone looked at Juice. "Me being the one out in the open makes sense. I'm the one who can get away the quickest by flying out of arm's reach of the devil."

"Then I'm standing with him," Gard said. "I'm the fastest sprinter here, so I'm the best chance at avoiding being grabbed. Besides, there's no way I'm letting Juice stand out here by himself." The Hogs admired the two's courage. Hayden then handed Gard his hunting knife with the diamond-fused chips in it.

"In case you need it," Hayden said softly. Gard gave a heartwarming thank you when he reached for the knife.

"Hayden, I want you in one of the trees next to me. If that beast tries to blast me with its fire to keep me away from him, shoot him. And if the bullets you made hurt it, then you may be able to weaken him long enough for me to stab him," Cain instructed. "Father, I want you in the same tree as me. When I make my charge, I want you to pile that defense spell on him. That attack seemed to knock the devil off balance. That would make it harder for him to stop my attack with his arms." Cain didn't even realize that he just called Logan father at that moment. But Logan heard it and was so touched by it, he couldn't even reply with words; he just gave a nod. "As for the rest of you, I want you in the other trees. If the devil tries to run away, I want you to block him and push him back into my kill path. Since we're in the garden, any attack on you that won't kill you right away will be something you can shake off, so keep that in mind!"

The group had their plan and was shocked to realize how easy it sounded. With everything said and planned out by Cain, they were left thinking that they were going to make it out of this alive. But they knew that was not guaranteed. They had seen firsthand how powerful the devil was, and they knew that any one of them could be the next one killed.

"Guys, if we don't succeed, if I don't make it to the end of this...I just want to say that it's been an honor to be your friend," Juice said. At this moment, it was time to think realistically that the times of saying it was going to be all right were now over.

"Thank you all for helping me," Miles said. "I was sick, dying even. You guys wanted to save me, and you gave me the powers from the cube."

"We unknowingly put a target on you, Miles," Hayden said with guilt.

"I don't see it that way. I see it as a chance for me to return a lifesaving act to my friends. I'll do all that I can to give you all the extra time that I can, just as you have done for me," Miles replied with utmost earnestness.

"I don't want to see any of you guys die, all right! I die first if any of us go!" Gard shouted.

"We'll just look out for one another. Watch each other's backs and all that," Eric replied.

"There is no one out there whom I would rather fight with," Hayden stated.

"I'm proud to be a part of this group. Not many people would want to do this, but us being together makes us stronger people," Timber added. After that, Will grabbed the shoulders of two of his friends, and everyone circled around for a prayer. Will asked for God's help in this battle and to keep his fellow fighters safe until the end.

As the Hogs were praying, Logan and Cain just watched and waited for them to finish.

"I do thank you for your sacrifice," Cain said to his father. "Being chased by that thing for all these years, being away from the ones you love, I can't imagine how hard that was for you."

"Not a day went by without me thinking of you and your mother," Logan replied.

"She would be proud of what you did. She always spoke highly of you, even when I didn't. She never stopped loving you," Cain reported.

After the Hogs finished their prayer, everyone gathered up to say another prayer—this time to the devil. Will asked if it was even possible to pray to the devil. Logan stated that there have been tons of cults that have tried speaking to the monster for years, and it was not a far-fetched idea. He said he knew the devil would respond to their prayer and instructed everyone to say a prayer to the monster, giving him permission for him to kill them right there and then.

"Devil, I give you permission to kill me, a human who is stronger than God intended! You have permission to come kill me!" Cain shouted. This phrase was repeated by each person after Cain. Once everyone gave their consent, they all rushed to their positions as they had no idea how much time they would have before the beast arrived. Once they were in place, they waited.

The devil did hear their prayer. He immediately teleported toward the tunnel that he used to escape from the garden and stood at the same edge that the Hogs and the Renshaws were just at earlier that morning and saw that the wooden ramp was a new addition. The devil hated this place, and it took him years to call upon that meteor from space to blast him out of the confines of his personal prison. But his victims were inside the garden, and he figured he knew why. The land had a nonending heal spell for the humans, blessing the land. The devil knew the humans were leading him into a trap, so he set up a trap of his own.

The devil turned and pushed the boulder back into place, blocking off the exit. He knew he was strong enough to move the rock out of his way when he was ready to leave, even with the magical lock on it. Once the rock sealed up the hole, the spiritual realm was now shut down within the garden. The barrier around the garden kept anyone with an active Loomation from teleporting. But if there was a hole in the barrier, or even a small crack, the spiritual realm would return. Over by the humans, both Logan and Miles felt that same feeling they once felt last time the devil was able to shut down the spiritual realm. Both knew that the power to teleport was now blocked.

The devil knew where everyone was, but he didn't want to go there just yet. He didn't like that he was heading into a trap, so he wanted to turn the tables on them. The devil went to the cave where the diamond was located, walked up to the diamond, and placed his hand onto it. The devil's hand created red veins that crawled over the diamond. The veins stretched around the object; outside the cave, the bright sky turned to pitch black, the gentle breeze suddenly stopped, and the water stopped flowing.

At the four trees, the humans saw the bright shining sky turn into a screen of black as any life that was in the sky was suddenly snatched away without warning. The humans all wanted to scream, but they grew silent. They all felt a shiver crawl from their shoulders all the way down to the bottom of their feet. They were trying to picture their surroundings in their heads to remember where everyone was. None of them could move as it was as if they forgot how. The hearts of the humans all first skipped a beat then started to pound heavy and fast. Then in the sky, lightning struck without warning. For a moment, everything was visible. Then they heard the loud bellowing of thunder, and another lightning strike went off, followed by a second one. The lightning was their only source of light. The flashing light showed off the land for a moment, but the beauty of the place was now gone. The place looked terrifying and felt cold and lifeless. The humans were stuck in an incredibly flourishing wide body of land that suddenly seemed to turn into a vast wasteland, with lightning being their only source of light, as they were being hunted by the devil himself. The paradise had turned into a true nightmare.

CHAPTER 35

A True Nightmare

The Loomation carriers were all close by one another. Juice and Gard were standing in the open with their backs to the four trees curved behind them. In the tree to their far left was the hiding place of Timber and Eric. Logan and Cain were in the tree directly behind Juice and Gard. To the tree next to that one was where Will and Miles were, and Hayden was in the final tree on the far right.

"Is this bad?" asked Juice.

"Does it look good?" Gard shouted. In the trees, Eric shouted over to the tree Cain and Logan were in, asking if either of them had seen this before. The answer was no, and there was fear in their voices. Will asked Logan if pain could leave a lasting feeling now that the garden had turned dark. No one was sure of this, so Will tested this out himself. Will used his pocketknife and gave himself a small cut on his finger. The cut caused a drop of blood. The cut should have healed up, and the minor pain should have gone away. Will's theory that the nonstop heal spell the land once possessed was now turned off was true. Will and Miles were huddled in the same tree, so Miles checked if he could still perform the heal spell by using it on Will. Will's cut healed up as if it was never there after Miles successfully placed the spell on his friend.

"Good news is that the heal spell still works on the ones with the active Loomation," Will reported.

"Yeah, but that only works when they're touching us," Eric pointed out. "This isn't a good idea. We should bail!" Eric shouted over to Cain and Logan.

All the Hogs agreed with that plan because the place was so dark that fighting under these conditions would have been troubling and lead to an easy defeat. But Logan reminded everyone of the threat at hand. Now that they all had given the devil permission to kill them, nowhere was safe. Cain, on the other hand, saw that leaving the garden would have been an act of retreating, so he chose to stay. Miles didn't help the case of retreating when he warned everyone that he couldn't seem to teleport now. Logan also couldn't teleport, so now they felt even more stranded in the middle of nowhere. Tensions were high for the Hogs, desperate for someone to decide with which they all could agree.

Before the argument went any further, a new sound arose. The chilling crackling sound from far away was closing in on them, getting louder with every second. From the light of the lightning strikes, the men were able to see a fissure in the ground growing toward them at a high speed. With every blast of lightning they saw, the crack in the earth kept slithering toward them like a deadly snake. Then the light stopped, and the sound of the cracking ground seemed to be beneath them. Then lightning struck to reveal the very ground Juice and Gard were standing on had suddenly given way, and the line in the ground had continued to go on past them, branching off into multiple cracks.

The events that followed happened so fast it was unreal. The humans witnessed these events as if they were looking at blurry photos due to the lightning flashing on and off so fast. The noise was nonstop. The cracking and shifting of the ground, the people screaming, and the thunder from the lightning made it hard to focus on how to handle the situation. This was a massive unexplained earthquake, one that appeared to have been created by the devil himself.

The ground Juice and Gard were standing on turned into a pit. Huge chunks of ground all around them fell into a deep hole. Juice managed to fly above the hole and snatched Gard from the growing gap before he fell. One of the cracks in the ground directed its way toward the tree where Timber and Eric were hiding. The tree started to tip downward toward the pit. Eric looked over and saw that the ground over by Logan and Cain was still intact. "TIMBER! JUMP!" Eric yelled as loud as he could, pushing Timber over to solid land. Timber made the jump and landed safely on the ground. Eric, however, lost his footing while pushing Timber; and when he tried to jump, he tripped and fell into the branches of the falling tree. As Eric felt that he was stuck in the tree branches and that the tree was falling into the pit, he desperately tossed the cube over to Timber. Eric felt that he was going to die and knew that the cube could still be useful. Within a flash of lightning, Eric's and Timber's eyes met up. Eric threw the cube in Timber's direction before the light was out. Timber snatched the cube in flight before the light went out and helplessly heard the tree fall with Eric still in it.

"JUICE! LOOK OUT!" Gard shouted as he was dangling from Juice's hand above the pit. Gard saw through the lightning that a tree was about to fall right on top of Juice. The tree hit Juice's back and started to shove him down the pit. The top of the tree slammed into the side of the hole, causing it to snap. Juice, Eric, and Gard were now stuck within the branches of the tree as it slid all the way down the very large chasm.

Will, Hayden, and Miles were trying to get over to Logan and Cain where the ground seemed the most stable. Then the ground started to let go, and the area they were running toward suddenly started to lift in the air like a drawbridge. Will knew that they were going to be the next to fall into the pit, so he instinctively grabbed Miles by his belt and chucked him up to the high-level patch of land where the others were out of danger. Miles hit the section of the land hard and took a few rolls but didn't mind, for he felt that he was now on safer ground. Miles looked over and saw Timber running up to him, telling him to move away from the cracks of the ground.

Will waited for Hayden to catch up to him because he didn't want to jump to the higher ground without him. Hayden was running as fast as he could carrying his rifle in his right hand. Then a new rupture emerged. The ground Hayden was standing on was pushed away from Will, causing a new trench to separate the two. Hayden felt his left foot to be weightless as the ground under him started to sink into the ever-widening trench. Hayden had to back up as he could not make the leap across the trench. Will then turned and saw the land he just threw Miles on was drifting farther and farther away from him.

Logan, Cain, Timber, and Miles now felt as if they were on an iceberg drifting in the ocean. The trench between them and Will soon turned into a canyon. They were now well out of shouting distance. Will looked across the distance between him and Hayden with a panicked look, as Hayden was the only friend Will could see. Then the land under Will mercilessly started to crumble, causing Will to slide down. Will turned and grabbed the shrinking ledge with his hands and elbows.

"WILL! GET UP!" shouted Hayden.

As Will was lifting himself back to the ground, more and more of the land started to fall faster and faster all around him. Will just kept grabbing the grassy dirt on the edge and used his feet to desperately push himself back up. In time, he got his feet back on the ground but still wasn't out of trouble. He now had to run faster than the crumbling ground to avoid the pit. Will ran until the sound of the ground falling had finally subsided. When he finally stopped, Will turned in despair and saw a huge canyon with no friends in sight.

The three boys on the falling tree fell deep into the hole created by the quake. The trench started to grow narrower the deeper they fell. The tree fell sideways; the top and bottom edges of the tree started to rub against the sides of the solid dirt walls. Wedged between the two sides, the tree started to slow down as if it was a high-speed car that just slammed onto its brakes. The tree cut streaks into the side of the walls, with the friction giving off some light for the three Hogs stuck in the tree who were hanging on for dear life. The tree slowed down enough to gently crash when it reached the bottom.

There was a moment of silence when the tree came to a complete halt. "Are you guys okay?" shouted Gard, breaking the silence.

"I'm good," Eric quietly replied.

"Juice, where are you!" Gard said as he reached for his cell phone. Gard turned on the flashlight built into his cell phone. The light from the phone didn't provide much light. Gard shone it where Eric's voice came from and spotted him in the light. Eric was still on the tree and was able to walk over to Gard. "Juice, say something!" Gard shouted with panic in his voice.

Juice was able to release a soft growl. Gard and Eric moved with haste over to him. When they found him, they saw that he was stuck between the bottom of the trench and the large tree. The tree wasn't completely crushing Juice. The ground was uneven, allowing for some of the tree's weight to spread out on the rough surface of the ground. It was hard for Juice to breathe with the tree lying on top of him, which was why he couldn't respond very well to Gard's call. When Gard pointed the light toward Juice, both Eric and Gard were stunned at the first sight of him. Juice was gasping for air, only getting enough air to barely fill his struggling lungs. His eyes were bloodshot, and his head was sweating like a pig. Juice's arms were pinned across his chest, so he couldn't even get his hands under the tree to attempt to push it off him.

"Juice, we're going to get this tree off you, don't you worry!" Gard said with a reassuring tone. Gard placed his phone onto the side of the rough chunky rock wall so that the light was shining on Juice. Both Eric and Gard got close to Juice and placed their hands under the tree and lifted with all their might. They tried lifting it from different angles, yet it didn't budge. Eric broke off one of the branches of the tree and attempted to pry the tree over. Eric shoved the stick under the tree at an angle; he and Gard pushed down on the limb in hopes of the tree turning over off Juice. The limb snapped like a twig almost immediately.

"Eric, start digging!" Gard shouted as he dove to the ground and started to dig his fingers into the bottom of the surface. Gard thought if they couldn't move the tree, they would increase the ground under Juice so he could slip out. The ground, however, felt as if it was solid marble rock, and neither Gard nor Eric could produce even the slightest scratch in the unyielding stone. After that plan failed, Gard picked up the phone and brought the light up close to the ground where Juice was stuck. There was no way to pull him out. The only body part of Juice they were able to pull on was his head, and that would most certainly kill him.

Gard, troubled, looked over to Eric, who was lost for words and devastated at seeing his friend in pain. Gard shone the light onto Juice and saw that tears were streaming down his face due to the mass of the tree crushing his chest and cutting off his ability to breathe well. "Juice, don't worry. We'll find a way to get you free, and you'll be able to fly us back to the rest of group," Gard said, using his best bedside manner.

Juice was able to nod, for he believed Gard. He then struggled to say something out loud, and Gard brought his ear close to Juice.

"I think we all earned the nickname Timber now," Juice said, making a joke. Gard laughed slightly. Gard then looked up and saw that they were so far down the pit that the lightning in the sky was barely noticeable. "How deep do you think we fell?" asked Gard.

"Deep," Eric simply replied. Eric could have calculated an educated guess, but his mind wasn't up for it. At the moment, he was both mentally and physically at rock bottom.

Getting stuck within the branches of the tree saved the boys' lives. If the tree hadn't wedged within the trench, it would have completely shattered on impact. Gard and Eric considered themselves lucky. Juice, on the other hand, wasn't feeling the same about the lifesaving tree at the moment.

"Did you see anyone else fall?" Eric asked Gard.

"It all happened so fast. After I saw the hole open under me, all I saw was the tree crashing into us," Gard stated.

"I helped Timber jump over to Cain and Logan. I was planning on heading that way until I got stuck. After that, things turned fuzzy, and I didn't see what happened to the others," Eric added. Gard and Eric had the frightening thought that others may have fallen down the pit as well. Gard instructed Eric to wait with Juice because he was going to explore the pit. He figured if they survived the fall, then someone else could have also. And if that was the case, that would mean an extra person to help lift the tree off Juice.

The patch of land Logan, Cain, Timber, and Miles were on was still drifting farther and farther away from its original spot. When the land finally stopped, it felt like a crash landing causing everyone to tip over and hit the ground or at least bring them down to one knee. Everyone took a moment to catch their breath and relax.

Cain took steps toward his father and started to yell, "What in God's name was that?"

"I don't know," Logan shamefully said.

"First the *Great Garden of Eden's* sun goes out, then the place tries to gobble us up!" Cain shouted.

"I'm aware of the dramatic situation that just happened. I was standing right beside you when it took place!" Logan replied, not appreciating his son's tone. The truth was that they were both scared, and that had them both tense.

"Logan, was that caused by *him*?" Timber asked, referring to the devil.

"Yes, I believe so," Logan sadly replied, bowing his head.

"Do you know how he could have pulled something like that off?" wondered Cain.

"The diamond…the grand diamond in the cave acts as a type of battery for this place. The devil must have found a way to somehow infect it, causing the land's blessing features to be shut down," Logan tried to explain.

"Could you find your way back to the cave?" wondered Cain.

"Yes, I believe I know how to get there," Logan answered.

"Then that's where we're heading. Weapons check, you two." Cain ordered the two Hogs. Cain still had the sword strapped to his side, and when he looked over to the boys, he was distraught to see that the one with the gun wasn't with him. Both Logan and Miles were relying on their active Loomation for their weapons. All Timber had was the cube his friend tossed to him when he was falling down the abyss. As far as Timber knew, Eric's last actions were him tossing the cube over to him. So Timber felt that the cube was important somehow.

"You want to go towards the person who just threw an earthquake at us?" Miles asked, bewildered.

"I'm done setting up traps. They haven't worked yet. And besides, I've always been a straightforward type of guy!" Cain said fearlessly.

"But there are only four of us. We should try to regroup," Timber pleaded. Cain told the men that he had an idea how the devil was setting up his plan of attack. Cain said that if he were in the devil's shoes, he would be making the same play.

"I don't believe the devil sent the earthquake to kill us. I think he wanted us separated. Heck, anybody that died from the experience would have just been a plus for him. Now that we're in the dark, on broken ground, he expects us to waste tons of time playing Marco Polo while he picks us off one by one." What Cain was saying sounded like the harsh truth. "Since we have an educated guess on where the devil last was, I say we take the fight to him."

"What about the rest of our friends?" Miles asked.

"One of them is a flyer. He'll find us before we find him. If that happens, we'll work on regrouping," Cain replied.

"What about the garden? This place was meant to give us the advantage of taking the devil's hits without the nagging pain," Miles added.

An idea came to Timber, one that would allow him to vote yes to Cain's plan on heading toward the cave. The sky turning from light to dark due to an infection by the devil reminded Timber of when Juice was infected by the Havocs and the plan the Hogs made in an attempt to cure him. Timber, with the cube in hand, spoke up.

"Logan…," Timber called out to the wise old man. "If the devil did something to the diamond, do you think a blast of its own energy would bring it back to normal?" Timber knew that the cube was made from a chunk of the grand diamond, and once the cube had all its connected pieces touching, it would generate Loomation and release once the cube was recoiled. Logan's eyes brightened, for he had faith in this idea, stating it was the best attempt to bring the garden back to the way it was. Timber wanted the sun and nonstop heal spell blessing of the land back more than anything, so he voted to head to the cave. Both Logan and Miles were on board for heading to the cave, and off they went.

Will was walking in the direction where he last saw his friend Hayden. The flickering lightning made his walk disturbing. Will made sure he was at least half a football field away from the giant gorge to his left; he just wanted to reunite with Hayden. After that, they would work together to find the others. Will knew that Miles and Timber were safe being with Logan and Cain. Will was worried about Juice, Eric, and Gard. Will saw them fall into the abyss when the earthquake started. Will wouldn't allow himself to believe that his friends who fell down the chasm were dead. He had to hold on to hope that Juice was able to pull them all out, and they were out there in the dark somewhere. Will thought if you were going to fall down the hole, it was good to have the one who could fly down there with you.

After a short walk forward, Will started to hear an unpleasant sound amid the thunder. He turned his head to the right, and when the lightning struck, he saw that there was a long curvy hill in the distance. The sound came from that direction, and it was growing louder. Will stopped in his place and kept his eyes on the hill. The lightning at first strike revealed the hill from afar. Then after a quick pause, complete darkness came, once again blinding his view. After another flash of lightning struck, Will saw something on top of the hill. The flash of lightning came and went so fast that Will couldn't make it out. As Will waited for the next flash, he had an idea of what that sound was. Then another quick flash of lightning appeared, and it became clear to Will that there was a very large pack of Sasquatches charging straight toward him. As Will ran for his life, he glimpsed to his right and saw that he was successfully keeping the threat away. But they were closing the gap fast.

On the other side of the canyon, Hayden heard the stampede. He rushed toward it and stopped at the edge of the ground. The lightning revealed to Hayden that Will was on the other side of the canyon with a herd of Sasquatches closing in on his tail. Hayden looked around the edge of the cliff, trying to find a way to help his friend. Hayden managed to spot a section of the edge that leaned over to the other side far enough for Will to make a jump. Hayden started to run to the section of the land while yelling at Will to get his attention.

Hayden hollered as loud as he could, but with the thunder and deafening roar of the stampede, his loudest attempts to catch Will's attention were drowned out. He stood on the edge of the land sticking out the closest to the other side. Hayden had to come up with a way to get Will's attention before Will missed his opportunity to make the jump. Hayden threw his bag on the ground, took a knee, reached into his bag, and pulled out a small bottle of lighter fluid. Once Hayden had the bottle in his hand, he used his teeth to rip the right sleeve off his shirt. Hayden wrapped the torn-off sleeve around his exposed arm and drenched it in the lighter fluid. He then pulled out his lighter and torched the fabric into flames.

Will spotted the fire from the other side of the canyon right away. In this darkness, any new source of light would catch the eye immediately. Will saw Hayden waving his burning right arm at him, urging him to come over. Then another lightning streak revealed the close ledge of the canyon that Hayden was standing on. Will knew that this was his best chance to get over to the other side. He didn't have time to fully prepare for his jump because if he slowed down just a little, he would have been trampled as he could smell the foul odor of the beasts looming ever closer. Will knew how far he needed to jump due to Hayden standing on the edge giving off light from his burning arm. It was a long jump, so he knew he would have to reach the edge of his side before he made his leap.

Because it was so dark, Will didn't even know where the edge of the land was. He had no time to wait for another lightning strike to reveal the edge as the beasts were breathing down his neck. He had no choice but to make his way to the destination. Will sprinted blindly to the edge of the land, with only Hayden on the other side in sight. Will wanted to leap, but he knew that he still wasn't close enough to make the jump. So he had to keep moving forward, praying that there was still ground under his feet for his runway. A few steps closer, Will now believed that he was close enough to make the jump. He wanted to wait just a step or two closer before he jumped, but he had a gut feeling that it was now or never.

It was a good thing that Will made the jump when he did because just one step closer would have sent him past the edge, and he would have sprinted right off the cliff without any jumping effort at all. At that moment, another lightning flash occurred, and Hayden saw Will airborne as a few of the Sasquatches right behind him had run straight off the edge, screaming as they plunged helplessly to the bottom of the canyon. Will could hear the screams of the falling beasts behind him fall down the pit.

Will slammed hard into the cliff on the other side of the canyon. His fingers drove into the dirt wall to keep him from falling. Hayden got to his belly and looked down the pit. Will was very close to the top, so Hayden reached out his hand to pull him up.

"OTHER ARM, HAYDEN!" Will shouted because Hayden reached out to Will with his burning arm. As Hayden pulled his arm back, he heard one of the animals land on his side of the canyon. Hayden couldn't believe that one of the creatures made the jump, so he hurried to his feet. As he moved, he peeled off his burning shirt from his arm. Hayden grabbed his rifle and pounded the butt of the rifle at the Sasquatch, knocking it down into the pit. The last thing Hayden needed right now was a vicious killing animal trying to attack him while he was trying to rescue his friend.

A second Sasquatch leaped over. This one wasn't so lucky. It didn't make the jump, and as it was falling, it grabbed Will's leg. The squeezing pressure from the hand of the beast was very painful. All Will could do was let out a loud scream. He had to use all his willpower to keep himself from flinching from the pain. Even the slightest movement would have caused his fingers to slip from the holes dug in the dirt that Will was desperately clinging to.

Hayden swung his gun and aimed down, ready to shoot off a round. Now that his torch was out, Hayden couldn't see anything, but he heard Will's screams and knew there was a beast on him. Then lightning flashed, and Hayden saw the bigfoot on Will's leg. Hayden only had milliseconds to aim and fire before the flash of lightning was gone. By the time Hayden pulled the trigger, the light was gone. Will saw the spark from Hayden's gun, and then he heard the impact of the bullet go through the creature that was grabbing his ankle. The grip of the monster's hand around Will's leg grew instantly weaker and then was completely gone. The weight of the beast dropped, and Will was safe. Then lightning went off again, and Will saw the handle of Hayden's rifle reaching out to him. Will grabbed the gun, and Hayden pulled him up. Once Will was safe on the ground standing next to Hayden, he asked him what happened.

"There was a Sasquatch on your leg, so I shot it off you," Hayden said, acting nonchalant about the event.

"Did you hit your target?" Will questioned.

"Trust me, if I would have missed, that thing would have pulled you down," Hayden replied. Then Will realized that Hayden used a diamond bullet. Will was outraged that Hayden wasted a diamond bullet on a Sasquatch. Hayden told Will that he fully knew what he was doing when he used that bullet. He explained that he knew a simple regular bullet wouldn't have released the creature's hold. Hayden added that multiple shots from a regular bullet would have done the trick, but there wasn't time to fire off more than one shot because the creature would have pulled him down. He also admitted that it was very hard to aim his shot, given the fact that Will was pretty much in his way when he was aiming. If he would have fired more than one round, it would have increased the chances of Will getting hit. Hayden finally stated that he only had time to aim one shot, and he had to make sure that the shot would have saved him right away.

"I still have one more shot for the devil," Hayden mentioned.

"Yeah, but no room for error anymore," Will uttered as he limped over to the edge to look at the cliff. Between the flashes of lightning, Will was able to see how deep the pit was. He saw how far he had to jump and how many Sasquatches were on the other side. Will who just barely escaped death was yelling at the person he should have been thanking. "Thank you, Hayden. If it wasn't for you, I would have been a goner."

Hayden walked up next to Will to watch the herd of animals on the other side start to wander away. Hayden said, "You're welcome," to Will and then said that they should go and find the rest of their friends.

Logan, Cain, Timber, and Miles were on their way to the cave. The huge hole in the ground was close on their right as they walked. These four hoped to reach the cave without bumping into the devil on the way. They also hoped that one of the missing Hang Out Group members would unite with them on the way. But these hopes were quickly overshadowed by the inevitable threat they were walking toward. The devil was just at the cave they were heading to, so expecting not to see the monster on the way there would be very foolish.

Cain walked next to his father to discuss strategy. He asked his father if he remembered the spell he placed on Ray when they first met. Logan sadly didn't remember, so Cain had to elaborate. He explained that Logan was able to increase gravity's force on Ray after he hit him with one of his spells. Logan now did recall that, but he sadly didn't expect it to work on the devil, claiming that the devil was too strong and could overpower it right away. Logan informed Cain that he used that spell on the unicorn, and it wore off quickly due to the beast's might.

"Did you teach Miles how to use the spell?" Cain asked. Logan explained that Miles did know how to activate that spell. He went into detail about how Miles's active Loomation was still young, fresh, and nowhere on the same level as his. Logan was strong enough to use the gravity spell on someone with a dry Loomation for ten minutes while Miles could keep a regular human down for almost two full minutes. Cain said that if they both teamed up on the devil with that spell, it may hold the beast down long enough for him to get the killing swing in with the blade.

"If Miles and I join forces and we give it all that we got, and I mean all that we got, we may be able to keep him in place for a little more than five seconds," Logan reported.

"Five seconds would be plenty," Cain stated fearlessly as he looked back and saw the two Hog members behind them. "You better relay the plan to the boys. They seem to listen to you better than they do me."

Logan stepped away from his son and walked with Timber and Miles. Logan first asked Miles if he still remembered how to perform the gravity spell.

"Yes, but I thought you said it wouldn't work on the devil," Miles said.

Logan told Miles that with their combined forces, they may be able to keep the devil still long enough for Cain to stab him. Logan instructed Miles that he wanted him to be at 100 percent when he delivered that spell, and when he fired it to make sure he used all the energy in his body to maximize his results. Logan added that when the fight began, he should not perform any defense spells, for that would just be a waste of energy. Logan warned Miles that using all his might on one attack would greatly exhaust him to a point where he wouldn't be able to stand for a few moments after the action. The final instruction was that Logan and Miles both had to strike the beast at the same moment in order to give Cain the most amount of time to kill the monster.

Miles said that he was ready for this, reassuring the others that this was why he had been training all this time. Timber, on the other hand, felt lost with what he would do when it came time to fight. He knew Logan and Miles were going to hit the monster with their active Loomation powers, and Cain was going to go in for the kill. Timber felt that he had to do something to earn his place with these fighters. Then he noticed the sword in Cain's hand start to glow. Cain was a few steps in front of the rest of the pack. When the sword started to glow, he stopped and looked at it with a confused glance. Timber then remembered the last encounter with the devil they had. He saw the sword start to glow when Will got it close to the beast. And now that it was happening again, that could only mean one thing.

"HE'S HERE!" Timber shouted as loudly as he could.

"Logan, light it up!" Cain shouted.

The four eased in close to form a circle, while Logan started to fire off light violet defense spells all around them. Logan released the weakest form of this spell in order to save his energy for the attack that really mattered. The purpose of these attacks was to cover the land with a dash of light to provide the location where the devil was coming from. Timber watched one of the beaming violet lights fly past the devil who was standing by the edge of the cliff. Timber was the only one who noticed the devil, as he was the only one looking in that direction at that moment. The devil didn't see Timber spot him, so he still believed that he was hiding in plain sight. Timber quietly snuck around the rest of the pack, acting like he still didn't know where the devil was.

Once Timber was out of the circle, he slithered his way toward the devil, approaching him from his left side. A flash of lightning went off, and Timber saw the devil walking up to the circle. The devil didn't even notice Timber to his left side. This was Timber's chance to make the first move, and he pounced at the devil, hitting him across the forehead with the cube. The sharp corner of the cube drove under the devil's skin and left a large gash across his forehead. The devil let out a surprising painful howl. With his right hand, he touched the large cut on his forehead and felt blood.

"NOW!" Timber shouted to Logan and Miles. At that moment, both Logan and Miles pointed their right hands at the devil and with all their might delivered the gravity spell. The spell dispersed out of their fingers like a stream of gushing water. Normally when they fire off defense spells, the length of their attack is the same length of their arm. But since they were giving this attack everything they had, the length of this attack was three times that size. Logan's attack looked yellow, while Miles's blast emitted a dark-blue shade. Delivering his attack had exhausted Logan, causing him to fall to one knee while Miles had gradually fallen to his chest on the ground.

The devil got hit with the full blast from both of them. The amount of pressure he was feeling from the concentrated gravity brought by the spell had caused him to freeze in his position. Cain saw his moment to attack, and he charged in strong, gripping the sword tightly in his hand. The devil still had his right hand up on his forehead and was already shaking off the effects of the spell. He quickly regrouped and aimed his right hand at Cain, blasting out his fiery flow toward his attacker.

As Cain continued to approach, he used his left hand to pull his coat over his body and shield himself from the oncoming flames. The devil was really pouring the heavy flames in the direction of Cain. The coat had now reached its limit of protection and started to wear away. Cain could feel the coat start to decay, but he didn't care; the coat enabled him to rush right up to the devil and violently swing the sword as hard as he could at him.

The devil used all his might to move his back away from the thrusting blade. Cain was attempting to slice the devil across his upper torso, but due to his vision being obscured by the coat and the shooting flames, he missed though he still managed to sever the devil's right arm at the elbow. The devil then leaned in and drove the claws of his left hand right into Cain's heart, killing him immediately. The sword dropped to the ground, and Cain's lifeless corpse dropped next to it.

"NO!" Logan shouted in great anger. He got to his feet, using whatever strength he had left to push himself onward. Logan picked up the glowing sword, placed it in front of his chest, and delivered a strong defense spell from his chest. Delivering a defense spell from one's chest provided a much stronger force. The attack seemed to infuse with the glowing light from the sword, increasing the might of the blast. The devil was hit hard and knocked down into the pit that he stood so close to.

The devil hit the ground hard, and it took him a while to get to his feet. He knew he could climb out of the hole; it just would take him a long time now that he only had one arm to climb with. The devil had never been hurt like that before. Until now, he never thought it was possible. The devil was so full of rage that fire was literally shooting out of his entire body. He let out a loud shout in high frustration, which released so much fire from his body that the entire canyon started to fill up with flames.

Down in the pit, Gard saw the red flames and felt the hot violent heat coming from a great distance. He could tell that the flames were coming right toward them. It felt to Gard that it was the flames of hell charging right toward them, and he turned and sprinted to Juice and Eric.

"We need to get Juice free now!" Gard shouted as he was running over to them. "Eric, start smashing up the tree now!" he shouted.

Eric started pounding his fist repeatedly against the trunk of the tree. Wood chips were flying all around Juice as Eric's fist started to be covered in splinters and blood. When Gard made it to the weakened tree, he pulled out the knife Hayden gave him earlier and started to furiously hack at the trunk of the tree as fast as he could.

When the tree was chopped up more, Juice was able to spread his arms out to free himself from the remaining binding strands of the tree trunk. Juice had no time to catch his breath as the flames were so close the heat was getting unbearable, so he reached out for Eric and Gard. They both jumped on Juice's arms and held on tightly. Juice was able to soar out of the pit, avoiding the oncoming flames. Once Juice was over the edge, he flew over the ground and crashed into the grass. The three boys saw the flames rise high above the pit and knew that there was no way they could have survived that fiery blast. They got out just in time. As they stayed on the ground trying to catch their breath, Eric asked, "What happened?"

"I think we made the beast angry," Gard replied. The three knew that their fellow fighters were not all dead, because someone had infuriated the beast.

CHAPTER 36

The Battle Ends

From the cracks in the earth, the burning flames were shooting high up in the air. Everyone in the garden saw them reach up as high as mountaintops. The fire was shining so brightly that the darkness was blotted out. The conflagration was making everything visible appear in a red glow. Will and Hayden were on top of a hill where they could see the fire burning from multiple places all around them. Standing in what felt like the middle of nowhere, surrounded by burning pits, made them feel like they were standing in hell. Hayden had never seen so much fire in his life, and even he thought it was a bit frightening.

"Over there," Will said while tapping on Hayden's shoulder. Will was pointing to Timber and Miles from afar. Timber and Miles were also standing on top of a hill doing the same thing Will and Hayden were doing. They were using this constant lightning of the garden to attempt to find each other. After they knew where the others were, they looked around to find the ground that would lead them back together. There was a trench between the two, but it required a slight hike around the trench nearby that would unite the two groups. It would be only ten minutes if both groups started walking toward one another. Will and Hayden waved over to the two, signaling them that they are heading over now. Will and Hayden hustled down the hill and started to make their way toward them.

Timber and Miles ran down their hill back to Logan who was kneeling next to his dead son. Timber and Miles wanted to express their deepest condolences to Logan after his son was murdered. But the fire came out of the pit so quickly that they knew that they needed to take the chance of spotting their friends right away. It paid off and just in time too because the fire blazing from the pits had ended, and the darkness along with the cold had taken over the garden once again.

The feeling of being in hell was truer to Logan than the others at the moment. Hovering over the body of his dead son was the worst feeling imaginable. Miles placed his hand on Logan's shoulder and said that he was sorry. Logan spoke slowly, with long pauses between his words. He just couldn't believe that his son was really dead. Timber complimented and respected Cain's courage and his will to fight until the final moment. His bravery was something he would always admire.

Logan told the boys that he felt that he had failed his son. He told them that throughout Cain's entire life, all his father had ever done for him was keep the devil from killing him. Logan pounded the ground yelling that it was all for nothing. He would have done anything to trade places with his son. Timber and Miles passed worried looks to each other. They both felt that they should give Logan a moment; the man just witnessed his only son being murdered right in front of him. But at the same time, they knew that with every second that passed, the devil grew closer to climbing out of the hole.

"He fought for the love of his daughter," Logan stated. "He risked his own life in order to make sure Kate would be free from this same fate."

"Logan, we know where Will and Hayden are. If we hurry, we can reach up to them soon," Miles said kindly.

"I thought the boy was ready. He had the right motivation powering him for this fight," Logan said, staring down at his son. "It wasn't enough, I guess. His emotions were clouded by hatred, revenge, and cockiness. He never fully experienced gratitude, not without a level of hate attached to it. That really messes up the heart in a way. His heart wasn't strong enough to beat the devil."

"Logan, please, we must go," Miles said softly with the utmost compassion.

Logan looked over and saw the sword resting next to him by his son. He picked up the sword by the blade and turned the handle over to Timber. "You two take the sword. I'll take the cube to the cave and try to get the sun back on."

"No, we should all go together," Timber pleaded.

"Logan, you can't leave us. We don't have a chance without you," Miles added.

"I'm in no condition to fight. I don't have it in me anymore. My whole reason to fight is gone." Logan felt so empty right now. He didn't even let out any tears, for he was so broken now. "You two, find your friends. Protect one another and save each other."

Timber and Miles knew that there was no talking the old man out of his decision. Timber stared at the sword with an uneasy feeling, as he hadn't carried it before. "I don't think I'm the right man to wield it," Timber sadly stated.

"You have the devil's blood on your hand, which makes you overqualified!" Logan proudly said.

Timber looked at his hand holding the cube and saw that it was indeed stained with the devil's blood. He couldn't believe that he was able to attack someone as powerful as the devil. Timber looked over to Miles, and Miles gave him a nod. Timber took hold of the handle and felt that boost of positive energy that whoever held it felt. Timber then handed the cube to Logan.

"All you need to do is crunch down on it to ignite the Loomation. Once that happens, it'll emit a white glow. After that, you just need to ease off it, and that will release the blast," Timber instructed.

"The blast will send out a shock wave that will knock you back off your feet," Miles added. Logan took hold of the cube and took a quick look at it before placing it in his jacket pocket. He said that it sounded easy. "You'll meet up with us after, right?" Miles asked.

"Once the sun returns, I'll be able to find you guys quicker, and by then, I'll be ready to fight," Logan replied.

"We're going to win this fight for him," Timber said talking about Cain. "We're going to win this fight for all of us!" After those inspiring words, the three men all left Cain's body and started moving. Timber and Miles went to meet up with Will and Hayden while Logan made his way to the cave.

After the fire subsided, Eric and Gard got to their feet while Juice stayed on the ground. "Any idea where the others are?" asked Eric.

"The fire originated in that direction," Gard said, pointing with the knife.

"Then that's where we're going," Juice said, getting to his feet.

"Juice, if you need to take a minute to rest, we can wait," Gard replied.

"Someone might need our help. And I promised myself that I would not just sit by and do nothing ever again!" Juice's words were inspiring and the right motivational statement that the others needed to hear right now. He said that he was still feeling sore from the tree slamming on him, and he admitted that he barely had the strength to pull Eric and Gard out of the pit. Eric and Gard once again mentioned to Juice how grateful they were for that. Juice felt well enough to take flight; he just didn't have the strength to lift the others right now. Gard told Juice to take the bird's-eye view but to stay in shouting range, saying that he and Eric would keep a running pace to stay up with him.

Logan ran to the cave alone with the cube secured in his pocket. He was thrilled to see the cave right where he expected it to be. Logan was scared to enter the cave because the lightning wouldn't give off any light inside. He would be walking in completely blind, so he took a moment outside the cave and did his best to remember the layout of it. He was trying to figure out how many steps between the entrance and the location of the diamond. But given his terrible memory, he knew that he was going to have trouble.

Will and Hayden were now in shouting distance from Timber and Miles, and that brought them so much joy. They were running toward each other. When they were united, they exchanged hugs, for they were thrilled to see they were all alive.

"Hey, look over there!" Miles shouted out among the group. The group all looked over to where Miles was pointing. As soon as the next lightning flashed, they all spotted Juice in the air with Eric and Gard running below him. Everyone ran up to each other, and all embraced in one big group hug.

"I thought you guys were dead!" Timber stated to Juice, Eric, and Gard.

"Of course, you did," Gard said with a laugh.

"I didn't lose hope!" Will added.

"Of course, you didn't!" Juice said with a grin.

Miles used the heal spell on Will, Juice, Eric, and Gard. The limp in Will's step was instantly gone. The deep cuts from the splinters of the three who fell down the hole had all healed, and all four of them felt as if they were at 100 percent again.

"Hey, where are the Renshaws?" asked Hayden, just now realizing that they were not all together. Timber delivered the sad news that they went up against the devil, and Cain hadn't made it. Timber then informed them of Logan's mission.

"If we can get the sun back on, we can regain our advantage!" Gard stated.

"Yeah, that heal spell felt great. If we could have that on full-time, pain wouldn't be a problem!" Eric mentioned.

"The heal spell won't save us from a kill move, though," Miles pointed out. The possibility of being killed was still on the group's mind. Now that one of them had died, the Hogs felt that any one of them could be next.

"If any of us die, I would rather it be me than any of you," Hayden stated.

"I would be willing to give my life if it would save any of you," Will added. The theme around the circle was that each one was willing to give his life for the others. This was said by each of them with a complete sense of sincerity.

"Well, let's just make sure we don't let any of us die. Sound good?" Juice said.

Then the sword in Timber's hand started to glow. Each Hog knew that the devil was there. A quick flash of lightning came to reveal that the devil was standing close by. He released his fire-burning flame from his remaining hand and aimed it right at the circle. Hayden shoved his way between the circle and the flaming attack. He stretched out his hands to widen himself as much as he could to block the coming attack from hitting his friends. The fire charged into Hayden's back, causing flames to fly all around. The Hogs were safe standing in front of Hayden, but they could hear him scream. The fire was much hotter than Hayden had ever encountered before, and it was hurting him badly. Once the fire flow ended, Hayden fell face-first into the ground. He landed on his gun, too weak to move, and was barely breathing.

"GET HIM!" shouted Will.

Right on command, every standing member of the Hang Out Group charged at the devil. Gard was the first to get to the beast. He swung the knife he carried right at the devil's face. The devil was able to catch Gard's arm before getting hit and then twisted Gard's arm, breaking it as easy as snapping a twig. The devil then charged at Timber who was holding the sword on guard. He moved so fast that Timber didn't have a chance to make a move. The sword was once again glowing when the devil got close to it, but he swatted it out of Timber's hand and delivered a mighty kick to his chest. Timber was drilled into the ground with his chest feeling as if it had collapsed. Juice came in and struck the devil's right shoulder, flying by with his fist out in front of him.

"A human flyer...now that's just insulting!" the devil said right before he threw flames from his hand at Juice. Juice did his best to dodge as many flames as he could, but his legs were hit, and he crashed down to the ground. Just after that, the devil was bombarded by defense spells fired by Miles. At the same time, both Will and Eric came in to attack, but the defense spells weren't strong enough to slow the beast. The devil was able to swing his elbow at Will, launching him right into Miles and knocking them both down. The devil then used his hand to punch Eric in the face. Eric fell back, and the devil dug his claws into Eric's leg and broke it.

The Hogs spent so much time working on their attack strategy for this very fight, and they all failed. Most of the attack plans were striking the target from multiple areas, one person at a time. But due to the lack of good visibility, they performed extremely poorly. No one could see who was attacking at the time; they just followed the screams from the devil's last victim. They were defeated so fast it left them looking pathetic and helpless. The devil continued inflicting as much pain as he could onto the Hogs. He tossed them around, and he kicked them while they were down. He was smiling as he was snapping the bones of their limbs by stomping on them.

Logan finally made his way through the cave and reached the diamond. The diamond's glowing presence was very faded but still there, and it was covered with dark-red veins. Logan figured that the veins were keeping the diamond powered down and responsible for the garden's hellish surroundings. Now holding the cube with both hands, Logan remembered the instructions Timber told him. He just had to turn it, and it would release the blast. Logan turned the top row clockwise, but nothing happened. He couldn't believe that he made it this far just to forget the simple instructions for this task.

At this time, the devil had beat the Hogs to a bloody pulp. They were scattered about, too sore and defeated to get to their feet. The devil felt proud of what he did and enjoyed every second of beating them senseless. "You know, I like killing humans. It's more personal entertainment for me rather than strictly business. With you, I can take my time, savor each punch, and pour on as much pain as I want!" the devil said. "But I've had my fun. Now to complete my vow." The devil walked around the area where the helpless injured Hogs lay. When the devil walked by Will, Will saw the sword glow, showing off how close it was to him. Until that happened, Will didn't know that the sword was that close to him, and he was hurt so badly that he couldn't even reach out for it.

"Let's start with the one with the active Loomation," the devil said. The devil then lifted Miles up by the throat with his one hand. The monster let out a grin because this was the part he enjoyed the most.

Back at the cave, Logan now remembered that he must crunch down on the cube then release. But the cube wouldn't crunch down now. He turned the top row of the cube back to where it was at first and then crunched down, and the cube illuminated with a white glow. The shining cube was beautiful to Logan as he looked up at the diamond and brought the cube up close to it. Logan then released the pressure he had on the cube, and a blast of energy was emitted immediately. The blast pounded the diamond, the cave walls, and Logan hard. Logan fell back onto the ground, and the whole place started to shake as if the blast set off a cave-in.

Rocks from inside the cave started to rain all around Logan, but he didn't care about that. He watched the blast wave sink into the diamond. After the blast was absorbed into the diamond, the shock wave crawled upward, wiping away the red veins as it went up. The diamond wouldn't be healed until the veins were completely gone. The veins were slowly disappearing, so the plan was a success. Logan got to his feet, turned, and ran to the exit. But a giant rock came down and blocked his way out. Logan backed up, pressing his back to the diamond, watching the place get smaller and smaller due to the rocks now starting to bury him alive. The last rock that completely covered Logan dropped right before the diamond was completely healed.

Outside, the sun turned on immediately, as fast as a light being switched on. As soon as the light came back on, the place returned to its former glory. All the humans still alive became fully healed. The light turning on caught the devil off guard and signaled the Hogs to attack. Miles fired off a defense spell from his chest, and since he was being lifted by the devil, Miles's chest was pointing right at the devil's face.

The attack knocked Miles out of the devil's hand, and the devil tipped backward, losing his balance and rubbing his eyes with his hand due to the attack hurting his sight. The devil started to get fire to come out of his hand to set up an attack, but before he could send it toward anyone, he was shot in the center of the forehead by Hayden's diamond bullet. The bullet lodged deep into the devil's head, piercing the outside of his skull. The devil was howling in horrible pain from this attack.

Gard charged in and stabbed the devil in the throat, causing the devil to hold on to his bleeding wound from his neck. Then Timber and Eric ran in from behind the devil, sliding their feet right into the back of the devil's knees. At the same time, Juice came down from the sky, slamming his feet into the devil's chest and pinning his back to the ground. Juice flew past the devil's face; and the next thing the devil saw was the sword, wielded by Will, being shoved into his heart. Will released the sword and quickly took a step back. All the Hogs were now circled around the devil with the sword still in his heart. The Hogs all stood on guard as an odd hush washed over them.

"Is that it? Is he dead?" an unsteadied Juice asked after a moment of silence.

"I think so," Timber replied.

"He's not moving," Hayden pointed out.

"Hey, are you dead?" Gard shouted. The Hogs grew silent again to check if they could hear any breathing from the monster.

"We did it," Will stated.

"No final dying words or anything?" Juice felt that this was odd, that the beast died just like that. Eric said that sometimes people didn't get a final word. Sometimes when a person died, they just ended. The Hogs felt uncomfortable being that close to the devil. One asked if they should remove the sword, but they were all too leery to go up close to the monster's dead body. They all backed away and just stared at the corpse. The belief that they defeated the monster still hadn't fully sunk in.

"Guys, we won...," Gard stated. Just then, everyone cracked a smile, and all let out a huge cheer. They jumped for joy and gave each other high fives. They had managed to kill the monster, freeing them from its wrath forever.

CHAPTER 37

Moving On

The Hogs saw that the ground was once again whole. The land must have shifted back to its normal radiance after the sun came back on. The Hogs sent Juice out to locate the cave Logan went to, as they couldn't wait to tell him the good news. Juice found the cave, but it wasn't a joyful sight. The joy that so enveloped the group had suddenly dropped out of them and disappeared. Juice led his friends to the cave, and they all saw that it had collapsed. Still hopeful, the Hogs acted fast, removing the rocks blocking the entrance. They frantically dug their way into the cave and found Logan's dead body. It was easy to figure out what happened; the cube's blast caused a cave-in and buried the old man alive. The Hogs owed this man their lives. If Logan hadn't done what he did, the devil would have been the victor, and they all would have been lifeless corpses scattered about on the ground.

A few members of the group went to retrieve Cain's body while others located a good place to bury them. They found a large tree that stood out alone in a grass field and dug the two graves by hand. Will, Juice, Hayden, and Gard were digging the graves; so Timber did his best to clean up the bodies. He tucked in their shirts, straightened their collars, and checked their pockets for any personal effects. Cain had nothing on him. Logan had only one object in his pocket, a letter. On the envelope were the words *For the Hogs.*

"Guys," Timber said, getting everyone's attention. Everyone looked over to Timber as he showed off the letter. "It's addressed to us," Timber added. The Hogs felt a little uncomfortable seeing the letter. It was the last message, the last words they would receive from the man who believed in them so much. The guys told Timber to open it and see what it said, so he carefully opened the envelope and removed the letter inside. He stood up, faced the Hogs, and started to read.

Dear Hang Out Group,

I have brought you a challenge that no one should ever face- a threat that sounds unbeatable, an opportunity that most people would rather not ever receive. But I believe that you are the ones who can defeat this beast. I've studied the powers of Loomation ever since I discovered it inside me. The power thrives and falls with emotion. The Loomation's effectiveness is dependent on how the carrier of this power feels. There are some emotions that will keep you strong: courage, pride and resilience. My son Cain Parker Renshaw remained fearless his whole life, and that has kept him strong. Ray relied on his confidence and that kept him strong.

I knew that these emotions were strong, but the Devil had all that power and more. To defeat the Devil, you need to attack him with something he doesn't have-something that you all have. The first time I went up against the Devil, my best friend Parker fought by my side. And my friend was able to inflict pain on the monster. He was fighting for the safety of his friend and wanted his fallen friends before him to be avenged. My friend was a warm-hearted man and found the good in all people; he fought very bravely.

I've discovered that the strongest emotion is the power of friendship and love, which was what I saw in

*all of you. You carry a very powerful feeling, and that
Loomation will work at its strongest when you all fight
together. You fought with love, friendship and honor.
This is something the Devil doesn't have. This was why
I've picked you for this challenge, and why I still believe
in you all.*

-Logan Charles Renshaw.

The Hogs all bowed their heads in silence as they were all very touched by what the letter said. They felt that they had known a great, wise man, and it was very sad to see him no longer with them. After the graves were finished, Timber and Hayden gently placed Cain's body in the right one, while Eric and Gard placed Logan in the left one. They covered the bodies up with dirt, and Will placed a cross that he made of two sticks in the ground as a headstone. The names of the men were carved in the cross: Logan Charles Renshaw and Cain Parker Renshaw. With their bodies being buried in the garden, they would never rot nor decay to bones. The Hogs felt that they should say something on behalf of the two.

"Logan had to spend almost all of his son's life away from him. I think he'll be happy to forever be at his side," Juice stated.

"Cain may have been bossy and rude, but he did have love in his heart. He wanted the devil killed for his daughter's safety. I hope he knows that Kate will never suffer any attack from the devil, and that way he will be able to rest in peace," Gard mentioned.

"Logan thought that he failed when the devil murdered his son. But that's simply not true. Cain was able to live a long life and even became a father. Logan passed the mission of keeping his child safe to his own son. And they both gave up their lives for their children. That's not the outcome of a failure," Eric said.

"Logan was my teacher and my friend. Without him, I would be still terrified of my own power. But Logan showed me the way. He helped me out when he was the only one who could. I hope to repay his actions by helping someone like me someday," Miles brought up.

"The bravery these two and even Ray showed was something we needed to see. Logan willingly being chased by the devil for decades wasn't something a scared person could keep up for long. Both Cain and Ray fought the devil without hesitation. That type of courage is inspiring and has made us all stronger," Will stated.

"Something none of us will forget," Hayden added. The Hogs felt bad that Ray wasn't buried next to his friend Cain. They got the idea of putting the cube in the ground between the two graves. This way, the cube would be out of their hands, in a place that no one could ever get to it. The cube represented Ray. They felt that he would have been wanted to be remembered by his intellect, and the cube was a symbol of that. After that, the Hogs headed to the door. They followed the river right up to the wooden ramp.

On the ramp, they saw that the boulder was covering the exit. They remembered how to open it; just two people who carried Loomation needed to touch it. No one wanted to touch it. Juice pointed out a scary fact, asking, "What if the devil killed all but one of us? That person would have been trapped in here forever!" No one liked that thought, so they told Juice to shut up.

"I touched it on the way in, so I'm not doing it on the way back," Timber stated with Juice agreeing to that idea.

"Oh wait. We need a picture!" shouted Juice.

"Come on, Juice, we all just want to get out of here," Will pleaded.

"Will, when are we ever going to be here again?" Juice asked. Juice left his phone back at the chemical plant, so he took Eric's phone because his had the nicest camera on it. Juice placed the phone on the boulder, keeping it facing toward the group with the view of the garden in the background. "Okay, I set the timer!" Juice said as he backed up from the camera. "Will, why are you in the back?" Juice asked because Will was the shortest in the group, and he was standing behind the tallest of the group. Juice placed everyone, and they all just stood and waited for the click.

"Juice, are you sure you set that thing right?" questioned Gard.

"He probably didn't," Hayden stated.

"This thing better hurry. I'm getting bored here," Timber added.

"Maybe I missed a button. Let me go check," Juice said as he walked away. Juice took one step forward when a sound came from Eric's phone; the sound was the five-second warning, so Hayden yanked on Juice's arm, pulling him back as the camera flashed. This action made everyone laugh, which put smiles on their faces for the photo.

Later, back at the swamp, the sun was setting. The Hogs were now packing up their belongings into the two vehicles. When they returned to the swamp, they knew it was time to return home. There was no one last night at the campsite nor one last large fire to burn up the rest of the gathered firewood. They just wanted to go home and return to their lives. For the first time in two months, they all felt truly safe. No more Havocs, no more Cain and Ray, no more creatures of the garden, and no more devil. The cube was locked away in the garden, so there was no more responsibility of keeping it protected by guarding it.

The pop-up camper was folded down and already strapped to the back of Hayden's truck. The bug net, the canopy, the shower tent, the folded chairs, the coolers and tables, along with all their luggage, were being loaded up now.

"Miles, have you finished your letter yet?" Eric asked. After the Hogs left the garden, they returned to Ray's chemical plant. They made sure any information on them was burned before they called the police to inform them of Ray's dead body at the plant. The Hogs wanted the body to be found by the police because Ray's death had to be declared for Kate to inherit all his belongings according to his will. As they searched the place, they found Cain's belongings. He had a cell phone, and a scrap of paper was taped to the back of it. The paper had the address where Kate was currently living. The Hogs took some time at the chemical plant to write out a letter to Kate.

None of them had the courage to call her to let her know that she had lost her father. There was so much they wanted to tell her, but they worried that their words would get too jumbled. The fear of getting overloaded with tons of questions made them afraid that they would grow speechless. They saw so many negative ways this phone call could have gone, so they wrote her a letter telling the story of the devil and how her grandfather managed to keep her safe from harm her entire life. They went over every detail of how both her grandfather and her father fought with tremendous courage and how they were both fully committed to sacrificing their lives for the sake of her safety.

After the major details of the death of her family were written, each member added a heartwarming letter for her detailing the positives of their time spent with Logan and Cain. Kate knew nothing of her grandfather, and they felt sad that she would never get a chance to learn about him on a personal level. Each member had a story to share; they thought anything would help Kate with this tragic news. Most of the Hogs finished their letters at the plant, but some needed more time. Miles teleported everyone back to the swamp after the time at the plant. When they returned, Juice asked Miles for a teleporting ride because he had a few errands he wanted to do. They weren't gone long. Only some of the camping equipment was packed up by the time they returned.

When they got back, both Juice and Miles returned to their letters. Miles spent the most time with Logan, so he had the most to share. He talked about how Logan was a wise teacher and that Miles would never forget all that he learned from him. Juice was the only one who knew Kate prior to her kidnapping, so he had a lot to write also.

"Yeah, I just finished my letter, Eric," Miles stated.

"Good, because I need your chair," Hayden replied while standing right behind Miles. Miles hopped out of his chair, and Hayden folded it up right away; it was the last chair that needed packed up in the truck. Miles handed over the letter to Eric. Eric was the one in charge of sending the letter, so he gathered them all up. Miles then reached into his book bag and pulled out the book called *The Power of Loomation*. Miles wanted Kate to have it since it had been written by her grandfather. Eric asked Miles if he still needed to learn anything more from the book. Miles smiled and said that he now knew everything in the book by heart.

"Juice, you done?" Eric shouted over to Juice who was standing by the cabin. Juice nodded, Eric rushed over, and Juice handed him the letter and sniffled. It was clear that Juice was still grieving over the recent deaths. After Eric grabbed the letter, Juice said that he had something he wanted to add to the letter as he bent over his bag and pulled out a photo. He said that he took a photo of the newspaper clipping from inside the cabin a while ago, and he made a copy of it at the store (which was one of the errands he wanted to get done). Juice said that the newspaper clipping was still hanging inside the cabin; he didn't want to remove that. But he wanted Kate to have the photocopy, saying that it may be the only photo of her grandfather in existence. Eric looked at the photo. The photo was of the seven travelers holding the diamond that they took from the garden and sold at an auction. Eric saw that Logan looked very similar in this photo to when he died. "It's perfect, Juice."

Juice then removed a hammer and nail from the bag. Juice hammered the nail into the front of the cabin. This got the Hogs to stop what they were doing and watch Juice. Juice then took out a second photo from his bag. This one was rolled up as it was very large. Juice also had a large frame inside his bag. When Juice placed the photo in the frame, the Hogs saw that the photo was the one that they all took together before leaving the garden.

"Juice, why are you putting that photo up?" asked Gard.

"Because we found this place in a time of need," Juice said as he placed the frame onto the nail. "And maybe one day, someone, or some people may find this place when they're in a time of need," Juice said as he straightened the photo. "And they would know"—Juice then put his hands down to get a good look at the photo hanging on the nail—"that we were once here." The Hogs took a moment to look at the photo and did find it pleasing in a way.

"Well, I don't plan on going too long without returning here for a night or two," Will stated.

"I agree. This place is my home away from home from now on," Hayden added.

"Maybe we can come back later in the summer," Juice suggested. Hayden mentioned that as soon as he got home, he'd be heading out of state to spend time with his uncle and cousins for pretty much the rest of the summer. Gard said that he started texting a girl who was going to the same college he was going to, so he had plans on spending most weekends getting to know her better. Eric said that he was taking early college classes at his college, so he was heading off much sooner than the others. Timber said that he'd be working every weekend until he also left for college.

"Well, we can be here during fall break, right?" Juice asked.

Gard said that since his college was so far away, he wouldn't return until Thanksgiving. One of them mentioned that he'd be visiting his mother's side of the family out of state this year for Thanksgiving, so he wouldn't be able to hang out that holiday weekend. And another one added that his entire family was taking a Christmas vacation, so he'd be out of town the entire winter break.

Just like that, the Hogs couldn't even figure out the next weekend they'd all be together again. Someone pointed out that the whole camping trip was to prepare for this. They knew finding the time to all get together after high school would be hard, so they wanted time to make this a summer they would never forget. They all agreed that this would, indeed, be a summer none of them would ever forget. They admitted that even though some of them were running for their lives from wild massive killing monsters, it was the most fun any of them had ever had. They were so grateful that they got to experience it all with each other.

It didn't take long for the rest of the supplies to get loaded. After that, the Hogs took one last look at their campsite with their minds at ease. It was sad leaving the place, but they knew it would always be there for a weekend getaway in the future. The Hogs got into the cars and drove away on the muddy road, leaving the place behind. There was nothing but the cabin, the fire ring full of ash, and a small leftover woodpile. Due to the remaining diamond chip pieces still buried under the cabin, the place would look just as they left it when the Hogs did return. The only change that they wouldn't even catch was the photo that Juice hung. Not too long after the Hogs left the campsite, the frame tipped slightly to the right, causing it to become unbalanced.

CPSIA information can be obtained
at www.ICGtesting.com
Printed in the USA
LVHW020405191021
700735LV00001B/4